WAYNE STINNETT

FALLEN HERO

A JESSE MCDERMITT NOVEL

Caribbean Adventure Series
Volume 10

D0841455

2016

Published by DOWN ISLAND PRESS, 2016
Travelers Rest, SC

Library of Congress cataloging-in-publication Data
Stinnett, Wayne
Fallen Hero/Wayne Stinnett
p. cm. - (A Jesse McDermitt novel)
ISBN-10: 0-9981285-2-X
ISBN-13: 978-0-9981285-2-8

Cover Photo by Fotomak
Graphics by Wicked Good Book Covers
Edited by Larks & Katydids
Proofreading by Donna Rich
Interior Design by Write.Dream.Repeat. Book Design

FOREWORD

There comes a time in every warrior's life when he knows it's time to finally step aside and leave the heavy lifting to younger men. There are also times when men of good conscience are ordered to step aside. The setting for this book is just before the 2008 Presidential election. Politics have no place on the battlefield, yet political winds are constantly influencing and changing the way international conflicts are handled.

This will be the final novel in the Jesse McDermitt Caribbean Adventure Series, and the end of the Caribbean Counter-terrorism Command. But, don't worry; the story ain't over yet. Next year, Jesse and most of his friends will be back in *Rising Storm*, the first novel in the Jesse McDermitt Caribbean Mystery Series.

As always, my greatest source of inspiration, ideas, and support for my writing comes from my wife, Greta. She'll sit and listen to the same plot points over and over, offering suggestions and tweaking ideas, as I work the story out in my head. Without her as a sounding board, her continued support, as well as the support from the rest of family, none of this would ever have happened.

Much gratitude to Detective Adam Richardson, for all his help with the day-to-day life of a police detective. I've gotten so much insight from his blog on www.writersdetective.com.

To my Aussie buddy, Gary Cox, I owe many thanks for the idea of having two old Conchs sharing different sides of a common story over a beer. I truly appreciate it. Also thanks to one of my readers, Erin Finigan, who suggested the name for Jesse's Noserider.

My beta reading team went above and beyond on this one. These folks are the polishers. Much gratitude is owed to Mike Ramsey, Marcus Lowe, Katy McKnight, Dana Vihlen, Dave Parsons, Gary Cox, Charles Hofbauer, Karl Schulte, Debbie Kocol, Ron Ramey, and Dr. John Trainor. I rely on the vast experiences and knowledge these folks bring to the table, as well as their sharp minds and attention to details, to find all the holes in my stories. The writing process takes months, and they devour my work in hours, spitting out the bones of discordance, then re-reading it to find all the things I'd forgotten about weeks or months earlier.

Today is November 20th, and this foreword is the last thing I'm writing for this project before it goes for editing. It also happens to be a warm, sunny day. So I'm gonna fork the Hog and get some wind therapy. See you in the spring.

DEDICATION

To my eldest granddaughter Kira, who aspires to one day be a writer and spend half of every day in front of her computer, bleeding her heart out.

"There comes a time in every rightly constructed boy's life when he has a raging desire to go somewhere and dig for hidden treasure."

- Mark Twain

If you'd like to receive my twice a month newsletter for specials, book recommendations, and updates on coming books, please sign up on my website:

WWW.WAYNESTINNETT.COM

THE CHARITY STYLES CARIBBEAN THRILLER SERIES
Merciless Charity
Ruthless Charity
Heartless Charity (Spring, 2017)

THE JESSE MCDERMITT
CARIBBEAN ADVENTURE SERIES

Fallen Out
Fallen Palm
Fallen Hunter
Fallen Pride
Fallen Mangrove
Fallen King
Fallen Honor
Fallen Tide
Fallen Angel
Fallen Hero
Rising Storm (Late 2017)

The Gaspar's Revenge Ship's Store is now open. There you can purchase all kinds of swag related to my books.
WWW.GASPARS-REVENGE.COM

FALLEN HERO

MAPS

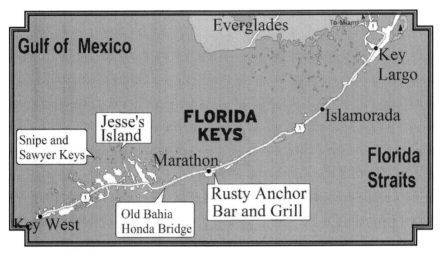

The Florida Keys

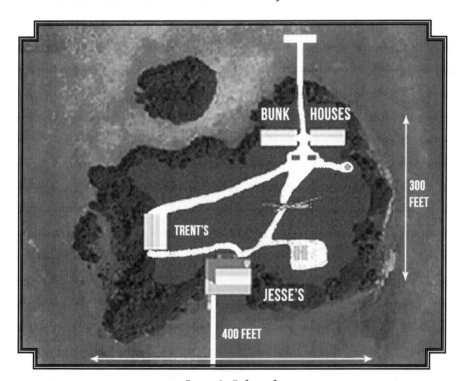

Jesse's Island

CHAPTER ONE

Water stretched to the horizon in every direction, so clear that I could easily see a small crab moving across the sandy bottom, twenty feet away. The shallows in the distance were punctuated here and there by flat, mangrove-covered islands, seeming to float just above the glassy surface. I knew the mirage was caused by the calmness of the water, but it still looked a bit surreal, kinda like a Salvador Dalí painting. The scent of iodine and brine, mixed with the low-tide smell of the exposed flats, filled my nostrils with every breath. Above a few of the larger islands, the fronds of coconut palms hung limp in the warm, still, tropical air, silhouetted against a cobalt-blue sky.

What many parts of the country call *fall* is my favorite time of year down here. To Keys' locals, it's the quiet time between the different tourist seasons. The rowdy college-aged tourists are gone, pulled back to their campuses by schedules they have to keep. The annual influx of snow-birds has yet to arrive and for a few weeks, the water is uncongested and all is quiet in the back country of the Florida Keys.

We just don't have the changing of four distinct seasons that other parts of the country enjoy. It's dry from December through April and rainy the rest of the time. It doesn't rain every day in the rainy season, but it can.

The dry season was still almost two months away. I was in calf-deep water, several hundred feet from my boat. On a day like this, I'd have been surprised if there was anyone within five miles of where I stood. And if there was anyone around, I'd probably have known them. The back country was my backyard.

The warm, slow-moving current gently parted around my ankles. Tiny swirls of water moved slowly away from where my feet were planted, as if the current were agitated or confused by this interruption of its twice-daily commute. My bare feet had been sucked down into the sand by the movement of the water and then covered over by the fine yellow-white crystals.

"Do you see him?" I whispered to Finn, who stood motionless beside me.

At just over a year old, Finn still had many of his puppy mannerisms. Physically, he was a muscular, full-grown, ninety-five-pound mixed-breed yellow lab. His previous owner had told me that he was three-quarters yellow lab and one quarter German short-haired pointer. Sometimes though, I couldn't help but think that the quarter of him that wasn't lab was actually clownfish.

He looked up at me for a moment and whined, before returning his gaze to the horizon. Both of us scanned the water ahead for any movement.

It was so quiet and still here, miles from anywhere, that I heard the gentle dripping sound, and again looked down at Finn. His left paw was raised out of the water, his body rigid, his eyes locked on something off to the right.

Okay, so maybe he is part pointer.

I followed his gaze out over the water, but at first I didn't see anything. Then, almost imperceptibly, a slight shadow moved. It appeared like a ghostly gray apparition in the water, about forty feet away. I guess that's where the "gray ghost" nickname comes from.

Bonefish came to this sandy flat to feed when the tide was falling, and they were one of the hardest fish to catch, for a number of reasons. We'd seen this particular guy on three outings now, and each time we saw him he just seemed to vanish in the gin-clear water. He was one of the biggest bones I'd ever seen—and whenever he was there, the other fish left. The times Finn and I had fished there and not seen a single fish, we agreed the big guy was there, but he was just so good at concealment that neither of us could detect him.

I knew a thing or two about cover and concealment. As a Marine sniper instructor, it had been my job to teach Marines how not to be seen, to stay alive. That seemed like a lifetime ago, though it had been only nine years.

Again, the shadow evaporated.

It reappeared for a moment, a good twenty feet from where I'd been looking; I began casting ahead of it, trying to anticipate which way he might go. Before my third whip of the lightweight fly rod, the great bonefish had disappeared again. I continued the whipping motion, keeping the fly in the air and not letting it touch the water, hoping he'd reappear. He didn't.

Finn whined again; when I looked at him, he had his head cocked to the side, which I'd come to understand was his way of asking a question.

"I don't know where he went, buddy." That seemed to satisfy Finn's curiosity and he went back to scanning the water around us.

I live in the Content Keys, on a little island that's barely two acres at high tide. It sits at the western end of Harbor Channel, where the channel turns south and disappears into a maze of flats and cuts that only those who know the water can navigate.

The sand flat we were fishing is just north of Crane Key and Raccoon Key, both uninhabited. Slightly deeper water can be found in Cudjoe Basin to the west, and my island lies about four miles to the east. At low tide, I can walk home.

To get to either my house or this flat, you have to first know where they are and *then* know how to get out there. The old joke about "you can't get there from here" is apropos for the back country. Sure, it looks like water everywhere, but the unmarked deeper cuts are the only place a boat can go and you have to have a boat to get out here. And not just any boat—it has to be a shallow draft boat. Or you have to come down Harbor Channel, in full view of my island for several miles.

There are no roads or bridges up in the back country. The islands all around look much the same as they did when early Spanish explorers first found them and deemed *los cayos* unworthy of settlement. They also determined that the waters around the Keys, known collectively as *Los Martires*, were too treacherous to sail. So, for the most part, they remained uninhabited for a couple hundred years after their so-called discovery—well, apart from the occasional Indian visitors who had been coming here for centuries, and a few piratical attempts to settle.

I let the fly drop into the water, dejected once again. Bonefish aren't any good as a food fish, but they are tremendously exciting to catch, regardless of size. Their fighting ability is on par with fish twice their size, and they're one of the smartest fish I've ever stalked. The inside of a bonefish's mouth is bony, and you can't set a hook. A barbed hook is useless for bonefish. The only way you can catch one is by keeping constant tension on the line and the point of the hook against his bony palate. If he charges toward you, and you're not ready for it, the line will go slack and the hook will simply fall out of his mouth.

"He wins again," I said to Finn, as I reeled in the line. "It's getting late anyway, close to beer-thirty. Why don't we get back to the boat?"

Finn barked once, his big tail wagging from side to side. I hooked the fly in one of the rod's eyes, and together we started walking back through the shallow water toward my boat, swinging on its anchor line in about two feet of water almost a quarter mile away.

Finn beat me to the boat, scaring a couple of gulls, who'd chosen my T-top for a perch, into noisy flight. Finn's feet barely touched the bottom, so he half swam and half lunged to the stern, where he scrambled up the "doggy ladder" a friend had built for me, and over the transom.

Just as I pushed myself up onto the gunwale, I heard a gunshot ring out. I immediately tumbled ungracefully forward into the cockpit of my little Grady-White, grabbing Finn and pulling him down. I've heard enough gunshots that I wasn't confused that it might be a car backfiring, or kids playing with firecrackers. Besides, the nearest car was a good ten miles away and the only kids were the two on my island.

I reached up and opened the storage box under the seat. Feeling inside, I pulled out my Sig Sauer P226, stripping it from its holster and thumbing the hammer back. I didn't need to check if there was a round in the chamber.

The gunshot had come from over my shoulder, to the northwest. It sounded like it was a long way off, but the only thing out there is Sawyer Key, Snipe Key, and a few smaller islands, all uninhabited. I raised my head over the gunwale and looked around carefully. Seeing nothing but the islands that lay nearly a mile away, I raised myself to a crouch and went to the side box of the console for my binoculars.

Scanning the horizon to the northwest, I couldn't see anything. Sound travels really well over water, and the gunshot might have been five miles away or it might have been ten. There wasn't another sound, except the tiny waves rippling against the hull and water dripping from my body to the deck.

Gunshots weren't normal out here in the back-country, but they weren't unheard of either. Lots of valid reasons to shoot out there; I did it all the time.

Lots of less than valid reasons, as well.

Finn put his feet up on the gunwale, looking over the side of the boat toward the northwest. "You heard it, too?"

The big yellow dog glanced at me with amber eyes, made a motion with his tail that might have been a partial wag, then looked back to the northwest, his ears lifted and cocked forward.

"You're still hearing something, aren't you?" I said.

Finn whined once, never moving his head or eyes. Whatever it was out there, rednecks blowing off steam or a drug deal gone south, it was completely quiet now—at least to my ears it was. Obviously, Finn could still hear something. I put the binos away, decocked the Sig, and put it back in the holster and then back into the rear-facing storage box.

Whatever it was, it was none of my business. I glanced at the compass and noted the direction that Finn was intently staring. Whoever it was out there, they were a long way out in the Gulf, at a heading of about three-hundred-twenty-degrees, from where we were near Crane Key. I started the engine and went forward to pull the hook. Finn barked at me once; I turned and saw that cocked-head, questioning look on his face.

"Not my circus, buddy," I said, stowing the anchor. "Not my monkeys."

CHAPTER TWO

Working the southeast quadrant of a fifty-foot grid of red-and-white interconnecting pipe, Jenny wondered again how she'd gotten herself roped into this job. Not that it was a bad gig—the money was good—but the days were super long.

Up before the sun every day, she then had an hour-long ride in a slow boat to the spot she and James had been working for three weeks now. One of them was in the water not long after first light, and they'd alternated throughout the day for the last twenty straight days: one of them on the boat, off-gassing what little residual nitrogen their bodies absorbed, while the other worked on the bottom.

The dives were shallow, meaning nearly an hour of bottom time. Then an hour surface interval, while the other was in the water. Six dives in a day weren't a problem, physically, but the repetition very quickly became boring. When one of them was on the surface, they'd refill their scuba tank from the onboard compressor and keep an eye on the other diver in the water. Whoever was in the water last would be on the boat first the following day.

At first it had sounded exciting—even romantic, in a swashbuckling kind of way. James wasn't unattractive, and he was quite charming. The fact that they were looking for a lost treasure that was reportedly worth millions of dollars certainly added to the excitement level.

James was all business, though. Over six feet tall and a trim but muscular two hundred pounds, with sandy hair and a bushy mustache, he had a laid-back approach to most things most of the time. He was an easy guy to like and Jenny had bought a couple of new bikinis to entice him. But on the water it was all about the job for him.

At twenty-seven, Jenny could pretty much have had her choice of guys. She took good care of herself, and it showed. Her long light-brown hair had turned golden blond in the tropical sun, and her skin was deeply tanned by the same sun. Tall and slim, with long legs and a shapely figure, she turned men's heads wherever she went.

The man who'd hired James rarely joined them on the dives, preferring to stay in Key West, researching the wreck or working at his regular job. Nearly everyone in Key West had more than one job. Jenny didn't know him personally, but knew who he was and knew that he took good care of his friends.

It hadn't taken long for the excitement of the search for sunken Spanish treasure to turn into a monotonous j-o-b, the very thing she'd come to Key West to get away from in the first place—well, that and a verbally abusive boyfriend.

Though it was early fall and the days were getting shorter, there were still a good thirteen hours of daylight each day. That, combined with the twice daily boat trip, meant a laborious and boring fifteen-hour day. To date, they'd found some nails, a few beer cans, tons of fishing tackle, and a rusty New Jersey license plate. Considering they were nearly fifteen miles from the nearest road, she wondered how the plate had arrived there.

The man financing the search was certain this new spot was the one that would finally make them rich. He'd hired James at a fixed daily rate for both boat and crew, with a percentage of the cut, when the treasure was found. James's crewman had disappeared on him two days before James accepted the job—also a common occurrence with the Key West work force. Desperate for someone reliable, he'd found Jenny through a recommendation from a friend.

Back home in Galveston, Jenny had worked for an accounting firm, just one of dozens of bean counters employed by the company. She'd paid her way through college at Texas A&M by working nights as a bartender. Bored with the daily grind after only two years, she loaded a few meager possessions into her ten-year-old Nissan and drove to Key West in three days. She'd quickly found work as a bartender at the outdoor Tiki bar at the DoubleTree Resort, and soon added a second job as bartender at The Rum Bar in Old Town.

Jenny was eager for extra cash, and the hundred and fifty per day James said he could pay was very tempting. Tourist season had dried up, and she hadn't been getting a lot of shifts at either job. She had no commercial diving experience, and explained that when James had contacted her about the job.

At first James was skeptical about hiring her. He wanted a more experienced commercial diver. She explained that her dad was a commercial diver on the oil platforms in the Gulf, and she'd been certified as a sports diver before she'd even learned to drive a car. She loved the sport and had continued taking classes, working her way up to divemaster and becoming certified in a number of specialties, including mixed gas diving and equipment repair. Once James learned that, he made her an offer and she told both her employers she was taking some time off and they could give her shifts to the other girls.

Throughout the last two days, Jenny and James had moved and reassembled the red and white pipe grid from its previous location, just fifty feet away. They were now doing a preliminary survey of each individual two-foot square of the intersecting grid. First, each grid had to be digitally photographed with a high-resolution dive camera. Six hundred and twenty-five individual grids, each with a corresponding digital image, always with north at the top of each image.

How can this possibly get any more boring? Jenny thought, hovering just above the next grid. James barely seemed to notice her when they were on the boat, and by the end of the day they were both too exhausted to care. *Maybe he's gay*, she thought.

A faint buzzing sound caught Jenny's attention as she snapped the picture and moved very carefully to her right for the next one. Maintaining neutral buoyancy in the water was critical; any sand or silt she kicked up would have to settle before she could take the next picture. Tiny particles suspended in the water would cause backscatter on the image, appearing huge from the camera's flash. She wore a belt around her narrow waist, with eight pounds of lead in a pouch at the small of her back. With her buoyancy compensator half-inflated, she was able to move easily while maintaining a partially upright position.

The buzzing grew louder and Jenny recognized it as the sound of an outboard engine. They heard them all the time; boats were always coming and going and the buzzing sound carried a long way under water. Occasionally, the project's financier came out on his own boat to check their progress, but that was rare. As the sound grew closer, Jenny took the picture and moved carefully to the next grid. The pitch of the outboard changed, as the boat slowed, approaching James's big workboat.

Must be the money man, Jenny thought. *Or a Coast Guard skiff, come to harass us.*

Hovering over the next grid, Jenny paused and looked up. The water was clear enough that she could easily make out the underside of James's workboat, and the smaller boat as it came alongside.

Not the Coast Guard, she thought. Their boats were bigger and she imagined the bottoms were just as clean as the rest of their equipment. The boat pulling alongside looked to be about the same size as the boss's, but she'd been the one out of the water the two times he'd visited, so she had no idea if the dirty, barnacle-covered hull above her was his or somebody else's.

Assuming it was him, Jenny went back to work, taking the next picture and moving slowly to the next grid. The man had sunk an awful lot of money into this project already, with absolutely nothing to show for it. Last week, when they'd found the nails, they'd thought the discovery might be significant. The nails had been scattered over an area covering more than two dozen grid squares.

But the nails had turned out to be nothing more than a bunch of fifty-year-old carpentry nails, not the seventeenth century shipbuilding nails they'd all hoped they were. Probably a bucket of nails that fell off a passing workboat.

Jenny was slowly moving to the next grid when she heard a splash and noticed a shadow pass over her. She started to turn and look up, and something hit her hard in the middle of her lower back and tugged viciously at her weight belt, yanking her upward.

Her first thought was that she'd been surprised by a shark. They'd seen quite a few over the last three weeks. She immediately began twisting her body to get free, thankful the shark had grabbed the single pouch full of tiny lead shot.

But suddenly her mask was violently ripped from her face, a clump of hair from her right temple going with it. Something wrapped around the outside of both her thighs and locked around her lower legs, as a large mass pressed against her bottom.

The man's legs, wrapped around hers like a boa constrictor, prevented Jenny from kicking with her fins. She grabbed wildly for her second stage, which should be dangling on her right side, but it wasn't there.

The man's arms encircled her, trapping her right arm in a tight grasp, leaving only her left hand, flailing uselessly. The bulk of Jenny's scuba tank prevented the man's arms from reaching all the way around and locking together for a full bear hug. As usual, Jenny was wearing only a bikini, since the ninety-degree water was more than warm enough to work without a wetsuit. The man's large hands instead grabbed both her breasts, the fingers sinking deeply into the tender flesh; pain shot through her body.

Slashing with her left hand, Jenny pawed at the water, trying to get free. But the man was too strong, and he held her breasts in a vice-like grip and began thrusting against her. She could feel the bulge in his groin as he drove himself into her, using her own legs for leverage.

Reaching back as far as she could with her free hand, she tried to grab the man's mask, but there wasn't one on his face. When she tried to gouge at his eyes, he twisted his head and she raked her long nails across his cheek.

With her right arm trapped, she could grab her octopus, the backup second stage of her regulator, though it did little good with her arm trapped. She pushed the button on the front of it anyway, releasing a purge of air in a free flow.

This seemed to distract the man for a moment, but then he squeezed harder. Jenny distinctly heard the cracking sound when her right arm broke, and a sharp pain shot up her arm. She heard the muffled sound of the man laughing, as he began thrusting his pelvis against her again.

Through her distorted vision, she made out a large hand as it flashed in front of her. The second stage of her regulator was yanked violently from her mouth and Jenny went into full panic mode, thrashing wildly and struggling to get to the surface.

A lucid part of her mind grasped that this wasn't a sexual act. She wasn't being raped by the Creature from the Black Lagoon. She felt a pull on her regulator hose, where it was attached to her buoyancy compensator. Too late, Jenny realized that the man attacking her wasn't wearing his own scuba gear, but was now breathing from her second stage. He also wasn't wearing fins, but was instead using his legs to power *her* fins, driving both of them toward the bottom.

Forced downward through the grid of interconnecting pipes, Jenny impacted the rough, sandy bottom face first, forcing her lower jaw open and driving sand into her mouth. She pushed against the bottom with her one free hand, again twisting her body and gyrating wildly in a last-ditch effort to get free, each movement causing excruciating pain in her broken right arm. She managed to push hard enough against the bottom to cause them both to slowly rise up out of the grid.

The man continued thrusting his groin against her ass and she could feel him growing larger, becoming aroused by her twisting movements and his hands on her breasts. Her lungs burned with the need for air as her face was again slammed into the bottom. This time, it wasn't the coarse, but yielding sand. The man had driven her face into a small piece of rough brain coral.

The jagged, dome-shaped coral didn't yield; instead, it gouged out chunks of flesh from her cheek. The wounds burned, competing in intensity with the other pain the man was inflicting. He continued levering her legs, spreading them apart. His swimsuit did little to hide his now hard manhood pressed against her. His hands pawed at her breasts, pulling her bikini top up and allowing him to grip her soft flesh even tighter.

Her face again buried in the sand, she felt the man release his grip with his right hand, but keep his grip on her left breast, squeezing so hard she thought she would scream.

Roughly, he continued thrusting with wild abandon. His free hand grabbed her hair and yanked her face up out of the grid. Jenny's neck was strained backward, and the regulator's first stage tore another hunk of flesh and hair from her scalp.

With her body bent backwards, the man seized the dump valve at the top of her BC and pulled it, releasing all the air from her compensator.

With no air in the BC, the heavy lead weights pulled Jenny to the bottom, the man riding her down as a gray haze seemed to cloud her vision. Her body fell over one of the pipes, and the man grabbed her hair at the back of her skull, smashing her face into the bottom over and over, showing no mercy at all. Her whole body was in agony as he yanked her head sideways and shoved it down hard to the bottom, his hand planted firmly against the side of her face.

As blackness descended over her mind, Jenny saw James next to her. He had a purplish hole just above his right eye, oozing blood. Somewhere in the back of Jenny's mind, she knew there was no way of escaping. As the man continued to bash her head against the rocks and coral on the bottom, she took a sharp breath, inhaling water, sand, and bits of seagrass. As she did so, a rough hand pawed at the bottom of her bikini, grabbing it and ripping it away, the cloth cutting deep into the tender skin of her inner thighs before breaking.

The pain she felt from the numerous gashes on her cheek and head, the broken bone in her right arm, and the vice-like grip kneading and twisting her breast was nothing like the agony in her lungs as seawater flooded them.

The pain lasted only a second. Jenny convulsed once as everything went black, then once more as the life force left her body. Her attacker continued to slam her face against the rough seabed, then slowed his merciless treatment, taking his time now that her body had stopped twitching. Her blood mixed with the silt that enveloped them both.

When he was finished, hoping to stage things to look like something else, he inflated Jenny's BC so he could drag both corpses up to the boat. There, he hooked a tether to one body and let the other drift away.

CHAPTER THREE

"Heard something like a gunshot about twenty minutes ago," Carl shouted from the south pier, as I idled *Pescador* into the little basin in front of my house. I'd named the boat for a dog I'd given up nearly a year ago when I found his original owner, adding the name—which is Spanish for fisherman—in big letters on both sides,. "Sounded like it was way off," Carl added.

Getting the little Grady-White turned around, I backed in under the house and Carl helped me with the lines. "We heard it too. Sounded like it came from out beyond Snipe Key."

Carl frowned. "That *is* a long way off. But, the barometer is high today, so sound'll carry further."

Carl Trent and his wife, Charlie, are the island's caretakers. Together with their kids, Carl Junior and Patty, they live on my island and keep things running.

"Thought it might have been you," he said, with a wry grin. "I was about to head out to find Finn and retrieve your body."

Tying Pescador off, I took Carl's offered hand and stepped up onto the little dock under my house. "It'd be kinda difficult for someone to get that close to me out there," I said, grinning back. "But we both appreciate the thought."

Finn jumped onto the dock and streaked past us, heading for the open door on the west side of the dock area.

"He still hasn't learned to relieve himself in the water?" Carl asked, as we followed Finn up to the deck.

"He will, sooner or later. We were out there for five hours."

We both sat down at the table on the corner of the deck overlooking the interior of my island. Below and to the east, the pump came on in our little aquaponics system, moving water from the reservoir on the vegetable tank back up to the fish tank—we grow an assortment of vegetables in one, and raise crawfish and tilapia in the other. After a moment, it shut off.

Carl reached into a cooler and took out two Red Stripes, placing them on the table between us. "You see that big bone out there again?"

"Yeah," I replied, picking up the metal bottle opener and opening both our beers. "We stopped by Cudjoe Basin on the way back. Saw him twice before he disappeared."

"I take it you didn't catch him," Carl said. "Mac stopped by a little while ago."

"He say what he wanted?"

"Spoke about as many words as he usually does. Said he was just stopping by to say hi."

Mac Travis lives in Marathon, on Boot Key. He runs a small salvage business from the workshop under his house and sets a string of lobster traps during the season. He used to work for Bill Woodson, who built or repaired a good many of the bridges that connect the Keys from Islamorada to Key West, before Wood was killed up island some time back.

"Mac's not the social type," I offered.

"No, he sure isn't. Seemed worried about something."

"He *is* the worrying type, though." I said, taking a long pull from the ice-cold beer.

"He only stayed a few minutes. Not even long enough to shut down his outboard. Said he'd catch up with you later. You catch anything?"

I couldn't help but wonder what it was Mac had wanted. He was sort of a loner and kept pretty much to himself, since his girlfriend, and late boss's daughter, Mel had gone back up north. He was the opposite of his Cajun crewman, Trufant. Anywhere there was trouble, Tru and his polished ivories weren't far away.

"Yeah," I answered. "There's about thirty or so grunts in the live-well. They'll keep until we finish these beers."

"You ever give your buddy down in Key Weird an answer?" Carl asked, referring to an offer I'd gotten to do some treasure hunting.

"Yeah, told him I was too busy and wasn't interested."

"Too busy?" Carl scoffed, as his wife Charlie came up the rear steps to the deck. "Hell, man, you haven't chartered since Kim went back up to Gainesville last month."

"I'm taking off to pick up the kids," Charlie said. "Hey, Jesse."

"Hey, yourself," I said, looking at the angle of the sun. "I thought they'd be back from school already."

"They had a play date with friends. The other kids' momma was taking them to Big Pine Key Park, to burn off some energy."

She leaned in and kissed Carl, then headed down the steps to the docks. We have a whole fleet of boats below the house, ranging in size from *Pescador*, a seventeen-and-a-half-foot Grady, to *Gaspar's Revenge*, my forty-five-foot charter fishing and dive boat. With Kim gone, her flats skiff was now stored up on slings, making room for *Pescador*.

"Kim's the one that runs things," I told Carl, after Charlie left. "She's a lot more organized than me."

Kim's my youngest daughter. She'd spent the last two summers here, much to the chagrin of her mother, my first wife. She'd returned to her studies at University of Florida, where she was majoring in Criminology, much to my own chagrin. She had a good head for business and I felt she was wasting her talent, wanting to be a cop. But she was a grown woman, and I wasn't going to stand in the way of her doing what she felt she needed to do.

As we enjoyed our beers, I heard the engine on Carl and Charlie's own Grady-White start up, and a minute later Charlie idled out the short channel to deeper water. Knowing it was high tide, she continued straight south in Harbor Channel, bringing the twenty-footer up on plane, zig-zagging her way toward Big Pine Key, seven miles south of here.

"So, why'd ya really turn down the chance to get in on the big treasure hunt?" Carl asked, taking the last pull from his bottle and standing up.

Draining my own beer, I rose with him and we started down to the dock area to clean the fish. "I don't know. Lawrence is a good friend and I guess I just don't want to work for him. Does that make sense?"

"We're good friends," he said, descending the stairs. "I got no trouble taking your money."

"That's different. At the end of the day, you always have something to show for the work you do. A treasure hunt doesn't have any guarantee of success."

"True dat," Carl said, picking up a cooler from under the cleaning station and stepping aboard *Pescador*. "I guess I can see your reasoning behind it. Think he found someone else?"

Carl opened the live well under the forward seat of the boat, then using a little catch net, began to dip the small grunts out and dump them into the cooler.

"Yeah." I picked up the first fish and quickly filleted it, then dumped the carcass in the water. "I heard on the coconut telegraph that he hired a guy out of Ramrod Key—a young fella named James Isaksson. Ever hear of him?"

Dipping the last of the fish into the cooler, Carl joined me at the cleaning table. "I know a Dwight Isaksson in Ramrod. He's a little older than us, maybe mid-fifties. Used to run a salvage boat, but had to give it up when he lost an arm to a boat prop. Might be related—don't know if he had any sons or not. Didn't know him that well."

We continued cleaning the fish, making quick work of it, and filled a small metal tray with the tasty little fillets.

"Ya know," Carl said, looking down in the water below the dock, "we could just drop a trap right here. Them lobster have gotten pretty used to getting fed here every day." I frowned at him and he said, "I know, I know, it ain't sporting."

"It's also illegal," I reminded him, though the thought had crossed my mind a few times on stormy days. We kept a line of lobster and stone crab traps along the deeper part of Harbor Channel and when a gale blew in from the east, pulling the traps became a real chore.

"Yeah, well, it's only illegal if you get caught." Carl picked up the tray of fillets, and we went back up the steps. "You got any room in your freezer?" he asked.

"Maybe for half of them. Charlie say what she was planning for dinner?"

Carl grinned. "Yeah, she did. Grunts and grits. Let's put half of these in your freezer and the rest I'll put in our fridge."

"How the heck does she know?" I wondered out loud.

"I keep tellin' ya. She's part fish and part witch."

CHAPTER FOUR

"We got a floater," Detective Ben Morgan said, leaning through Captain Pete Simpson's open door.

"A floater?" the captain asked. Though Key West had the reputation of being a wild and lawless town, there were surprisingly few murders in the southernmost city, and a body floating in the water wouldn't be good for tourism. "Where?"

"A boater found the body of a diver about half a mile north of Snipe Key."

Relieved that it was a possible diving accident and not a homicide, Captain Simpson said, "We're shorthanded, Ben. You're gonna have to take lead. Grab Evans out of the bullpen."

Morgan frowned. "She gets seasick."

Simpson opened his drawer and tossed a small pill bottle, which Morgan deftly caught in his left hand. "Tell her to take two Dramamine. By the time you get down to the dock, they'll kick in. Jefferson's already out on a domestic disturbance with shots fired, and Clark won't be back from vacation till tomorrow."

Morgan turned to go back to the squad room. He'd been a Monroe County Sheriff's deputy for nearly twenty years, moving up from water patrol to the detective squad ten years before. Five years ago, he'd been promoted to lieutenant. As Captain Simpson's second-in-command of the small investigative unit, he oversaw the work of the other detectives, but rarely went out into the field anymore.

In his early forties, Ben was one of only a handful of lieutenants in the department. Unlike the others, he wasn't looking forward to his next promotion. In a town known for rum drinking, a Captain Morgan would become the brunt of many jokes.

"Evans," Ben shouted as he entered the squad room and found her at her desk. She looked up from her computer, her light-brown eyes sparkling with excitement. The woman always seemed to be upbeat and smiling. Ben walked across the small squad room she shared with three other detectives. Evans's partner was out on sick leave for at least two more weeks.

Ben placed the pill bottle in front of her. "Take two of these. You're with me."

"What do we have?" Devon Evans asked, standing and picking up the pill bottle, looking at it. "Dramamine? We're going out on the water?"

Ben rolled his eyes at the young blond detective. "You live and work on an island. How can you not be a boater? Never mind, take two of those and let's go. A fisherman found a floater up near Snipe Key."

"Ugh," she replied, twisting off the top and shaking out two of the little orange pills. Obediently, she popped them in her mouth and swallowed them down with a gulp of water from an Evian bottle. She'd been prone to motion sickness since she was a little girl. Not just on a boat, but planes, cars, even amusement park rides.

The drive from the administration building on Stock Island to the nearby marina where the department kept their two patrol boats only took a few minutes. They could have walked it nearly as fast, but given the increasing girth of his waistline, Ben preferred the air-conditioned comfort of his county-issued Crown Vic.

At the marina, the two detectives walked out to where a patrol deputy waited on a brand new twenty-three-foot Mako center console. Drug arrests were common in the Keys, and many times the dealers had their financial assets seized, as well as their boats, cars, and drugs. The boats and cars were auctioned, and the money kept the department's equipment updated on a regular basis.

The deputy wore gray shorts, along with his gray uniform shirt and black utility belt and holster—typical of water patrol deputies, but in sharp contrast to the light gray suit and black tie Ben wore and the black skirt and dark gray jacket of the junior detective.

"Welcome aboard," the deputy said. "I'm Deputy Martin Phillips."

"Detective Ben Morgan," Ben said, shaking hands with the young deputy. "This is my partner, Detective Evans."

Ben stepped down into the cockpit and pointed forward. "Take the forward seat, Evans."

Devon stepped down and went forward as the deputy started the big Yamaha outboard, then tossed off the lines.

"I used to be on the marine patrol squad," Ben said. "I thought I knew everyone. You're new?"

"Filling in for Quail," the deputy said, as he put the boat in gear and idled away from the dock. "His wife's having a baby any day and he's taking some comp time. I usually patrol out of the Middle Keys."

"Ah, you're Ben Phillips's boy. Heard you'd joined the department. How's your dad?"

"Doing well, sir. The other patrol boat is anchored on-station where the body was found. He has a line on it, but hasn't pulled it out of the water yet. Waiting for the ME."

"Doc Fredric on his way?"

"He's finishing up an autopsy in Marathon," Phillips replied. "Said he'd be out there in under an hour. That was about twenty minutes ago."

"It'll be close to dark when he gets there."

"I don't think Doc sleeps much," the deputy replied, bringing the boat up on plane and accelerating across the shallow flats to the north.

Twenty minutes later, the deputy slowed as they approached another sheriff's patrol boat, identical to his own. The other deputy motioned them to tie up on his port side. As they neared, Ben could see why. In the water on the starboard side, a scuba tank was in the water, tied off to the boat. Attached to the tank was a body, floating face down.

Once the two deputies made the boats fast, Ben stepped over and asked, "Whatcha got, Deputy Cantrell?"

John Cantrell pointed a long arm toward another boat, anchored a hundred yards away. "Fishermen found her about an hour ago, sir." Then stepping over to the other side, he nodded down at the body. "She's naked, except for the BC and fins."

"Naked?" Devon said, stepping over to the other boat and leaning over the rail. "I know it's the Keys, but isn't that kind of odd? Scuba diving in the nude?"

"Not as strange as you'd think," Deputy Phillips said, joining the others at the rail.

"Have you moved the body at all?" Ben asked, pulling a pair of blue latex gloves from his pocket and snapping them on. Evans, following his lead, did the same thing.

"No, sir," Cantrell replied. "Dropped a noose around the first stage and tied it off."

"Well," Ben said, leaning over and reaching a hand down, "let's see what she looks like." Grabbing the woman's dark-blond hair, he pulled her head up for a closer look at her face. "Good God!" he exclaimed, releasing his grip and letting the woman's cracked and torn face drop back into the water. He'd seen his fair share of victims involved in scuba diving accidents, car accidents, beatings, and nearly a dozen murders. But, he'd never seen anything like he'd just witnessed.

Devon went to the back of the boat and leaned over the transom, vomiting into the water. Phillips quickly grabbed a bottle of water and took it to her, offering her a towel that was draped across the back of the seat.

"Thanks," Devon said, wiping her mouth and taking a long pull from the bottle. "It wasn't the body. I get seasick pretty easy." She returned to the side of the boat, all three men staring at her. Ben rolled his eyes.

To prove her point, she leaned over the gunwale and peered down at the body. "Something's not right here."

"You mean about a woman who lives on an island and gets seasick?" Ben asked.

"No." She glared at him. "Look at her right arm."

All three men looked over the side. The body moved in the light chop and, just as Devon had indicated, the right arm moved strangely.

"Her arm's broken," Phillips said. "The upper arm."

Just then, the sound of another boat could be heard. Ben looked to the east and saw a patrol boat, with blue lights flashing, coming out of Cudjoe Channel, just beyond Sawyer Key. As it approached, he recognized Doc Fredric standing in the bow, one hand holding the bow line, his white hair pulled straight back by the wind. There were three others on board with Doc Fredric, Ben noted.

"ME's here," he said to nobody in particular.

Cantrell went forward and motioned the other boat to the port side as well. The deputy at the helm expertly guided the boat alongside, making a threesome of twenty-three-foot Makos, all lashed together, with their collective bows pointing north into the current.

When it was secured, the doctor stepped lightly over onto Phillips's boat, belying his age, then again onto Cantrell's. "Nice to see you again, Marty," he said, shaking Phillips's hand. He nodded to the other deputy, shook his hand and greeted him by his first name, also.

"I don't believe we've met," the old doctor said to Devon, extending his hand. "I'm Leo Fredric, Monroe County Medical Examiner. But please, just call me Doc."

"Detective Devon Evans," she replied.

"You're a breath of fresh air in the department," Doc said, extending his hand to Ben. "Too many of these ugly, old detectives in the department to suit me. What do we have, Ben?"

Ben grinned at the old-timer. He'd been the ME for Monroe County since before Ben had joined the department in 1991, and everyone liked him. "Doing about as well as an ugly, old detective can, Doc." Nodding over the side, he continued. "Female Caucasian, completely nude except her fins and buoyancy compensator. Multiple cuts and abrasions on her face, and what appears to be a broken upper right arm."

"A broken humerus?" Doc asked, a quizzical expression on his face, as he leaned over the gunwale for a closer look. "Some lividity around her outside bicep, as well. She must have been hit pretty hard. A boat perhaps. But, I'll know more when I get her to the lab."

Unlike the detectives, Doc always talked of the dead, as if they were still alive, using the pronouns *she, he, him,* or *her,* instead of "the body," as the detectives were accustomed to. If he knew who it was, he'd refer to the victim's body by name.

"May we borrow your—" Doc began, turning to Cantrell, who already had his backboard out, a line attached to the top of it. "Oh, I see you anticipated me, John. Very good." He turned and nodded to the two men in the back of the boat, who were both wearing department issue scuba gear.

The two men rolled off the gunwale, disappearing with a splash. A moment later, their air bubbles announced their arrival next to the body and Cantrell lowered the backboard to them.

"Face down, gentlemen," Doc said. "Leave her equipment on her. There may be trace evidence on it."

The two men worked quickly, strapping the body onto the backboard as they were instructed.

When they had it secured, Doc nodded to Marty and John. "Haul her up, boys. Let's see what we can see."

Marty and John pulled up on the line attached to the backboard. As the top of it reached the gunwale, Marty held on firmly as John grabbed the handhold on the top of the board. When John nodded, Marty joined him at the gunwale and they both reached down to grab other handholds on the sides. The divers in the water pushed the foot of the board away from the boat and the two deputies hauled it up, and then maneuvered it around so that the woman's upper body was on the casting deck and her feet on the center console's front seat.

"The BC is fully inflated," Doc noted, walking around the body. He squatted down to examine the woman's face. "Oh my, what happened to you, dear?"

"Looks like her face was hit by a prop," Ben offered.

Doc looked up, a wry smile on his face. "Oh no, not a propeller, I'm afraid. Come closer, Ben. You too, Devon."

The two detectives moved around to either side of the ME and knelt next to the platform. Marty and John leaned in behind the two detectives for a closer look, as well. Taking a pair of tweezers from his pocket, Doc carefully removed something from the side of the woman's face. At first, Ben thought it was a bone fragment.

"Coral, I do believe," Doc said. Then he extended it to Marty, who he knew to be an avid sport diver and aquarist. "Would you agree?"

"Absolutely, Doc." Marty pointed. "What's that in her mouth?"

From another pocket, Doc pulled out a small magnifying glass. "Good eye, Marty," he said, opening the woman's mouth and looking inside. "Coral sand and sea grass, I believe. All the way back into her esophagus. Note also the foam back in there. This poor girl probably drowned."

John whipped off his sunglasses and did his best Richard Dreyfuss impression. "Well, this is not a boat accident!" His impression of the line from the movie *Jaws* was less than stellar, and he received a stern look from Ben.

Doc and Devon both chuckled and she whispered softly, "I loved that movie."

Doc grinned at her and said in a low voice, "That picture ruined tourism here for two years. I'd just been made assistant ME at the time and it was the most boring two years of my life."

She giggled softly, getting her a stern look from Ben as well. "Can we get on with this?" he said.

Marty handed Doc two heavy plastic bags. The ME glanced up at the young deputy and winked. "Better watch out, Ben. I think these young deputies are bucking for your job."

Doc did a quick inspection of the victim's right hand then, putting the bag over it, he secured it with a rubber band. "What's this?" Doc said, peering closely at the left hand, before bagging it, as well.

"What is it, Doc?" Ben asked.

"Probable COD is drowning," Doc replied. "I won't know for sure until I get her to the lab, but there's something under the fingernails of her left hand. My first guess is skin tissue. Possibly from someone else."

"Homicide?" Devon asked, her eyes sparkling just a little.

"I can give you more information in the morning," Doc said. "But my guess is yes, a homicide. Do we know where the dive boat is?"

Ben glanced at Marty, who spoke up. "Dispatch is checking, but no dive boats reported a missing diver today."

Doc Fredric looked toward the bow, and beyond it to the northern horizon. Like most people in the Keys, he instinctually knew the rise and fall of the daily tides. "It will be low tide in less than an hour," he said, still staring off to the north. "This poor girl may have drifted on the current for miles."

CHAPTER FIVE

The following afternoon found Finn and me slowly idling the *Revenge* along the canal at the *Rusty Anchor*. Reaching the turning basin at the end, I used the throttles to slowly spin her around as I scanned the tiny marina. There wasn't anyone on the dock, nor in the yard. Unusual at the *Rusty Anchor* on a Friday evening.

Gaspar's Revenge is my forty-five-foot beast of a fishing boat. I'm a horsepower junkie, and the *Revenge* has it in spades. It's powered by twin eighteen-liter diesel engines, each producing just over a thousand horses when they're new. But they'd been highly modified and supercharged by the previous owner, who was also a power nut. Now, each engine put out a whopping one-thousand-three-hundred ponies.

Letting the boat drift slowly toward Rusty's big barge, tied off at the end of the turning basin, I quickly scrambled down from the fly bridge and tied the *Revenge* off to the barge's big deck cleats.

Leaping the gunwale, I crossed the barge to the gang-plank, Finn trotting ahead of me. I recognized most of the boats docked here—live-aboards, for the most part, plus a few boats whose owners lived in normal accommodations but didn't have their own dock.

For the weekend, this would be home for Finn and me. Rusty and I had gone through boot camp together at Parris Island, and had been close ever since. Next year, we planned to celebrate the thirtieth anniversary of our graduating and becoming Marines.

I paused at the top of the gangplank and took a slow look around the yard and parking lot, while Finn relieved himself on a banyan tree. Looking at my surroundings was an old habit born of necessity. Seeing no threats—not that I expected any—I strode toward the door of the bar.

Inside, I paused for a moment, letting my eyes adjust to the lower light. The Thurman family had owned this land for generations, and the bar had been many things over those years. Out back, Rusty's grandfather had made rum during the Prohibition years. The rum shack was now home for Rusty's cook, Rufus.

"Hey, you old coot," I heard Rusty shout from behind the bar. "Drag your sorry ass over here."

Spotting a couple of empty stools near the far end of the bar, I took the furthest one, against the wall. Another old habit. There were a few more patrons than usual at this time of day, and everyone's attention was glued to the TV, which was currently showing a commercial.

"What's going on?" I asked Rusty as he placed a cold Red Stripe in front of me and popped the cap off.

"Weather channel," he replied. "There's a 'cane out in the Atlantic. But a course you wouldn't a heard anything about that."

He was right. We don't have television on my island, though I guess I could watch it in the *Revenge* if I were inclined. Which I'm not.

"Bad?" I asked, taking a long pull of my first beer of the day.

"Cat four," he replied.

Category four meant it was a major hurricane, with winds over a hundred and thirty miles per hour. Bad news any way you looked at it.

"Last night it was heading in a straight line toward the Carolinas, but earlier today, it turned a little more westerly."

"How far out?"

"A hundred or so miles north of Puerto Rico right now. Heading west by southwest, toward Cuba."

Double bad news. South of Cuba is the warm waters of the Caribbean and north of Cuba is the Gulf Stream, more warm water. The Florida Keys lie just north of the Stream.

"Shit," I muttered. "I was looking forward to some fishing."

"Ain't gonna happen, bro. Rain bands'll get here by morning. They keep saying it'll move through the southern Bahamas on Sunday and make landfall on the northeastern Cuban coast some time on Monday. Weather here's gonna be crapped out for a week. The governor's already issued a state of emergency."

"You making any plans?"

"Ordered a special beer delivery, that's about it. Was gonna call ya to see what your plans were for the *Hopper*, but figured I'd see you before you saw your phone."

Right on that count, too. If I hadn't lost it again, my phone was somewhere on the boat, probably with a dead battery.

The door opened, and Jimmy Saunders walked in with his girlfriend Angie. Jimmy was my first mate for a time, and Angie was Carl's daughter from his first marriage. The two joined me at the bar, Jimmy pulling out the stool for Angie.

"*Que pasa*, Jesse?" Jimmy said, clapping a hand on my shoulder as Angie sat down next to me. "What're you doing down here, dude?"

"It's Friday, Jimmy. I'm always here on a Friday."

"Friday already, man?"

Rusty gave me a sad look. "About that. Kim called and said to tell you she was staying in Gainesville. Something to do with Marty having to work this weekend."

"Nothing to do now but have a hurricane party," Jimmy suggested.

"And speaking of that," Rusty said. "Where you been? I thought you'd be here with that beer order a coupla hours ago."

"Sorry, *compadre*. We had to run all the way up to Islamorada to get everything. Seems you're not the only barkeep with that idea, man. I'll start bringing it in."

"Anything I can do?" I asked.

"Help Jimmy?"

I drained my beer and got up. "Sure," I told Rusty. Then to Angie, I said, "Hold my seat for me?"

"Sure thing," she said with a smile, and I went out the back door after Jimmy.

I caught up to him at Rusty's old Chevy pickup. "Damn, that's a lot of beer."

"Booze too, man. Rusty figured he might not get a chance to get more for a few days. 'preciate the help, bro."

Rusty's big walk-in cooler had an exterior door, and Jimmy had the pickup backed in close to it. Since he knew better where to put stuff, I handed cases to him at the door and he put them away. We had the pickup empty in just a few minutes.

Jimmy brought me a cold Kalik, the national beer of the Bahamas, when he came back out of the cooler. "Last of the cold Stripes is in the bar cooler, man. Those we just unloaded are warm."

I opened it and said, "Thanks."

"You mind?" Jimmy said, taking a small plastic bag from his hip pocket. Without waiting for a reply, he produced a rolling paper and quickly rolled a joint.

"Why do you waste your money on that?" I asked, putting the tailgate up on the Chevy.

"You never tried it?" he asked, lighting up and taking a long drag.

"Not in this lifetime," I said.

"Well, you shouldn't knock something you never tried, dude," he croaked while holding his breath.

Jimmy exhaled a cloud of blue-gray smoke, which drifted upward in the light wind. I caught a whiff of it, the smell strong and kind of sweet. I'd tried cigarettes once when I was a teen. Nearly expelled a lung. I knew others in the Corps who smoked regularly and it didn't seem to diminish their ability to run or fight. Marijuana was completely out of the question, though. A Marine caught with even a small amount would be severely punished and probably discharged.

"I'll stick to beer," I said, raising my bottle to him. Jimmy was a good man, the pot smoking notwithstanding. When he worked for me, he always arrived sober and never brought it on board. The one time he had, I'd snatched it from his hand and tossed it overboard.

We sat down on a couple of upturned buckets, me drinking my beer and him smoking his pot. Ours was an unlikely friendship, but like I said, he was a hard-working man and very reliable—two things that are hard to find in the Keys.

"What ever happened to that Linda chick?" Jimmy asked, licking his fingers and smushing the joint out halfway through.

"She moved upstate. You know that."

"But what happened between you and her?" he prodded. "Seemed like you had a pretty serious thing going there."

"Yep," I said, standing up and heading toward the door. "Right up to the point when I found out she was screwing someone else."

"Buzzkill, man," Jimmy said, following me back inside the bar.

"So, what are you gonna do about the *Hopper*?" Rusty asked again. *Island Hopper* is my vintage 1953 deHavilland Beaver amphibian, which I keep down by Rusty's boat ramp.

"Guess I ought to find a place to move her inside," I said. "Or at least further upstate out of danger."

"Ain't gonna find any empty hangar space in the Keys," he said. "Best bet, fly her up to Billy's place in LaBelle. Might be some hangar space there. I doubt the storm's gonna make landfall here, but we will get some pretty strong blows come Tuesday and Wednesday."

"You up for a road trip?" I asked Jimmy.

"No can do, man. Rusty's got me for the duration. New class was supposed to start Monday, but we had to cancel on account of the storm."

"Can I borrow your—" I began. Rusty placed the old rotary phone on the bar. "Thanks."

I hadn't talked to Billy in several months. He answered and said, "Rusty Thurman, how are ya, you old Conch?"

"Hey, Billy," I said. "It's not Rusty."

"Well, hey there, Kemosabe," he said. "What can I do for ya? Need some guns?"

"I need to fly my plane out of here for awhile. Can I hire you to give me a ride back?"

"Hell, no! But if you pay for the gas, I'll come down and see how you whites handle a storm. Tomorrow?"

"At the airport around nine?"

"Done," he replied. I heard a click and then a dial tone.

"You're bringing that crazy-ass Indian down here?" Rusty asked.

"He's mellowed out now," I told him. "He can stay on the boat and go back after the storm."

Planning for a hurricane in the Keys is more of a waiting game than anything. Until you know where the storm's headed, you just wait and pay attention to the weather experts. I glanced up at the TV, which showed the projected path of Hurricane Ike. The cone extended out west-southwest of the storm, passing over some of the islands in the southern Bahamas and then, depending on which side of the cone the storm took, it would either cross Cuba at the eastern end and go into the Caribbean, or skirt the northern coast. The line down the center of the cone had it crossing and then moving along the southern coast of the communist island nation.

Over the next couple of days, folks here would just watch and wait. We'd experienced many hurricanes here. Or I should say, others had. I'd only lived here for nine years and was still considered an outsider by most Conchs, the people who were born here. Everyone had their own plan, in the event of a hurricane and everyone always had provisions laid up at the start of the season. For Rusty, I knew that no part of his plan involved evacuating. He and his family had weathered the worst that Mother Nature could throw their way, and they'd survived. Most Conchs had the same mindset.

"Reckon what he's doing here?" Rusty said, pointing with his chin out the windows along the west side of the bar. I followed his gaze and saw Mac Travis tying up at the gas dock.

"A couple of Red Stripes," I said to Rusty.

He pulled them out of the cooler, popped the caps off and handed them to me. I carried them out the back door, and when I reached the dock Mac was just stepping up onto it.

"Mac," I said, extending a beer bottle.

He took it from my hand and sucked down a third of it. "Jesse."

We walked out to the deck behind the bar. The sun was still high in the western sky, but big white clouds had it partially blocked. Sitting down at one of the tables, away from the few people who were enjoying the cooler air, Mac took his sunglasses off and laid them on the roughhewn table. His face was dark-tanned, with little lines around his eyes. What the sunglasses covered was less tanned, giving him a raccoon look.

"Figured you'd be here today," Mac said.

"Guess I'm getting too predictable. Carl said you stopped by yesterday."

"Gotta leave for a few days," he said. "Was wondering if I might ask you to keep an eye on Wood's old place."

Bill Woodson used to live on an island not far from mine. The terms of his owning it were shady at best, but he'd built a little stilt house out there, not much different from my own.

"Wouldn't expect you to be one to evacuate."

"I'm not," Mac replied. "Just got some business to tend to."

"Wood's island belongs to Mel now?"

"She don't want nothing to do with it," Mac replied. "Or the Keys, for that matter. But yeah, it's hers. I've been kinda looking after it, while she's up in DC."

Melanie Woodson is an attorney. She and Mac had once been an item, up until Wood was killed. Mac turned to lobstering then, doing occasional salvage work during the off-season to get by, and Mel went off to play environmental advocate. An unlikely pair, at best.

"I can see the island from my deck," I offered. "And can hear anyone out there for miles around."

"I appreciate it. Doubt there will be any trouble this time of year. I just finished boarding everything up, it should ride the storm okay, even if it's a direct hit."

"How long will you be gone?" I asked taking a long pull from my beer bottle.

"A week at most."

"I'll buzz over after the storm and make sure everything's okay."

Mac offered his bottle, and I clinked mine against it. He stood up and looked out over the long backyard toward where the Hopper sat, near the boat ramp.

"I expect you'll be moving that?"

"Flying up to LaBelle tomorrow," I replied. "But I'll be back by mid-afternoon.

He picked up his sunglasses and put them on. "Appreciate it. And thanks for the beer."

"Don't mention it," I said.

"See you around." He turned and walked back down to the dock. A moment later, he was idling down the long canal toward open water. His house was over in the maze of canals along Sister Creek, near Boot Key Harbor, about ten minutes away by boat.

"What'd Mac want?" Rusty asked, when I went back inside.

"Asked me to keep an eye on Wood's place. He's going out of town for a few days."

"Hope he's going up to DC to make nice with Mel," Rusty said. "Those two need each other and she don't belong up there."

CHAPTER SIX

B en and Devon arrived at the ME's office in Marathon early the next morning. Doc Fredric had been working on a particularly troublesome case there and had taken the female victim's body there, instead of Key West. It meant a drive for the two detectives but getting out of the city, even for just a day, was always a welcome diversion for Ben.

"Look, I know this is your first possible homicide case," Ben said as they approached the door. "But, you *have* witnessed an autopsy before, haven't you?"

"Five. Relax, Lieutenant, I'll be fine."

"Good." Ben opened the door and walked inside. "We don't want a repeat of yesterday."

Behind his back, Devon did her own impression of Dreyfuss, giving Ben the finger then hooking her pinkies in her mouth and wagging her tongue at him.

Doctor Fredric stood just inside the doorway and grinned at her display. "You're much too young to have seen that."

Devon's cheeks colored as Ben turned to face her. He turned back to the ME and said, "Seen what?"

"Oh, nothing," Doc said, turning toward the hallway leading back to the morgue in the rear of the newly built structure. "I have the preliminary autopsy findings. Follow me, please."

They paused at the reception desk, where the two detectives signed the log, then Doc led them further down the hall and stopped in front of a large doorway. He tapped some buttons on a keypad next to the door and Ben heard a gentle whooshing sound as the door opened, breaking the airtight seal.

Doc went straight to his desk and picked up a clipboard, then went to one of two cadaver tables in the middle of the room and pulled back the sheet from the body.

Ben felt bile rising in his own throat. The woman's face was horribly disfigured. Devon stepped up closer to the body, eager to learn the precise cause and manner of the victim's death.

"The tox report hasn't come back yet," Doc began. "But, judging from her overall physique and appearance, I'd wager it will be negative. The scrapings from under her fingernails were indeed skin and blood tissue, along with two strands of hair. But of course the DNA results will take even longer."

Ben approached the other side of the table. The woman's body had been opened up. A Y-shaped incision had been made from each shoulder to a long lateral cut from between her breasts to her navel. She'd already been sutured back together, but there was little Doc could do for her ruined face. The right side wasn't as bad and, looking at her profile, Ben could see that she'd been a beautiful young woman, probably in her late twenties. She'd had medium-length hair, turned a light golden-brown by the sun. Aside from the incisions and sutures, she had an exceptional body, he noted. Fit and athletic.

"Nothing out of the ordinary with her heart and other organs, but as I expected, her lungs were filled with sea water. I also found bits of biological material and fine, powdery sand in her lungs."

"Biological material?" Ben asked.

"Some type of algae or sea grass. I sent samples to a colleague at Mote Marine Lab, up island for identification."

"Death by drowning?" Devon asked, sounding somewhat disappointed as she bent to examine the wounds to the victim's face more closely. The woman's left cheek had literally been torn from her face, and hung on by a small thread of skin below the left ear. Her left eye socket was empty.

"She probably would have died from wounds incurred anyway," Doc said. "Drowning was faster. Her scuba tank had nearly a thousand pounds of air and I found nothing wrong with either the first or second stage of her regulator."

"You dive, Doctor?" Devon asked.

"Please don't be so formal," Doc said. "Everyone just calls me Doc or Leo. Yes, I have a master scuba diver rating and I'm also certified in equipment repair and testing."

"So, if she had air, how'd she drown?" Ben asked.

"Note the bruising on her breasts?" Doc picked up a round Styrofoam cylinder about the size of a scuba tank and walked around behind Devon. "If I may demonstrate?"

Devon turned her head and nodded. Doc placed the lightweight cylinder against her back and stepped closer. "Raise your left arm, please."

When Devon lifted her arm, the ME wrapped his arms around her, sandwiching the make-believe scuba tank between them. He was careful to keep his hands away from her breasts, though.

"With the cylinder on her back, her attacker was unable to clasp his hands together for a proper bear hug. So, he grabbed what he could. Holding her breasts and squeezing, he fractured her right humerus, wedged at her side. He'll be a very powerful man."

When Doc put the prop back on the table and looked at Devon, her face flushed. She quickly recovered and bent to examine the victim's breasts. "Yes, I see bruising in the pattern of a hand on both breasts, and scratch marks. Possibly from his fingernails?"

"Exactly!" Doc said.

"The left breast seems a bit more deeply bruised."

"Very observant, Devon," Doc said, smiling. "Once her right humerus was fractured, he released his hold on that side and pulled the second stage of her regulator from her mouth. It all happened in a matter of seconds."

He opened the woman's mouth to show several crooked teeth, the front ones in both the upper and lower jaws were pointing slightly outward, one on the bottom was missing. Other than that, her teeth were pearly white and straight.

"How do you know it was a man?" Ben asked. "A strong woman could have done the same thing."

"Ah, yes. You're absolutely right, of course. There are a couple more things." Doc stepped to the foot of the table and took both the victim's ankles in his hands. "Please don't be embarrassed," he said to Devon, and then moved the legs apart, exposing the woman's genitalia.

"See these abrasions on the inside of her upper thigh?" Doc asked.

Devon leaned over the body. She'd been closer to another woman's vagina in college, though she'd never tell either of these men.

"Her bathing suit was forcibly ripped away," Devon said.

Ben glanced quickly where Doc was pointing. "Still doesn't mean it was a man."

"That's where we get to the troubling part, Detective."

Ben knew the ME was about to tell them something important. He always used a person's title when he became dramatically serious.

"The vaginal swab came back positive for acid phosphatase."

"Semen?" Devon asked.

"Very good," Doc replied.

Ben's brow furrowed. A murder was one thing, but a rape *and* murder was something else altogether. "You're saying she was raped and then murdered by drowning, by someone who yanked out her reg and held her under?"

"No, he's not saying that," Devon said, looking closer at the bikini abrasions. "The skin here is broken, but she didn't bleed, or bled very little." Slowly, Devon stood erect and shuddered.

Doc looked at her and solemnly nodded.

"Oh my God," she muttered. "You're saying this woman was murdered by drowning and *then* raped."

"You're looking for a large man," Doc said, moving methodically around the table, covering the body. "About six feet tall. He'll be powerfully built, with great upper body strength. If you find him, and he has a computer, I'd be surprised if you don't find pornographic material on it depicting acts of necrophilia."

CHAPTER SEVEN

The flight to LaBelle took a little over an hour. I'd left just after dawn, having first called Carl to let them know what was going on. He'd said not to worry; he'd take care of things there. Gray clouds had been building to the east when I left, blotting out the sunrise, but at least it hadn't been raining. I'd left Finn with Rusty; I wasn't sure how Billy would react to a dog in his car. Landing at the small airport, the sky was clear and sunny, though it was only a hundred and forty miles north of Marathon.

Billy strode out of the little terminal building as a small motorized cart approached from a row of hangars. "A buddy has room in his hangar," Billy said, pointing at the approaching cart with his chin and extending his right hand.

Putting my flight bag down, I gripped Billy's forearm in the Indian way he'd taught me when we were kids. He was dressed in his usual jeans, western shirt, and boots, his long black hair tied back under a well-worn cowboy hat.

"I appreciate this, Billy."

"Ain't nothing, Kemosabe."

Billy Rainwater and I had grown up together, hunting and fishing all around the Fort Myers and LaBelle areas. His mother was half Seminole and half Calusa, and his father was one of the few remaining full-blooded Calusa Indians. This meant nothing back in the sixties and seventies, but Billy's Calusa heritage gave him special recognition today. A year younger than me, he'd followed me into the Marine Corps, when he'd graduated high school.

Billy introduced me to Steve Carter, as the man climbed off the little cart and walked toward us.

"That is one beautiful ole Beaver," Steve said, after we shook hands. "Fifty-four?"

"Close," I replied. "It's a fifty-three."

"I got plenty of room in my hangar, but she's gonna make my old crop duster look even uglier."

"I'll be back after the storm," I said reaching for my wallet. "How much for four day's storage?"

"Nothing," Steve replied. Then to Billy he said, "We're square now?"

"On the first thing," Billy said.

The man nodded and went back to his cart, where he attached a long vee-shaped boom to the lower cross member between the *Hopper's* pontoons, then hitched it to the cart.

"What was that all about?" I asked Billy, as the man started pulling *Island Hopper* toward his hangar.

"He owes me a few favors," Billy replied. "You ready?"

A few minutes later, we climbed into one of Billy's big off-road trucks, a Chevy Blazer. He owned a shop on the outskirts of town, where he worked on other people's off-roaders, a very popular activity in South Florida. I noticed a pair of surfboards strapped to the roof of the big truck. Turning out of the airport parking lot onto Cowboy Way, we drove a short distance and then turned south on US-29. As the big truck gathered speed, the oversized tires began to hum on the pavement.

"You still driving that thirteen-letter shit-spreader?" Billy asked, referring to my 1973 International Travelall, aptly dubbed *The Beast*.

"Got no reason to buy anything newer," I replied. "What's with the surfboards?"

"I feel like going surfing in a hurricane."

"You surf? Since when?"

"Not all Indians ride only horses," Billy replied.

"You know there aren't very many beaches in the Keys, right?"

He shrugged. "I'm sure you know where all of them are. Just take me to one and I'll teach you how to ride, too."

I laughed. "Me? Surf?"

"Never too old to learn new tricks, Kemosabe. When you stop learning new ways to have fun is when you start dying."

"Pretty deep for a red man," I said, paraphrasing a line from Gunsmoke, a TV show the two of us used to watch all the time, in which Marshall Matt Dillon was talking to the red-headed saloon owner, Miss Kitty Russell.

Billy grinned, remembering also. "I'm a pretty deep red man."

The drive took a lot longer than the flight, but soon we turned off Alligator Alley onto the Sawgrass Expressway, going around Miami. Traffic in our direction was pretty light, but there was a steady stream of cars headed north. The stream got heavier when we merged onto US-1 off the Reagan Turnpike.

"Looks like they might have issued an evac order," Billy said.

Ahead, on our side of the highway, there wasn't a car in sight as we approached Card Sound Road just south of Homestead. The northbound side, though, was nearly at a standstill.

"Turn left," I said. "Let's get some lunch at Alabama Jack's."

Billy slowed the big truck and got in the turn lane. "Never been there, but I heard about it."

"Good food, but don't eat too much. When we get to Rusty's the food's a lot better."

As Billy turned onto Card Sound Road, it started raining. "This from the hurricane, you think?"

"Maybe an outer band," I replied. "The storm's probably still several hundred miles away. I'll call Rusty and find out."

Fishing my phone from the cargo pocket of my shorts, I turned it on. It had been in a drawer in my stateroom aboard the *Revenge*. I'd let it charge overnight, without turning it on. Now I saw that I had half a dozen missed calls, the most recent from my daughter, Eve, who lived in Coconut Grove. There was also a text message from Kim and another from Rusty, both sent at about the same time, two days before.

Ignoring the messages, but making a mental note to call both my daughters, I punched the icon to call Rusty. Jimmy answered and I asked what the latest was on the storm.

"Downgraded to a Cat 3, man. But still headed west-southwest. The Weather Channel predicts landfall on one of the islands in the Bahamas sometime late Monday night. Rusty still says it'll cross Cuba into *El Caribe* after that. They ordered tourists out of the Keys this morning. You on your way back?"

Something in Jimmy's voice told me he was asking for a specific reason. "Yeah. We're stopping for lunch at Alabama Jack's. Should be back there in about two hours. What's up?"

"That crusty old dude, Vince O'Hare? He was here looking for you a little earlier."

O'Hare? I thought. "He say what he wanted?"

"Grunted something about coming back later was all, man."

"All right, if he shows back up, tell him I'll be there by fourteen hundred."

"Later, dude."

I ended the call, wondering what Vince wanted. He was an old shrimper and lobsterman, who lived alone in a rundown old house on Grassy Key and kept pretty much to himself. Except for when he felt like tying one on—then he usually ended up in a fight or in jail.

"What'd Rusty say about the storm?" Billy asked, slowing to turn into the parking lot.

"His bartender answered," I replied. "Storm's still way out in the Atlantic, at least six or seven hundred miles from here, so this rain probably isn't from Ike. They did order all the tourists to leave the Keys, though."

We ate a quick lunch and got back on the road, stopping for gas in Key Largo. By the time we arrived at the *Anchor*, the rain had stopped and the sky was a deep azure, as if there were no threat of bad weather on the horizon.

CHAPTER EIGHT

The bar was dimly lit and the interior was dingy, even by Stock Island standards. The lack of windows made it perpetually nighttime inside. The ambiance, if one could call it that, seemed to be a mixture of a 1950s roadside dive and a 1970s strip club, with a little bit of biker influence. The wooden floor was uneven, making patrons that were unaccustomed to the place—even the sober ones—stagger as if they'd been on a weekend bender. In short, it wasn't the kind of place tourists flocked to, unless they were looking for trouble.

Rafferty's Pub had once been owned by William "Wild Bill" Rafferty, who'd bought the place in 1963. It had a very seedy reputation then, but Wild Bill introduced a whole new level of debauchery. Back then, Key West had in many ways still been a pirate town, lying on the outskirts of civilization. Wild Bill had been a well-known character in Atlantic City, New Jersey, during the fifties. His arrival in the Keys was shrouded under dubious circumstances and his connections with the syndicate were common knowledge. He'd operated a similar establishment on the Boardwalk with impunity.

Today, Wild Bill wasn't so wild. His current residence was a convalescent home in Florida City, the last town on the mainland before the Keys. He spent his days and nights much the same as the other people who lived there: sitting in a wheelchair, drooling into a cup. But Wild Bill had a secret, one that only a small handful of others had any idea about—and most of them were now dead. He'd shared part of that secret with his oldest son.

That son was the current owner of *Rafferty's Pub*, located a block off US Highway 1 just before the bridge to Key West. At fifty, Harley Davidson Rafferty was the oldest of Wild Bill's two sons. He was also the brightest, which really wasn't saying a whole lot. His little brother, Marion Morrison Rafferty, named after the legendary John Wayne, was ten years his junior.

Harley was the only one that ever dared called him Marion, though. The younger man preferred the name Duke, like his namesake. He'd pummeled many men, and more than one woman, to near death just for calling him by his given name. Duke wasn't a tall man, but he was unusually large, the product of steroid abuse in his late teens and early twenties.

"How'd it go?" Harley asked his little brother, as the freakish-looking man joined him at a table in the back.

A waitress wearing only a G-string quickly placed a beer and another shot glass on the table, before hurrying back to the paying customers sparsely scattered around the thirty tables strewn around the interior of the bar. In the middle of the large room, against one wall, was a small stage where a girl with long, dark hair gyrated naked around a pole, not even attempting to keep time with the techno music blaring from the speakers. Next to the stage, behind an elevated podium, sat a balding overweight man, who controlled the sound equipment and introduced the dancers.

"Went okay," Duke grunted, pouring a shot of whiskey from the half-empty bottle at his brother's elbow. "Why cain't we just go on out and find it?"

Harley's eyes rolled back in his head. "I told you a million times—not until the old man and his cronies are all dead. There's only him and the boss left, and the boss is in prison."

"Both of 'em are all dried up in da head, man."

"Don't matter, Marion. Others know what happened way back then. They just don't know where to look."

If Duke had had two eyebrows, they'd have been knitted together as he glared at his older brother. Instead, the single bushy brow just sort of dropped in the middle, as if two giant caterpillars had collided at high speed. "Why you gotta call me that?"

"Sorry, little brother." Harley poured more whiskey into his own shot glass and raised it in salute. "It won't be much longer. Here's to keeping secrets."

Duke lifted his glass and clinked it against Harley's. "Secrets."

"Did you take care of everything like I told ya?"

"Did just like ya said," Duke replied. "Cleaned everything up real good with a hose-pipe they had. Then I left an O-Z in the wheelhouse and set it adrift."

"*One* ounce?" Harley asked, slamming his shot glass on the table. "I gave you *two* ounces. What happened to the other one?"

Duke stammered for a moment, unable to put words together in his addled brain and get them to come out of his mouth. Finally, he just shrugged his massive shoulders. "I guess I partied with the other one."

"You tooted a whole ounce of coke?"

"Well, not just me, Harley."

The elder brother folded his fingers together and rested his chin on them, waiting. Sometimes, it was easier with Duke to just let him have some time to organize his thoughts. Any time his brother tried to lie, it was so obvious that a deaf, dumb, and blind man could tell.

The big man looked down at his empty glass sheepishly. "Me and Brandy and Jasmine, I guess."

"They weren't with you on the boat, were they?"

Duke looked up at his brother. "Course not. I ain't dumb."

"Calling you dumb would be an insult to dumb people."

"I did everything ya said, Harley. It's just, well, I had the two O-Zs and the girls wanted to party, ya know."

"These girls always want to party, Duke. It's why they work here."

"Sorry."

"So, you cleaned everything up, left the ounce of blow on the boat and set it adrift. Did you at least make sure the problem was taken care of? And what about the nigger you said was financing their dive? You leave his cash box, too?"

"Sure, Harley. There won't be no trouble there. Them two won't ever be seen again and the box'll be found just like ya wanted."

"Good," the older Rafferty said, motioning the waitress to bring him another beer. "I can't believe the three of you snorted up a whole ounce, though."

As the nearly-nude waitress delivered Harley's beer, Duke dug into his pocket and took out a small plastic bag half-full of white powder. "We didn't do all of it," Duke said, laying the cocaine on the table between them. "There's plenty left."

The waitress, a bleached-blonde from Oklahoma, eyed the bag of cocaine on the table hungrily, smiling at her bosses.

CHAPTER NINE

Ben was nearly home. It had been another very long day, and now there was a possible hurricane to deal with. As he approached the entrance to the parking area for Garrison Bight's houseboat community, his cellphone began to ring on the passenger seat. He had it set up to use a distinctive ringtone whenever dispatch called, and that was what he was hearing now: the "Bad Boys" theme song from the TV show *Cops*.

He considered ignoring it, but picked it up and hit the *Accept* button as he turned into the parking lot. "Lieutenant Morgan."

"Sorry, Detective," the woman's voice said. "I know it's late and you've been on duty all day, but we just got a call that might be connected to your homicide."

"Might be?"

"Well, it's a dive boat," the dispatcher explained. "Adrift and grounded on Knockemdown Key in Kemp Channel.

The marine unit on scene suggested it might be related to your case."

"Who's the marine unit on scene?"

There was a pause before the dispatcher said, "Deputy Martin Phillips."

"Jeez, does that kid ever sleep?" Ben muttered as he backed out of the parking spot in front of his little blue houseboat. "Never mind. Tell the deputy I'm on my way, but it'll be half an hour before I get there."

Forty-five minutes later, delayed by an overturned RV at the entrance to the KOA campground on Sugarloaf, Ben pulled into the back of the Sheriff's Department sub-station on Cudjoe Key. Getting out of the Crown Vic, he looked toward the building first, debating going inside to get a cup of coffee. Behind him, someone called his name.

He turned and saw Deputy Phillips standing on the dock by his patrol boat, holding a thermos in the air. "Got your coffee, Lieutenant," he shouted across the grass and crushed shell parking lot.

Ben walked over and accepted a plastic mug as he stepped aboard the deputy's boat for the second time in as many days. He was beginning to feel like he was back on marine patrol duty—except for the extra fifty pounds the desk job had put on him.

"Thanks, Marty. What ya got?"

"It's not really a dive boat," Marty began, as he tossed off the lines and started to idle the boat through the canal. "But it does have an air compressor and tanks aboard. It's more like a salvage boat or research vessel."

"Know who it's registered to?"

"Dispatch just called to confirm, not a minute before you got here. But I know the boat. It's registered to James Isaksson, a salvage diver out of Ramrod. I used to work for his dad, Dwight."

"Did you call Mister Isaksson?" Ben asked, as Marty turned a sharp left following the canal.

"No, sir. I figured you'd want to have a look first."

"Why'd you figure that?"

"When I tied off, there was a Kong tether attached to a jack line."

Ben glanced over at Marty. Kong was one of the more popular tethers that sailors used to keep from being lost at sea if they fell overboard while single-handing a boat in a storm.

"And?" Ben asked.

"The other end was in the water, sir. I figured you'd want to be first on scene, especially so close to the sub-station. Those guys won't turn out for an abandoned boat report; it happens all the time."

Marty slowly idled across the flats at the end of the canal, instead of following it on around another turn to the deeper channel and open water. He looked at Ben, a serious expression on his face. "Jim Isaksson's body is attached to the other end of the Kong."

Once the bottom dropped away, Marty brought the patrol boat up on plane, turning south into Pirate's Cove, then east past Gopher Key and into Kemp Channel.

Ben could see the salvage boat on the other side of the bridge. It was listing, and obviously stuck on the bottom. It would be several hours until the tide refloated it.

Marty quickly tied the patrol boat off to the forward part of the much larger vessel, and the two men stepped over onto the canted deck. "Right over here, Lieutenant," Marty said, walking to the stern.

"Pull him up," Ben said, looking down at where the tether disappeared into the water. It was already dark, the only light provided by a half moon directly overhead.

Marty went to the helm and, after a couple of seconds, he flipped a switch that turned on two spreader lights attached to the structure around the aft deck of the salvage boat. He then began pulling the tether up. It was made of an elastic material that kept it short and out of the way. Stretched to its full length, it would extend to ten feet if the wearer needed to move around while connected to the jack line.

A man's body broke the surface, rolling face up, bloated from the buildup of internal decomposition gas. A weight belt around the man's waist had probably kept the body from rising on its own. The man's skin was pale and stretched around the weight belt. There was a puckered hole just above the man's right eye, and both his eyes were missing.

"He didn't attach that tether," Marty said. "He's not even wearing a harness, and seas are flat, so there'd be no reason to wear one."

"This pretty much how you found him?" Ben asked. "The tether attached to his weight belt?"

"Yeah," Marty replied. "No reason for him to do that."

"What about his eyes?" Ben asked, to see how sharp the kid was.

"Scavengers go for the soft tissue first," Marty replied. "I doubt the bullet hole had anything to do with his eyes being gone. There'll probably be more soft tissue damage, too."

"Apparent bullet hole," Ben corrected him. "Aside from the fact that this might be another homicide, what makes you think this is related to the dead girl?"

"Dwight called me a month ago," Marty replied. "Said that Jim's deck hand had up and quit, and how Jim had just landed a big salvage contract. Wanted to know if I was interested."

"What'd you tell him?"

"That I'd think on it," Marty replied. "I have a couple of weeks' vacation time due me and thought I might be able to help him out until he could hire someone. The next day, when I got the okay to take the vacation time, I called Dwight back. He told me that Jim had already hired a diver. A woman named Jenny Marshall."

CHAPTER TEN

"You gonna ride it out here?" Rusty asked me, once Billy and I had sat down at the bar and the two had caught up on things.

"Probably." I glanced at the TV. Any time there was a hurricane, Rusty kept the TV on the Weather Channel. Hurricanes being what they are, the Weather Channel ran nearly continuous coverage, especially if it appeared to be heading toward the U.S. "Still too far out to say. If it stays on that course through tomorrow, the *Revenge* will be safe here. If it turns a little more westerly before then, I might consider bugging out for my hurricane hole."

Just about every large boat owner in the Keys has a hurricane hole, a place they could run their boat to and take shelter from a storm. Mine was up in Tarpon Bay, several miles inland on Shark River, which flows out of the Everglades. I'd hunkered down there a couple of times.

Or I could just go home. My stilt house was more than capable of withstanding even a category three hurricane and the dock area was completely enclosed. The down-side would be the storm surge. The top of the *Revenge* is just a foot below the floor beams of the house on a spring tide. If a hurricane arrived then, the accompanying surge could raise the *Revenge* right through the floor. Or, more likely, crush the fly bridge and push her under.

"So, Jesse says the food here is pretty good," Billy said.

"Pretty good?" Jimmy scoffed, coming out of the walk-in cooler behind the bar. "Best you'll ever eat, dude."

I introduced the two, and Billy asked Rusty what he recommended.

"Rufus—he's my chef—he can cook just about any-thing, and do it better than anyone else." Rusty turned to Jimmy and said, "Go see what he's got that's fresh."

"Heard from Julie lately?" I asked Rusty as Jimmy dis-appeared through the back door.

"They'll be here later this evening, as a matter of fact. Same reason, run the *James Caird* up to Tarpon Bay if it looks bad. Either way, they're taking a few days aboard the Whitby."

"Both of them?"

"They *are* married, bro."

"I meant, both of them are taking time away?" I said.

"Yeah," Rusty replied. "Deuce says things are slow and he has an announcement."

"Married?" Billy asked. "Your little girl's married?"

"Ya gotta come down here time to time," Rusty said. "Julie's a grown woman. She and Deuce Livingston been married for a coupla years now."

Billy laughed. "Guess we're all getting long in the teeth. Last time I saw her, she was a skinny little thing, no higher than a buck key deer. He a nice guy?"

Rusty grinned. "Couldn'a picked a better man to be my son-in-law. Used to be a Navy SEAL, now he works for the government. Julie's a petty officer in the Coast Guard and works for the same agency."

The back door opened and Rufus came in. "Rodney jes drop off some snappah, Mistah Rusty. Dey still alive and Jimmy be cleaning dem. How yuh doin' Cap'n Jesse mon?"

"Right as rain," I replied. "Rufus, meet an old friend of ours, Billy Rainwater. Billy, this is Rufus."

"Please ta meet yuh, Mistuh Billy," Rufus said, extending his hand, an odd look on his face. "I and I nevuh met an Indian before."

Billy bypassed Rufus's hand and gripped his forearm. "And I never met a Jamaican man before. You got a last name, Rufus?"

I suddenly realized that, while I'd known the wiry old Jamaican for quite a few years, I never knew his last name.

"A course," Rufus replied, with a gap-toothed grin. "Everbody got a last name. So, yuh be wantin' some a dat fresh snappah? How yuh want it cook?"

"Surprise me," Billy said.

Rufus's eyes widened. "Dat I and I can do, Mistuh Billy." Then he turned and went back out through the door to his kitchen.

Rufus's kitchen was built onto the back of the bar and had three big roll-up windows on two sides. Locals came and sat on stools to watch him cook. It had become sort of an attraction to the local islanders, and quite a few live-aboards at the marina.

I leaned over the bar. "So, what is Rufus's last name?"

"No idea," Rusty replied. "Never bothered to ask."

Just then, the front door of the bar opened and I instantly recognized Deuce and Julie as they stepped inside and made their way to the bar. As they approached, I couldn't help but notice that Julie's belly was much larger. *An announcement?*

Introductions were made, and I glanced down at Julie's swollen mid-section. "Is there something you guys haven't told me?" I asked Deuce.

He just grinned. When I looked across the bar at Rusty, he was grinning, too. "You're going to be a great-uncle," Julie said.

"Get out! Really?" I gave her a big hug and looked at Rusty, still grinning behind the bar.

"She didn't want Rusty to tell you until she could do it herself," Deuce said. "Russell the third will arrive in February."

My eyes began to sweat a little. Deuce's father and namesake had been my and Rusty's platoon sergeant when we were stationed in Okinawa way back in the eighties. Russ had been murdered nearly three years ago, and Deuce had come down here to spread his dad's ashes on a reef—and also to find his dad's killer.

That killer became responsible for my wife's death before he was brought to justice. His bleached-white bones are scattered on a little island not far from my home.

"A boy?" I asked, my voice catching a little.

Deuce slapped me on the shoulder. "And they say you Jarheads aren't very bright."

Jimmy came back in, carrying a platter of what I immediately recognized from the scent as blackened snapper. Rufus carried a large bowl of steamed vegetables with little chunks of sausage and crawfish, which he calls janga. They're actually the freshwater crawfish we raise in the aquaponics system on the island. In Jamaica, the locals call them janga and consider them an aphrodisiac. I didn't put a lot of stock in such claims. Jimmy took over for Rusty behind the bar as we all sat down to eat.

"Looks like I'll be looking for a job soon," Deuce said after we'd wiped out the platter of fillets.

"A job?" Rusty said, nearly choking on his last bite of sausage.

"The writing's on the wall. In a few months, we'll have a new administration in the White House. And he doesn't much like the DHS."

"That who you work for?" Billy asked.

Deuce gave me a quick glance, and I nodded slightly. Just like with his dad, Deuce and I could express volumes to one another without really saying a word. With just a glance, Deuce asked if Billy was good and I'd informed him that he was someone I would trust with my life. And I have.

"Yes," Deuce replied. "I'm the head of a counter-terrorism unit under Homeland Security."

"So why not just go back to the Navy?" I asked. "You only have, what, eight years to retirement?"

"I was under contract all through college," he said. "Less than five years left. Scuttlebutt says the Navy will be offering early retirement to a number of officers and upper enlisted men. I asked Colonel Stockwell and he made sure my name was on the short list. I'll be retiring just before Trey is born."

Stockwell is Deuce's boss. A former Army SpecOps officer, he'd taken the position of Homeland Security's Associate Deputy Director, Caribbean Counter-terrorism Command over a year before.

"What kind of job will you be looking for?" I asked.

"You remember what I told you just before you retired, Jesse?" Rusty asked.

I grinned, remembering the conversation we'd had just before I left the Corps. Turning to Deuce, I said, "Never mind. Just get down here, and we'll find out what kind of hustle you're best suited for."

"Well, I kind of already have an idea," Deuce said. "Security and personal protection."

"Not a lot of need for that down here, I wouldn't think," Billy offered.

"He's right," I said. "Maybe in Key Weird, working for the cruise lines or something."

"We were thinking up island," Julie said. "Since I'll be going back to the Coast Guard Reserves, I'd want to be near the station in Islamorada. From there it's a short commute to Miami, where Deuce could have an office."

"Deuce?" I asked. Julie was never big on nicknames.

She put a hand on her belly. "Well, I can't very well call my husband *and* my son 'Russell.' I think Ace would approve of Deuce and Trey."

Ace. I grinned at her. Russ would have loved being called that. He'd have loved taking his grandson fishing and diving for lobster, too.

"It'll be a struggle at first," Deuce said. "But I'm sure I can make it work."

I took a pull from my beer bottle. "No, it won't. I want in."

"No way, Jesse," Deuce said, holding up both hands, palms out. "I didn't come here looking for a handout. Besides, we have a pretty good nest egg, remember?"

Some time back, Deuce had played a pivotal role in helping locate a couple of lost treasures, one of which was what had gotten his dad killed. Against Deuce's protestations, Rusty and I had insisted on Russ getting an equal split, in the form of a savings account for a grandchild Russ would never know.

"That wasn't meant to be used for start-up capital," I said. "It's for Trey's and some possible siblings' futures, and for you two to retire on when you're old like me and Rusty. Besides, I'm not offering a handout. When I said I want in, I mean as a partner. A working partner or silent partner, I don't care. But I get a percentage."

"You want to work in the security business?" Billy asked.

"When you stop having fun, you start dying," I replied, clapping a hand on the back of my old friend's neck. "Your words, man. Besides, I know a good investment when I see one."

Deuce and I talked about it for a while longer and came to a tentative agreement. I'd foot the bill to get his new venture up and running, and in return I'd receive twenty percent of the net profits for two years or until I earned back my initial investment plus ten percent, whichever came first. I'd also be available for any kind of consult work that I might be suited for, on a per-piece basis.

"What about the rest of the team?" I asked. I'd grown close to most of them and enjoyed having them pop in and out on occasion.

"Most will either be absorbed into other jobs in other agencies, or return to the jobs they came from. Andrew said he's going back to the Coast Guard. He's only a little more than a year from full retirement."

"Tony and Art?"

"Art already has orders. He's heading to Coronado as an instructor in two months, and shipping over for his last tour. Tony and Tasha moved up their wedding and flew off to Vegas two weeks ago without telling anyone. They got back last Wednesday, and I sat down with him and Chyrel yesterday. He's up to ship over in December, and she's already said she won't be going back to the CIA. They're my first employees."

At midnight, the little party broke up. Julie and Deuce went down to their little ketch, and Billy and I headed to the *Revenge*. There was no change in the storm's status. The forecast models all showed it crossing eastern Cuba some time the next night. From the ripples in the turning basin, I knew from experience that the waves were really starting to build, out beyond the end of the canal.

"Where's the nearest sand beach?" Billy asked, as we sat down with a couple of beers on the couch in the salon.

"Sombrero Beach is just a few miles from here. You really want to surf in that chop?"

"Storms are the only time waves build up in the Gulf," Billy replied. "And *we* are gonna ride a few."

"You might be riding a few," I said, with a sideways grin. "Me? I might fall off one or two."

CHAPTER ELEVEN

Ben and Devon arrived at the Medical Examiner's office in Marathon early the following morning. *Way too early on a Monday, after working most of the weekend,* Ben thought. Doc Fredric ushered the two detectives into his work area. Neither James Isaksson's body nor any other was in sight.

"My findings were quite conclusive," Doc said, walking over to the stainless-steel doors of the reefer and pulling one open. He slid out the cadaver tray; Isaksson's body lay composed and peaceful on the cold steel. Doc indicated the gunshot wound. "A single GSW to the forehead was the cause of death. No water in the lungs. Death was instantaneous."

"No exit wound?" Devon asked.

Picking up a small plastic bottle from his desk, Doc handed it to Devon. "The murder weapon is a .38 caliber revolver."

"How can you be sure it wasn't a semi-automatic?" she asked, handing the bottle to Ben, who examined it closely.

"Did you know that ballistic forensics go back nearly eighty years?" Doc asked Devon, as Ben continued examining the bullet. "A man named Calvin Goddard first used his new invention, the comparison microscope, to examine ballistic evidence in the Saint Valentine's Day Massacre in 1929. The results of his tests proved that the Chicago Police had no hand in the shooting, and that it was a rival gang member by the name of Fred Burke."

Ben handed the bottle with the bullet in it back to Devon. "The gun that fired this bullet has a left-hand twist, most likely a Colt."

"Indeed, Ben," Doc said. "That narrowed the search considerably, since Colt Firearms are one of a very few manufacturers that use barrels with a left twist. The striations the gun barrel imparted on this particular bullet have a twist rate and groove spacing consistent with only one firearm: the Colt .38 caliber Cobra."

"Thanks, Doc," Ben said. "Anything else you can tell us?"

"Stippling around the entry wound suggests that the fatal shot was fired from close range. No more than a foot away."

Ben frowned. "Execution style," he muttered. *As if the murder of the girl weren't enough.* It took a special kind of killer to hold a gun to someone's head, look them in the eye, and pull the trigger. Add to that the sick circumstances of Jennifer Marshall's murder, and a really deranged psycho was loose in the waters around Key West.

As Ben and Devon left the building, her phone rang. She answered it, listened for a moment, and then said, "We'll be there within an hour." Turning to Ben, she said, "Forensics recovered a clear set of prints on the cash box and got it open. There was an ounce of cocaine inside. Walt's running the prints through IAFIS."

Walt Cantrell had been with the Department much longer than Ben and now worked only part time, only on major crimes, as the lead forensics technician. In his late sixties, he no longer collected the evidence in the field, but was very much respected among the field technicians who did.

Forty minutes later, the two detectives entered the forensics lab on Stock Island. "What ya got, Walt?" Ben asked.

The older man pushed his wheeled office chair from one examination table to another, spinning around as the chair rolled across the floor. "The box itself is just a cheap, standard money box. You can buy one in any Walmart or Office Depot. The key wasn't recovered at the crime scene, but they're really easy to pick."

"What was in it?" Devon asked.

"Four-hundred and ninety-three dollars and forty-seven cents in cash. There were also several bundles of business cards wrapped in rubber bands. Each bundle was for a different business on the island, mostly bars. A receipt book with no custom imprint, but the copies indicate it was a local cab driver's book. They get business cards from local bars, write their name on the back, and hand them out to tourists, along with one of their own. Bartenders base what cab they call for a patron on how many customers the cabbies send to them."

"What else?" Ben asked.

"An ounce of cocaine," Walt replied, removing his reading glasses and tossing them on the desk. "Which makes no sense to me at all."

"How come?" Devon asked.

"One of the bundles of business cards was for a cab company. The prints on the box match the owner of that company. Cab drivers in Monroe county are registered and their prints are on file. It didn't take the FBI's Integrated Automated Fingerprint Identification System long to find a match, as it searches outward from the area where the suspect prints are lifted. This money box appears to belong to Lawrence Lovett."

Ben's eyebrows came up. "Lawrence?"

"So you know him?" Walt said. "If you know him half as well as I do, you know something's not right here."

"Totally out of character," Ben agreed. "But he wouldn't be the first decent person to step over the line." Turning to Devon he said, "Contact property crimes with both the Department and PD. Find out if Lawrence Lovett has filed a stolen property or robbery report recently."

Devon walked to the other side of the room, taking her phone out of her purse as Ben sat down across from the older forensics man. "What about the coke, Walt? Can you tell me how many times it was cut and where it came from?"

Walt put his reading glasses back on and picked up a clipboard. "Very high grade. Eighty-nine-point-seven percent pure from Venezuela. The other ten-point-three percent is levamisole, a drug used to treat worms in cattle. Really easy to get in South America."

"Only stepped on once," Ben thought aloud.

"Yep, probably just before it went on the boat. Most interceptions made before delivery here in the States are about ninety percent purity."

"So, this ounce could be the personal stash of the importer?"

"Most likely," Walt replied. "Or someone high up in the chain." He tapped the little plastic bag. "This is definitely not street-level coke, Ben. Even kilo packages are usually cut to anywhere from seventy to seventy-five percent. A one-ounce package like this would be considered heavy street quantity and usually less than fifty percent pure. Something a street dealer would cut again to about twenty-five percent cocaine, and then break up two ounces into individual eighth ounce packages for sale. The size of the package is grossly inconsistent with its purity."

Devon came over to where the two men sat at the table. "No report of property crimes by anyone of that name."

Walt and Ben looked at Devon, then back at one another. "Why wouldn't Lawrence report that his cash box was stolen?" Walt asked.

"Maybe it wasn't," Ben said, standing up. "Maybe he forgot it on the salvage boat where he killed two people."

CHAPTER TWELVE

B illy and I arrived at Sombrero Beach just as the sun was rising beyond the tip of Tingler Island. Within a few minutes, it disappeared behind the clouds. The parking lot was mostly deserted, except for four cars, one of which was a sheriff's patrol car. The deputy got out as Billy parked several spaces away from him.

We got out of the Blazer, and Billy quickly released the catch for the boards on the roof as I opened the back door to let Finn out. On the other side of the high dune, I could hear the waves crashing on the shore, sounding like a train going by.

"Excuse me," the deputy said, as he got closer. He wasn't anyone I knew. Finn sat down next to me, watching the approaching deputy. "You know there's a hurricane out there, right?"

"Yeah, Deputy Arnold," I replied, reading his name tag and pointing to the southeast. "It's two hundred nautical miles that way."

"The water's dangerous," Arnold said. "The red flag is out and there's a tropical storm warning in effect."

"That's why we're here," Billy said, coming around the hood with a surfboard under his arm. "When else do the Keys see waves?"

The deputy glanced at Billy, then ignored him and addressed me again. "It's too dangerous, sir. Help might not be able to get to you in a timely manner."

I really didn't like the dismissive look he gave Billy. Aside from skin and hair color, we looked much alike. Both of us had bare feet, and wore shorts and tee-shirts. Billy's was a red *Rusty Anchor* shirt that Rusty had given him last night, and mine was a faded blue *Gaspar's Revenge* shirt, frayed around the neck. Billy, being Indian, had no facial hair, whereas I hadn't shaved in over a week and hadn't had a haircut in three months. Of the two of us, I probably looked more like a bum than Billy.

"Son," I said, looking down at the deputy. "I live here and this is my friend from Fort Myers. We've both been around the sea all our lives, and I make a living from it. If either of us ever needs help out there, it'll be beyond the capabilities of the sheriff's office."

Deputy Arnold squared his shoulders, propping one hand on his holstered Glock. "What's your name, sir? Do you have any identification?"

Just for the heck of it, I reached into my front pocket. Though I never needed it, I now kept a little billfold with me all the time. I showed the deputy the badge and ID that Deuce had given me some months back, up in South Carolina.

Deputy Arnold's eyes grew just a little wider, making him look even younger than he already looked.

"I'm Special Agent Jesse McDermitt, Homeland Security." Nodding toward Billy, I added, "This is my partner, Billy Rainwater. Unless you have something more to tell us, we'll be going surfing now."

The young deputy looked at Billy, then back at me. "No, sir. Just be careful out there, okay?"

Without a word, I grabbed the other board off the roof and followed Billy along a walkway, Finn leading the way. Ahead I could hear the pounding surf. I doubted anyone would be here, so I hadn't bothered to bring Finn's leash. Besides, he was already well-trained and I could call him off a chase with a seagull.

"You still get a hard-on when someone tries to push too much weight around," Billy said. "Admit it."

"I believe in personal responsibility," I said, admitting nothing. "I'm a grown man and don't need a twenty-something deputy looking out for my well-being."

"That why you live way out there on an island? So nobody else is responsible for you? Which, by the way, I'd like to see some day."

"Part of the reason," I replied honestly, as we reached the beach access. Having others responsible for me sometimes put them in harm's way, something I tried to limit. "If you can stay for a day or two, we can head up to my house once the seas lay back down."

Billy stopped and turned. "And what the hell's with the badge?"

"Deuce swore me in a few months back for an op," I replied. "Guess I just forgot to resign."

"Ha!" He turned and strode toward the beach access. "You just like pulling rank on the underlings."

I followed after him and looked out over the beach. "Well, it does tend to shorten some conversations."

An elderly couple was walking away from us to the right, and two guys were paddling out on surfboards. The sky was overcast, but so far it wasn't raining. Far out toward the southern horizon, the sky looked darker and I could see big waves breaking over the reef line. A steady wind of what I guessed was nearly thirty knots was blowing out of the east, building the waves and pushing the water westward. As the waves marched across the surface, they wrapped around Tingler island and came ashore here at an angle to the beach.

"Whoa," Billy murmured. "They aren't big, but look how long."

He was right. As a wave started to break far off to our left, its lip curled along the beach for several hundred yards, breaking in the shallows the whole length of Sombrero Beach. Other smaller waves moved around the north side of Tingler Island, causing a bit of chop in the near shore water as they collided with the larger waves off the ocean.

"Those are some pretty big waves," I said.

Billy glanced over at me and grinned that daredevil grin that had gotten both of us into so much trouble as kids. "They're only about four to six feet, Kemosabe. Smaller than you."

Together, we walked down to the edge of the water, where foam was collecting among a lot of vegetation that had been washed away from somewhere. Occasional clumps of foam broke loose from the detritus, dancing across the sand, propelled by the wind. Finn gave chase to each one, ripping the dastardly cretins apart with a single pounce.

"Finn!" I called, when he got too far away. He stopped in his tracks and looked back at me, head cocked quizzically. "Stay close by here. Don't wander off."

He loped back toward us and began chasing new clumps of foam. For the next twenty minutes, Billy explained surfing and I practiced going from a prone position on the long-board to a standing position. At the end, Billy said, "You're gonna fall down the first few times. Try not to ding my stick with that hard head of yours, it's the only Bing I have left."

"What's a Bing?"

"Bing Copeland was the best board maker of the sixties," Billy said. "That there is an original Noserider. It's over nine feet long, and the bottom is shaped kinda like a boat. Super stable."

Ordering Finn to stay close again, we waded out into the surf. The other surfers had wound up far down the beach and were now walking back. The two of us had the water all to ourselves as we began to paddle out.

The first wave nearly rolled me over. Then Billy showed me how to put my weight on the nose and dive the board below the wave. When we were finally out beyond the breakers, we stopped to rest for a minute.

"First time, try just riding on your belly and next time get up on your knees. Just like a small boat, you can steer left and right just by leaning that way." He pointed with his chin at the other two surfers. "But these long-boards aren't maneuverable like what those kids have. Take longer to turn, so don't run over them."

Billy started paddling hard, as a wave approached. When it lifted the tail of his board slightly, he sprang to his feet. The wave wasn't even breaking behind him, as he rode down the front of it and turned left, keeping just ahead of where the lip curled over into foaming white-water.

Alone on the water, I looked back and waited. The next wave didn't look like much, so I lay down on the board and began stroking hard. I continued paddling, waiting for the wave to lift the tail of the board, like it had Billy's.

It didn't. When I looked back, I realized too late that I'd paddled faster than the wave. Now I was too far ahead of it and in the break zone, with the crest of the wave bending down toward me.

Ten million gallons of water landed on top of me, rolling me off the board and tumbling my body ass over elbows. Something yanked at my left foot, then started pulling me for a moment—the leash from the surfboard. I tried to orient my body to go the right way, but the lightweight board bobbing on the wave kept pulling me around backward.

I finally stood up, gasping and snorting water out of my nostrils, just in time to see the two young surfers at the water's edge.

"What he lacks in style," one of the guys said to the other, "he more than makes up for in age. Hey, old man! What do you call that thing attached to your ankle? It kinda looks like a surfboard."

The two surfers ran past me, both yucking it up at their joke, diving on top of their boards over another breaking wave. In seconds, they'd paddled out far enough and turned to catch the next two waves, peeling off quickly to the left and ripping up and down the face of the wave, heading down the beach toward where Billy was now walking back. I paddled back out, determined. Turning around, I saw Billy paddling effortlessly toward me.

Over the next couple of hours, I managed to sort of get the hang of it. I even succeeded at riding one wave halfway down the beach. The chop got a little heavier, and the two kids had enough and left. Sitting on our boards, well out beyond the breakers, Billy and I were all alone on the water. Even the sea birds that usually fished here were gone.

"What do you think?" Billy asked.

I'd been watching the waves, waiting for my next ride. The adrenaline rush, once I stood up, was something I hadn't been ready for. Kind of like when I mash the throttle and bring a boat up onto plane, but far more intense.

I just grinned. "I don't think I'll start dying anytime soon."

It was nearly noon, with the wind blowing at a good forty knots, before we were forced to head back to the beach. As the two of us stood up in knee-deep water, the skies just opened right up. Cold, fat rain drops began pelting us as we waded ashore, washing the salt water from our skin.

Once we were up above the part of the beach where the waves now reached, far above the usual high tide line, we dropped our boards on the sand. Finn joined us and we plopped down in the sand to watch the squall come ashore in awe.

Finn was already soaked. I was sure he'd probably jumped into the surf a few times to play. The rain didn't seem to bother him in the least. In fact, he seemed to relish it.

The rain pelted us as we looked out at the turbulent water. The surf resembled the water in a washing machine. The regimented lines of the waves we'd seen earlier were gone. There was more flotsam on the beach, mostly palm branches and reeds—probably from some distant shore that had felt the full brunt of the storm as it crossed the Bahamas and approached Cuba.

Finally, we decided it would probably be prudent to head back to the *Anchor* for beer and surfing tales. When we got to Billy's Blazer, the deputy who had been parked there was gone, as were the other cars. We quickly strapped the boards back in place and got in the truck.

Ten minutes later, we arrived at the *Anchor*, dripping wet. We both carried our dry tee-shirts bundled up under an arm until we reached the door. I pulled on my shirt and looked out along the dock. A yacht in the traditional trawler-style, one I hadn't seen around before, was tied up on the far side. It looked to be about thirty-five or forty feet, with a long fly bridge that covered the entirety of the salon and a small cockpit. Obviously a live-aboard taking refuge from the storm. The name on the bow was *Leap of Faith*.

I pulled open the door and walked inside. The *Anchor* is that kind of place. No shoes, dripping wet, no problem. Finn made a bee-line for the bowl of water Rusty kept in the corner. He quickly and noisily lapped up most of it, then curled up in the corner for a nap.

"Thought I was gonna have to go rescue you two," Rusty said from behind the bar.

There were nearly a dozen people inside. A few of them were sitting at tables, but most were at the bar. All of them were known to me.

"The day I need to be dragged out of the water is the day you can carve my headstone," I said, as Billy and I pulled up stools near the end of the bar. Rusty placed two cold Red Stripes in front of us. "Any change in the storm?"

Rusty looked at the big clock on the wall. "Noon update should be coming on, any minute."

As if on cue, the station switched to a live broadcast. A young female reporter was standing in front of a sea wall, with huge waves crashing against it. Off to the side, palm trees swayed violently in a heavy wind. The subtext at the bottom of the screen said that she was on Long Key, not far up island. Dramatic backdrop, but the storm was still moving to the south-southwest and nearing the Cuban coastline.

"It'll cross Cuba," Rusty said. "After that, my money is on it turning west and then north, either crossing western Cuba or around the tip and into the Gulf."

"No chance it'll come this way?" Billy asked.

"Listen to the man," I told Billy. "Rusty's made a science of watching these storms."

"Not really a science," Rusty said. "I just remember things. No, there's no chance of hurricane winds here. But we're still gonna get some big gusts and probably constant fifty-knot winds tonight and most of tomorrow. By nightfall, it'll all be done here, and Ike will be a problem for folks in the northern Gulf."

The door opened and I turned to see who it was. Vince O'Hare stood in the door frame for a moment looking around. He spotted me watching him and nodded to-

ward the tables along the windows where nobody was
sitting.

"Save my seat, Billy," I said, picking up my beer.

O'Hare is a salty old lobsterman, accent on the old. I
have no idea how old, but he's well past seventy I'm sure.
He fought in the Battle of the Bulge in World War Two
and lived to tell about it. His long, scraggly gray hair and
unkempt gray beard framed a face that had been weathered by sun, sea, and time. Deep lines gouged his face at
the corners of his eyes, which were surprisingly sharp
and pale blue, like sea ice.

"Jimmy said you were looking for me," I said, as I spun
a chair around and straddled it. "What's up?"

"You know Lawrence, right?" the old man said in a
gravelly voice.

"Lawrence Lovett down in Key West? Yeah, why?"

"This can't go beyond this table, ya understand?"

I motioned Rusty to bring us a couple beers. "Whatever you say, Vince. What's on your mind."

He waited until Rusty put the beers on the table, then
leaned forward conspiratorially. "He and I got to talking
a few months back about the old days here. Back in the
sixties."

"He's been here that long?"

"And then some. The thing is, we started comparing notes about something that happened in sixty-six.
Things we knew from different sides of the fence, ya
might say. Something that involves a shit-ton of money
and could get us both killed."

"I was four years old then," I said.

"Have you ever heard of Dominic Russo?"

"Can't say that I have," I replied.

"He was originally out of Jersey," O'Hare began. "A made man in the Gambino family."

"*That* I've heard of."

"Yeah, well, Russo had a bit of a falling-out with the family and was sent to Miami. Back then, Miami wasn't like it is now. It was more like a mosquito infested frontier. Anyway, after a coupla years down here, the hate for what happened up there took over. The mob controlled most of the casino action over in the islands. Nassau, mostly. Nobody could touch them back then, and they became pretty brazen about their operation. Once a week, they flew cash out of the islands to Miami, where it was put on a truck and shipped north."

"I'm with you so far," I said, tilting my beer up. "What's this got to do with you and Lawrence?"

"I'm gettin' to that," he growled. "Anyway, one week they had a big haul in the casinos. New Year's weekend, it was. They couldn't fit all the cash in the one plane, so they chartered a second one. Russo had been waiting for just this opportunity. He had a pilot in Nassau, a real scumbag by the name of Bill Rafferty, who he knew from his Jersey days. So Russo clues Rafferty in on when and where the second load of cash was leaving from, then Rafferty kills the pilot and steals the smaller plane. Ripping off the mob is something you just don't do, but Russo and Rafferty did it. Woulda got away with it, too. Nobody saw Rafferty kill the pilot and his body was never found. The plane just disappeared. Flew right on top of the water toward Miami, but Rafferty got blown off course in a storm and had to ditch in the water."

"Lemme guess," I said. "You and Lawrence figured out where."

"Pretty close," Vince said, scooting closer to the table and taking a long pull from his bottle. "I went in with Lawrence fifty-fifty in trying to find it. Kind of a silent partner, you might say. We hired divers and they've been looking for it for a month, using an old Spanish wreck as cover."

"You found it?"

"Would you just let me get to it, boy?" Vince snarled. He'd always had a short temper, which got him into trouble with the law on a regular basis. "Lawrence called me yesterday. Someone left a message on his windshield last night saying only, 'This is a warning. Back off.' Last night, the divers never came back. Lawrence called some people he knew and found out they'd both been killed."

"This, I haven't heard about," I said. "Any idea who did it?"

"Cops think it was Lawrence."

"What?" I nearly shouted.

"Keep your voice down, ya damned Gyrene. Ya want every man jack in the place to know? I called Lawrence this morning. No answer. I checked around with some people I know down island and sure enough, Lawrence is in custody in Cayo Hueso, suspected of murder and drug trafficking."

"That's ridiculous," I said. "Anyone that knows the guy knows he wouldn't hurt a sand flea."

"Be that as it may," Vince said. "The cops got something on him. He hasn't been charged yet, but he hasn't been released, either."

"So why are you telling me all this?"

"I feel kinda responsible. Was hoping that, what with you being a Fed and all, maybe you could spring him?"

"I'm not a Fed," I said.

"Yeah, and the Pope ain't Catholic."

"How much was on the plane?"

Vince looked around. "Three and a half million in cash. And the mob wants it back. They got people all over with ears to the ground."

"That was over forty years ago," I said. "If that cash went into the drink, it's gone by now."

Vince grinned. "Cash money ain't made of regular paper. Ever leave a dollar bill in your jeans and run it through a washing machine? Besides, it was wrapped in plastic. It's out there, and it's still intact."

"And you want me to go down to Key West, pretend to be something I'm not, and get Lawrence out?"

"Yeah, something like that," he replied. "And then help us find the killers and the cash."

Just then, there was a loud screeching sound from outside. I looked out the window, just in time to see the wind lift the stage off the deck out back. It hesitated a moment and nearly flopped back down, then another gust got under it and sent it flying into the canal. Everyone in the bar went to the windows to see what had happened.

The stage was a five-sided raised platform that jutted out from the end of the deck like an arrow. It had flipped across the yard and into the canal, barely missing Deuce and Julie's Whitby, but landing right on top of someone's skiff tied off in the canal. The console must have been built better than the stage, because several of the stage's planks were broken, splintered upward, with the console sticking up out of the stage. Rusty stared in disbelief.

"How the hell did that come loose?" I asked, joining him at the window, looking out at the damage. I saw Deuce stick his head up out of the hatch in their ketch.

"My fault," Rusty said. "We built the stage as an after-thought, when we added the deck. Had plenty enough lumber left over, but we didn't have enough metal straps to anchor it to the underpinnings. It was only toe-nailed to the deck planks. I'd planned to fix it, but completely forgot."

"Hey, that's my damned boat," a fishing guide by the name of Dink Wilcox shouted. Dink wasn't his real name, but that's what everyone called him. It suited his looks a lot more than his real name, Brian. Dink's a tall, gangly-looking guy who's constantly bumping into stuff and tripping over things that aren't there. Kind of like a waterman might walk when he steps off his boat af-ter two whole days on the pitching deck. But on his boat, Dink was perfectly at home. He kind of reminded me of the country music singer, Mel Tillis, who could sing like nobody's business, but stuttered when he talked. Dink had permanent sea legs. Next to Julie and my late wife, he was probably the best guide the Middle Keys had ever seen.

"Sorry about that, Dink," Rusty said. "You ain't goin' nowhere tonight anyway."

"Dammit, Rusty! That's my bread and butter, right there."

"I'll make it up to you," Rusty said. "You ain't gonna be fishin' for a coupla days, what with this storm. Yeah, it's a hundred percent my fault. I'll put you in something identical or better as soon as this blows over, okay?"

That's just the way Rusty, like most other people around here, does business, and Dink knew he was good for it. The fact was, a lot of clients met Dink here at the *Anchor* for their charters. Rusty made a lot of money off charter fishermen in the form of cases of beer before they left and a ravenous appetite when they got back.

I had no doubt that Rusty would put him in a much nicer boat than the one that sat in the canal looking like a center console barge. It was a sound business move to keep Dink bringing his clients here.

Everyone returned to their seats, and I sat back down with O'Hare. Rusty continued to stare down at the wrecked boat, a puzzled look on his face.

"Something wrong, bro?" I asked him. "I mean, besides the twenty-thousand-dollar lesson in carpentry."

He stood there a moment, then turned suddenly, as if just hearing my voice. "Huh?"

"You all right?" Vince asked.

Rusty looked out the window again. "Yeah. I'm okay. That there just gave me an idea."

CHAPTER THIRTEEN

I n the observation room of the sheriff's Stock Island facility, Ben and Devon watched a closed-circuit TV monitor. The feed was from the room next door. Just outside that room's door was a sign: *Interrogation Room One*. It was, however, the only interrogation room in the building and it was also used to take statements and conduct witness interviews. The two detectives didn't have enough evidence to make an arrest yet, so the subject they were watching on the small black and white screen would be interviewed.

Someone above Ben's paygrade thought putting suspects in an interrogation room would have some psychological effect on the suspect and it would work to the benefit of the Department. Let them think they were being interrogated. In an interview, the subject is free to leave at any time.

On the screen, the prime suspect in the double homicide sat in a metal chair, anchored in place in front of a metal table, which was also anchored in place. Suspects sometimes reacted suddenly or violently, tipping over furniture. The chair was placed closer to the table than a person would ordinarily sit, unless they were eating. But, it was too close to get comfortable and cross your legs and it wasn't so close that you could prop your elbows without leaning forward. In other words, the furniture was intentionally arranged to create discomfort.

The two detectives had been watching him for ten minutes. As they let him stew, he'd gone from looking confused to looking scared. Everything in the room was designed to make a subject more and more uncomfortable. Yet the man sat erect in the straight-backed chair, both hands resting comfortably on his thighs. Though his face showed concern about where he was, nothing was evident in his posture.

"He's big enough," Ben said.

"Yeah," Devon agreed, concentrating on his face. "But he's a lot older than what I'd figured the man who killed the girl would be. How do you want to handle it?"

"I'll stand; you sit and ask the questions. Get him to relax and open up. Easy questions—he looks scared. Get him to establish where he was, what he was doing, who he was with. Get him to set a timeline. Then I'll hit him with the evidence. See if his story changes."

Ben picked up the metal box. On top of it were several file folders, all of which held unrelated paperwork. On top of the files was a fingerprint card, also unrelated. Just some clutter from Ben's desk.

"You ready?"

"Let's do it," Devon replied.

Together, the two detectives left the observation room, went a short ten feet down the hallway and entered Interrogation Room One, with Devon leading the way. She quickly crossed to the table and sat down, as Ben placed the box and folders on the far end of the table, separating them, then picking up one of the files and opening it. He leafed through the pages and pretended to be reading.

"Mister Lovett," Devon said. "You drive a cab here in Key West, right?"

"Yes, ma'am."

Devon had had people call her "ma'am" before, but the way he said it made her feel like it was simply his natural response, not a perp trying to suck up.

"What company do you drive for?"

"I own di company, ma'am," Lawrence replied. "Just di one cab."

"Must be kind of tough being an independent in a tourist town."

Lawrence seemed to relax a little. "Not so much. I treat people di way I want to be treated and a lot of di locals prefer ridin' with me."

"Can you tell me where you were yesterday from noon to four pm?"

"Yestuhday?" Lawrence said, his voice cracking slightly, in the sing-song accent of island people.

"Yes, sir," Devon said. Her face was calm, with only the slightest trace of a disarming smile. "Yesterday afternoon."

Though fairly new with the Monroe County Sheriff's Office, Devon had already established herself as the go-to interrogator to get people to relax and open up. She had the uncanny ability to make people feel as if she related to the problem they were facing.

"I was working, driving my cab."

"Any particular fares jump out at you? Anyone seem unusual?"

"Dis is Key West, ma'am," Lawrence replied, with a half-grin. "Jest about everyone here is a little unusual."

"Anyone in particular stand out yesterday afternoon? Seem a bit more unusual than others?"

Devon watched the man's face. His eyes strayed to the ceiling over Devon's right shoulder. "Well, lesse. Der was one couple, a young man and woman. Dey was very drunk and it was just after lunch time. She wanted to go back to di cruise ship, but he wanted her to dance at *Rick's* again. Dat was his very words, dance again. She was a pretty girl, but him not so much. I thought it a little weirder dan usual. She so pretty and him kinda ugly, but wantin' her to dance naked in front of strangers."

"Anyone else?"

"Itta be helpful if yuh tell me who yuh looking for."

"Just anyone out of the ordinary," Devon said, turning the smile up a bit and lowering her eyelids just a little. "I haven't been here long, but I've seen a lot of weird."

"Jest di usual tourists from di cruise ship, early on. Mostly normal folks from di mid-west taking a vacation. Den, 'bout three o'clock, I start my rounds."

"Your rounds?"

"Di local bars have a schedule for di girls, so dat I pick several of dem up at once, at staggered times, and get dem home safely at di end of dere shift. Dis takes me from three to five every day and again from two to four in di morning."

"What do you do between these rounds?"

"I staht my workin' day at noon, eat my lunch and take a nap while di island enjoys di happy hour, den I go back to work from midnight to four. About nine hours all together. After all di girls are home safe, I go home and go to bed. Den do it all over again di next day.

The girls? Devon thought. He said it twice.

"These girls?" Devon said. "Who are they exactly?"

"Jist di girls dat work as bartenders, waitresses, store clerks and all. Some don't have anyone to take dem home and it used to be dey sometimes got harassed or worse. Me and Mizz McKenna worked things out with all di bar owners and came up with a schedule, where dey could all get home safe and sound."

"Mizz McKenna?"

"Mizz Dawn McKenna, ma'am. She a spiritualist. And kinda di muddah hen for some of di locals."

"Do you know James Isaksson and Jennifer Marshall?"

Lawrence's gaze fell to the middle of the table. "Yes, and I know dey are dead."

It surprised Devon that he would admit that. No mention of the murders had been leaked to the press. "How do you know this?"

"Di coconut telegraph."

"Do you recognize this money box?" Ben asked, moving it to the center of the table.

Lawrence looked at it as if seeing it for the first time. "It looks like di money box dat was stole from my cab last night."

"You didn't file a stolen property report?" Ben asked, laying the file down and picking up the fingerprint card.

Lawrence looked up at the older detective. "No, suh. It not di first time I been robbed and di police can nevuh catch di crooks. I jest figure dey needed di money more dan I."

"This box was found on James Isaksson's boat. The boat he and Jennifer Marshall were killed on. Inside this box was a lot of money and an ounce of cocaine. Fingerprints were all over the scene of the murder." Ben tossed the print-card in front of Lawrence with a practiced hand. "Are your fingerprints going to be a match?"

It was an open-ended question, one Ben had used many times to trip up a suspect, if only in his own mind. A criminal might have used gloves and left no prints. They'd be smug and deny any match, which told him as much as a verbal answer. A guilty suspect who hadn't worn gloves would deny it also. But their reaction would be more vehement and they might exhibit a questioning look, wondering if they'd wiped down the scene of the crime adequately.

Lawrence's eyes grew wide. "I been on di boat a few times, suh. Cap'n James was working for me. I don't know anything 'bout drugs and don't 'sociate wit di druggies. Same wit Cap'n James."

"Were you on the boat yesterday between two and four?" Devon asked suddenly.

"No, ma'am. Not yestuhday. I was out dere three days ago. Do I need a lawyer, ma'am?

"Do you have something to hide?" Devon asked, skirting the question, since he hadn't demanded an attorney, only asking her advice. So far, this was just an interview, and Lovett was free to get up and leave at any time.

"All I can tell you is di truth," Lawrence replied. He began to tell the detectives about the search for the lost ships of the *Nuestra España* Fleet. Of the twenty-one ships in the convoy that left Havana in 1733, most were driven into the shallows around the Keys by a hurricane. Thirteen of the wreck sites were known, stretching eighty miles along the Keys. Lawrence went on to explain how he'd gotten a preliminary search permit for one of the wrecks that he believed to have been miraculously blown through the natural channels and into the Gulf, where it had finally grounded in what was now the Great White Heron National Wildlife Refuge.

"I hired James to do di surveys," Lawrence said. "If he found di ship, di law say we have to turn it over to di archeologists. When dey finish, we may get a small part of di value of di treasure. It be a small part, but more dan I make in di cab in a lifetime."

"And the drugs in your money box?" Ben asked. "It was locked when it was recovered on Isaksson's boat. The coke and money locked inside it."

Lawrence sat back in his chair and looked Ben in the eye. "I don't know anyting 'bout drugs, suh. Dat be di truth."

"Wait here," Ben said, nodding Devon toward the door.

In the hallway, Ben leaned against the far wall. "What do you think?"

"He didn't seem to be evasive about anything," Devon replied. "But I still think he's not telling everything he knows."

"I agree," Ben said. "If he did indeed hire Isaksson, and I believe that part's true, and he admits being on the boat numerous times, which makes sense if the dead guy was working for him, then we can't hold him on the prints at the scene. What about the coke?"

"Wasn't found in his possession," Devon replied. "The only way to tie it to him is his confession that the box looked like his, but was stolen."

"Seems fishy, him not filing a report."

"Fishy, maybe," Devon said. "Or complacent. Most property crimes don't get solved."

"Let's let him sit a while longer while you check his background. See if he was being truthful about being robbed in the past. And while you're on the computer, find out who this Dawn McKenna is."

"What are you going to do?"

"Go see a judge and try to get a warrant to search his home."

"Good luck with that," Devon said, and left Ben standing in the hallway.

CHAPTER FOURTEEN

J ust before sunset, with the wind holding at a steady forty-five knots out of the south-southeast, the power went out in the bar. The TV blinked off, and the sudden quiet was marked by the sound of the wind outside. It was still light out, though it was darkening quickly as another squall approached. We'd just been watching it on the radar loop on the Weather Channel. Still, there was more than enough light coming through the windows that surrounded three sides of the *Anchor* to be able to see easy enough. But it would be dark soon.

"Arm yourselves, gentlemen," Rusty said, reaching into a drawer and tossing several boxes of wooden matches onto the bar. He removed the globe from a hurricane lantern mounted to the wall beside his office door and struck a match.

Chairs and stools scraped. All around the bar, Rusty had identical hurricane lanterns placed between every other window. I picked up one of the dozen or so boxes of matches Rusty had tossed on the bar and went to the nearest table. Striking a match, I picked up the large candle holder sitting in the middle of the table. It was a green cracked-glass globe, wrapped loosely in a coarse, heavy rope. I turned it sideways and put the match inside and lit the candle. From there, I went to a hurricane lamp mounted between the dart boards on the wall, next to the men's and women's heads, and lit it.

More flickering firelight slowly rose inside the bar, as it got darker by the minute outside. More lanterns and candles were lit. The door opened and I glanced over. Outside, I saw a yellow Jeep Cherokee, and a lump suddenly came to my throat.

The Jeep had belonged to my late wife, Alex. It was on a night just like this, three years ago, that she came back into my life, as Hurricane Wilma approached. Our relationship rekindled, then burned into a white-hot fire. We were married less than a week after her return, and Alex was murdered on our wedding night. I'd given the Jeep to Julie a week or so later.

Deuce and Julie, followed by two other couples, came inside. They went straight to the bar, then Julie disappeared into the office and Deuce sat near the end of the bar, close to the office door.

I recognized one of the live-aboard couples that came in with them, but it had been awhile since I'd seen them. Mark, or Mike, and his girlfriend Melodi. I couldn't remember either of their last names. They took a table in the middle of the room.

The other couple, I'd never seen before. They stood at the door and looked around for a moment, then moved to the corner table nearest the door and sat down. I walked over to them.

"Can I get y'all something?" I asked.

The man, slightly gray and wearing glasses, looked to be about my age. The woman appeared to be a few years younger, with blond hair and slight laugh wrinkles at the corners of her eyes. Both were dressed like boaters, and looked capable enough.

"Are you the owner?" the man asked.

"No, I don't even work here. But everyone sort of kicks in when needed."

"Any idea how long the power will be out on the docks?"

Out of the corner of my eye, I saw Julie come out of the office with a set of keys on a buoy float. She and Deuce headed out the back door.

"Probably just a few more seconds," I said. "The kitchen, reefers, and shore power are on a backup generator. The bar lights aren't, though. My name's Jesse."

"Hi, Jesse," the woman said. "I'm Kim and this is my husband, Ed."

"Y'all just taking shelter?"

"We were heading for Boot Key Harbor," Ed said. "Meeting friends there to cross over to the Berry Islands. When we got in radio range, they told us the mooring field was full and suggested calling you guys. Seems a lot more secure here than swinging on the hook in Sister Creek."

I heard the generator start and watched through the windows as a few lights flickered on in some of the boats.

"You're welcome to hang out inside," I said, as the sound of rain began pounding on the steel roof. At the same time, the monotone voice on Rusty's portable VHF radio began to recite the current conditions at Key West. "Everyone here is a local or live-aboard."

"Anything we can do to help?" Kim asked.

Looking around, I saw that everyone had returned to their seats, taking the power outage in typical Conch fashion: ordering another beer.

"I think everything's under control. The kitchen will be open until the bar closes at midnight and the bar was stocked for the storm yesterday."

Rusty approached the table, weaving his considerable girth through several other tables with ease. "I'm the owner of the joint," he said, extending a hand to Ed. "Name's Rusty Thurman. Y'all must be *Leap of Faith?*"

Ed stood and took Rusty's hand. "Ed and Kim Robinson."

Rusty handed each of them a menu. "Around here, supper's on the house for first-time live-aboards. Hogfish and grouper are fresh today."

"That's very generous," Kim said. "Thanks."

I left Rusty to get their order and went back to where Billy sat at the bar, still nursing his second beer of the evening. In the distance, I heard the low roll of thunder out over Vaca Key Bight as Deuce came back inside.

"Where's Jules?" I asked him.

"Not feeling well," he replied, taking the stool next to me. "That thing with the stage shook her up. We were in the vee-berth when it happened."

"That's her momma-bear instinct growing stronger," I told him. "Women are fiercely protective of their babies. Things that she wouldn't consider risky before will be a non-starter now."

"She went in the house. Said we'd be sleeping ashore tonight."

"You might as well put the Whitby up for sale, dude," Jimmy said, as he stocked the cooler under the bar with beer. "Might as well start looking for a mortgage provider and a minivan, too."

Deuce ignored him and turned to me. "I had Chyrel check, and right now your friend hasn't been charged. But he's being held as a person of interest. They can hold him without charging him for twenty-four hours, then they have to release him or apply to the court to hold him without charges as a murder suspect. They can only do that for a total of up to ninety-six hours. How sure are you about this guy?"

"Do you mean would he kill someone if he had to?" I asked. Deuce nodded. "Yeah, but only in self-defense or defending someone else. There's no way he's the type that could plan out and execute a murder. And zero chance that he's involved in drugs. That, I'm a hundred percent sure about. As sure as I am about you."

The door opened and we both looked toward it. Marty Phillips, the young deputy sheriff who had been dating Kim for the past year, stood in the doorway, his uniform soaked from the rain. I couldn't help but notice Ed Robinson's furtive glance when he saw the uniform.

Marty came straight over to the bar, where Deuce and I sat. "Whew, glad this day is done," he said. "The sheriff ordered the boats in, and I was put in a cruiser with a road deputy for the rest of the day. Craziness out there."

"You saved me a quarter," I told Marty. "I was just about to call you." His puzzled expression told me the reference to a pay phone went right over his young head. "You know anything about the two murders?"

"How do you know anything?" Marty replied. Then he looked at Deuce. "Never mind," he said.

Marty grabbed an empty stool next to me and placed it behind our two stools. Deuce and I both turned away from the bar to face him. "I responded to both of them," he replied. "But it sounds like you probably know as much as I do."

"Where did it happen?" Deuce asked.

"They're working on that," Marty replied, as Rusty joined Jimmy behind the bar. "The first body was found in the water by fishermen out about a half mile past Snipe Key. The second was on a boat that drifted aground on north Knockemdown just about sunset."

I glanced at Rusty and he looked up toward the ceiling. I could almost hear the wind, waves, and tides moving through his mind. Rusty is the great-grandson of Conchs, and at least half of what flows through his veins is seawater.

"The bodies found about four hours apart?" Rusty asked.

"Yeah," Marty replied, leaning in closer to the bar. "How'd you know that?"

"Wind was out of the northeast yesterday, from the storm. Blew about fifteen knots all afternoon. Tide was ebbing, too, currents snaking through the backcountry at two knots. A body in the water will move with the current. Add a north wind to a southerly current and the boat will drift through the shallows faster than the body. I'd bet the body in the water got separated from the boat about three yesterday afternoon."

"I was fishing Cudjoe Basin yesterday afternoon," I said. "Heard a gunshot off to the northwest. It sounded like it was a good five miles away."

"You sure it was a gunshot?" Marty asked, but before I could answer he said, "Never mind again. I keep forgetting who you guys are. What time, exactly, did you hear the gunshot? This'll be important in determining exactly where it happened, and maybe the why."

"Afternoon is all I can tell you," I said. "I'd guess about fifteen hundred."

"What time was the body in the water found?" Rusty asked.

"Not much later," Marty replied. "about four-thirty or five."

"Jesse don't wear a watch, so this is just a guess based on his guess of the time he heard the shot, but a good place to start looking would be about four miles north-northwest of where the body was found. That'll be where it and the boat got separated and probably where the murders happened."

"What do you know about Lawrence Lovett being a suspect?" I asked Marty.

"I know Lieutenant Morgan has a person of interest in custody. No idea who it is, though."

"Morgan?" I asked. The name was familiar.

"Ben Morgan," Marty said. "Head detective in major crimes."

Ah, I thought. *The balding detective that responded when Stockwell and I shot up some drug dealers in Key West last year.*

"What's out there?" Deuce asked. "Five miles north-northwest of where you were fishing?"

"Nothing," I replied. "Just some shallows. It's part of the Wildlife Refuge."

"Great White Heron?" Deuce asked, arching an eyebrow. "That's a national refuge, isn't it?"

"Yeah," Marty said. "We patrol it, along with Fish and Wildlife, but it's actually under the jurisdiction of the federal government."

CHAPTER FIFTEEN

"We should cancel the pickup," Duke Rafferty muttered, nervously pacing the dock.

Harley tossed a canvas bag onto the foredeck of his twenty-five-foot Seapro center console. "Just get on the boat, Marion."

The big man stopped his pacing and glowered at his older brother.

"Sorry. *Duke.* It's just that these are the kinda guys who take punctuality real serious."

"There's a hurricane out there, Harley."

The elder Rafferty brother dropped onto the deck of the boat as it rocked in the choppy water. The dock was in a little canal behind Harley's house on Raccoon Key, just off Stock Island. "It's way down on the other side of eastern Cuba. Now get in."

Duke hesitated.

"Duke, look at me."

The heavily-muscled man looked at his brother.

Harley knew Duke wasn't totally stupid. "The hurricane is three hundred miles away and it's moving at fifteen miles per hour. How long will it take for the storm to get here?"

Duke's brow furrowed in thought for a moment, then he stepped down into the boat, grinning sheepishly. "It won't be here until tomorrow about lunch time."

Most would have counted the answer wrong, but Harley just tousled his little brother's hair. Technically, Duke was right, since the brothers usually didn't rise until early afternoon and ate lunch when most people were enjoying happy hour.

Harley started the twin Mercury outboards, then switched on the running lights and forward spotlights. The two quickly untied the boat from the dock and shoved off. Harley knew the seas outside the canal would be rough, but he also knew that the guy he bought coke from would be a lot rougher if they missed the drop.

As he steered the boat toward the opening to the Gulf, Harley turned on the chart plotter and entered the GPS numbers his contact had given him. The plotter displayed the course in a matter of seconds and Harley was glad to see that it was only two miles north, on Calda Bank.

"Hang on!" Harley shouted to his brother, as he pushed the throttles halfway, bringing the boat up on plane at the canal entrance.

Once they were outside the protection offered in the canal, it got rough really fast. Harley adjusted the boat's trim, raised the bow slightly, and throttled back to barely stay on plane. For the next fifteen minutes, the two men held tightly to the T-top rails as the boat was tossed left and right from one wave to another.

As they neared the pickup point, Harley saw the lights from another boat approaching from the northeast and turned toward it. He recognized the old trawler, its deck awash in bright spotlights, the rigging swaying back and forth in the heavy seas. It had once been used to catch shrimp, and still had all the nets and equipment aboard—but the nets hadn't touched the water in a couple of years, and the shrimp holds were loaded with cocaine or marijuana these days.

"Put the fenders over," Harley told his brother.

Duke quickly moved over to the gunwale, keeping one hand on the T-top frame. He tossed the fenders, already tied to the cleats on the gunwale, over the side. Harley maneuvered the smaller boat alongside the old trawler, which had come to a complete stop.

"Hurry up and tie off," Joaquin, the skipper of the old boat, shouted over the north wind. "You're my last drop and then I'm getting off this damned ocean."

Even with the fenders in place the two boats banged against each other several times in the dark. Harley heard a crunching sound and hoped it was the old wood of the trawler, not his fiberglass. The crewmen on the other boat caught the lines Duke tossed and quickly lashed the two boats together.

Harley moved around the port side of the center console and up to the bow, where he opened the two huge fish boxes. Duke positioned himself with his back wedged against the T-top's starboard cross member, his feet spread far apart against the inside of the hull, bracing himself against the tossing waves. One by one, the crew on the trawler dropped twenty individual packages down to Duke, each weighing twenty-five pounds and wrapped tightly in heavy plastic.

Duke had no trouble catching the heavy packages and tossing them gently to Harley, who more or less tried to deflect the packages to the right spot in the fish boxes. In minutes, the boxes were full and the crew on the trawler untied the lines, separating the two boats.

"The boss will make the pickup himself tonight," Joaquin shouted from the wheelhouse.

"Why not Milton?" Harley shouted, as Joaquin ducked back into the wheelhouse and engaged the bigger boat's transmission. Harley's words fell on deaf ears, as the shrimp trawler slowly chugged away, turning back to the northeast.

Putting his own boat in gear, Harley throttled up and tried to trim the boat again. With five hundred pounds of blow up in the forward fish boxes, the center console was sluggish in the heavy seas. But the twin Merc one-fifteens slowly brought the bow up. Both Harley and Duke quickly became drenched from the salt spray as the bow-heavy boat crashed down over each wave. The huge splashes from the bow were picked up by the north wind quartering their stern, blowing the white water right into the boat over the gunwale. It quickly drained out through the scuppers, but it was miserable ride.

It took twenty harrowing minutes to get back to the relative safety of the canal, and it was pouring rain when they got there. Harley and Duke quickly tied the boat up to the dock behind Harley's house and ran up to the storage area below the back deck. Harley was always careful, and never unloaded as soon as he got home. Better to check if anyone was hanging around or watching the place first.

"Let's check the yard and then get cleaned up," Harley said. "We'll unload after midnight, move the product into the lab, and go see how things are going at the bar."

Duke walked around one side of the house and Harley went the other way. They met in front and, neither having seen anything suspicious, went up the steps to the main floor.

"Why you suppose the boss is making the pickup tonight?" Duke asked, when they reached the door.

"I don't know," Harley replied, suddenly exhausted. "I just don't know."

An hour later, the rain quit and the two men went down the back steps. Harley unlocked the large storage area under the house, went inside, and came out with a small pull cart, like fishermen use to unload their catch.

Harley's house was built on stilts, like most of the homes on Raccoon Key. Beneath the house, a twenty by twenty-foot area encompassing nine of the concrete piers had been closed in. Originally built as a two-car garage, it had been remodeled into a small one-bedroom apartment by the previous owner. When Harley bought the place, he'd stripped the apartment's interior bare, leaving only the exterior walls and the bathroom in the corner. He'd sealed it up and turned it into a lab of sorts, complete with its own air conditioning system. The temperature inside was kept very low to keep the humidity down. This way, the bricks of coke they opened, cut, and repackaged wouldn't get damp.

The dock was completely dark as Harley moved the cart next to the bow of the boat. He looked all around. No lights were on in any of the houses across the canal, and the blue light of a TV shown from the old man's house next door. Harley kept watch while Duke went aboard and began unloading the product. They quickly moved it into the lab, closing the door behind them just as another squall started dumping rain again.

Inside, a single concrete pier stood in the center of the room, a large stainless steel table next to it taking up most of the space. Two smaller tables were against each wall.

Harley had called his chemist guy earlier in the day. Paul had told him he'd come tomorrow with the cut, so they didn't bother to put the product away. Instead, they just unloaded the packages on the big main table, leaving plenty of space for Paul to set up his equipment and do his work.

The chemist would bring two hundred and fifty pounds of procaine, a powdery substance used as a local anesthetic, for the cut. For several hours, he'd very carefully weigh out the coke in three-quarter ounce portions. He'd do each package individually, adding just enough of the procaine to make it a full ounce. This process would create about twelve thousand little one-ounce bags.

Cutting the coke effectively increased their product weight from five hundred pounds to around seven hundred and fifty, and still kept it above sixty percent purity—at least that was what Harley hoped for. The last few shipments had been less than the usual ninety percent pure. The chemist could only step on it so much before the purity would be below what his customers would accept. And these days every street dealer carried a test kit in his back pocket.

In minutes, the Rafferty brothers had the drugs unloaded, put the cart away, locked the door, and left. Harley drove his own car, a black Cadillac CTS, and Duke drove his red Jeep Wrangler. The drive was a short one. They both pulled into the rear parking lot of *Rafferty's Pub* just a few blocks later.

Harley went straight to his office in the back, telling Duke to keep an eye out for the boss. In the office, Harley opened a closet and squatted down. He spun the dial on the door of the safe anchored to the concrete floor and unlocked it. From the bottom of the safe, he pulled out a black valise and opened it. Then, from the top shelf, he started removing and counting out individual bank-wrapped bundles of hundred-dollar bills. The top shelf was nearly empty when he placed the two-hundredth bundle into the valise and closed it.

Two million bucks, Harley thought, lifting the valise and noting its weight before placing it on his desk. More money than he'd ever spent in his whole life. But after cutting the coke, packaging it in individual one-ounce bags, and distributing it into his pipeline, it would bring in six times that. He fronted a good portion to a lot of local dealers—only to those he thought were good for it, and he kept detailed records—but occasionally one would disappear, along with several thousand dollars of Harley's blow. Duke usually did an exceptional job of tracking those guys down. He was good at it, and usually made a decent example of the wannabe thief to deter others from trying. But now and then, one got away scot-free, costing Harley a few thousand dollars.

Not much of a loss, compared to the potential profit of ten million, he thought. It had taken him nearly two years to get deep enough into the boss's organization to make the pitch, all the while turning kilos and stashing the profit. And now it was finally gonna happen. This one big score was going to set him up for life.

There was a knock on the door, and Duke stuck his head in. "Mister Delgado is here, Harley."

"See what he's drinking and show him in."

The door was pushed open and Jack Delgado said, "I'm drinking Scotch."

"Come in, Mister Delgado," Harley said, coming around the desk. "Duke, get Mister Delgado a drink. And set his men up, too."

"They don't drink," Delgado said, crossing the short distance and sitting down on a small couch against the wall.

"I got everything right here," Harley said, as Duke closed the door. "Two mil, just like we agreed on. The drop went really smooth, too. Even with the bad weather, your man was right on time."

"Figured you'd be all set, Rafferty. You strike me as an intelligent man to do business with."

"Is something wrong with Milton?" Harley asked, opening the door for the real question he wanted to ask, but wouldn't.

There was another knock on the door and Duke came in. He handed Delgado his Scotch and left. "He's fine. I like to meet people I do a lot of business with. And I wanted to ask you something, and get the answer straight from the horse's mouth."

"What's that, Mister Delgado?"

"You're turning into a big player down here and gonna be coming into some really big money now, am I right?"

"Enough to hold me the rest of my life," Harley replied, "if all goes according to plan."

"How long will it take you to distribute five hundred pounds?"

Harley didn't like the direction the conversation was going. He only wanted to make this one big score. "A month, on the outside."

"I like a guy who knows how to take his time and do things right. I'd like to offer you a chance to do this on a regular basis."

"I sense a *but* at the end of that," Harley said. "And to be honest, Mister Delgado, I'm not real sure I want to do this continuously."

"Let me make this clear, Rafferty. If I *were* to want you to do it continuously, you would."

Harley swallowed hard. Delgado was the top of the heap in South Florida. Most of the people who became his enemy had a habit of disappearing. Harley wasn't sure he wanted to continue the risk of running a large volume of coke, but Delgado had a way of making people want to do what they thought they didn't.

"I still sense a *but*, sir."

"You're perceptive, too," Delgado said, as he stood up and took a long drink from his Scotch. He placed the glass on Harley's desk and opened the valise to peer inside. Closing it, he pulled the zipper shut. He looked Harley squarely in the eyes. "Why is an ounce of my product sitting in the Monroe Sheriff's evidence locker, connected to a double murder?"

Harley played poker once a week. The guys he played with weren't big stakes gamblers, but they were good and you had to be good just to sit down at the table with them. It was all about micro-expressions, Harley had learned. And he was good at it.

"An ounce?" he asked, raising an eyebrow in feigned interest. "And two murders? How are they connected?"

"That's what I'm asking you, Rafferty. How is an ounce of my uncut coke connected to these two murders here in Key West?"

"Uncut?" Harley asked, with just enough of a surprised look on his face. "Just an ounce? The one doesn't match the other. Whatever I buy from you is stepped on to about sixty-five percent. Just like most everyone else who sells ounces. There's a whole lot more profit down here at the bottom. I don't know anyone who sells higher purity by the ounce."

Harley seemed to ponder it, while Delgado studied his face. Harley snapped his fingers and said, "Hey, maybe the killer is a bigger dealer. Someone like me, who sells the ounces. And maybe that ounce was his own stash! I never touch the stuff myself, but I know a lot of guys whose profits go right up their own noses. I can put the word out, if you like. Maybe someone here in town knows something. Any idea where it came from or who the killer is?"

The corners of Delgado's mouth turned up a little. "I like you, Rafferty. Yeah, if you hear anything, you let me know."

"Absolutely, Mister Delgado. Can I have Duke get you another Scotch?"

"You got a VIP lounge here?"

"Yes, sir," Harley replied.

"The girl dancing now, and another one with similar features. Have a bottle of The Glenlivet brought to the VIP room, with three glasses. Four, if you'd like to join us."

Harley smiled and stepped over to the door, opening it. He looked out to the stage and then motioned Duke over. "Grab Brandy off the stage. Tell her and Jasmine to go to the VIP room with a bottle of The Glenlivet and three glasses."

Harley closed the door and turned back to Delgado. "I'd like to join you, but I have a lot of paperwork to catch up on here. Want me to put the bag in my safe until you're ready to leave?"

Delgado clapped his fat hands and rubbed them together vigorously. "Yeah, we won't be but an hour or so."

"No hurry, Mister Delgado," Harley said, putting the valise back in the safe. "Take your time and enjoy yourself. Brandy is the girl you saw onstage. She and Jasmine are like bookends, and they'll take really good care of you."

Opening the door again, Harley found Jasmine standing just outside, smiling. "Walk this way, sir," she said to Delgado.

The old boss stopped at the door and watched Jasmine's ass as she seductively crossed the back of the bar toward the VIP lounge, wearing only a thong and sheer negligee. "If I walked like that," he said, "I'd probably break something."

Delgado's two bodyguards followed him as he followed the retreating Jasmine like a hound on a deer trail. Harley motioned to Duke again, then closed the door. When Duke came in, Harley said, "We got trouble, little brother."

"What?"

"Somehow Delgado knows that the ounce you planted on the salvage boat came from him."

CHAPTER SIXTEEN

Ben Morgan dashed from the covered porch of his houseboat to his car, but was pretty soggy when he got in anyway. Hurricane Ike was paralleling the Cuban coastline on its southern Caribbean side, but Cuba was only ninety-six miles from Key West, so the Keys were getting a lot of the rain from it.

Ten minutes later, Ben parked in the Key West Courthouse parking lot on the corner of Fleming and Thomas Streets. He'd already spoken to the judge, and knew he'd only be inside a minute or two. When he came back out, the sun was shining and steam was rising off the sidewalk.

Welcome to Key West, Ben thought. *Don't like the weather? No problem, just wait ten minutes.* He walked to his car and drove to the suspect's address in Old Town. Walt's forensics guys were meeting him and Devon there, along with two patrol deputies.

When he arrived at the little house on Grinnel Street, the patrol car and forensics van were already there, the deputies and techs milling around at the gate, drinking coffee.

"The warrant's all signed off," Ben said, getting out of his car. Devon pulled up right behind him, climbed out of her car and joined him. They walked toward the two deputies.

One of the deputies held a clipboard. With a nod to Ben and a smile for Devon, he said, "The techs have already signed in, Lieutenant."

Ben handed the warrant to the deputy, who checked the address against the one on the porch post. He handed the warrant back and extended the clipboard. Ben signed the log and handed it to Devon, then put the warrant back in his inside jacket pocket.

"Let's go see what Mister Lovett has to hide," Ben said, and the two deputies fell in behind him and Devon.

"Morning, Lieutenant," one of the techs said with a smile. "Sergeant Evans."

"Wait here while we clear the house," Ben said to the senior tech, a man named Mitchel Bailey.

Unlocking the front door with a key the suspect had provided, Ben drew his sidearm and stepped inside. "Police! We have a warrant!"

Ben stepped inside, sweeping the room with his sidearm. He quickly moved to the opposite corner and glanced down a hallway. Covering the living room and little eat-in kitchen, he nodded to Devon. There were two doors off the kitchen, one with a window that obviously went out to the backyard and the other possibly a pantry or utility room.

"Check there," Ben said, nodding toward the solid door and lifting his weapon to allow her to pass in front of him.

Devon crossed quickly and stood at the side of the door, her Glock raised and ready. Ben glanced at the two deputies, who'd followed them in, then jerked his head toward the hall. As the deputies disappeared toward the bedroom area, Ben crossed the small kitchen and joined Devon. He positioned himself on the opposite side of the door and nodded. Devon turned the knob and threw the door open as both of them stepped back and aimed into a utility room, well-lit by a window.

"Clear!" Ben shouted over his shoulder.

Hearing the deputies call out that the bedrooms were also clear, Ben went back to the front door and waved the techs inside. It was clouding up and looked like another rain band was about to come through.

"Two bedrooms, one bath," Ben said to Bailey. "Plus a small kitchen, living room, and utility room. Typical Conch house."

"About an hour, Lieutenant," Bailey replied.

Ben nodded, and the techs set to work as he and Devon stepped outside. "Let's go get some coffee," Ben said.

The two detectives got in Ben's car and drove two blocks to the corner of Eaton Street, to a place called Old Town Bakery. They sat at one of only two tables, next to a window. Ben ordered a sausage, egg, and cheese biscuit and a large black coffee, and was surprised when Devon told the girl that she'd have the same.

"I just don't know about this guy," Devon said, after the waitress left their table.

"Me either," Ben agreed. "But it's not our job to know. We gather evidence and process it to its own conclusion. Never try to force things to go one way or the other."

"Really, sir?"

"What do you mean?" Ben replied.

"You seem to have it in for Lovett."

"Not at all," Ben said. "It's just that right now, the only evidence found has brought him into the focus of the investigation. We just follow the evidence, and if it tells us that Mister Lovett isn't our guy, then we look elsewhere. There's never anything personal, just a job."

"How long have you been a detective, Lieutenant?"

"Ten years in the Marine Patrol, ten years as a detective, with the last five as a lieutenant," Ben replied as the waitress brought their coffee. "What about you? What'd you do before joining the department?"

"Eight years in the Marines," she replied, "then two years in college, and four now with the Department."

"You were a Marine?"

Devon smiled. "I still am."

He chuckled. "Once a Marine, always a Marine, I get it. There's a guy up island you should meet."

"Not interested," Devon responded.

"I'm sorry. I didn't mean it that way."

Devon had been looking through the window at the people on the sidewalks. She'd always enjoyed people watching from an inconspicuous place. She glanced back at Ben. "I probably took it wrong. I'm sorry. I've been through a few ... what you might call turbulent relationships. Decent guys are hard to come by."

"You could have your pick of them," Ben said.

"Yeah, right."

"You don't notice the way guys are more pleasant when you're around? I've done a million warrant searches and never had a forensics tech or deputy smile at me."

"I didn't notice," Devon said.

"What did you do in the Marines?"

"Deployed twice to Afghanistan." Devon shrugged. "I was military police."

"That explains the rapid advancement," Ben said. "Some of the best and brightest cops I've known came from the military."

Their food arrived and the two detectives ate quickly while discussing the case. When they were done, they both ordered another large coffee, and four more in a go-tray, then returned to Lovett's house.

The deputies were leaning on their squad car and the fence, talking. Both smiled as the two detectives approached. Ben extended the go-tray and both men gratefully accepted a cup.

"See what I mean?" Ben said, as he and Devon approached the front door. Mitchel Bailey was just coming out with a desktop computer.

"I'll take this to the lab," Bailey said. "Our computer forensics guy will be able to recover anything, deleted or not."

"Anything else?" Devon asked.

"You're not gonna believe it," Bailey replied. "Huge rolls of cash, stuffed under the far side of the mattress in the bedroom. Kathy's bagging them now."

Ben and Devon went inside and found Kathy Jennings sealing a gray plastic bag with something heavy in it. There was an identical one sitting on the bed.

"Whatcha got, Jennings?" Ben asked.

Jennings looked up from what she was writing on the bag, as the two detectives entered the bedroom. "More cash than I've ever seen, Lieutenant. Twenty rolls, each big enough to choke a manatee."

CHAPTER SEVENTEEN

The morning sky was dark gray and threatening rain when I woke up. I dressed quickly for the cooler weather that I knew the storm had brought with it: jeans and a long-sleeved *Gaspar's Revenge* tee-shirt. Digging a well-worn pair of boat shoes from the bottom of my hanging closet, I slipped them on, too.

I'd never been one to have a large wardrobe. In the Corps, I could just about put all my clothes in a single sea bag. I owned exactly two pairs of jeans, a couple work shirts, four pairs of cargo shorts, a pair of flip-flops, and the Topsiders on my feet. I didn't own even a single pair of socks. Several months before, Kim had set up an account with a tee-shirt printing company and created what she'd called a virtual Ship's Store on our website, gaspars-revenge.com. She kept my tee-shirt drawer well stocked while earning a little walking-around cash on the side. She did the same thing for Rusty. He now has a display rack full of both *Rusty Anchor* and *Gaspar's Re-*

venge souvenir shirts, mugs, and hats. Some of the other guides had even asked her if she could do the same for them.

I went up to the salon and flipped on the coffeemaker. Finn rose from his spot next to the aft hatch and looked at me expectantly. I opened the hatch and he bolted outside. I'd already set the coffeemaker up the night before, but never set the timer. Deuce and I had come aboard to talk about helping Lawrence, and we'd been up late. He'd told me that the team was on a temporary stand-down, and Deuce felt sure he could take a few extra days, as there wasn't anything on their schedule other than personal fitness. He said he could probably get Stockwell to make a call and get us clearance with the sheriff's office to at least see what was going on and what they had on Lawrence.

Not that it mattered. I knew he hadn't killed anyone—at least nobody that didn't deserve it. He was a friend, and I was determined to find out who the killer was.

I'd thought about Deuce's plan after going to bed. Him opening a private security company was bound to be a success. Having Tony and Chyrel onboard was a good start. But none of us were investigators. And it sounded like we were about to start a private investigation. I doubted if Deuce even had a license yet, but, he still carried the badge, and under Stockwell the Caribbean Counter-terrorism Command had been transformed into more of a police agency.

"You awake?" I heard Deuce call from outside.

I opened the hatch to the cockpit and he came aboard, Finn right behind him. "Waiting for the coffee," I said and went back to the galley.

Deuce sat down on the sofa, with his own coffee mug. "I can come back later. When you're alive."

"He still grumpy before the first cup?" Billy asked stepping up into the salon.

Before the machine finished, I poured a cup and took the first sip. Rusty gets this really good coffee that's grown in the mountains of Costa Rica, and he shares some of it with me. The *Hacienda la Minita Tarrazu* is my favorite. I took another sip and set the mug down on the countertop.

"You talk to Travis?" I asked Deuce, as Billy poured himself a cup.

"Yeah, he already knows my plan to start a security agency, and he's not only good with it, but he said he discussed it with the Secretary and there may be an occasional job coming from the government, a security detail for VIPs visiting Miami, things like that. I won't be holding my breath, but he said he'd call the sheriff this morning."

"What's he gonna tell him?" I asked. "That the Feds are taking over his murder case?"

"I might have mentioned that the murders most likely took place in waters that fall under federal jurisdiction."

"Now, that'd be a reach," I said. "Sure, maybe the FBI would get involved. But Homeland Security?"

"The sheriff kinda likes us," Deuce replied. "Remember, we brought down a fugitive killer on the streets of Key West not long ago."

"Fugitive killer, he says," I said to Billy. "A hired assassin that was after me and him, is more like it."

Just then, Deuce's phone chirped and he pulled it out of his pocket. He answered and listened for a moment.

Then he said, "Thank you, Sheriff. We definitely won't get in the way of the investigation and I promise that anything we uncover; we'll report right away."

He listened for a moment more, then said goodbye and ended the call. "The director called the sheriff. We have a meeting with the local medical examiner in an hour. Both bodies are at the morgue, here in Marathon."

"Doc Fredric? You'll like him."

"You know the ME?" Deuce asked. "Why does this not surprise me? How far is it?"

"Just over on Grassy Key," I replied. "About ten minutes."

"Mind if I tag along?" Billy asked.

Billy and Deuce had gotten to know each other last night and, just as I figured, they'd become friends. "Sure," Deuce replied.

"We have a little time," I said. "Let's go up to the bar and get some breakfast."

Less than an hour later, bellies full of shrimp omelets and grits, we started out to the parking lot. I told Finn to go back to the boat and stay there. He dutifully complied, but the look on his face wasn't happy.

"We can take Julie's car," Deuce said, then stopped in his tracks and looked at me. "I mean, if you're okay with it."

"It's just a car, Deuce," I replied.

But it was anything but that. I opened the passenger door of the bright yellow Jeep Cherokee and got in. I hadn't been in Alex's car in three years. My mind flashed back to the first time I'd sat in this seat. My truck had broken down on the side of the road in a pouring rain. Alex stopped and offered a ride. I remember that I'd hardly recognized her that day. I'd seen her around quite a few times, and she'd always been dressed as a fishing guide, with her hair hanging out of a fishing hat in a ponytail. On the day we actually met, I was up to my elbows in dirt and grease, and totally drenched from the rain. She'd been wearing a floral print dress and had styled her hair a little.

The others got in and Deuce started the Jeep, snapping me out of it.

It's just a car, I told myself.

When we arrived at the medical examiner's office, Doc Fredric met us at the reception desk. I introduced everyone, and Doc had us sign in, then escorted us back to the morgue.

"Billy Rainwater?" Doc said, as he punched a keypad beside a large metal door. "Are you related to Leaping Panther Rainwater?"

"He's my father," Billy replied. "Did you know him?"

"Not exactly," Doc said, as the door made a whooshing sound and opened slightly. He pushed it open and entered, waving us inside. "You favor him quite a bit. No, I met Leaping Panther a few times professionally."

"Professionally?"

Doc chuckled. "His profession, not mine. Your father was the best Everglades tracker and guide there was. I was saddened to hear about the accident and his condition afterwards. I guess you're the leader of the Calusa people now?"

"Yes," Billy replied, humbly. There weren't many people left with any Calusa blood, but being three quarters and the son of the chieftain automatically made Billy the leader.

Doc led us to what looked like several large stainless steel refrigerators joined together. "The sheriff called me this morning, Agent Livingston. He asked that I bring you up to speed on the investigation from my end and his detectives would meet with you later today to tell you what they've uncovered. I'm just at a loss as to what Homeland Security's interest is in this case."

"Just the over-reaching hand of the government," Deuce replied, with a grin, clearly liking the old man immediately. "Actually, it's more personal, Doc. A friend of Agent McDermitt's is currently a suspect in these murders."

"*Agent McDermitt?*" Doc said, looking over at me. "Somehow, I always thought that to be the case."

Doc opened one of the doors and pulled a long tray out. On it was a body, covered with a sheet. He pulled back the sheet to the man's chest. "Victim one is a young man from Ramrod Key, positively identified as James Isaksson. He was shot once in the forehead at close range."

"He's a salvage operator," I said. "Lawrence approached me over a month ago to go treasure hunting. I declined, and then I heard that he'd hired James."

"Did you know him?" Doc asked.

"Only by reputation and to say hi," I replied. "He and his dad are—or were—good and decent people."

Doc opened another door and pulled the tray out. A woman's body was outlined under the sheet. "This might be difficult for you," he said, and pulled the sheet down to just below the woman's shoulders. "Victim two is a waitress and bartender down in Key West. She's been identified as Jennifer Marshall, originally from Galveston, Texas. She's lived in Key West for just under two years."

The woman's face was battered severely on one side. So much so that her left eye and a lot of skin and tissue was missing. The right side of her face was fairly undamaged. She'd obviously been a very beautiful young woman.

"Miss Marshall's official cause of death is drowning. But she would likely not have survived the trauma inflicted."

"Any evidence recovered with either body?" Deuce asked.

"Yes," Doc replied. "Not so much with Mister Isaksson. The bullet I removed from his cranium has striations consistent with a Colt .38 caliber Cobra."

Nodding toward the woman's body, Doc said, "I found quite a bit more evidence with Miss Marshall. She was forcibly drowned. There were traces of sea water and microscopic plant life found in her lungs. I've been able to determine that the killer is a large man and quite strong. He grabbed Miss Marshall from behind while she was scuba diving. He ripped the second stage of her regulator from her mouth, loosening a number of teeth and dislodging one. While holding her tightly in a bear hug, he fractured her right humerus."

"Takes a lot of strength to do that," I said.

"Quite," Doc replied. "She put up a good fight, though. I recovered blood and hair samples from under the fingernails of her left hand. We haven't yet received the DNA results on those. There was biological material in the form of semen recovered from a vaginal swab and more biological material—microscopic plant life—in her mouth, throat, and lungs."

"She was raped and drowned?" Billy said.

"I'm afraid not," Doc replied and pulled the cover back up over her face. "Miss Marshall was drowned and *then* her body was violated."

"That's a special kind of fucking sick," Billy mumbled.

"I see you inherited your father's propensity for subtlety," Doc said, with a wry grin.

"What about the skin and hair?" I asked. "You don't have any DNA report yet, but can you tell anything else from those?"

"Yes, quite a bit," Doc replied. "The blood type is O-positive. Miss Marshall was A-negative. Basically, there are only three types of human head hair: European, African, and Asian. The hair samples under Miss Marshall's fingernails came from a person of European descent, with curly black hair, a powerful physique, and type O-positive blood."

"Did you say European? Not African?"

"Definitely European," Doc replied. "But that's the majority of the people in this country."

"Yeah," I agreed. "But it totally rules out Lawrence."

"Who is Lawrence?"

"He's a black taxi driver in Key West," I said. "A friend of mine. The detectives down there are holding him as a suspect."

"Oh, my," Doc said. "I don't think I'd examined the hair sample when I gave Lieutenant Morgan the autopsy findings. Only that it was black and curly. Are you on your way down there now?"

"We are," Deuce replied. "Can you relay that finding to the detective in charge of the investigation?"

"I certainly will," Doc said.

We left the morgue and decided to go straight to Key West. Though it was normally only a forty or fifty-minute drive, we were hit with a blinding squall halfway across the Seven Mile Bridge, and again on Summerland Key. Both of them had traffic slowed to a crawl, so it was noon when we finally crossed the bridge onto Stock Island. I directed Deuce to the sheriff's main office, and we parked and got out.

"The ME said the lead detective is a guy named Ben Morgan," Deuce said. "Why is that name familiar?"

"You probably read it in a report," I replied, as we walked along the sidewalk. "He was the cop that investigated the shooting at Key West Bight. The one that me, Travis, Scott, and Germ were involved in." Scott Grayson and Jeremiah "Germ" Simpson were also members of Deuce's team. Both were Marine Combat Divers, and were planning to return to their units.

"You've been busy, Kemosabe," Billy said with a grin. "Done gone off the reservation."

We both laughed at our inside boyhood joke. Whenever one of us had gotten mad about something, that was what we'd called it: Going off the reservation.

Once we were inside the building, Deuce flashed his badge at the desk sergeant and asked to speak with Lieutenant Ben Morgan. "He should be expecting us."

"He and his partner just returned from executing a search warrant and are in interrogation. You'll have to wait."

"Does the suspect have an attorney present?" Billy asked.

"I never said he was a suspect."

"But you did say he was in an interrogation room," Deuce said, picking up on Billy's hint. "Not being interviewed."

The desk sergeant dismissed it, waving his hand like he was after a fly. "He hasn't asked for one." He pointed to a long bench seat against the wall. "You can wait over there, or come back later. The lieutenant doesn't like being interrupted."

"Interrupt him," Billy said. "Tell him that his *suspect's* counsel is here."

"You're a lawyer?" the sergeant asked.

"Yes," Billy replied. "My client may not be aware of his rights. Please inform the lieutenant that he needs to stop questioning him unless I am present."

The desk sergeant stood up and walked across the office to another desk, where he spoke to a uniformed deputy.

"What the hell are you doing?" Deuce whispered urgently. "Pretending to be an officer of the court can get us back there all right, but not in a good way."

"I am a lawyer," Billy replied. "Being the leader of a nearly extinct Native American tribe has certain advantages. I was fast-tracked through law school in a year, and passed the bar a month ago." Billy turned to me and shrugged. "Probably coulda passed it without the school, just from all the courtroom drama shows we used to watch."

"And you never thought to bring this up?" I asked.

Billy just shrugged again. "I would have, if Deuce hadn't said I could come along." He grinned broadly. "I was thinking of going to med school next."

CHAPTER EIGHTEEN

"It's all circumstantial," Devon said, while watching Lawrence Lovett on the closed-circuit TV. A person's body language and reaction to questions always told her a lot more than the words they spoke. Everything about this man told her he had nothing to do with the murders, other than having hired the victims.

"We have another hour," Ben said. "Then we have to release him, charge him, or present enough evidence to a judge to get an extension."

"You know as well as I do, Lieutenant, it's not enough and DNA results only come back in a day on TV."

"Then we go in hard," Ben said. "Get a confession out of him."

"The trouble with that is, neither of us thinks he did it."

Ben stood up and began pacing. "Doesn't matter what we think. We follow the evidence. Mister Lovett, the nice old man that he is, wouldn't be the first to have a hidden life. He's connected to the victims, he's the right size to be able to do what he did to the girl, he's got curly black hair, and the bullet from the guy's noggin came from the same kinda gun we just learned he owns. There's only a little more than a dozen of those registered in Monroe County."

Devon looked up at Ben from the TV monitor, arching an eyebrow.

"Okay, okay," he said, "there's probably three or four times that many in the county that aren't registered. Still, all of that together means you and I might be wrong about Lovett." Ben pointed to the screen for emphasis. "That guy might be some kind of sicko killer that likes to screw dead girls."

"So we go in hard," Devon said. "Ignore our own instincts, and try to force a confession?"

"If we're wrong, and we don't do everything in our power to keep him off the streets, he could disappear. He could kill again. We'll have the DNA evidence in just a few days."

"Then let's do it," Devon said, walking to the door.

Ben picked up a file folder from the desk. Inside were just three sheets of paper. This time, they were directly related to this particular case. He followed the younger detective down the hall to the next door and entered.

The two detectives sat down at the table across from Lawrence, and Ben opened the folder. He took the first page out, turned it around and pushed it in front of Lawrence. "This is the report from the medical examiner on James Isaksson's autopsy." Ben stabbed a finger at a spot on the page. "Cause of death: single gunshot wound to the forehead."

He removed the second page and spun it around, pushing it to a spot next to the first page.

"Ballistics report on the bullet taken out of James Isaksson's head. The striations imparted on the bullet by the rifling grooves in the barrel match only one kind of firearm: a Colt .38 caliber Cobra."

Lawrence's face fell as Ben took the last sheet out and put it next to the others.

"This is a copy of a gun registration for a Colt .38 caliber Cobra. Is that your signature at the bottom?"

"Yes, suh," Lawrence muttered, without even looking at the document. "It was in di box dat was stolen."

"The same theft you didn't report?" Devon asked, thinking that this was too easy. "The same box that was found on the boat where the murder took place?"

"Why did you kill them?" Ben roared, slamming an open palm on the folder.

"I did not do dese things," Lawrence cried out, looking up at Ben, tears welling in his eyes. With a deep sob, his head fell to his chest and he quietly repeated, "I did not do dese things."

Just then, the door buzzer interrupted. "What the—" Ben muttered, standing up quickly. Crossing the room in two strides, he yanked open the door to find a uniformed deputy on the other side. "This better be good!"

"Sorry, Lieutenant," the deputy said, as Ben stepped out of the room and closed the door. "Your suspect's lawyer is here, along with two federal agents. The lawyer's demanding to see his client."

"Frigging perfect timing," Ben muttered, reaching for the door knob. "He was about to confess." He opened the door. "Evans, grab the reports and follow me."

CHAPTER NINETEEN

After a few minutes, the uniformed clerk returned. I recognized Lieutenant Morgan with him, and a woman detective following. Both Morgan and the woman detective had removed their jackets; their shields and empty holsters were clearly visible.

Lieutenant Morgan and the woman stepped through the door and faced us. "Which one of you is the lawyer?" Morgan asked.

"I am," Billy replied, digging his wallet out of his jeans. He produced a laminated ID card and handed it to Morgan.

"IDs?" Morgan said, looking at me and Deuce. He examined Billy's and handed it back. Looking at Deuce's badge and identification, he said, "DHS? Why's a special-agent-in-charge coming down here about a murder case?" Morgan handed Deuce's ID back and took mine.

Deuce ignored his question. "Did you get the fax from Doctor Fredric?"

Morgan took a cursory glance at my ID and started to hand it back. He stopped and looked at it again. "Special Agent McDermitt? We've met before?"

"About a year ago," I replied. "A surveillance op in Key West Bight. We were working with DEA and the bad guys decided to turn it up a notch, into a shootout. Did you get Doc Fredric's fax?"

"Didn't even recognize you with all that man hair," Morgan said, handing my ID back. "What fax?"

"Right here, Lieutenant," the clerk said, handing him a sheet from an inbox on his desk.

Morgan took it and started to read. He got halfway down and stopped. "European?"

"That's right, Lieutenant," Deuce said. "You've got the wrong man."

"Maybe on the murder of the girl," Morgan said. "But Lovett owns a gun exactly like the one that the guy was shot with."

"Exactly *like*?" Billy asked.

"We haven't found the actual murder weapon yet," the woman said.

"Circumstantial at best," Billy said. "A judge would laugh you out of his chambers."

Morgan glared at Billy. Finally, he relented the point and jabbed a finger at him. "You can come into interrogation." He turned to Deuce and said, "Unless the federal government has an interest here, you two can wait right here."

Without another word, or waiting for a reply, Morgan opened the door to the inner office and motioned Billy inside.

"Doesn't matter," Billy said, remaining where he stood. "My client won't be answering any more questions. Not even what time of day it is. Which, by the way, is now twenty-four hours after you brought him in for questioning. Charge my client or bring him out here. Now."

Morgan stood with the door open for a long moment. "What the hell," he finally said. "Neither of us thinks he did it, anyway. Evans, go get Mister Lovett and bring him out."

After Detective Evans left, Morgan turned to me and Deuce. "So, what's the Fed's interest in this case."

"Purely personal," I said. "Lawrence is a friend of mine."

"Not entirely personal," Deuce said, as Detective Evans returned with Lawrence. "The department I currently head will be dissolved soon, and Agent McDermitt and I are opening a private investigation and security company. Mister Lovett will be retaining our services to find whoever killed his employees."

"Cap'n Jesse!" Lawrence said, when he saw me. "Yuh look like a boat bum."

I laughed. "Good to see you, too, Lawrence."

"Thanks for gettin' me out, Cap'n."

"Wasn't me," I replied. "Your lawyer, Billy Rainwater, got you released."

Lawrence looked at all three of us in turn, then picked up on the ruse, extending a hand to Billy. "Thanks for coming, Mistuh Billy."

"Billy," Deuce said, "would you mind catching a cab with Lawrence to his home and stay with him? I'm sure he wants to get cleaned up and back to work. We'll catch up with you later this evening."

"Always wanted to see what it was like hanging out with a cab driver in a tourist town," Billy said, and the two of them walked out the door.

"You want to find out what we know," Morgan said, after they left.

"Not really," I said, grinning at Morgan. "We probably know as much or more than you already. We were thinking that we might be of some help in your investigation."

"Well, it's after lunch time," Morgan said. "We can compare notes while we eat."

"*Hurricane Hole*?" I asked. "My treat."

"You're on, McDermitt."

Ten minutes later, Deuce and I were seated at a table on *Hurricane Hole's* back deck, right next to the water. The storm must have kept most people inside, as there wasn't anyone else on the deck. At the moment, it was sunny and fairly cool.

"They obviously know more than we do," Deuce said. "What do we have to bargain with?"

"The location where the murders took place," I replied, as a waitress approached. We both ordered bottles of Kalik.

"All we have to go on is Rusty's guess."

"You'll find that in matters of wind, wave, and current, your father-in-law's guess is better than most any oceanographic computer model. We can find it with the *Revenge*."

Morgan and Evans came out onto the deck from the protected bar area, and Deuce and I both stood up.

"We might have gotten off on the wrong foot," Deuce said. "We really do want to help, and I think we have information that might be important. Please, just call me Deuce, okay?"

Morgan extended his hand. "Ben," he replied. "My partner, Devon."

I shook hands with both of them. The woman detective had a firm, dry handshake. She looked to be in her late twenties, but I'm never good at guessing a woman's age.

"Jesse," I said, and we all sat down. Deuce gave me a slight nod, giving me the go ahead. "We might have a good starting point as to where Isaksson's boat was when the murders took place," I said to Morgan.

"This is the guy I told you about, Evans," Morgan said. She gave him a puzzled look and he added, "The *Marine* I told you about."

"How'd you know I was in the Marines?"

"I didn't recognize you with the hair and beard," Morgan said. "But, that boat of yours sticks out and I checked you out after that shooting. Couldn't get deep enough to learn anything about you being a Fed, though. Good cover."

"You're a Marine?" I asked Evans.

"Ninety-five to oh-three, sir," she replied.

"Can the sir, okay?" I said. "I retired in ninety-nine. Infantry."

"MP Company, Headquarters Battalion, Second Mar-Div."

"Lejeune?" I said. "My last billet was there. Scout-Sniper Instructor with Force Recon." We surveyed each other a little closer, a bond already formed. She had the beginnings of tiny crow's feet at the corners of her light-brown eyes, but didn't wear makeup to try to hide it. I realized my initial estimate was probably off by a few years. Looking closer, I guessed she was at least thirty. "Deuce here is a former SEAL commander. Or will be pretty soon."

"Not sure I follow," Morgan said, looking at Deuce. "You're with DHS *and* in the Navy, but working on the side as a private detective?"

"I was recruited out of the SEALs to head a small unit down here," Deuce said. "Originally, we were to have only a loose attachment to DHS. Last year, Homeland Secretary converted our covert little operation into an overt police force, with many of the same duties and powers of the FBI."

"But you're working as a PI?"

"Long story," Deuce said. "And I don't want to get into politics, but it appears that our organization's days are numbered."

"Pretty much what the sheriff told me on the phone, while we drove over here. Said that you being here in any capacity has the blessings of the president himself."

Deuce shrugged as the waitress arrived to take our orders. "Jesse took him fishing a couple of years ago."

Both detectives arched their eyebrows at that. We placed our food order, and after the waitress left Morgan asked, "So, how is it you know where the boat was when Isaksson was murdered?"

I explained how I was on the flats that afternoon and heard the shot and knew what direction it came from, because my dog's part pointer and was locked onto something he could hear, but I couldn't.

"Wait," Ben said. "You're relying on a dog?"

"Not completely," I replied. "But I know it was a gunshot and Doc said it happened about the time I heard it.

And I know the direction it came from. You spend much time on the water?"

"When I can," Morgan replied. "I was a marine patrol deputy for a few years."

"So you know it's hard to judge how far away something is based on the sound." He nodded, so I continued. "I have a friend who grew up on the water here. His dad and grandpa, too. He knows instinctively what the wind and tides are doing. He gave us a pretty good idea where the woman's body and the boat had drifted from based on the locations of where they were found. Using a chart, I can show the direction I heard the sound from and he can pinpoint the channels and how the currents flow that would have put the woman's body where it was found, and the boat where it was found. Where the three lines intersect is where Isaksson's boat was when it and the woman's body parted company."

"I think you're really enjoying this," Deuce said. "I don't think I've ever heard you speak that many words at one time."

"We have techs working on the wind and current data," Morgan said. "What I want to know is, how is it you guys know where the bodies were found? That information hasn't been released."

"The federal government isn't without resources," Deuce replied.

We continued to discuss the case as we ate. Devon had a surprising appetite for a woman so slim. I couldn't help but wonder what all that fuel might power, under her business suit and slacks.

Morgan finished his last bite and wiped his mouth, wadding the napkin and dropping it on his plate. "So, we're going on the assumption that both victims were killed on or near Isaksson's boat, while they were working together as salvors, which Mister Lovett hired them to do. He's only been out there a couple times, always following his GPS, so he's unable to tell us where to look. The anchor line on the boat was cut and the boat set adrift after the murders, for whatever reason. Maybe the killer thought they'd just float out into the Gulf, instead of drifting toward shore."

I took the last bite of a pretty decent grilled snapper sandwich and chewed quickly. "I have a dive boat. Deuce and I are both qualified search and recovery divers, and have done some treasure hunting as well. We'll go up to Snipe Key tomorrow and start looking around. From what my friend tells me, the area Isaksson and Marshall were diving is probably four to five miles north of there. If the killer cut the anchor line at their dive spot, we can probably find something. The water's very clear in the Gulf during a falling tide. It might take a few hours, but I bet we can find the spot where his boat was anchored."

"I don't know," Morgan said. "The sheriff prefers to keep a tight lid on investigations, particularly major crime scenes."

"Including a crime scene that's outside the three-mile limit?" I said.

"And in a national wildlife refuge?" Deuce added.

The detective thought for a moment and seemed to come to a decision. "You find anything—" he began.

"You'll be the first to know," I interrupted.

"Mind if Evans goes with you?"

Devon looked nervously at Morgan. "Out on a dive boat?"

"Are you a diver?" I asked.

"No," she replied. "Not even a boat person."

"Take some Dramamine," Morgan told her. "I want you with them."

"What will you be doing?" she asked.

"Old-fashioned cop stuff," he replied. "We know the guy is big. We know he's a white guy with dark curly hair. He had to have gotten out to the victims' dive site by boat. I'm gonna put together some road deputies and start canvassing boat rental places. I don't think he's much of a boat person, and he probably rented a boat. Someone might remember renting to him."

CHAPTER TWENTY

Harley and Duke sat at Harley's slightly elevated private table in the corner, with Jasmine sandwiched tightly between them. Unlike the other tables in *Rafferty's Pub*, there was no candle in the middle of this one and the stage lights didn't reach it, leaving the three of them in near total darkness but able to see the whole bar floor and stage.

The club's patrons were otherwise occupied anyway, as a new girl spun around on the pole. Her full name, or at least the name she gave Harley when he hired her, was Jenae Saequa. She'd told him it was French for "a little something" and she sure was. No more than five feet tall, she couldn't have weighed a hundred pounds wearing a wet jacket. Her tiny body was firm and well-toned, and she performed with an athletic grace, spinning around the pole and even hanging upside down from it at times. She was obviously not a newcomer to pole dancing, and no stranger to performing in the nude. The men in the bar—as well as a couple of women—were enjoying the show and oblivious to the goings-on in the darkened corner.

Harley rarely touched the product he sold, preferring alcohol. But when his brother slid the tiny mirror toward him, with half a dozen lines of white powder on it, he picked up the small gold-plated tube and snorted one of them. Below the table, Jasmine was rubbing him through his jeans. Everything was going smoothly and, for the first time in a long time, Harley felt satisfied with where he was in life. So he leaned back, tossed down a shot of tequila, and let her slender fingers perform their magic on him.

Duke's eyes were glued to the new girl on the stage. When she'd first come in, earlier in the day, he'd escorted her to Harley's office. Standing next to her made Duke feel even larger. The top of her head didn't even reach his chin, and he guessed that he probably weighed nearly three times what she did. Jenae had told Harley that she'd just arrived in Key West and was staying with a friend, but only for a few days, and she needed some fast cash.

Harley had told her that Wednesday nights were usually pretty busy and she accepted the one-night, tips-only trial gig, but would need to leave at midnight for another job.

The raucous music ended, and Jenae picked up a sheer white negligee and put it on as she left the stage. The music started again as the DJ introduced Brandy, who took the stage wearing brown-and-white chaps, knee-high white boots, and a white cowboy hat.

Duke's eyes followed Jenae as she moved through the bar, talking to several patrons, until one nodded and stood up. She took the man by the hand and led him toward the VIP room in back.

"I gotta head out in a little while, Harley," Duke said.

Jasmine had tugged Harley's pants open and was now stroking him slowly under the table with one hand, while she held the gold tube to her nose with the other and snorted up another line.

"Where you gotta go?" Harley asked, tilting his head back, enjoying Jasmine's manipulative fingers.

"Just got some personal stuff to take care of," Duke replied, tossing down a shot of tequila.

Before Brandy finished her third dance, Jenae returned to the bar, again circulating around the tables, as the man she'd gone to the VIP room with headed for the front door, smiling. In minutes, Jenae was leading another half-drunk shrimper to the back room.

Harley tapped out a little more dust onto the mirror from a glass vial. Using a small razor blade, he quickly chopped up any large pieces into powder and then deftly cut them into several long straight lines. He was amazed at Jasmine's dexterity, as she one-handed the gold tube, then leaned back, sniffing, and drank down half her shot glass—all while not missing a single stroke.

Several minutes later, the shrimper Jenae had taken to the VIP room staggered out and returned to his table. Duke watched as he quickly drank what was left in his glass, opened his wallet, and looked in it. The shrimper shrugged, tilted his glass again, and headed toward the door, munching on the ice. Duke knew that these men would tell their friends about the new girl in town, and they'd come back in droves. Nothing brought in business like good word of mouth.

Duke checked his watch and saw that it was almost midnight. He waited a moment more, and when Jenae didn't return to the bar he knew she was in the dressing room, getting ready to leave. "Gotta run," he said to his brother, who was now putty in Jasmine's hands.

Harley grunted as Duke stood up, pocketing the little glass vial with several grams still in it. He went straight to the back door and out into the small employee parking lot. Duke knew all the cars there, and walked quickly to his Jeep. He climbed in and waited. Jenae had arrived earlier that evening with a friend, and the other girl had left immediately.

Hope the other girl's late, Duke thought, as he sat in the dark in his beefed up red Wrangler, watching the back door.

A moment later, Jenae stepped out and lit a cigarette while looking around the parking lot. She was wearing tight jeans, slung low on her hips, that hugged her legs all the way down to her ankles. Black three-inch heels added to the illusion of very long legs. Above the low-cut jeans, her tight belly was visible below a cut-off football jersey with the number sixty-nine on it.

Duke smiled and started the engine, revving it a few times, so Jenae would know he was there. He flicked on the lights and pulled out of his parking spot, turning toward her.

Duke stopped just a few feet from where she stood and killed the engine. "You got someone coming?" he asked, innocently, as if he were just a boss looking out for one of his new employees.

"I just called her," Jenae replied, recognizing the giant man in the Jeep and smiling. "Said she's running late, but she'll be here in like twenty minutes, so I came out for a smoke."

"Call her back," Duke said, trying to be cool and in control, like his brother. "I'll be happy to give you a lift."

"It's way up on Big Coppit Key," she said, taking a tentative step closer. "I wouldn't want to put you out or anything."

Duke grinned, like he'd seen his brother do to seduce women. "No big deal. I'm going up island to Sugarloaf anyway. Big Coppit's right on my way."

Jenae smiled and stepped up beside the Jeep, trying to lift a leg to get in. But she was too short, her jeans too tight, and the Jeep's oversized mud-tires too tall.

"Hang on," Duke said, setting the brake. He reached up and grabbed the roll bar, lifting himself from the seat and swinging his legs out.

Duke quickly moved around to the passenger side, where he easily scooped Jenae up like she was nothing. She squealed, wrapping an arm around his neck and hanging on. Duke gently placed her on the Jeep's passenger seat.

"You're sure strong," Jenae said, smiling.

"You're really small," Duke said sheepishly, somewhat embarrassed. "I work out with a lot more weight, I bet. How much do you weigh?"

"Never ask a lady her age or what she weighs," Jenae replied. Then she bounced in the seat and giggled at the discomfort she saw on Duke's face. "Just kidding. I'm four-foot-eleven, and weigh ninety-three pounds. You work out with more than that?"

Duke grinned and walked around the car. Climbing in, he said, "I start out with about four times that."

"Wow!" Jenae said, impressed. "I bet you weigh over two hundred."

"Six-one and two-eighty," he said, climbing in. "I'm three times your size." Emboldened, he added, "Speaking of that, how'd you like to make three times what you already have?"

Jenae turned in her seat as Duke started the engine. She smiled seductively and twirled her blond hair. "What do you have in mind?"

"My boat and you, all night."

Jenae opened her purse and pulled her phone out. "Let me text my friend."

CHAPTER TWENTY-ONE

K evin Montrose fished just about every morning. He'd retired thirty years before from his job as a letter carrier with the post office, and was proud of the fact that in that whole time he'd never missed a day of work. For the next twelve years, he hadn't missed a day at his part-time job fixing old outboards at the marina. He'd finally fully retired nearly twenty years ago, and had been fishing ever since. He had little else to do but fish and care for June, his wife of fifty-four years, who'd passed away six years before. At eighty-three, his boat and the fishing were about all that he had left that brought him pleasure.

Kevin fished and lived by the tides. When the tide was high, he fished the mangrove roots for snapper. When it was low, he fished the deep cuts in the back country for grouper. He slept when he was tired and ate when he was hungry. The rest of the time he was fishing, selling his catch, or sleeping. Once the sun came up, he'd motor up and down canals, delivering his catch to some of the older shut-ins.

Now, in the dark, still hours before dawn, the sturdy little wooden boat with its high stiff bow cut easily through the choppy water near shore. Kevin had built the boat when he returned from the war in Europe, using scrap wood. There was a lot of it available after the 1945 Homestead hurricane. He'd built the boat using plans for a Chesapeake style rowing bay boat, so he could get out to the patch reefs north of his parent's home on Key Largo, but it was big for a rowboat and he'd built it with the idea of saving up and putting an outboard engine on it. After landing the job as the Vaca Key letter carrier in 1948, he'd moved there, built his own home, and met his wife the same year. The engine on the back of the boat, a brand-spanking-new 1949 Kiekhaefer Mercury twenty-five-horsepower Thunderbolt, had been a wedding gift from his parents. Kevin had meticulously rebuilt the engine six times since then, and kept it in top-notch condition.

The Thunderbolt purred quietly in the pre-dawn hours. Kevin was heading to a favorite fishing spot not far from the fancy houses on the other side of Overseas Highway. He could have had one of those houses if he wanted, but stayed in the home he'd built sixty years ago. At one time, he could have bought the whole piece of land the fancy houses were on, back when it was still a mosquito-infested mangrove marsh. Instead, he'd saved his money in the bank. The value of that property, which he now wished he'd bought, had now far surpassed his savings account. His only living heir, a twenty-two-year-old granddaughter, would be graduating college in the spring. He'd already told her that the old homestead was hers, if she came back to Marathon to live.

Dreguez Key was on the Gulf side of the highway, not far from Sugarloaf Marina, where he'd once worked. The engines got to be too sophisticated and the older outboards, like his Thunderbolt, had all but disappeared. A few old-timers stopped by now and then with an engine problem. But it wasn't enough work to keep him on at the marina. That didn't matter to Kevin. His social security check was more than enough to pay his bills, and his fishing put food on his table, as well as a few other locals' tables.

Kevin steered the little boat into the shallow creek mouth separating Dreguez from Upper Sugarloaf. A moment later, he came out into the large shallow bay and turned west, following the shoreline of the little uninhabited island. The interior was impenetrable, covered with a thick tangle of mangrove and buttonwood. The island was mostly underwater right now, with the tide almost full. The prop roots of the mangroves were barely showing along the shoreline. Lots of smaller fish and babies use the mangroves to hide in, and at high tide the predators could usually squeeze in among the roots, too.

Cutting the motor twenty feet from the mangroves, Kevin picked up a long, slender metal rod and walked up to the bow. Slipping one end through a big eye ring screwed into the bowsprit, he dropped it until it reached the sandy bottom, four feet below. Then he hoisted it and rammed it down as hard as he could.

The little boat drifted around slowly in the current, like a flag on a pole, until the stern was pointed toward the creek he'd just come through. Satisfied that his makeshift anchor would hold against the light current, he sat down and laid his favorite rod and reel across his knees, removing the hook from the rod's lower eye.

Opening the bait box, Kevin reached in and snagged one of the little three-inch mud minnows swimming around inside. He baited his hook and cast his rig toward the mangroves. The trick to getting the bigger fish to come out was to offer them something easier, and no snapper could resist a struggling mud minnow. Once you had a fish hooked, the trick became keeping the snapper out of the roots, which were covered with sharp edged barnacles and oyster shells. The little mud minnow began tugging against the rattle float a foot above it on the fishing line, straining to get to the safety of the roots. The rattle float would get any nearby snapper's attention. Kevin slowly gave the mud minnow more line, letting it get closer to the mangrove roots.

Suddenly, the water rolled just beyond the float, and the rod bent. The old man raised the tip and tightened the drag, trying to angle what he figured to be a big snapper away from the roots.

The fight lasted only a few seconds before the big fish reached the safety of the roots. A second later, the line went slack, and Kevin knew he'd lost another hook. He slowly tried to reel the line in, hoping that he hadn't lost the rattle float, too. The line hung up, telling him the float was still there and snagged in the roots. He placed the rod in one of the rod holders and pulled the starting cord on his fifty-nine-year-old engine. It started instantly, and Kevin went forward to pull the pole up.

Idling slowly to where he knew his expensive float was tangled, he reeled the line in as he got close. Easing up to the mangroves, Kevin killed the engine and grabbed a branch to hold the boat steady. A moment later, he had his steel rod firmly planted in the bottom again and stepped over the gunwale into knee deep water.

Shuffling his feet on the sandy bottom to avoid stepping on a stingray, Kevin walked to the bow and took hold of the fishing line, following it to where the float was caught up in the roots. But the float wasn't caught on anything. Knowing there were dangers to sticking one's hand into mangrove roots, he did it anyway, feeling for the fishing line beyond the float. He followed it down and found the swivel with the steel leader still attached.

"Damned fish musta threw the hook," he muttered.

Figuring that it was the hook that was fouled, Kevin eased the tension on the line and felt slowly along the leader, not wanting the hook to pull loose and jab his finger.

His hand met something soft and yielding instead, and he jerked his hand back. "What the hell?"

Reaching down cautiously again, he found and ran his hand along whatever it was. It was a lot larger than a snapper, and it was soft and smooth, so he knew it wasn't a shark. He squeezed it, but the thing didn't move. Kevin started, as he suddenly realized what he had his hand on. It had been many years since he'd touched the firm flesh on a young woman's bottom, but he remembered it well.

Kevin jumped away from the mangroves, bumping his little fishing boat, and quickly climbed in—as quickly as an eighty-three-year-old man can, anyway. Fumbling with the seat bottom, he finally got it open and pulled out a powerful spotlight that was connected directly to a twelve-volt battery under the helm.

Kevin stood at the rail and turned the light on. "Holy Mary, Mother of Christ," he muttered.

Caught in the beam of the spotlight, just below the surface of the water and wedged deep behind mangrove branches, a half-naked woman stared vacantly upward at him, her blond hair streaming around a pretty face. Her legs, encased in black nylon stockings, were pulled up to her chest, which was bare. Other than what she was wearing, she looked like a child who'd climbed into the bough of a tree for a nap.

Kevin looked around quickly. The marina was only half a mile away, but he knew the office wouldn't be open yet. He decided he didn't want to risk going to one of the live-aboard people in the marina, or the few scattered at anchor in the shallow bay. There were only a handful, and any one of them might have been the one that did this.

Or she might have just come out here to drown herself, he thought. *Or maybe got drunk and fell off a boat.*

He looked down at the body again. On her feet were a pair of black shoes with impossibly high heels. *No,* he decided, *she didn't come out here on her own or fall off a boat. Not in those shoes.*

West of the marina, Kevin heard an airplane engine crank, spit, and come to life. He realized he was close to the little Sugarloaf Shores Airport where skydivers took off from. They sometimes did a morning jump right at sunrise, still more than an hour away. He knew there was a small beach there, and a path to the airport gate.

Kevin quickly retrieved a bright yellow float from his tackle box and peeled a few more feet of fishing line from his reel. Using his pocketknife, he cut the line and tied the yellow float to it, draping it over a branch so he could find it again. Then he started the engine and pulled up the anchor pole.

A few minutes later, he rounded the end of the island where the runway thrust out into the water. He knew the water was shallow here, but he also knew he could get within a few feet of shore at high tide, right near the airport gate. Kevin slowed as he neared shore, pointing the bow at the lone streetlight by the gate. When he felt the keel touch bottom, he shut off the engine and set his anchor pole firmly in the soft sand.

An airplane sat idling in front of the hangar as Kevin hurried across the road. He went through the gate and approached the office, where several people were milling around.

It didn't take long for the police to get there. A Monroe County deputy was the first to arrive, and Kevin explained to the young man what he'd found. A few minutes later, an unmarked car pulled through the gate and a man and woman got out.

Kevin explained again to the two sheriff's detectives about the woman whose body he'd found stuffed into the mangrove roots. They began asking questions about what he'd been doing out there at this hour and how he'd found the body.

The sun was just lighting the eastern sky when a sheriff's boat arrived, and Kevin recognized the young deputy on the sleek center console. "Marty, tell these detectives I'm just a fisherman."

"Sergeant Evans," Martin Phillips said, nodding at the female detective and then at her partner. "Detective Clark, dispatch said you needed a boat."

"You came all the way from Key West?" Evans said.

"No, ma'am," Marty replied. "I was assigned there temporarily, while Randy Quail was out with his wife in the hospital having a baby. I usually work out of Marathon, but I live on Ramrod and take the boat home."

"Do you know Mister Montrose, Deputy?" Clark asked.

"Yeah," Marty replied. "He's delivered our mail and fixed my dad's outboards since before I was born. He's harmless, except to the fish he stalks every morning."

"We'll need you to come with us, Mister Montrose," Detective Evans told the old man. "To show us where you found the body."

Kevin turned to Marty, his eyes pleading. "You can't miss it, Marty. I tied a yella float to the line that she's snagged on. I'd like to get my tackle back, though. If it ain't too much trouble."

"I think the detectives kinda want you to stick around, Kev," Marty said, winking at the old man. "At least until they get the body out of the water, okay?"

"Ah, there goes a day of fishin'."

The two detectives climbed into Marty's boat with the old man. Marty had tied up to the dock of a vacant vacation home just outside the airport's gate.

"Go up around Dreguez," Kevin said. "Waves filled the cut with sand during the storm. You'll have to use the creek to get into the bay."

Marty nodded, steered the boat out of the dredged canal, and turned north, bringing the boat up on plane. Several minutes later, with the powerful outboards burbling at an idle, Marty navigated through the creek mouth.

"Can't stay here long," Marty said. "Tide's falling and it'll be too shallow for my boat soon."

"Over there," Kevin said, shining Marty's flashlight. "See the yella float in the tree branch I told ya about?"

Checking the current and his depth sounder, Marty aimed the bow of his patrol boat at a spot twenty feet to the left of the float. With the bow a few feet from the over-hanging mangroves, Marty stopped the boat and flipped the switch to release the anchor. The splash seemed un-usually loud in the still predawn air.

The boat drifted sideways in the current, turning slowly into it. When they neared the float, hanging in the tree, Marty flipped the switch the other way, lock-ing the windlass. The Danforth dragged a little, then dug into the sand, stopping the boat just a few feet from the marker.

"How long before Doc Fredric gets here?" Marty asked, noting the two feet of depth the sounder displayed.

"An hour," Evans replied. "Maybe longer."

"We'll be sitting on the bottom in an hour," Marty said. "This bay will be six inches in two hours and we won't be able to get the boat out for ten."

Both detectives were shining lights down into the wa-ter on the starboard side, where the body was. "What do you think?" Clark asked Evans. "I don't see any blood or obvious trauma. Maybe she fell off a boat."

"No boater I know would let a floozy prance around on his deck in those shoes," Kevin said.

"We should wait for the ME," Evans said, looking around.

"The way we came in is the deepest," Marty said. "If we can't get out, Doc won't be able to enter in another boat and it'll be afternoon before he can."

"We'll have to get the body out of the water ourselves," Evans said.

Marty quickly unbuckled his holster and stored it in the overhead compartment, locking it. He never carried anything in his pockets when he was on the water.

"Hand me the backboard when I get in," Marty said, stripping off his uniform shirt and tee-shirt. He quickly swung his legs over the gunwale and slid into the water. Moving toward the body, he noted the blond hair and the top of her head above the water. He took the backboard Clark handed him and moved closer.

"Tie the line off to the bow cleat," Marty said. "The board'll float alongside while I get her out."

Approaching the body, he examined the roots. The woman looked like she'd contorted herself through an opening a few feet to the left and wedged herself in a sitting position with her legs drawn up to her chest and leaning slightly.

Or someone stuffed her in there, Marty thought.

It took some work, but he managed to unfold the body and pull it toward the opening. When he finally had her floating free, he quickly placed the board on her back and reached around to buckle the straps, which were hanging off the sides.

With little time to spare, Marty did the same with the woman's feet, then turned the board over, so the woman was floating on it. Clark hauled on the line and Marty pushed, bringing the board to a standing position. The woman's head hung down, her hair covering most of her exposed breasts.

Marty scrambled to the stern and boarded the boat. The two men lifted the body and backboard out of the water and placed it face up on the foredeck. She wore only black nylons, black high heels, and a red-and-black garter belt.

Hooker underwear, Marty thought, though he didn't recognize her. Most hookers worked the tourists in Key West. There were a few in the Middle Keys, but he knew who most of them were.

"Looks like a working girl," Clark said, shaking out a blanket to cover the body from onlookers.

"Not from around here," Marty said. "Unless she's new, or a call girl from up island. We better get out of here while we still have water." Trimming the engine up a little higher, he started it and eased the boat forward as the windlass took up the anchor line.

When the anchor broke from the bottom, Marty spun the wheel away from the mangroves and put the boat in reverse. He waited until the bow would clear the branches, and idled toward the creek mouth. The engine bumped the sandy bottom twice, but they made it through.

Clark's phone rang and he answered it. He said where they were and that they were headed in, then ended the call. "Tim's at the airport."

"Good," Evans said. "Ben and I are covered up with two murders, you guys can take this one."

"You don't think they're related?" Marty asked, bringing the center console up on plane in deeper water. "We don't get a lot of bodies here, and Isaksson's boat was found only a mile and a half away."

"I doubt it," Evans said, standing next to him, trying to send a text with one hand while hanging onto the T-top frame with the other. "We're working on the theory that Isaksson and Marshall were killed on a salvage site, somewhere out in the Gulf. That doesn't fit in with a prostitute."

CHAPTER TWENTY-TWO

The next morning, I was up before the sun. It was going to be a busy day. Chyrel and Tony were supposed to arrive shortly, and we'd move her computers and stuff up to my island. One of the bunkhouses is set up as sort of an office. Chyrel uses it when she stays over, as does my daughter, Kim, since that half of the bunkhouse has four bunks.

Deuce had asked Billy if he'd be willing to stay in Key West with Lawrence, and added him to the payroll, which I hadn't even written a check for yet. Billy agreed and would stick with Lawrence, day and night, in case the killer decided to come after him. Knowing Billy as I did, I didn't bother to ask if he was armed. He probably had a second gun in his boot, a knife in the other, and probably more. As far as being able to protect Lawrence, there are few men I'd trust more with my own life.

As I stepped out into the cockpit with my morning coffee, Finn leapt over the gunwale onto the barge and then over to the dock, nosing around for a place to pee. I saw a white van creeping slowly into the parking area from under the driveway's overhanging gumbo limbo trees. I stepped over to the barge and walked across the deck to the gangplank as Tony and Chyrel got out.

"Just in time for breakfast," I said, approaching the van.

"Hey there, Jesse," Chyrel said, giving me a big hug.

Tony came around the front of the van and I took his offered hand. "Been awhile," he said. "Deuce told me you were going to be a part of his new company."

"More like a silent partner," I said, leading the way to the bar. "With you two on board, it's bound to be profitable."

As we reached the door, I could hear Rusty and Deuce laughing inside. Holding it open for the other two, I followed them in. Jimmy was telling a story.

"And then the other dude says, 'What shark?'" Jimmy said from behind the bar.

Deuce, Julie, and Rusty all laughed. Rusty turned toward us as we approached. "Hey, y'all. Saw you pull in. Hope you're hungry. I just told Rufus to put on some more breakfast burritos. Should be done in a minute."

The three of us joined them at the bar. "I'll be staying here," Deuce announced. "I got a lead on an office that might be coming available. It's only a half mile from the Coast Guard station, and when the call comes I need to get right up there."

"Tony can dive with me," I said.

"Sure, why not?" Tony agreed. "But who's gonna stay on the boat?"

"A lady cop from Key West," Deuce said. "Once you get Chyrel's equipment up to the island and unloaded, you and Jesse can pick her up at Old Wooden Bridge Marina."

"I thought we were going to pick her up at Garrison Bight," I said.

"She texted me about an hour ago. Said she was on her way to Sugarloaf on another case," Deuce said. "I told her to meet you there. Figured I'd save you some gas."

"It'll be low tide about noon. Call her back and see how early she can get there."

Deuce picked his phone up from the bar and walked over toward the back door. Rufus was just carrying in a tray of food, which he slid onto the bar.

"I and I try something new," Rufus said. "I blacken some janga and chop dem up in a omelet, wit goat cheese and peppers." We tore into the little burritos.

Deuce returned, holding his phone away from his ear. "She can be there in less than an hour. Turning the case over to another detective."

"It's only a few miles further to get here," I said. "If she doesn't mind going up to the island for about an hour, so we can unload, it'd get us out on the Gulf a lot sooner."

Deuce put the phone to his ear again. "You heard? Okay, turn right at the first rural mailbox you see after passing Kmart in Marathon. You can't miss it." He ended the call and laid the phone back on the bar. "Said she's on her way."

Rusty turned up the volume on the TV as we ate quickly. The latest update on Hurricane Ike showed it now moving northwest and nearing the western tip of Cuba. From there, the steadily widening cone of probability had it moving into the middle of the Gulf of Mexico over the next several days, and away from us.

Tony and Chyrel only ate a couple of the small burritos, saying they'd eaten before leaving Homestead a couple hours earlier. They went out to unload the van and put their gear on the *Revenge*.

"I'm gonna get the engines warmed up," I said after my fifth janga burrito.

Deuce and Julie walked out with me, Finn trotting ahead of us toward the boat, as a brown Ford Crown Victoria parked next to Tony's van. I never could figure out why they call them unmarked police cars. The big sedan *screamed* cop.

We angled away from the docks and met Devon as she was getting out of the driver's side. I don't know why, but I'd assumed Morgan would be dropping her off.

"This isn't gonna work," I said, looking her up and down. She was conservatively dressed as she had been yesterday, except her jacket and slacks were blue. On her feet were hard soled shoes. "Those shoes don't go past the pier. And it's gonna be hot out on the water this afternoon."

"I have a go-bag she said. "But the only change of clothes in it is another suit like this one." She smiled and added, "You'll just have to bear with the stench."

I glanced at Julie, and then back at Devon. They were close to the same height and, outside of Julie being pregnant, were about the same build. "Can you help her, Jules?"

"What?" Julie asked, "Have you run out of women's clothes on that boat of yours?" She extended her hand. "Julie Livingston, Coast Guard."

When Devon shook her hand, Julie leaned in and loudly whispered, "Jesse's boat sometimes makes women's clothes fall off."

"Tequila does that for me," Devon said, winking at Julie. "Devon Evans, Monroe County Sheriff's Department and former Marine."

"Ha!" Julie exclaimed. "I like you already, Devon Evans. My dad and Uncle Jesse are both Marines. Come with me. I'll let you get into my shorts."

As the two of them walked toward Rusty's house, Deuce and I could only stare after them with our mouths open. "Is it just me," I asked, "or has Jules gotten a bit saltier since picking up petty officer second class?"

"I think she's just exhibiting her true colors to me now, after a lifetime spent living among knuckle-dragging Jarheads."

I clapped him on the shoulder, and we walked down to where Rusty's big barge was tied up at the top of the turning basin. The sun was above the horizon, but not yet above the trees. There wasn't a cloud in sight, and it felt like the weather would hold. But there were still a few wind gusts reaching twenty or so miles per hour.

Tony and Finn came out of the salon as we crossed the barge's deck to the *Revenge*. "We got everything secured," Tony said, as Finn curled up by the transom door for a nap. "I just checked NOAA. Sounds pretty sloppy out in the Gulf, seas two to four. But it should start laying down soon."

"Need help with anything?" Deuce asked, as I climbed up to the bridge.

"I don't think so," I called down, noticing for the first time that my sat-phone was in its cradle and fully charged. "I'll call you if we find anything. Good luck with the office."

I started the two big supercharged diesel engines, letting them rumble at idle to warm up. Finn barked as I climbed down, always anxious to go for a boat ride. I went into the salon and found Chyrel pouring the contents of the coffee pot into a big Thermos bottle. "Ah, thanks," I said. "That's what I was just coming down for."

She followed me out, and I climbed back up to the bridge. I poured a mug of coffee and stowed the Thermos in one of the upper storage bins. When I looked down at Tony and Deuce on the barge, they were both staring across the yard. I followed their gaze and saw Julie and Devon walking toward us.

Devon had changed into a pair of Julie's faded cut-off blue jeans and a white tank top, with the *Rusty Anchor* logo on the front. She filled both out quite nicely, I noticed. In her left hand, she carried a gym bag with one of Julie's old, faded-denim work shirts draped over it. Her feet were bare and tan, like the rest of her legs.

"Cast off the lines!" I shouted down to the barge.

Deuce looked up and grinned, then started toward the bow lines. Tony was frozen in place for a second before going to the stern. Devon stepped down into the cockpit, seeming unsure of herself, and Chyrel took her inside to find a spot for her bag.

The lines were tossed, and Deuce pushed the bow out. Tony stepped aboard and walked along the side deck to the forwardmost fender, pulling it up and putting it in its holder. I engaged the transmissions, away from the barge, as Tony went aft and secured the rest of the fenders and coiled the dock lines.

"You didn't say she was a *hot* lady cop," Tony said, climbing quickly up the ladder. At thirty-four, he had the strength and stamina of a teenager, with the same loose, wiry build. "Good thing Tasha didn't see *her*. The woman gets a little jealous around other hotties."

"Hottie?" I asked. "She's a police detective."

"Yeah, kinda like us, huh?" Tony said, his big white teeth gleaming in his dark face. "Only with curves."

"Shut the hell up, you animal," I said. But my grin betrayed my thoughts and he laughed.

A moment later, as we idled down the long canal, Chyrel and Devon joined us on the bridge and I introduced her to Tony.

"I thought Agent Livingston was coming," Devon said.

"Tony's filling in for him," I replied. "He used to be on Deuce's SEAL team. And Chyrel's former CIA."

"Hey," Chyrel said, sitting down and waving a hand. "Just a cyber spook. None of that Mitch Rapp kinda stuff."

"Just how big a security company do you have?" Devon asked.

"Just the five of us, right now," Tony replied. Then to me he added, "We've got two more coming—Paul and Andrew—which will make seven."

"Our two DHS teams comprise twenty individuals each," Chyrel added. "All of Deuce's new employees are coming from there."

"Andrew's in?" I asked. "I thought he was going back to finish his thirty."

"He looked into it," Tony said. "Even the Coast Guard is offering a sweet early retirement package right now. I'm getting almost a year's pay to retire four years early. Regular retirement will kick in then."

Passing the last of the boats tied to the dock, I bumped the throttles up just a little. The big twin diesels responded instantly.

"I know Julie was kidding when she said that bit about women's clothes falling off," Devon said, sitting on the port bench, next to Chyrel. "But it's not really a stretch. This is a gorgeous boat."

"Thanks," I replied. "You said you'd never been on one?"

"A few times," she replied. "Whenever the job requires it, but nothing this big. Actually, this is the second boat I've been on today."

"The second?"

"I had to go out on another boat very early this morning."

I glanced at her for a second. She did clean up nice and, judging by those legs, she was a runner. That'd be what all that food fueled.

"How big is this thing?" Devon asked.

"She's forty-five feet of pure Wisconsin muscle," Tony said, as we idled out of the canal, encountering the first small waves. Checking the radar and sonar, he added, "Ten feet under the keel, Skipper. Nothing on radar."

Here in the bight, it was usually flat calm in October, sheltered from the prevailing northeasterly breeze. In summer, the wind was off the water, but with a shallow barrier reef just a few miles offshore, there was rarely much wave activity. Now, there were a few whitecaps. Compared to the waves right now on the other side of Cuba, these were nothing, and were barely felt against the sturdy hull. I pushed the throttles forward enough to get the big boat up on plane at twenty-five knots. The *Revenge* responded as she always did, eager to challenge the sea. I started a wide hundred and eighty degree turn to the west that would loop us around the end of Boot Key and Knight Key, lining up on a northerly heading toward the big arch in the Seven Mile bridge.

"What's the other case you were on up here?" I asked Devon, as the *Revenge* began dancing her way through the slop in the deep channel. "Anything to do with the two murders?"

She was looking up at the high span of the bridge as we passed under. "I never realized it was so high," she said, then turned around in her seat to look at me. "A woman's body was found in the water on Sugarloaf Key. Possibly a prostitute, but even though it was only a few miles from where the salvage boat was found, I doubt if they're connected to our case. But, I was on call last night, so I went. I left another detective with it, when his partner arrived. They're waiting on the ME."

"Ever met Doc Fredric?" I asked.

"A few times," Devon replied. "You know him?"

"He likes fishing the back country. I've taken him out a few times."

"Where exactly *is* this back country?" she asked. "I've heard it mentioned a few times."

"Look behind you," I said, pointing over her shoulder. "That long stretch of land is Big Pine Key. See all those islands way in the distance ahead of us? That's the back country. My house is on the outer edge of it. It's part of the Content Keys group of islands."

Navigating the back country is more about knowing where the shallows are than following any markers. The natural East Bahia Honda Channel runs mostly ten feet deep and is very wide, going roughly north from the bridge. After a few miles, it angles north-northwest toward Horseshoe Banks.

Fifteen minutes later, we cleared the banks and I turned slowly toward the west, avoiding the shallows of Monkey Bank and Bullfrog Banks. The light at Harbor Key Bank came into view, and I adjusted course to the north of it. When I was sure I was clear of the shallows at Turtlecrawl, I slowed and turned southwest, entering Harbor Channel near its northern end. Harbor Channel was another natural deep water cut. It was a good twenty feet deep at the northeast, where it flowed into and out of the Gulf. Here in the middle, it got a little deeper and it was here that we ran a line of lobster and crab traps in the deeper part. I slowly backed the *Revenge* down off plane, approaching the first lobster pot float, and Finn trotted forward to sit down in the middle of the foredeck. Ahead, the channel curved to the south next to my island and disappeared into a maze of shallow, narrow cuts through the back country.

Devon looked all around. The water in the channel was a deep blue, and I could just make out the shapes of small coral heads and seagrass interspersed on the yellow sandy bottom. Straight ahead lay the Content and Water Keys, beyond which only a small skiff could go, and only at high tide.

"Past those islands," I said to Devon, pointing ahead, "is a maze of small islands, sandbars, and mangrove flats that only a kayak can get into at low tide."

"Is that your house?" Devon asked, as I brought the *Revenge* down to idle speed near the entrance to the channel I'd dug out with a shovel more than seven years ago. I'd deepened and widened it since then, using Rusty's barge and backhoe. The roof of my house was just above the mangroves on the south side of the island. I made a mental note to do some pruning next week. I like to see all the approaches, even if you have to be a local to try the cuts to the south.

"My island," I corrected her. "There are four houses on it. But, yeah, the one you can see above the trees is where I live."

We entered the narrow channel and didn't see anyone on the dock. Tony and Chyrel went down to put the fenders over and tie off. I eased the bow close to the pier, and Tony used a boat hook to snag the line coiled on one of the posts. I shifted the port engine into neutral and the starboard into reverse. The big boat gently drifted back alongside the pier. While Chyrel tied off a second dock line to a stern cleat, Finn leapt the gunwale and raced up the steps.

"We'll be here only as long as it takes to unload Chyrel's gear," I shouted down to Tony.

"Roger that," he replied, dropping into the cockpit and disappearing into the cabin.

"What's behind those big doors," Devon asked, as I glanced over the gauges and shut down the engines.

"Dock space," I replied. "For the *Revenge* and a few other boats."

"How many boats do you need?"

"Each has its own purpose," I said, "and none can do it all. The *Revenge* is my primary charter vessel. But some clients don't want to go way out to the Gulf Stream and she burns sixty gallons of fuel an hour, so I have another, slightly smaller boat called *El Cazador*."

"The Hunter?"

"*Si*," I replied with a grin. "*Para peces de caza*. Neither of them can get back into the flats south and west of here for bonefish, though. So I have a shallow-draft skiff for those clients. Then a couple of boats that are just for knocking around in and fetching supplies."

"We'll be taking this one to look for the dive site?" she asked.

I'd noticed a little color draining from her face when we'd entered Harbor Channel and had slowed in the two-foot chop coming in off the Gulf. The *Revenge* takes waves on the bow effortlessly, but rolls some when she's going slow and the waves come abeam. Her bridge, being higher, rocks violently at times.

"You prone to sea sickness?" I asked, going down the ladder.

"Prone would be an understatement. But I took a Dramamine."

I helped her down and said, "Better take another one. Out on the Gulf, it'll be a little choppy until late afternoon."

Wondering where Carl was, I trotted up the steps to the deck and found him coming up the other side. "Wasn't much of a blow," he said. "We're cleaning up some debris that washed up on the east side and around the base of the north pier."

"Brought some guests," I said and introduced him to Devon as Tony lumbered up the steps with a large, white box slung on his back with shoulder straps.

"Hey, Tony," Carl said. "Good to see ya. Whatcha got in the box?"

"My new mobile comm center," Chyrel said, following behind Tony. She had her usual oversized computer bag on her shoulder and was carrying a basket, which was full of several kinds of cables and a bunch of electronic gizmos. I try to stay out of the comm shack.

"Hey, Chyrel," Carl said, taking the basket from her and giving her a hug. "Glad to have you back. Charlie misses you when you're gone."

"Aw, well I miss y'all, too."

"Tony," I shouted, as he was going down the steps. "Change of plans. Go ahead and help Chyrel set up. We're gonna be on the east side, helping clean up for a while until the seas subside a little more."

"It's beautiful," Devon said as we walked down the back steps. "What's that?"

"That's our aquaponics system," Carl replied. "We grow vegetables in one tank, the one with all the empty cages, and we raise crawfish and tilapia in the other."

"You took everything in for the storm?" I asked.

"It did get a little breezy up here," Carl replied, as Chyrel took the basket and followed Tony. "Everything's in the eastern bunkhouse."

"We're going to do some looking around up above Snipe Key," I said. "But we have some time to pitch in, before we have to leave."

For the next two hours, Devon got a working tour of my island. I introduced her to Charlie and the kids, then we all went about cleaning up the shoreline. We dragged small branches to the fire pit, leaving the bigger stuff in the water to cut up later. Carl Junior and Patty were out of school due to the storm. They seemed to be making a game of dragging sticks with Finn's help.

Mostly, we picked up trash. Wind and waves from even a small storm will shake all kinds of trash loose.

Then it floats out into the Gulf and the tide carries some of it into Harbor Channel, where it usually washes onto my shore at the bend in the channel. Plastic bags, bottles, trap floats, gas and oil jugs, along with all kinds of other detritus from the civilized world, finds its way here. We've even had boats float up on the eastern shore after storms. Some stuff we find, we can't even figure out what it is. Other stuff, we have to make up what it is in front of the kids, like when we'd found one of those blow-up dolls after a storm the year before.

We kept any usable lumber we found. Driftwood in the form of tree branches soaks up salt and minerals in the water and makes for an entertaining bonfire. Bamboo is best, as it absorbs more. Carl leans cut bamboo against a log and fills the ends with seawater. When the water evaporates and the bamboo dries, it creates an eerie green flame. Charlie has decorated the area around the bunkhouses, stone fireplace, and tables with different colored trap floats.

I showed Devon the north pier, where I sometimes keep *Island Hopper* tied up, then we helped move the plants from the bunkhouse to the garden. One by one, we each stepped up into the huge, shallow-water trough, returning the plants to their individual support stands.

"They've only been out of water since yesterday evening," Charlie said. "They should all be fine."

The plants ranged from three-foot-tall tomato plants in cages to broad squash plants, cucumber, peppers, and other vegetables, each with its roots tangled through, and hanging below, the crushed coral in the baskets. Carl had laid a number of four-by-four posts on the deck in the bunkhouse for the baskets to sit on without damaging the roots.

Tony came out and helped with the last of the plants. "Chyrel's just about set up," he said. "Told me to get outta her way."

Once we were finished, Devon asked, "How many people can you feed here?"

"Barely ourselves, with the fruit and vegetables," Charlie said. "If you don't mind seafood and help catch it, we're pretty much unlimited there."

"The vegetable plants are more to filter the water than anything," Carl added. "They flourish on the nitrogen waste from the crawfish and tilapia and provide oxygen for them in return."

"Is that a mango tree?" Devon asked, pointing to one of the fruit trees on the clearing's perimeter.

"Yeah, pick a couple to bring with us, if you like." I glanced up at the sun, still the only object in the pale blue sky. "We better get out there," I said. "There's maybe eight hours of daylight left."

Devon shook hands with the Trents and we started up the back steps together. "The techs still haven't come up with where the boat might have drifted from," she said.

"Eggheads try too hard to be precise with stuff," I said. "All we need is a vague location to start looking. And Rusty gave me that." I stopped at the door to my house. "Tony, go ahead and start up the engines. I want to show Devon something."

I turned the knob and walked inside. In the corner, I pulled a few charts out of a slotted cabinet until I found the right one. Rolling it out on the dining table, I put salt and pepper shakers on opposite corners to keep it from rolling back up.

"Take a look." I pointed to a spot on the chart as Devon approached the table. "This is where the boat was found." I traced my finger up the chart, following deep water. "A boat drifting on a falling tide would come down these natural channels, maybe bouncing off the shallows and being spun back into the deeper current. The numbers show water depth."

I poked my finger at Cudjoe Channel, near Sawyer Key. "This is where the boat most likely drifted into the back country. About five miles west of here. Beyond this, currents don't matter much. On a falling tide, it's only moving about two miles per hour in the open Gulf. The prevailing northeast wind and the current pushed the boat to where it drifted into Cudjoe Channel. Rusty says the current and wind working at angles to each other would probably push the boat due south."

I went over to my fly-tying table and grabbed a pencil. Drawing a line from the top of the page, due south to Sawyer Key, I said, "Most likely, it drifted this way."

"How can you tell how far it drifted along that line?"

"Good question," I replied. "It ran aground and was stuck at low tide. So, odds are it went adrift sometime after the previous high tide, which was just about the time Doc Fredric says they were killed, and when I heard the gunshot."

"I remember you said distance was hard to figure, but not direction. Where were you, when you heard it?" she asked, apparently grasping my trigonometry.

"Right here," I said, pointing to another spot. "We were on the flats just north of Crane Key and the direction we heard the shot come from was a few degrees north of northwest."

I drew another line, at a three-hundred-twenty-degree angle from Crane Key, until it intersected the first line. The spot where the lines met was just beyond the three-mile-limit line in thirty feet of water.

"It's not," I said, tossing the pencil on the chart. "But engineers will try to pinpoint it to within ten feet and take days to do it. All we have to do is go to that spot and start making ever widening circles until we see something."

"What do you expect to see?"

"Isaksson's anchor, for one thing. If you know you'll be anchoring up in the same place over and over, most people will use a heavy anchor with a mooring ball attached and floating above it, so they can always come back to the exact same spot. Morgan said the anchor line was cut, but maybe the anchor line was tied to a mooring ball, which could still be there. Failing that, Isaksson only had a survey permit, so there might be survey grids on the bottom. Harder to find, but they should still be there."

"You make it sound so simple," Devon said, looking around my living room.

I lived alone and had simple needs, so my living room wasn't much to look at: a recliner and reading lamp, the dining table the chart was on, a small couch, my fly-tying bench, and a small bookcase filled mostly with assorted manuals and a few novels. Here and there were parts from outboard engines, dive equipment, and odds and ends.

"Obviously," I said, noting her gaze, "simple works for me."

"Yes, I see that." Devon said, then turned around quickly. "Oh, I didn't mean that the way it sounded. I actually like it. Simple, manly, and functional."

I heard the engines on the *Revenge* start and took a sheet of paper from a drawer in the chart cabinet. I wrote down the latitude and longitude of the spot on the chart and folded the paper into my pocket.

Once outside on the deck, Devon looked once more out over my island. "You know what you have here?"

"What's that?"

CHAPTER TWENTY-THREE

"She said I was running a hippie commune," I told Tony, as I idled the *Revenge* into Harbor Channel and turned northeast.

"Obviously, the lady doesn't know you very well, Skipper," he replied with a grin, sitting next to me at the helm. He shook his head, looking at Devon on the port bench.

"Straight out of San Fran," Devon added. "Maybe without the weed. But I stand by that comment."

Leaving the relatively sheltered water of Harbor Channel, with the sun straight above us, we encountered the first big waves in the Gulf. I turned the *Revenge* west around Harbor Key Light. While the wind was a lot lighter and out of the southeast, as Hurricane Ike made its way into the central Gulf, the predominant direction of the bigger waves was out of the northwest. The light, steady breeze sheered the tops off the larger whitecaps. Waves slapped the wide Carolina bow flare, launching salt spray high into the air. The spray was picked up on the wind blowing across the foredeck and pushed away from the boat.

Devon looked better than she had when we first entered Harbor Channel just a few hours ago. I'd made her take another Dramamine before leaving the island and planned to remind her to take one every few hours, just to be sure. Nothing ruins a boat trip faster than girl-vomit.

Tony leaned in toward the dash, watching the screen of the chart plotter. "Eighty-one-degrees, thirty-three-minutes longitude."

I turned the wheel to starboard and brought the throttles up just a bit to thirty knots, to make the math easier. I straightened the *Revenge* on a due north course. "Keep a sharp eye out, Devon," I said. "I'm sure the dive site is still a few miles, but something else might be in the water."

The lady detective turned sideways on the bench and leaned an arm on the forward dash to look ahead, which also afforded me a nice unobstructed view of a shapely thigh. She wasn't going to see anything, but I knew that staring intently at the horizon while the boat is rocking is the best way to *teach* the inner ear that you're moving side to side and it's normal. Fluid in the inner ear works like a carpenter's bubble level to give us balance. As the boat rocks, the inner ear picks up on the motion and sends signals to the brain. The eyes, seeing the horizon tilt back and forth, tell the ears to shut the hell up. If you're inside the cabin, or on deck and looking at a fixed object on the boat, it sends mixed signals to the brain and you get to taste breakfast again.

I held the *Revenge* on a due north heading, checking the speed. At thirty knots, we'd reach the three-mile limit in about six minutes. The target spot was only a mile be-yond that and was programmed into the GPS chart-plot-ter.

When the GPS indicated that we were five hundred feet from the spot I'd programmed as a waypoint, I pulled back on the throttles, bringing the heavy boat down to settle into the water at ten knots. I cleared the chart-plot-ter, dropped a pin at the start point, and turned the wheel to starboard just as we crossed near the target.

With no visual reference, that pin on the chart-plotter would become the center of an ever-widening circle, and I'd be able to use the plotter's track function to keep each ring of the circle about sixty to eighty feet apart.

"Look sharp outboard of my turns," I said. "The first couple of circles will be tight."

After a couple of hours, the circles became wider, reaching a half mile in diameter. I was about to give up and move north. The seas had calmed slightly, but it was still sloppy. Wave heights were now less than three feet.

"There!" Devon shouted as we neared the original lon-gitude line. "I saw something white on the water."

I looked in the direction she was pointing and slowly turned the wheel that way. At first, I didn't see it.

"I see it," Tony said. "About a hundred yards, dead ahead."

I saw something pop over a wave momentarily, and turned the wheel toward it.

"Go down and get ready to snag it," I told Tony and he was down the ladder in a flash.

"Do you think that's from Isaksson's boat?" Devon asked, as she stood and went to the forward rail of the fly bridge in front of the forward bench.

She braced herself on the rail, leaning slightly, as she watched Tony making his way up to the bow with a boat hook. I couldn't help but admire her form in those cut-offs. Definitely not your typical cop.

"Might be," I replied, slowing to idle speed as we neared what I now recognized as a mooring ball. "Or someone's lobster honey hole."

When Tony lunged with the boat hook, I slipped both transmissions into neutral. He quickly hauled up the heavy anchor rode that the ball was attached to, used one of my dock lines to loop a bowline knot around it, then dropped them both over the side. The *Revenge* drifted back in the current, and I could tell by the sudden stop that the anchor to which the float was attached was either very heavy or set deep on the bottom.

"Come back here a minute," I said to Devon. While Tony began to get our dive gear ready, I went over the basics of how to operate the *Revenge*, in case there was an emergency and we needed to be picked up.

"I can't drive this thing," she said.

"Sure you can," I encouraged her. "Just like driving a car, and you won't have to move it at anything more than an idle."

"What if I hit something?"

"Look around," I said. "There isn't anything for miles to hit. Well, except me and Tony." I grinned and gave her a wink. "Please don't run me and Tony over."

I pointed out the ignition keys, told her how start the engines, shift the transmissions, and turn the boat. "If there's any trouble, just start the engines, go forward and toss the line, then idle the boat close to us. The odds of you needing to do this are almost zero, but you should know how."

"How will I know if you need help?"

"We'll surface and blow a whistle," I said. "Otherwise, just enjoy the sunshine, and work on your tan."

Her face colored slightly, but she recovered quickly. "My tan's the same all over. Is this a clothing-optional cruise?"

My eyes went wide and I stuttered a bit. "Well, um, not right now."

Yeah, that was smooth, McDermitt.

"All set," Tony shouted from the cockpit.

I climbed down to join him, wondering if there was any seriousness in what she'd said, or if she was just trying to get a rise out of me.

"Grid search?" Tony asked, slipping his fins on.

"No," I replied. "We don't have a lot of daylight. Vis is surprisingly good. Anything we're likely to find, I'm thinking is gonna be close and obvious. We'll go to the anchor and then split off fifty feet to the east and west. We'll do a half circle counter-clockwise to the other's start point, staying up ten feet off the bottom. We should be able to see each other easy enough. If there's anything to be found, it'll probably be within the three-hundred-foot circle we'll be able to put eyes on."

Tony nodded and we checked each other's gear while Finn looked at us curiously. He knew what we were about to do, and he'd surprised me a few times by showing up right beside me on shallow dives. He liked to dive the shallows for clams. I told him to stay on the boat with Devon, and he looked up at her on the bridge and barked.

Tony stepped through the transom door and did a giant stride entry, with me right behind him. We gave each other the okay sign, neutralized our buoyancy compensators, and started finning against the slow current. Reaching the anchor line, we followed it to the bottom. What Isaksson had used to anchor the mooring ball was the rusted block of a big marine diesel engine. We hovered a few feet above the engine block for a moment, checking our compasses. I attached a strobe to the block and switched it on. We both signaled okay, turned away from each other, and began kicking.

Searching underwater isn't difficult if you know how. But there aren't any roads, nor any visual clues as to where you are, where you're going, or how far. I extended my compass and swam due west, counting my fin strokes. I knew it took three kicks to cover ten feet at a relaxed speed, so when I counted fifteen kicks, I turned due south and started my end of the circle, using the strobe on the engine block as a visual clue for distance.

When I looked to my left, I couldn't quite see Tony, a hundred feet away. But I could see his bubbles flashing silver in the distance and knew he'd be doing exactly the same thing I was.

I slowly continued finning in a wide circle to the south and then east, looking left and right for anything that wasn't supposed to be there. I was just astern the *Revenge* when I heard the clanking sound of steel on an aluminum tank. I turned due north and kicked hard, swimming past the *Revenge*. When I neared the engine block, Tony came into view, kicking slowly into the slight northwest current, a few feet off the bottom.

As I got closer, I saw what he'd signaled me about. On the bottom, about ninety feet from the engine block and directly in front of him, was a survey grid made of red-and-white snap-lock pipes. Isaksson's dive site.

I joined Tony and looked down at what might be the spot where Jennifer Marshall had been murdered.

I noted the direction of the current over the dive spot and signaled Tony to return to the boat. I wanted to move the *Revenge* up current enough to put her directly over the dive spot.

CHAPTER TWENTY-FOUR

Harley heard the bell ring. "Damned phone," he muttered, answering it again. Again, there was only a dial tone. He put it back and bent to his task once more, slurping tequila from Jasmine's belly button. Just as he bent his lips close to her skin, the phone rang yet again.

Slowly the fog lifted, and Harley realized the ringing was his alarm clock, not the phone on his office desk. He'd been dreaming about Jasmine lying back across his desk. He reached over and fumbled blindly on the night-stand, finally finding the source of the offensive noise and knocking it over before he could turn the thing off.

Slowly opening his eyes, Harley looked around his bedroom, his eyes finally coming to where Jasmine lay next to him, her long black hair tangled and spread all over the pillow. The blanket was pulled down, twisting over her hip and disappearing between her thighs. It covered only one leg, the rest of her hard little body on display for his eyes only.

This could get complicated, he thought.

"Never screw the talent," his dad had told him a million times.

Dad had never had the talent available that Harley had today. There weren't many men's clubs in Key West, but there were a lot of drop-dead gorgeous young women to choose from. Though *Rafferty's* was mostly a local's dive, every night there were at least a dozen half-drunk tourists, eager to part with their dollars. If a girl wanted to make good money fast, she took off her clothes.

There weren't many jobs in the world where a man in his mid-forties could bed a different hard-body, half his age, every week. He leered at the naked Jasmine. Five-nine and maybe one-twenty-five, she had legs that could wrap around a man twice and was almost flexible enough to do it. He considered waking her up for another round, but didn't think he'd survive it.

Instead, Harley rose and put on a clean pair of boxers from his dresser. He walked stiff-legged to the bathroom, rolling his shoulders, trying to get the kinks out of his spine.

Leaving Jasmine to sleep off the effects of the booze and coke, Harley went into the living room and turned on the TV. She was smaller than him, at least in weight, but had matched him shot and line, all through the night.

He clicked the channels until he found the local station, which usually showed a short news update at noon. The lead-in story was about a missing twenty-two-year-old. Harley thought it weird that they were showing an artist's sketch instead of the woman's actual photo.

"Hey, that's that girl from last night," Jasmine said, coming into the living room.

She wore only the silk button-down shirt that Harley had worn the night before. The shirt was completely unbuttoned, exposing her flat belly and tiny exclamation-point-shaped pubic hair. Harley was distracted from the news story.

"You remember," Jasmine said, pointing at the screen. "The hot one that just got to town. The one that turned me on so much I gave you a handjob under the table. She had a French name. What was it? Janet something?"

Harley looked back at the sketch on the TV screen again and the memory of the tiny, athletic dancer came back. She'd done only one set, turned a few quick tricks in the back room and left at midnight. He'd wanted to talk to her about coming back, but Jasmine delayed him and when he'd gotten to the dressing room later, she was already gone. Duke had left at about then, though Harley hadn't noticed at the time. Jasmine had held his full attention.

Had to be a coincidence, Harley thought. Duke was no lady's man, though he had muscles on muscles. The French girl was way out of his league.

It dawned on him that the cops might be using a sketch because the girl wasn't missing. *Maybe her face was too fucked up to show on TV*, he thought. Duke had a mean streak sometimes, and when he was a kid, he'd killed a couple of stray cats in the neighborhood with a BB gun. But Harley doubted he'd hurt a person, especially a girl.

"Says she's missing, huh?" Jasmine said. "Hey, I thought someone had to be missing for twenty-four hours before you could do a missing persons thing."

"They do," Harley said, reading the description. Four-eleven, blond hair, blue eyes, ninety-five pounds. *Damn, it is her.*

"Think we should, like, call the cops or something?"

"And tell 'em what?" Harley said. "That she was dancing and turning tricks in my club, while you were tooting coke off my dick?"

"Yeah," Jasmine said, pushing him back on the couch and straddling him. "Probably not a good idea, huh?"

It was two in the afternoon and Harley was an hour late when he got to the club. Kenny and Wendell were already there and waiting.

"Sorry, guys," he said, unlocking the back door. "I got held up. Kenny, I noticed some hiss in one of the speakers last night."

"Yeah, one of the sub-woofers is about gone," the DJ replied. "I got a new one on order. Should be here before five."

"If you can't get it hooked up in time," Harley said, "how about just cutting the one speaker out completely?"

"Sure thing, Boss," Kenny replied, wandering toward the DJ booth.

Wendell went straight to the bar and started checking the beer coolers and liquor shelf, making notes in his notebook. Kenny put on a CD and turned the volume to about half what he usually had it on. It wasn't the techno crap he played when the girls were dancing. Instead, a local trop-rocker started singing about drinking Mekongs, missing his girlfriend, and screwing four-dollar Thai hookers.

Harley went to his office and opened the door. The only thing on his desk was a nearly empty bottle of Patrón Añejo, two shot glasses, the mirror, and little gold tube. He closed the door and shook his head, surveying the mess. Everything that had been on his desk, had been swept to the floor and a red G-string hung on the closet doorknob.

There was a knock and Jasmine stuck her head in. "Shit, Boss, did we do this?" She came into the office and snatched the G-string, looking around at the disheveled office. "Sorry, I got kinda carried away."

The phone started ringing and Harley looked around for it. Seeing the cord disappear into a drawer, he yanked it open and answered the phone, motioning Jasmine out the door. He listened for a minute, then said, "Thanks for letting me know. Stop by anytime to collect."

Harley removed the phone from the drawer and put it on the desk. He dialed Duke's number and waited.

When his brother finally answered, Harley said, "Where the hell are you?"

"At home," Duke replied. "What time is it?"

"It's after two. You shoulda been here an hour ago." If Duke had been on time, Harley would have been the one arriving late. "Where'd you disappear to last night?"

"Sorry, Harley. I was partying with a girl I met."

"The girl from last night? The little spinner with the French name?"

There was silence on the other end. Duke was a pitiful liar, and Harley really didn't want to know the truth.

"Look, I just got a call. Someone's snooping around the spot."

"Who?" Duke asked.

"That's what I wanna know," Harley said. "Rent a boat from the marina and head out there. I at least want to know who it is. Scare 'em off if you can."

CHAPTER TWENTY-FIVE

"**I** was beginning to worry," Devon said, when we surfaced at the swim platform. "You were down there a long time."

I looked at my dive watch. "Twenty minutes isn't all that long," I told her, handing my fins up. She took them and tossed them on the deck.

"Did you see anything?"

I unhooked my BC, dropped underwater to get out of it, and levered myself up onto the swim platform. "Yeah, I think this is the spot," I replied, pulling my BC and tank out of the water and laying it on the deck in the cockpit. "There's red-and-white grid pipe assembled on the bottom, about two-hundred feet ahead. That's what salvagers use to survey a possible site. We'll move the boat so it's directly over the spot, and dive it again."

Reaching down, I took Tony's fins and tossed them on top of mine, then grabbed his BC and tank by the regulator's first stage and laid it on the deck next to my own.

Devon and I climbed up to the bridge, and I started the engines as Tony went forward and untied the line holding us on the mooring ball. Slowly, I idled straight ahead, watching Tony on the foredeck.

He turned and yelled, "We're over the grid now."

As we passed over the spot, Tony released the brake on the anchor chain. I continued idling forward until we were about a hundred feet beyond the site. There, I released the lock on the windlass and dropped the anchor. Tony went aft and stood on the swim platform, looking down into the water. The current slowly carried us back toward the survey site.

"That's good!" Tony shouted.

I locked the windlass, and Tony went back up to the foredeck and set the brake on the anchor line. The *Revenge* drifted back slightly further, lifting the line, dragging the chain, and setting the hook. I reversed hard, to make sure it was set, then looked down over the starboard rail. The survey grid was almost directly below us.

"I don't suppose you dive, do you?" I asked Devon.

"No," she replied. "I'm a good swimmer, but I've never even tried snorkeling."

"Tony and I are good divers, but we're not investigators. What should we be looking for and what do we do with it when we find it?"

"I have some evidence bags and latex gloves in my gym bag," she said, heading to the ladder. Tony and I joined her in the salon. "Ideally, this would be done by forensics tech divers," she explained. "But, as you pointed out at dinner, we're outside territorial waters and the sheriff doesn't have jurisdiction out here. So it's us or bring in the FBI and Coast Guard."

"I doubt we'll find anything that might be useful in the shooting," I said. "I understand the gun was a revolver, so there won't even be a shell casing. If the girl was also drowned here, what should we be looking for?"

"I know it'll be like looking for a needle in a haystack," Devon said. "But, you saw her, right?" I nodded and she continued. "She's missing a tooth, one eye, and quite a bit of tissue from her face."

"Find a tooth on the bottom of the ocean?" Tony asked.

"Or whatever blunt object he used to smash her face," Devon replied, digging into her gym bag. She placed a box of latex gloves on the settee. "Wear these," she continued, pulling out another box, "and take a few of these evidence bags. Anything you find goes into a separate bag. Usually the forensics people will write where the object was found on the front of the bag, but I guess we'll just put 'Survey Site' on all of them."

I looked at Tony and pointed with my chin toward the water. "Southwest corner of the grid is square one and we go left to right, bottom to top?"

"Top right corner will be number six-twenty-five?"

"Good idea," Devon said. "Write on the bag what the grid number is where you find anything. If you find something outside the grid, just estimate the distance to the nearest one."

"We could be here a few dives," I said. "Maybe a few dives for several days." I took a number of the evidence bags from the box and stuffed them into my pocket. "Why the gloves? Can you get fingerprints from something that's wet?"

"They can in the lab, at least sometimes. I read about a case where they were able to lift prints from a postcard that'd been mailed in the nineteen-forties. Mostly, the gloves keep you from cross-contaminating evidence."

Snagging several pairs of the gloves, I stuffed them in another pocket and headed out to the cockpit.

"We only have about three hours of daylight left," Tony said, following behind me. "Two more dives, and we'll have to start doing some deco stops."

"What's that?" Devon asked, following us out into the sunlight.

"Air is mostly nitrogen and oxygen," I explained, as Tony changed the tanks out and hooked the empties to the compressor hoses. "Too much of either isn't good. At depth, you're breathing compressed air at a greater volume, equal to the water pressure. At thirty feet, the pressure's almost twice the normal atmospheric pressure we breathe at the surface. Oxygen is burned off easy enough in the muscle tissue, but a decompression stop at a shallower depth is needed when the nitrogen level gets too concentrated in the body. No big deal. We'll just cut the third dive short and hang out ten feet below the boat for a few minutes, to bleed some nitrogen off."

"What?" she asked, looking puzzled. "You have to test your blood or something?"

Tony and I laughed. "Nah," I said, lifting the gauge cluster attached to my regulator. "Dive computers calculate all that now. But once you've done a few thousand dives, you know the depths and limits."

We geared up and were back in the water in minutes, agreeing that we'd work the grid from opposite sides. We descended to the bottom, then split up. I went over to grid one, and Tony started at grid twenty-five.

Visibility was nearly a hundred feet, but when I got to the first grid and actually studied the bottom, I realized the enormity of our task. On pleasure dives, you're just looking around to see what can be seen. I'd never really studied the sea-floor through the eyes of a person looking for something out of the ordinary. As I adjusted my buoyancy and pulled on the latex gloves—not an easy task in the water—I realized it would be difficult to find anything at all. Studying the bottom beneath the first grid, I didn't see anything at all that shouldn't have been there, and moved on to number two.

Tony and I soon met in the middle, both shaking our heads. We moved up one grid to the north and then started moving apart. Isaksson and Marshall had obviously taken a lot of time to set the survey grid up so that it was perfectly square on a north-south axis. Knowing Isaksson's dad a little better than the son, I wouldn't have been surprised if one of the corners was at a precise one-hundredth of a second in both latitude and longitude. Now Isaksson's and Marshall's grid was being used to find clues to who killed them.

I slowly moved back to my left, studying the bottom closely. We did this sideways thing several times, meeting in the middle and going back the other way. When I was down to four hundred pounds of air, I signaled Tony and we headed up to the boat. The next dive would require a safety stop, and if there was a fourth dive we'd need a fifteen-minute decompression stop.

Without getting out of the water, we quickly switched the tanks out and connected the empties to the compressor, telling Devon that we hadn't seen anything. Five minutes later, we were back at the grid square each of us had left off at.

It wasn't until we were ten minutes into the fourth tank that I heard a clanking sound and looked to find Tony motioning me to him. He was at the fifteenth row, near the east side of the grid.

Tony pointed as I got closer. Laying below the grid was an underwater camera with a double strobe attachment. I noticed that the pipe I had my hand on was bent slightly downward. Before I could examine it, I saw a small brain coral, no bigger than a ripe cantaloupe. It was more the position of it than the dome shaped coral itself that caught my eye; most people might not have noticed it, but I saw instantly that it had been disturbed. One side was pushed down into the sand, and there was a crack in the dome.

I motioned Tony closer. We each stuck our heads down into adjacent grid squares. I could see that something had discolored the area between several polyps and quite a few of the tiny animals were dead.

Tony scribbled on his dive slate and showed it to me. *Skin?*

Holding a dive knife against a dead spot on the small brain coral, I was able to keep it from being further disturbed, while Tony carefully used his own dive knife to remove as much of the soft, spongy substance between the coral polyps that he could. Somehow, we managed to get most of it into an evidence bag. We had plenty of air and worked cautiously, trying to collect as much of the substance as we could without doing any more damage to the fragile little coral.

This was one of the many things that Tony and I had in common, and something we both took very seriously: a deep, abiding love of the sea and all its creatures. This small cluster of polyps, grouped to resemble a human brain, had taken years to reach this small size, starting from just one or two polyps clutching onto a clam shell or rock. I'd seen brain coral domes that were up to fifteen or twenty feet across, covered with millions of tiny polyps, which are the living part of the coral. Successive generations are added onto the calcium skeleton of earlier generations. Large brain corals could be thousands of years old.

So, yeah, we were being careful. Probably not what the forensics guys might have done—they'd likely have bagged the whole coral—but we were watermen first.

Then I saw it. At first, I thought it was just a broken piece of long-dead coral turned white. But when I picked it up I realized it was a human tooth. One of the smaller front teeth from the bottom jaw, if I had to guess.

We bagged the tooth and had to take the camera and strobes apart to fit either into the largest evidence bag. I looked closely at the bottom. I remembered Doc Fredric saying that he'd found microscopic plant life and small sand crystals in the girl's lungs. I didn't know if he could compare them or not, but I decided to put some sand into an evidence bag, then I closed and sealed it.

Hovering there, I shuddered with the realization that this was where the girl had died. Several grid squares to the north, I spotted something unusual. While Tony continued sifting through the sand where the tooth was found, I finned over to the object.

I knew what it was before I even got close. I know a thing or two about guns, and a black-and-silver revolver looks way out of place on the sea bottom. It was just a few feet from where I was now sure Jennifer Marshall had been murdered. I looked up and realized I was probably thirty feet below where James had been shot to death. I carefully put the revolver in a bag, but instead of putting the bag in one of the deep cargo pockets of my shorts, I shoved it into the inside pocket of my BC and swam back over to Tony. He was inspecting the grid pipes around where we'd found the tooth and what we'd guessed was skin tissue.

He looked up at me, then pointed to two parallel sections of the grid and made a motion with his hand like a bridge. I nodded and pointed to the pipe I'd noticed was bent and made the same motion, but inverted, telling him that it was bent downward.

Tony studied the bent pipes and moved slightly around, until he was above the one that was bent down and had his hands on the two that were bent upward. I'd given him all the details on the murders during the ride out here. Even behind his mask, I saw the look of revulsion in his face, at the same time that I realized what had happened here.

The killer hadn't hit the woman with the brain coral, he'd forced her head down through the grid and smashed her face on it. Probably more than once, to do the amount of damage that was done. Then, after she'd drowned, he'd used the two pipes for leverage while he raped her lifeless body so hard that the pipe the body was hanging over was bent downward. I shuddered again as we rose a few feet.

I checked my air pressure gauge and, seeing that I was down to nearly twelve hundred pounds, I motioned to Tony that it was time to leave. We finned north, passing under the *Revenge*, slowly rising to intercept our anchor line. Leveling off at ten feet, we swam to the line and grabbed it, dumping some air from our BCs to hang on the thick braided nylon.

Safety and decompression stops are boring and tedious, but they're a necessary part of repetitive diving. Hanging there by one hand and looking around, I thought about the gun I'd found. I hadn't taken the time to inspect it or anything. I didn't need to; I'd known it was a Colt Cobra when I picked it up.

Could I be wrong about Lawrence? I wondered.

I only knew him as a cab driver, and didn't really know much about his personal life. I usually went with my gut instinct about people, and Lawrence had helped me out on more than one occasion. My gut had always told me that he was a decent person.

But I don't believe in coincidences. Usually when two seemingly unrelated events occur and seem to be linked only by the circumstances of their occurrence, there's some underlying and unseen connection between them.

Lawrence hired Isaksson, of that there was no doubt. Treasure hunting being what it was, I felt pretty confident that only Isaksson, Marshall, and Lawrence knew where they were searching—and now two of the three were dead and the third was being framed for the murder. I was equally certain that both had been killed right here. The cops had determined that James was killed with a Colt Cobra and Lawrence owned one, though he'd said it was stolen. I'd just found the same weapon at the murder scene. These connections seemed to add up to be way more than coincidental. And they all pointed to Lawrence as the killer.

Or did they? The wild card in this whole thing was why Lawrence hadn't reported the theft of his money box and gun, if it had really happened. If it had, then obviously, someone was taking steps to try to make it look as though Lawrence was the killer.

I had to decide what to do about the discovery of the gun. I still believed Lawrence to be innocent, so I should hand the gun over and hope that the facts bore that out. If he really was the killer, I knew I *had* to turn it over, friend or not. But what about the hair under the girl's nails? Lawrence definitely hadn't killed the girl, but he wouldn't be the first person convicted of something he didn't do.

In the distance, I heard a buzzing sound, recognizing it immediately as an outboard motor getting closer. I could tell Tony heard it as well, and we both started looking around. Though sound travels a lot further underwater, it's impossible for the human ear to figure out what direction it's coming from. We've lived on land for so long our brains have adapted to the speed of sound through air. We determine direction by the nanosecond of difference it takes for sound waves to reach both ears. In water, sound travels four times faster than it does in air. Sea creatures' minds are better adapted to determining direction underwater.

The pitch of the outboard remained high as it neared. Being close to the surface when a boat is approaching under power can be more than a little unnerving. Then I saw the boat, perhaps a hundred feet away. The pitch changed as the boat slowed down. Tony looked at me questioningly, and I checked my watch. I held up my fist, then extended four fingers, telling him we still had four minutes of decompression time before we could safely surface.

The other boat was small, maybe eighteen or nineteen feet. The bottom was covered with barnacles and fine, stringy algae. It obviously hadn't been out of the water in some time and used infrequently. The boat drifted alongside the *Revenge* for about a minute, then roared away at top speed.

Curiosity got the best of me. I signaled Tony to stay put and I'd be right back. I let go of the anchor rode and swam back toward the *Revenge*, passing directly under it, but remaining at ten feet. Below the swim platform, I turned into the current and kicked toward the surface. I just wanted to pop my head up, make sure everything was okay, then drop back down to finish the deco stop.

CHAPTER TWENTY-SIX

Duke's head hurt. The previous night was a blur when he tried to recollect the events after having left the club. He went up the ladder from the salon of his twenty-nine-foot sloop, squeezed his wide shoulders through the narrow hatch, and looked around.

Duke wasn't a sailor and had no intention of learning. The boat was cheap, and the dock fees were a lot less than renting an apartment. He'd bought it two years ago, and it hadn't left the dock since then. He didn't even know if the little motor would start. He ate his meals out so, as with the motor, he didn't know if the alcohol stove would work or even how to operate it. The boat was connected to shore power, fresh water, and cable TV. He'd installed a little air conditioner in the forward deck hatch that more than cooled the tiny interior. It was a place to sleep and have some privacy away from Harley.

Stepping over to the dock, he went up to the marina office to see if they had any coffee and a boat he could rent.

The mid-afternoon sun was already hot, though it was the middle of October.

Twenty minutes later, Duke idled the dirty seventeen-foot center console under the US-1 bridge and followed the channel markers to the man-made cut to Cudjoe Bay. He crossed the bay and turned north into Kemp Channel. Going under Overseas Highway again, he almost brought the boat to a stop. A salvage boat was aground on the right side of the channel, with yellow police tape around the whole deck.

Not seeing anyone, he continued on his way, glancing back nervously at the big boat. He followed Kemp Channel out into Cudjoe Basin, then northwest in Cudjoe Channel, until he finally reached the Gulf waters.

Duke turned due north and accelerated. It wasn't his first time making this trip, and it wasn't his first time at the wheel of this particular boat. At least once, sometimes twice a month, Harley had him go out here to see who was snooping around. Most times, he never found anyone. He'd never figured out how Harley knew anyone was out here. It was miles from anywhere.

Ten minutes out, and nearly soaked by the salt spray, he spotted a boat in the distance. It looked like a big offshore fishing boat had anchored up. Duke turned wide, angling away from the boat slightly. When he was nearly abreast of the bigger boat, he turned suddenly and headed straight toward it.

Still a hundred feet away, he saw a blond woman in the back of the boat. She was waving both arms over her head and pointing at the red and white flag on the roof. Duke didn't know what the flag meant, and didn't care.

This was close to the spot that Harley wanted to keep secret.

Slowing the boat, Duke turned until he was broadside about fifteen feet away from the bigger boat. He looked it over carefully. It was a beauty, as was the girl. She had blond hair pulled back in a big, puffy ponytail and was wearing cut-offs and a work shirt tied below her boobs. Just like the girl in Dukes of Hazzard.

Yeah, Duke thought. *Now that's a hot one. Boat probably cost a ton of money, too.*

"Are you nuts?" the woman shouted over the water. "There are divers in the water!"

"You can't dive here! It's a sanctuary!" Duke shouted back, realizing the woman was alone on the boat and trying to figure out a way to get her off it. It wasn't about satisfying a need, just an opportunity that he couldn't pass up.

"We're not sport diving, sir," the woman said, an irritated and suspicious tone in her voice. "I'm with—"

"It don't matter!" Duke yelled, cutting her off and waving his arms. He moved to the front of his boat, where he opened a fish box. "This here is a sanctuary! You're not allowed to do *anything* in a sanctuary!"

Duke reached into the fish box and lifted a twelve-gauge shotgun out, racking a shell into the chamber. Duke knew that particular sound always scared the hell out of people, especially girls. *Hell*, he thought. *I'll just ride over there and take her.*

When Duke looked up, long before he had a chance to even raise the shotgun, he realized he'd made a serious mistake, as he was now looking down the barrel of a big gun in the woman's hands. He froze.

"As I was trying to tell you," the woman said, "I'm with the sheriff's department. Now, real slow, extend that shotgun out to your right and lay it on the deck. Don't think about it, mister. Just do it. I'll shoot you before you can move an inch."

Duke knew he was screwed, and he also knew that Harley would be very angry. The woman's boat was rocking in the small waves, but not nearly as much as his was, and her gun barrel never wavered from his chest. Slowly, he did what she said and leaned to lay the Remington on the foredeck.

A wave hit Duke's boat the wrong way and threw him off balance—only slightly, but enough to lose his grip. The shotgun clattered back into the fish box, where the anchor rested haphazardly on top of the life vests and anchor line in the box. One of the anchor's flukes wedged into the trigger guard and the shotgun went off with a boom, blasting a big hole in the side of his rental boat.

Duke saw the woman duck behind the side of the boat. He moved back to the wheel and jammed the throttle as far as it would go. A shot rang out and Duke instinctively ducked his head. A few seconds later, he was safely out of range and turned to the east and then south, speeding away toward shore. There was no way a boat that big could catch him.

He had to get to the club as fast as possible and tell Harley what happened.

Harley's gonna know what to do, Duke thought. *He always knows what to do.*

CHAPTER TWENTY-SEVEN

As soon as my head broke the surface, I knew something was wrong. Devon's service pistol being swung toward me was a dead giveaway.

"Whoa!" I shouted, raising my hands. "Easy now. What happened?"

"Some idiot came flying up in a boat!" Devon said, bending over and coming up with her holster. She slid her weapon into it and clipped it to her belt. "He fit Doc Fredrick's description, powerfully built with dark curly hair. He started yelling about this being a sanctuary and waving his arms around like a lunatic. I already had my weapon on him when he brandished a shotgun. When I ordered him to drop it, the shotgun went off and blasted a hole in the side of his boat."

"Are you okay?" I asked. "Can you see him now?"

"Yeah, I'm all right," she said, her shoulders lifting as she blew out a long breath. "Just some adrenaline. I got a shot off at him as he sped away, but I don't think I hit anything but water." She pointed toward the Contents, just off to the southeast. "He disappeared south, just before that bigger island."

"He's gone now," I said, trying to calm her. "And he'll play hell getting across the flats that way. We still have a few minutes of decompression time. Will you be okay alone until Tony surfaces?"

"Yeah, but how can I signal you if he comes back?"

"We'll hear him before you," I said. Then, realizing she was out of her element here and could use some added security, I said, "See that hatch, right beside the ladder? Open it and you'll see a panel to the left with a switch marked 'Diver Recall.' Flip that on, and we'll hear it and come up in a few seconds."

She seemed to be relieved that there was a plan, and nodded. I dumped some air from my BC, quickly descended to ten feet, and swam forward to where Tony was still hanging on the anchor line. I signaled that everything was okay and checked my dive computer. That short surface time had added three minutes to my decompression time. Using basic dive signals, I told Tony to surface alone when his time was up and I'd surface when my own decompression stop was finished. Surfacing before finishing a deco stop is inadvisable at best, but I'd been near the end of the prescribed period and repetitive dive tables are way over on the conservative side.

A minute later, Tony's dive computer beeped and he nodded at me, signaling he was surfacing. He let go of the anchor line and drifted away toward the *Revenge*.

Alone with my thoughts, I wondered if the guy who'd come out with the shotgun was in fact the murderer returning to the scene of the crime, or if he was just another Keys whack-job that happened to fit the general description. The odds leaned heavily toward the latter, but I couldn't discount the former.

Hanging there on the anchor line, with nothing around me but water, I thought about the lady cop. She was a looker, so how come she was unattached? Thinking on it, I realized that most of the cops I knew were single. I guess being a cop is about as conducive to a stable relationship as being a Marine. Unannounced deployments had wrecked my first two marriages. Right now, I wasn't looking for a relationship, but it had been several months since I'd even been on a date.

My own computer beeped and I checked it, confirming it was now safe for the average diver to surface. I released the anchor line and made my way back to the swim platform.

When I surfaced, Devon was talking animatedly to Tony about what had happened. I tossed my fins through the open transom door, then shrugged my BC off. Tony lifted it out of the water and placed it next to his on the deck of the cockpit.

Ducking underwater, I levered myself up onto the swim platform, swung a leg up and stood. I glanced toward the sun, now sinking closer to the western horizon. "Less than an hour of usable daylight. I think we're done here today."

"Did you find anything?" Devon asked.

"I think so," Tony replied. "We might have found the where and how of the girl's murder. There was a substance lodged in some coral that might be skin tissue, and Jesse found a tooth."

"You're kidding!" Devon exclaimed, shoving Tony with both hands in excitement. She looked at the water all around us. "What are the odds of finding a tooth in the ocean?"

"Finding the dive site narrowed those odds a lot," I said, bending over my dive gear and opening the inside pocket. "Then it's just a systematic search. I also found the gun that probably killed James."

"Can I see that?" Devon asked, extending a hand for the evidence bag. I handed it to her and she peered at the gun through the clear window, moving it around until she could see the serial number. "This is the gun that's registered to your friend, Mister Lovett."

"Be that as it may," I said. "There's no way Lawrence had anything to do with what happened here."

"And what do you base that *opinion* on?"

"Twenty years of measuring not just the abilities, but also the morals and convictions of men I trained for combat," I replied. "And before you ask: yeah, my skills at it are crazy good."

"Your opinion is noted," Devon said. "And it happens to be aligned with my own judgment of the man. But this evidence could convict him anyway." She stepped closer, appraising me with those sparkling brown eyes. "You could just as easily have buried this in the sand and nobody would have known."

"I'd know." I shook my head as I dried off with a towel. "That'd be like doubting myself. I know he didn't do it and I trust that your investigation of the evidence will bear that out."

"You sound like Ben," Devon said. "You'd have probably made a pretty decent cop. I'm a good judge of people, too."

Tony lifted the two larger evidence bags out of the goodie bag he'd carried. "This is an underwater digital camera."

"Probably what they were using to survey the site with," I said. "Be worth looking at the images. They might be time stamped."

"Want me to refill the empties?" Tony asked.

"That's up to the detective," I said, grinning and not breaking eye contact. "We can come back here tomorrow, or just spend the night out here and dive again early in the morning."

"I don't have a cell signal out here," Devon said. "And I need to get this evidence to the lab rats." She didn't break eye contact, either. In fact, those big brown orbs positively danced with mischief. "Besides, your friend Julie didn't loan me any extra clothes. Not even PJs."

"You could probably find something to fit in the guest cabin," I offered. "No pajamas, though."

Devon smiled. "So, women's clothes really do fall off on this boat?"

Way off to the south, I heard an outboard and looked over her shoulder, toward the sound. "No," I replied absently, scanning the horizon. "A lot of clients forget stuff. Any clothes left behind, I wash and put away in case they come back."

From behind Sawyer Key, a white center console with a blue T-top appeared. When it turned toward us, a blue light on the roof came on.

"Probably best to get this evidence to the lab as soon as possible, anyway," Devon said.

"I thought you didn't have a signal," I said, nodding toward the approaching police boat. "How'd you call for backup?"

Devon turned and looked. "I didn't call anyone."

The blue light on the approaching boat stopped flashing as it got closer. I recognized Marty and waved him to the port side, where I put two fenders over.

Marty tied off quickly and nodded to Devon. "Detective Evans, surprised to see you out here."

"What are you doing out this far, Marty?" I asked.

"You know each other?" Devon asked.

"Deputy Phillips is dating my daughter," I said. "Come aboard, Marty."

He stepped over the gunwale, scratched Finn behind an ear, and shook hands with the three of us. "Good to see you again, Agent Jacobs," Marty said to Tony. Then he turned to me and said, "I spent a little time looking at the charts this morning. After Rusty explained where he thought the two murder victims had been diving, I calculated wind and current and it looked like he was probably right. So, I just came out after my shift was over to have a look around. Spotted the *Revenge* on radar, from back in the channel."

Devon explained about the boat that had shown up while we were decompressing. Though she was able to give a pretty good description of the man, she hadn't gotten the registration number off the side of the boat; by the time she thought to look, the shotgun blast had obliterated it.

"No signal out here," Devon said. "If you'll call it in for me, tell dispatch to inform Lieutenant Morgan that the guy looked like what Doctor Fredric suggested the killer would look like."

"It's a grungy-looking boat," I said. "At least from the bottom. Odds are the guy's not much of a boater. The shotgun might have caused fifty dollars of *improvements* to it."

Marty stepped back over to his boat and radioed the incident and description to the sheriff's dispatcher.

"Why can't I get a cell signal?" Devon held her phone up and turned around in a circle, then went to the gunwale and waited until Marty finished talking to the dispatcher. "Also relay to Lieutenant Morgan that we found the murder scene and collected some evidence. I'll be bringing it in later tonight."

While Marty was busy calling that in, and with Tony down in the engine room putting our gear away I asked, "So, we're not spending the night out here?"

Devon smiled seductively and leaned closer to me. "Some other time, maybe?"

"*Cualquier momento*," I replied with a wink, flirting back just a little. "*Mi barca es tu barca.*"

Some women are a little more aggressive than others. Most of the women I'd known in Devon's line of work tended to fall into that category. They also tended to back off, if the man was more aggressive.

Getting serious, I said, "The fastest way to get the evidence to the lab would be to take the *Revenge* to Key West."

"You don't have anyone to get home to?"

There was a loaded question, if ever I heard one. Maybe she was serious. "Not a soul," I replied, as Tony came up from the engine room. "But Tony does."

"Tony does what?" Tony asked.

"Needs a ride from Deputy Phillips," Devon said. "So you can get home to your wife, and Captain McDermitt can take me and the evidence straight to Key West."

CHAPTER TWENTY-EIGHT

ater occasionally splashed through the hole in the side of the boat as Duke sped south toward shore. He'd lost his bearings in the confusion that followed the shotgun blast, and now he didn't know where he was. All the islands looked the same.

Mistaking the bigger island of the Content Keys for Sawyer Key, he entered Content Passage, thinking it was Cudjoe Channel. When he approached the other side of the shallow passage, he knew he wasn't going the right way. Expecting the wide and empty Cudjoe Basin, Duke was surprised to see two large islands ahead.

Just then, the boat ran aground. The engine kicked up and raced as the boat ground to a stop, sliding partially sideways and leaning over. The sudden stop threw Duke off balance, and he nearly went over the side. The boat's unexpected appearance frightened a flock of seagulls into flight; they all seemed to laugh at the big human's antics.

He quickly shut off the over-revving engine and looked around. There wasn't much of anything to see, except water and islands. About a mile away to the east, Duke saw a pier extending out to the north from one of the smaller islands. He could barely make out someone on the pier and retrieved his binoculars from the forward fish box, returning the shotgun.

Training the binos on the pier in the distance, Duke turned the little knob on top, until it came into focus. Two women and a man sat on the pier, looking in his direction. In the water in front of them, Duke could make out two kids splashing around.

I better get out of here, Duke thought.

A quick glance over the side revealed a shallow bottom, but further ahead of the boat it seemed to be a little deeper. Duke didn't know anything about tides, or when the next high tide would be. For all he knew it could be high tide now, but in his mind running aground meant it was low tide. Unfortunately for him, the tide was already near its peak and would be falling very soon.

Not wanting to get his shirt wet, he pulled it off and tossed it on the foredeck. Then he stepped over the side of the boat and dropped down into the water. It barely reached his knees. Walking straight ahead, he found that it did get deeper, and in just twenty or thirty feet the water was up to his waist.

It was at that moment that Duke remembered he still had his cellphone in his pocket. Pulling it out, he tried to turn it on, but got nothing. Muttering expletives, he marched back to the boat. If he had to, he'd lift it and carry it to deeper water.

First, Duke tried pulling the boat using one of the dock lines. Looping the end around his right hand, he spread his feet wide, his left foot toward the boat, and pulled with all his might. It didn't budge.

Realizing that the heavy end would be where the engine was, Duke went to the back of the boat. "Maybe I won't have to carry the whole thing," he muttered, rolling his head from side to side and flexing his muscles.

Duke pushed the button on the side of the engine and the hydraulic system made a gurgling and grinding noise, but eventually raised the lower unit out of the water so it wouldn't drag the bottom. Duke didn't know a lot of things, and another of the things he didn't know was that things weighed less in the water than out of it. By raising the engine, he made the boat heavier.

One thing Duke did know was that when he put his shoulder against something, it usually moved. He squatted down low, grabbing the lower unit of the engine with his left hand and the transom with the other. In an explosive burst of strength, he planted his left shoulder against the spot where the hot water came out and heaved. He burned his shoulder and neck on the hot aluminum cowling.

"Shit, shit, shit!" Duke yelled, dancing around in the knee-deep water.

A few of the black-headed gulls that had been frightened by the sudden grounding had returned. Hearing his shouts, some spread their wings, ready to take flight if need be. All of them laughed raucously at him. One of the gulls, between fits of laughter, seemed to call his given name over and over, as if mocking him. "Marion! Marion! Hehe, hehehehehehe! Heee-heeeeeee!"

This angered Duke. He did his Incredible Hulk pose, flexing his powerful shoulder and arm muscles. He roared back at the gulls, his muscles bulging and rippling with the strain. As adrenaline coursed through his veins, he grabbed the lower unit again, threw his shoulder against the engine's hot lower cowling, and pushed with everything he had. The heated aluminum seared the tender flesh where his bulging neck met his massive left shoulder. The pain caused him to bellow like an enraged bull, and he pushed harder. The huge muscles in his back and arms strained against the more than one thousand pounds of boat.

Suddenly, the suction effect of the sand released its hold on the boat, and it moved forward a few inches. Duke roared again, lunging forward and digging his feet deeper in the soft sand. The boat began to move and the giant power-lifter growled with a guttural animal-like noise, pushing even harder, until the boat was free of the sand and floating once more.

With a final grunt and a huge shove, he pushed the boat into deeper water, then scrambled aboard. His shoulder felt like it was on fire, and when he touched it his fingers came away wet and sticky with blood and burned flesh.

"That bitch is gonna pay for this," Duke muttered, pushing the button on the throttle to lower the engine. It was then that a cloud of mosquitoes located the heat source and swarmed down on him.

The prop was barely in the water when Duke started the engine and put it in forward, slapping at the bugs biting him. The prop shot a geyser of water into the air behind him as he raced the engine, but the boat began to move into deeper water.

Looking over the side, Duke saw that the water depth was probably okay and lowered the engine enough to stop the big rooster-tail. He throttled up slowly, to keep from dragging the prop on the bottom.

Duke turned and looked back at the gulls on the sandbar. He raised his fist and extended his middle finger to them as the boat slowly came up on plane. He kept the engine trimmed high in case there was another sandbar. The mosquitoes were quickly left behind.

Keeping the setting sun to his right, he continued south, picking his way blindly through the shallow water. Off to the right, he saw two channel markers close together, one red and the other green. They'd always been on his left, coming back in, so he knew he was close to where he was supposed to be. The markers weren't in the channel he usually used, so he ignored them and continued straight ahead, knowing that he'd encounter the highway sooner or later.

The boat grounded again, and once more Duke had to get out and push. At least this time he'd been going considerably slower, and he could push it off the sand without burning himself.

Mosquitoes swarmed in again as he climbed into the boat. The sun was completely gone now, but he could see light in the distance, and idled the boat that way. Using a flashlight he'd found in a storage bin, he shined it in front of the boat like a headlight.

Duke grounded the boat twice more in the shallows next to Raccoon Key, though he had no idea what it was called. Had he bothered to stop and look around, he might have found the bleached bones of another steroid abusing gym-rat.

Finally, the flashlight illuminated a green marker ahead and to the left. Duke angled the boat toward the marker and entered Niles Channel. It was several hours past sunset when he idled toward the bridge, watching the cars pass over it.

Knowing he couldn't return the boat to the marina with a hole in it, he brought it up onto a small beach surrounded by mangroves, right at the foot of the bridge. He didn't know what bridge it was, but he was pretty sure he was east of where he wanted to be.

Putting his shirt back on, Duke got out of the boat, slapping away mosquitoes, and trudged up the steep incline toward the road. It was a Thursday night, so traffic heading toward Key West was pretty light, but he stuck his thumb out anyway. All he needed was a ride to the marina, where he could get his Jeep.

Several cars drove past in a group and one honked, but none of them stopped. Duke turned and started to walk. As he approached an overhead streetlight, he looked down at himself. His black jeans had mostly dried out. He could never find regular shirts or even tee-shirts that fit. A size 5X fit across his shoulders, but they always ballooned out at his narrow waist. So Duke wore only tank tops.

Maybe they just didn't see me, he thought. Duke hadn't hitchhiked since he was a kid in high school. He remembered another kid telling him that when you hitched at night you should stand under a light. Hearing another car coming, Duke hurried through the cone of light so that it fell on his face when he turned and held out his thumb. The car was alone on the road and slowed down.

Duke smiled and did his best to look harmless. The car pulled to the edge of the pavement and came to a stop next to him. It was a throwback to the sixties, a red Ford Falcon.

"Where you headed?" the driver asked. He had curly brown hair, a big mustache, and wore one of those fruit-juicy kind of tropical shirts, all bright colors and flowers.

A pretty woman sat in the passenger seat, wearing a tee-shirt over a bikini. She opened the door and got out, tilting the seat back forward. Her bikini bottom was a thong and left nothing at all to Duke's imagination.

"Would you mind wedging my purple beach ball behind the other seat?" she asked. The top of her head didn't even reach Duke's chin.

"Thanks," Duke said, stepping into the backseat and jamming the ball behind the driver's seat, so the wind wouldn't blow it out of the car. "I'm going to Stock Island, but if you ain't going that far I'd appreciate a ride to Sugarloaf Marina. That's where my car is."

As Duke sat down in the little backseat, the woman started to put the seat back and the man stopped her. "Slide it forward first, babe. He needs a bit more leg room than you."

She adjusted the seat, giving Duke as much room as possible, but it was still cramped. At least they had the top down.

"What's your name?" the man asked as he pulled back into the middle of the southbound lane and accelerated smoothly through the gears.

"My friends call me Duke."

"Pleased to meet you, Duke. We're going all the way to Key West, heck we might even jump this sucker to Havana. Sort of a party weekend. Be happy to drop you at Stock Island. Or on Sugarloaf, if you want to get your car."

CHAPTER TWENTY-NINE

After Tony and Marty left, I took Devon up to the foredeck, Finn following behind us. I showed her how to lock the anchor in place. Then I went up to the bridge, started the engines, and engaged the windlass. A couple of minutes later, she joined me on the bridge and Finn curled up in the corner of the cockpit by the transom door.

I brought the *Revenge* up to twenty-five knots, engaging in one of my favorite diversions: chasing the sun with a pretty girl beside me.

"It's beautiful out here," Devon said, sitting on the port bench and looking out over the water. It had calmed considerably since morning.

"No need to sit over there," I said, jerking my thumb at the second seat. "You don't have to crane your neck from over here. Just maintain three points of contact when moving around."

As Devon squeezed between the aft bridge rail and my seat, two of the points of contact she maintained were on either side of the back of my head. The contact was warm, soft, and inviting.

"Will we get to Key West before dark?" she asked, finally settling in beside me.

I'd already entered Key West Bight into the GPS and reached over to tap the bottom of the display. "At this speed, Mister Garmin says we'll arrive in Old Town about half an hour after dark. How are you feeling?"

As if she'd suddenly remembered her sea-sickness, her eyes widened. The setting sun on her face accentuated the brown-orange glow of her eyes. "I hadn't even thought about it. The last pill I took was hours ago."

"You have your sea legs now," I said with a sideways grin. "When we get to the dock, you might experience some dizziness on land for a little while."

"That's a real thing? Sea legs?"

"One of the reasons I put you to work looking for stuff in the water. It helps to train your brain that the boat's moving and you're in it."

"I'm suddenly starved," Devon said. "Beer and a steak after we drop things off at the lab? My treat."

Beer and a steak? I thought, glancing at the gun still in its holster on the front of her hip. If she could get over the seasickness, Devon just might be the perfect woman.

"There's beer down in the fridge," I offered.

"But you're driving."

Switching on the autopilot, I rose from my seat. "I won't tell the cops if you don't."

Devon grabbed the wheel. "Are you nuts?"

"It's on autopilot. Nothing to worry about."

"What if there's a boat? You stay. I'll get us a beer."

I sat back down at the helm, but left the autopilot on. "There's a small cooler in the cabinet under the sink."

Devon carefully moved around behind me, placing a hand on my shoulder instead of the seat back, as her breasts again brushed the back of my head. I could still feel the warmth of her touch after she'd disappeared down the ladder.

A few minutes later, I was about to get up and see what was keeping her when I heard the hatch open and close again. I went to the rail and reached down to take the cooler. Devon also handed up a small bowl of sliced fruit.

"I couldn't find any munchies," she said, climbing up the ladder and moving behind me. "You're one of those nutrition nuts aren't you."

I laughed. "I wouldn't go that far. I like a steak as well as the next guy, but never been a big fan of chips and snacks."

"Well, the fruit can only hold me over for so long," she said, dropping into her seat and popping a chunk of pineapple into her mouth. "Is this as fast as your boat goes?"

Never one to ignore a challenge, I pushed the throttles to the stops. The whine of the super-chargers kicked in, as the *Revenge* surged ahead, reaching its top speed of fifty-four knots in a matter of seconds.

I leaned over closer to Devon, to be heard over the screaming engines. "We'll miss the sunset at this speed."

She had a death-grip on the arm rests of her chair. "Let's not miss the sunset," she nearly shouted.

I slowed the *Revenge* to thirty knots, figuring that at that speed we'd near the channel just about the time the sun reached the horizon. Devon relaxed and opened the cooler. I let her try to twist the top off the first Red Stripe she took out, then pointed to the bottle opener mounted to the side of the dash. She opened it and handed it to me, then opened one for herself and closed the cooler.

"What's in the evidence bag marked 'Grass'?"

I looked over at Devon as she took a long pull on the cold beer. "I remembered Doc Fredric saying that he found sand and microscopic plant life in Jennifer Marshall's lungs. Plants grow in sand, so I collected some from the spot where Tony and I think she was murdered."

"Smart move doing that. You know about plant DNA?"

"I don't know about any kind of DNA," I replied. "I just figured Doc might be able to identify the same kind of plant from the sample. Maybe it'll help prove the girl was there."

Devon turned her seat toward me, pressing her knee lightly against my thigh. "The lab can do better than that," she said, her eyes sparkling. "Plant DNA is the same as animal, unique to each individual organism. Since plants don't move around to reproduce like we do, they share some of the same DNA strands with other plants in the same general area. If there's any microscopic plant life in the sample, the lab can positively identify whether the location it was collected from is the same spot where the plant life entered her lungs. That'll put the victim at the survey site when she died."

I grinned. "So moving around a lot is important for us?"

She slugged my shoulder.

I knew that they could match the ballistics to the gun I found, and that would put James and the killer there, linking the two murders to the one spot James was surveying. Proof that both murders took place at the same spot would make it more likely that it was just one killer.

Still a few miles from Man of War Harbor, with the sun nearing the western horizon beyond, I slowed the *Revenge* to idle speed. There weren't any clouds to the west, but a thin line of high clouds stretched off to the northwest, the end lit up in a fiery orange-red like a glowing cigar tip.

"Have you ever seen the green flash?" I asked Devon.

"Heard about it," she replied.

"Conditions are good. Just as the top of the sun is about to slip below the horizon, sometimes it looks like a little inverted teardrop of it breaks loose and hangs on the edge of the world, then it flashes green, before it disappears."

"You've seen this?" she asked doubtfully, but sat up higher in the seat anyway.

"A few times. It's a rare sighting."

Just before the water seemed to reach up and grasp the bottom of the sun, I shifted to neutral and shut off the engines. The only sound was the gentle lapping of small waves against the bow as the *Revenge* drifted forward.

"They say if you make a wish and the green flash appears, your wish'll come true."

Slowly, the great orange orb slipped lower and lower, seeming to flatten out at the bottom. Its fading light illuminated the high clouds overhead, changing them into pink and yellow cotton candy. I glanced over at Devon just as she closed her eyes. Her mouth moved a little, as if she were whispering something. When she opened her eyes, the light from the setting sun made them look like amber glass. Devon's breath seemed to catch in her throat for a second as the top of the sun slipped below the horizon without fanfare.

"Doesn't happen all the time," I said.

"I don't think I've ever experienced a sunset like that," Devon said. "Thanks for taking the time."

"I try to take life out of gear about this time every day and just coast, while watching the sun go down."

"Coast, huh?" Devon turned toward me, the reflected light of the high, wispy clouds shining on her skin. "Seriously, though, if I don't get some medium-rare protein soon, you're gonna have to carry me."

I started the engines and put the boat in gear. "Yes, ma'am."

Contacting the harbor master, I got a slip assignment and asked for a dock hand to help with tying up. I also called Lawrence. Once we were tied up, I paid for the slip for one night and a possible second night.

"Stay and watch the boat," I told Finn, after he'd returned from the only tree near the dock. "I'll bring you back something."

Devon was carrying her gym bag with the evidence in it. As she and I reached the foot of the pier, Lawrence's big, black Crown Vic rolled to a stop and Billy got out.

"We've been having a good time," he said. "Lawrence has been teaching me the finer points of being a Key West cabbie and showing me around the island."

"We're going to the sheriff's office," I told Lawrence, as I held the back door open for Devon.

"Seems kinda weird," Devon said, climbing into the backseat. "Taking evidence in with the possible accused driving the car."

Lawrence turned in his seat and smiled at Devon. "You'll find di right mon," he said. "Yuh seem like a very bright young lady."

She laughed as I sat down next to her and Billy got back in the front seat. "Follow the evidence, huh?"

"Detective Morgan called me a few minutes ago," Billy said. "He's been watching security camera footage from all over. Did you know that just about every bar in town has a sidewalk cam? Anyway, the footage meshed with Lawrence's version of making his rounds that afternoon. He was definitely here in Key West when the murders occurred."

"Wonder why he didn't call me," Devon said, taking her phone out of her purse as Lawrence turned left on Eaton Street. "Ah, he must have called when I didn't have a signal out there." She tapped the screen and put the phone to her ear. I could make out the tinny sound of the voicemail. It was short.

"He confirms that," she said, putting the phone back in her purse. "He also said to take the evidence to the lab, that he's going home and not to bother him until morning."

"So, what do you tell folks who get in the taxi and find two cabbies?" I asked.

"I'm a driver in training," Billy said, with a grin.

A few minutes later, Lawrence stopped in front of the big government building on Stock Island. "Wait here," Devon said, as she got out of the car. "It'll only take a few minutes to check this in and get the forensics people working on it."

After Devon walked off, Billy turned in his seat. "Why are we waiting for her?"

"We're going out for steak and beer," I said.

"We? As in, all of—"

"No," I replied. "*We*, as in me and her. I want you to stay with Lawrence until we get a handle on this."

"Not a problem, Kemosabe," Billy said. "Just that a steak sounds good, right about now."

"I usually eat 'bout dis time, too," Lawrence added with a grin.

"I'll be sure to tip you enough to cover your meals," I said. "Someplace other than where we're going."

Billy turned his head and grinned. "Ain't she a little young?"

"She's maybe eight years younger than me," I replied, watching Devon walk back toward the car. "Not like she's a schoolgirl or anything."

"Outback okay with you?" Devon asked, sliding into the backseat.

"I thought you said you were hungry," I replied. "Best you'll get there is an eight-ounce sirloin."

"You know a better place?"

"The Strip House, Lawrence," I said.

Fifteen minutes later, Lawrence pulled to the curb at the south end of Simonton Street and we got out. I handed Lawrence two hundred-dollar bills, which he of course tried to refuse. I finally convinced him that it was to cover the fare and Billy's meals for the next couple of days. I wanted Billy with him day and night.

Inside, Devon and I both ordered the sixteen-ounce New York strips, baked potatoes, and draft beers. Halfway through the meal, Devon's phone rang. She looked at the caller ID and answered it.

"What'd you find out, Mitch?"

She listened for a few minutes, said thank you, and ended the call.

"That was Mitchel Bailey," she said, attacking her steak again. "Our top forensics guy. I asked him to look at the pictures on the camera, do the ballistics test, and look at the sand you collected first. No prints on the gun or the camera. The only pictures on the camera were of the bottom, each one framed by red and white pipe."

"Photographic survey," I said.

"Mitch said the last picture on the memory card was the underside of two boats. A big one and a smaller one."

"The killer's boat," I said, spearing a piece of meat. "If we can find it, an underwater picture of it could be matched to that, right?"

Devon nodded. "You catch on fast. It's all about matching one thing to another, putting events, people, and objects together in a timeline."

"The gun?"

"Ballistic tests positively matched the gun you found as the one that killed Isaksson. And the serial number matches your friend's registration. He's lucky he was on those security cameras."

"What about the sand?" I asked.

"You hit a homer, Gunny. The micro-organisms in the sand you collected are a visual match, too. It's been sent off for DNA analysis, but we probably won't have the report back for at least a week."

I swallowed a bite of my steak, washing it down with the beer. "I thought DNA testing was done in just a few hours."

Devon wiped her mouth, shaking her head. "Only on TV," she said. "In real-life, a fast turn-around on a major case will take several days. Plant DNA related to a murdered diver? No, that's going to be a week at the earliest."

I took the last bit of my potato skin and swirled it around in the juices on my plate, then chewed it slowly, while I thought. "So some unknown person went out to where Isaksson was diving," I said. "He shoots James, and then dives down to murder Jennifer. Why? A crime of opportunity?"

Devon washed her last bite down and wadded her napkin on her plate. "A random act of violence and the perp just happens to be the one that stole Mister Lovett's cash box and gun? And then just happens to leave it on the boat?"

"Yeah, you're right," I agreed. "Way too many coincidences."

"A more likely scenario would be that someone who Lawrence pissed off, stole his gun and money box, then decided to frame him for a double murder."

I shook my head. "I'm betting you could turn this rock upside down, shake it, and not find a single person with any kind of grudge against the man."

"He knows something that he's not telling us." She said it as though it were a proven fact.

"How do you know this?"

Devon smiled. "You're not the only one good at reading peoples' moral compasses."

"I've known Lawrence for several years and I've never known him to lie."

"Could be something he doesn't even know he knows," Devon said thoughtfully. "I get the sense that this thing goes a lot deeper than just two dead divers. Could be a rival treasure hunter or cab company."

I thought about that for a moment. I knew first-hand how millions of dollars' worth of treasure can change a person. And there were treasure hunters out there with far fewer scruples than most people.

"There is someone else involved," I said. "Lawrence's silent partner in the treasure hunt."

"The computer techs didn't find any deleted emails where he discussed the treasure hunt with anyone."

"Doesn't surprise me," I said. "Lawrence is in his late sixties and his partner is at least eighty, a World War Two Vet. They probably communicate with old rotary phones."

"You know who he is? This silent partner?"

"Yeah," I said. "I know who it is. Have Morgan bring you to get your car tomorrow about noon. I'll arrange for Lawrence and his partner to both be at the *Anchor*, ready to tell all."

Devon looked at her watch. "Wow, it's after ten already."

"You have someone to get home to?"

She smiled. "Not a soul."

CHAPTER THIRTY

Harley slammed his desk phone in the cradle. He'd been trying to call his brother since nine o'clock and for four hours his calls had gone straight to voicemail, like Duke had turned his phone off.

More likely, he broke it, Harley thought. There was a knock on the door. "Yeah!"

The door opened, and Brandy stuck her head in. "That creep Joaquin Hernandez is here, Harley."

"Take him to the VIP room and make him happy."

"C'mon, Harley," Brandy said, pouting. "He smells."

Harley pulled his wallet out and took two hundred dollars from it. Extending the bills, he said, "Joaquin is a hard-working man. I need his eyes out there on the water every day. Which means he needs to leave here happy tonight."

Brandy entered the office, dressed like all the dancers when they were on the floor: high heels, panties, and a skimpy negligee. She snatched the bills from his hand.

"This is the last time I'm gonna do him, Harley. He tastes the same as he smells."

As Brandy opened the door to leave, Duke stepped inside, forcing her to squeeze past him. "Where the hell have you been?" Harley asked. "Close the door."

"We got a problem, Harley."

"What kinda problem? Did you run that boater off, like I told you to?"

"That's the problem," Duke said, sitting in one of the chairs in front of Harley's desk. "There was a cop on the boat."

"A cop?" All kinds of scenarios popped into Harley's head.

Duke went on to tell his brother about the big fishing boat, the cop getting the drop on him, the shotgun blasting a hole in the boat, and his ordeal in getting back to civilization.

"Did it sink?"

"No," Duke replied. "I got it stashed a few miles from the marina."

"Good. Taking it back to the marina is asking for trouble we don't need right now."

Harley thought for a moment. If the cop got the registration number and even half a look at Duke, they'd be snooping around the marina very soon.

"What's the number of the marina?" Harley asked.

Duke dug through his wallet, which thankfully he'd left on the boat when he went aground. He took out a business card and handed it to his brother.

"I need a new phone," Duke said. "Mine got wet."

Harley rolled his eyes and pulled the bottom left drawer open. In it were half a dozen boxes of brand new prepaid phones. He took one out and slid it across his desk.

Duke was amazed at how easily Harley spun a story about an engine fire while the two of them had been out night fishing. He threatened to sue the marina owner, since they'd barely escaped with their lives. By the time he hung up, it sounded like Harley could have gotten the marina guy to pay him to keep him from going to the cops.

Harley hung up the phone. "That's taken care of. He's gonna report the boat was stolen, and file it with his insurance. That's what he'll tell the cops, if they come looking. But you gotta get back up there and get it sunk for real, though. If the cops find it, they're sure to connect you."

"Right now?" Duke asked. "I ain't had anything to eat since this morning."

"No, wait till after we close," Harley said. "I gotta make a cash drop and I want you with me. Tomorrow, I need you to find Waldo. He didn't bring in his front money today."

Duke grinned. Harley knew it made the kid feel good about himself to be the only one that Harley trusted when he went to the bank to make a night drop. And he truly was good at hunting people down, almost like a savant.

An hour later, the music died and the lights came on in the bar. There were only a handful of drunk fishermen and tourists still in the place. Duke and his weightlifting buddy Ray, who worked part time as a bouncer, herded the drunks toward the door.

Harley was at the bar, going over the receipts with Kenny, when Jasmine came out of the dressing room, ready to go home. Whose home, they hadn't discussed yet.

"You gonna be long?" Jasmine asked.

"Maybe an hour," he replied, inhaling the citrus smell of her perfume. "I have to go to the bank first. I'll call you a cab and you can hang out at my place till I get there?"

"Hang out by the pool or on the porch?" she asked, her lips pouting.

Harley dug in his pocket and handed her the spare key to his house. "The pool, the bedroom, or even the kitchen," he said. "I'm gonna be hungry for a lot of things when I get there."

Taking the key, Jasmine dropped it in her purse with a wink. Harley motioned to Kenny for the phone. The bartender lifted it from below the bar and turned it toward Harley, sliding a business card from a cab company across the bar.

Harley spoke on the phone for a moment and hung up. As Jasmine started to turn toward the back door, he stopped her. "Wait at the back table," he said. "He'll blow the horn when he pulls up and I'll walk you out."

"Well, aren't you the gallant horny old goat," Jasmine said, walking to the elevated back table.

"None of my business, Boss," Kenny said, his tone low, so the dancer couldn't hear. "But you're never gonna get that key back."

"You're right," Harley said, watching Jasmine's ass as she went up the steps. "It's none of your business."

Duke returned and said, "All locked up, Harley."

Kenny loaded the last stacks of cash into Harley's bag and closed it, handing him a slip of paper. "Fourteen-hundred and change in credit card receipts, and an even fifteen grand in cash, mostly from your street team. I got a couple hundred in small bills and change still in the cash drawer for tomorrow."

A car horn honked twice from behind the building. Harley picked up the bag and nodded at the bartender. "All this money was from the legal sale of beer, wine, and booze, Kenny."

"Whatever you say, Boss," Kenny replied, as Duke and Harley started toward the back.

Jasmine was two steps ahead, teasing Harley with every step, all the way to the back door. Outside, Harley handed the bag to Duke, along with his car keys. "Start her up, I'll be with you in a second."

Duke, took the keys and started toward Harley's car, as the cab driver powered the dark tinted window down. He smiled at Harley and Jasmine. "You order di cab?"

Harley leaned and looked inside the cab at the driver and another man in the front seat. "I'd hoped it'd be a private ride."

"Double di security," the black driver said. "Dis is a new mon, I been showing him di ropes."

Harley gave the driver the address and opened the back door for Jasmine. Handing the driver a twenty, he said, "It's just a few blocks away. Wait at the curb until she gets inside?"

"Di lady will be safe inside before I leave, suh."

Harley had a thought. Cab drivers knew a lot of people, and saw and heard a lot of things. "Say," he said, leaning a forearm on the roof of the car. "You wouldn't happen to know of a fishing boat named *Gaspar's Revenge*, would you? A big offshore fishing boat?"

The driver smiled, his big white teeth seeming to glow in his black face. "Never heard of a boat by dat name, mon."

Harley started to reach for the back door handle, when the long-haired guy in the passenger seat spoke up. "I know that boat."

Harley opened the door and Jasmine slid in, her bare thighs below her short cut-off jeans squeaking on the vinyl seats. He closed her door, then leaned down to look at the man who spoke.

"Where do you know the boat from?" Harley asked.

The man just stared back at him for a moment, his dark eyes blank, then he rubbed his thumb and fingers together. Harley took his money clip from his pocket and peeled off another twenty. He folded it lengthways and extended it to the man with his fingers. "Where?"

"Runs out of Marathon," the long-haired guy said. "No idea who the guy is, but I seen him around Boot Key Harbor a few times, picking up clients."

CHAPTER THIRTY-ONE

Detective Ben Morgan's phone rang only moments before the alarm was set to go off. It had been Ben's first good night's sleep in several days. He was fully awake when he sat up on the edge of the bed, picked up his phone and answered it. "Lieutenant Morgan."

Ben listened for a moment and said, "Okay, we'll both be there at eight." He listened another moment. "Okay, we'll all be there then. You call the other two, and I'll call her."

He said goodbye and ended the call, then scrolled through his contact list until he found Evans's number. She answered on the third ring.

"Have fun out on the boat yesterday?" Ben asked. Before she could answer, he said, "Doc Fredric just called. Meet me at the coroner's office in an hour. Jefferson and Clark are meeting us there."

"All four of us?" Evans asked.

"I don't ask why," Ben said. "Just get your butt in gear. See you at eight."

Ben ended the call and went straight to the small shower in the equally small bathroom of his little floating house. He showered quickly and dressed in one of his usual suits. Clipping his shield and holster in place, he was out the door less than half an hour after waking up.

When Ben arrived at the coroner's office, Evans's car was already in the parking lot, as was Jefferson's. He parked and was just getting out when Joe Clark pulled in and parked next to him.

"What's going on, Lieutenant?" Clark said, as he got out of his car.

"You know as much as I do, Joe," Ben replied, looking over the other detective's shoulder. "Is that the captain's car?"

Clark turned to look. "Yeah, I think it is."

They went inside, signed in, and Doc's assistant led them back to the door to the morgue. The assistant pushed a button on the keypad, waved at Doc Fredric, and went back to his desk.

Doc pulled the door open. "Please come in, Detectives. We're ready to get started."

Ben and Clark followed Doc over to where Evans was standing beside a covered body on a gurney. Jefferson was in the opposite corner, talking to Captain Simpson. The sheriff himself stood next to them, arms crossed, as the Captain explained something to Jefferson.

"Gentlemen, if you please," Doc said, loud enough to get the sheriff's attention.

"How'd you get here so fast?" Ben asked Evans in a low voice.

"I run every morning at five," she replied. "I was just getting dressed when you called. I've been talking to Doc until everyone else got here."

"What's going on?"

"He wouldn't say," Evans whispered, as Sheriff Roth turned and approached the group by the gurney.

"Tell us what you've found out, Doctor," the sheriff said, brusque and to the point, as always.

Doctor Fredric pulled the sheet down, exposing a young woman's face and shoulders. Even in death, Ben could see that she had been very beautiful. Her skin was flawless, except for the very visible bruising around her throat. Looking down, he saw that her feet weren't anywhere near the end of the table. She couldn't have been more than five feet tall.

"This is Miss Janet Sawyer," Doc said. "Her stage name is Jenae Saequa. She was a resident of San Fernando, California, where she worked in the adult entertainment industry. She is originally from Green Bay—"

"Can we cut to the chase, Doctor Fredric?" the sheriff asked.

"Certainly," Doc replied, without appearing ruffled. Ben knew the old ME was eccentric and tended to be wordy and dramatic, but he also knew Doc did this for the benefit of the junior investigators. It put them more at ease in the unfriendly environment of the morgue. He told stories, but with the heart of a teacher.

Doc looked across the gurney at Ben. "The cause of Miss Sawyer's demise was manual strangulation. Like Miss Marshall, she was murdered while having sexual intercourse."

"Rape kit?" Ben asked.

"Yes, well, she wasn't raped, Ben. At least not at first."

"How can you tell that?" Jefferson asked.

"No vaginal tears, bruising, or abrasions, Doctor?" Evans asked.

"No," the medical examiner replied. "And the swab showed traces of a personal lubricant."

"So, more than likely, she was strangled while having consensual sex?" Evans asked.

Doc's eyes locked on hers for a moment. "Yes, Devon. It's a fetish wherein the woman is choked to near unconsciousness during sex."

"Sick," the captain mumbled.

"Different, yes," Doc said and then continued. "Assuming she was put in the water soon after the murder, I estimate the time of death was between two and four, yesterday morning."

"If the old fisherman had arrived at his favorite fishing spot just a little earlier," Clark said, "he might have seen the guy."

"Or he might have been another victim," Ben said.

"The biological samples have been sent for DNA analysis," Doc continued. "After speaking to Sheriff Roth very early this morning, he called the lab and our samples are now being fast-tracked. Although Mister Isaksson's murder was different from the two women, it was connected to the murder of Miss Marshall. I also believe, and Sheriff Roth agrees, that all three murders were done by the same man."

Doc looked slowly from one detective to another. "We're now dealing with a serial killer, and I believe he will strike again."

Outside, Ben and Devon watched as the captain's SUV left. The sheriff had stayed back to talk to Doctor Fredric.

"A serial killer?" Devon said. "It doesn't make sense."

"They never do," Jefferson quipped.

The door opened, and Sheriff Roth came out and walked toward the group of detectives.

"Bring me up to speed, Ben," the sheriff said, joining the circle of investigators.

Ben glanced at Devon and saw the sparkle she always got in her eye when she'd discovered something in an investigation.

"Yes, sir," Ben said, waving a hand slightly toward Devon. "Detective Evans spent most of yesterday with a private salvage investigator, trying to locate the original murder scene."

"There's more to this than a guy who likes to screw dead girls," Devon said, bluntly. "Yesterday, we found the place where the first two murders occurred. It's about four miles north of Sawyer Key, out in the back country."

"Four miles?" Roth asked. "That's beyond the limit."

"The private contractor that Devon was with is a special agent with the federal government." Ben said. "They offered the resource as a pro bono private contractor, and I accepted."

The sheriff nodded at Devon, and she continued. "Evidence found at the murder scene included a Colt .38 Cobra that is a ballistic match to the bullet removed from what we believe is the first victim's head."

"Jimmy Isaksson," Roth said. "I went to school with his dad."

"My condolences, sir," Devon said. "The weapon is registered to Mister Lawrence Lovett, a cab driver in Key

West. The first two victims had been employed by Mister Lovett in a treasure hunt. A cash box containing money and drugs was discovered on Isaksson's stranded boat, with room enough for the gun. It's been determined that the cash box belonged to Mister Lovett."

"I sense a *but* coming," Clark said.

"But," Ben said, "we know the cash box was planted. Everyone I spoke to yesterday described Lovett as not just law-abiding, but willing to go out of his way to help others. Security videos from half a dozen bars put him in Key West at the time of our double homicide out in the Gulf."

Roth crossed his arms. "How certain are we on the time of death? Both bodies were in the water."

"Doc Fredric gave us a possible window from immediate immersion of the body to minutes before they were found, and a witness reports hearing a gunshot in that area at three o'clock that afternoon. Based on that, Lovett couldn't have been involved."

"Can't be in two places at once," Roth said. "How'd his gun and cash box get on the boat?"

"He says the cash box was stolen," Ben said. "Didn't cop to the gun until later."

"What's he hiding?" Clark asked.

"We might get a chance to find out this afternoon," Devon said.

All four men looked at her, waiting for her to continue.

"Captain McDermitt brought me and the evidence back here, yesterday," Devon said.

"McDermitt?" Roth asked. "Jesse McDermitt?"

"Yes, sir," Devon said. "He's the DHS agent that helped find the murder scene and recover the evidence."

"Good man," Roth said. "But be careful. He doesn't play nice with bad people, and the Feds he's with have been known to take some shortcuts."

"We will, sir," Devon said. "Over dinner, McDermitt told me that Mister Lovett has a silent partner in his treasure hunt. He's arranged for the Lieutenant and I to meet with Lovett and his partner, who will divulge more information. We're meeting them in two hours."

"Very good," Roth said. "Update Captain Simpson with any new developments. I want this psycho in custody as soon as humanly possible, Ben. You're authorized any overtime you need."

The sheriff left the group without another word.

"Over dinner?" Ben asked.

"Neither of us had eaten since breakfast," Devon replied. "Look, I knew Lovett was hiding something and had a hunch that McDermitt might be useful. Turns out, he's pretty sharp for a PI and apparently has unlimited resources and funding. He found the exact spot the murders took place, recovered all the evidence, and even took a sand sample. Bailey said the sand and the plant-life in it are microscopically consistent with what was found in Marshall's lungs. DNA results of the plant life, along with the gun, which was found just eight feet away, will put both murders in the same place."

"Seems you had a very productive day," Ben said. "Anything else?"

Devon opened her purse, took out an eight-by-ten photo, and handed it to Ben. "Marshall was doing a photographic survey of a possible Spanish treasure site. Mc-

Dermitt found her camera. This was the last picture on the memory card."

Ben turned the photo in several directions. "What is it?"

Devon took the photo from him, oriented it correctly, and held it up to the sky. "You're looking up at the underside of James Isaksson's boat at the time that Marshall was attacked. Right next to it is the underside of the murderer's boat."

CHAPTER THIRTY-TWO

My phone woke me not very long after I'd gone to bed. Judging from the shaft of moonlight on the foot of my bunk just below the hatch, I figured it was still several hours before dawn.

The caller ID showed it was Billy calling, and I answered it.

"Someone's is looking for you," Billy said.

"Who?"

"A guy that owns a strip club called *Rafferty's*, across the bridge from the rock. It's just off the highway on the Gulf side."

Rafferty's, I thought, recalling what Vince had said about the guy who stole the casino plane.

"An old guy?" I asked. "Maybe seventy or older? What'd he want?"

"No, not old," Billy said. "About our age."

Not a real common name, I thought. But common enough, and decades separating the guy from Jersey who stole a fortune in mob cash.

"Billy, it's the middle of the night," I said. "What? He was looking for a charter?"

There was a moment of silence. "I wouldn't wake you and the lady cop for that."

"The lady cop isn't here," I said. "We had dinner and then I walked her home."

"Then you're a dumbass, Kemosabe," Billy said, and I could see his grin in my mind. "Anyway, this guy didn't strike me as the fishing type. More like a middle-aged biker."

"What'd you tell him?"

"Lawrence told him that he'd never heard of your boat," Billy replied. "Knowing you'd prefer to meet trouble—and he looked like trouble—on your own turf, I told him I'd seen the boat around Boot Key, and knew you chartered out of there."

I only knew a handful of people down here at the end of US-1, and none of them owned or even worked at a topless joint. I probably hadn't been in one since I was a corporal.

"He'll have to wait in line," I said, dismissing it as someone just looking for a charter, or at worst, to run pot or something. "While I got you, I need both you and Lawrence at the *Anchor* tomorrow, er, today at noon."

I heard him and Lawrence talking, then Billy said, "We'll be there."

"And tell Lawrence that he needs to call Vince and have him there, too. Tell him that both he and Vince need to let the cops know what it was they were *really* looking for out there off Snipe and Sawyer Keys."

I ended the call and went up to the salon. I poured two fingers of Pusser's rum and sat down on the settee with my laptop. Sipping from the glass, I looked over at Finn, lying by the hatch. He lifted his head, cocking it sideways.

"It's not morning yet," I told him. "I just need to think a bit."

Finn lay his head on his outstretched paws, as I powered up the laptop. He didn't go back to sleep, but just watched me, with those intelligent-looking amber eyes, as if saying he was ready for any adventure I could come up with.

Waiting for the computer to boot up, I sipped my rum and thought about the girl. After dinner, we'd wandered around Old Town, even stopped in a small jazz club I knew for a nightcap. We'd talked about our time in the Corps, but the only people we came up with in common were those the other only knew by name.

When we finally strolled down Carsten Lane, near the old Key West Cemetery, it was after midnight. She stopped at a cracked sidewalk that led to a small covered porch. The little porch and the house beyond were almost hidden by lush tropical vegetation.

"I'm not going to ask you inside," she said.

Though she'd been flirting throughout the day, that statement had at first made me think that flirty was just the way she was, and she wasn't really interested. Then she grabbed my short beard in both hands and asked if I was always so shaggy.

"I wore a high-and-tight for a good five years after I retired," I told her. "Guess I've just gotten lazy in my old age."

Then Devon laughed and told me she liked the scruffy look. She pulled my face to hers and kissed me. I'm not surprised easily. And the only people who seem to be able to make me feel like a blithering idiot are women.

She'd left me standing there in astonishment and had only glanced back just before closing the door. I'd wandered aimlessly back down Southard to Duval Street, taking the long way back to the Bight, and stopped at *Sloppy Joe's* for one more beer.

When the screen came up, I clicked on the Google icon and searched for *Rafferty's*. That got about a billion results, so I added more keywords to the search, until I found *Rafferty's Pub*, over on Stock Island. The top results were links to Google Maps, Yellow Pages, Yelp, and Manta, which I knew meant only one thing. Sure enough, when I scrolled further, I didn't find a website for the place. All of the first two pages of results were websites that mentioned it.

Clicking on the "News" tab, I wasn't surprised to find a lot of news stories detailing arrests and disturbances at or involving *Rafferty's*, but nothing more recent than a year ago. Glancing at each story's summary, I quickly noticed a common theme: drugs, drunks, derelicts, and hookers. I clicked on the most recent news story in the Key West Citizen about a shooting that had occurred there. There was only a picture of the bar, probably from the newspaper's archives, but no details about the owner, though it did give his name. The shooting had happened in the parking lot, between two drunk bikers. Both were locals, both were shot in the leg, and both had been taken to jail.

"Exciting place," I said aloud. Finn lifted his head slightly—one side of it, anyway. Sort of a chilled head-tilt. "Not our kind of exciting, boy."

He put his head back down as I searched through several more news stories. I did find the same archive photo a couple of times. But I didn't find any picture of the owner, Bill Rafferty. I wrote the name down on a pad and turned off the laptop. I'd been in a lot of places like *Rafferty's Pub*. But not in a long time. Some places I'd visited would make this one look like a knitting circle. Even to my untrained eye, I knew there was prostitution and illegal drug activity going on there.

So, what did the owner of a nest of rattlesnakes want with me? Or more accurately, with the *Revenge*? Sure, she turns heads in any port. But a biker bar? Maybe the guy saw her in the Bight?

Or maybe he saw her out on the Gulf, I thought.

Lifting my glass, I drained the last swallow. It was late, and tomorrow looked to be a busy day. I used the head before going back to bed. Washing my hands and face, I looked in the mirror. The guy looking back was the same guy I'd seen there every day since I graduated boot camp and became a Marine. The kid I'd been before that summer had ceased to exist on that day.

I looked closer at my own face, separating the familiarity in my mind. The lines at the corners of my eyes were white, from a lifetime spent squinting in the bright sun. They hadn't always been there, nor had they been so deep. I'd first noticed them when I was in my early twenties. Back then, they were tan lines and the creases smoothed out under normal lights.

Damn, I thought. *That was almost a quarter of a century ago.*

The same green eyes stared back at me, though they now seemed to be a little less vigorous than I remembered. The biggest change was my hair and beard. There were a few grays at my temples now and if I'd had a shirt on, my hair would have been over my collar. There were quite a few more grays sprinkled down my jaw. I ran both hands through my hair, pulling it behind my ears.

At least I'm not bald, I thought, picturing Rusty in my mind.

I went back to bed and was asleep before my head hit the pillow, but not for very long. It seemed like I'd only just closed my eyes when the alarm—aka my coffee maker—went off, the smell of Costa Rica's finest filling my sleeping nostrils.

A hot cup on the bridge brought me back to life as I watched the rising sun silhouette Old Town in hazy gray shadows. As crazy and weird as it sometimes is, I still love Key West. Not for the rowdy tourist nightlife, but for moments like this. I can picture it like it must have been two centuries ago. Before *Useless One*, before the railroad, back when the *Revenge* would have been a schooner.

Movement on the dock caught my eye. It was early and few people were moving around yet, so the running woman drew my eye. I was pretty sure it was Devon. She had a long stride, and was obviously used to running along the sometimes-crowded waterfront. She glanced my way, saw me, and waved as she turned off the dock at

Schooner Wharf. She disappeared up William Street and I lost her. But I was sure it was Devon.

Finn and I walked a block to Pepe's on Caroline Street, where we both had a hearty breakfast of fresh eggs, bacon, and fried potatoes. Half an hour later, I tossed the lines and idled out of Key West Bight.

The sun was fully above the horizon now, as I turned south into the channel. I fished a pair of sunglasses from the overhead, put them on, and turned east around Whitehead Spit, speeding toward the rising sun at thirty knots. I wasn't in a hurry, but I did want to grab a shower when I got to the *Anchor.*

I spent the time mulling over why someone would want to kill Isaksson and the girl. Thinking like a criminal was difficult for me. The enemy on the battlefield, I could understand, but the civilian who commits crimes against other people for personal gain or a cheap thrill, I didn't get. Not naturally, anyway.

My friend Andrew Bourke would say their brains are wired differently; he'd been going to school to learn more about the criminal mind. He and Paul Bender would likely arrive today. Paul would be the closest thing Deuce's new endeavor would have to an actual investigator. He'd been a police detective before the Secret Service, and had since earned a degree in forensic psychology. Both men were very capable, and I trusted them.

Could the nut in the boat yesterday have had anything to do with it? Maybe someone did have a grudge against Lawrence. Maybe he'd stepped on some toes he wasn't aware of. I just couldn't draw a connection between the murders and the old Androsian. Well, aside from the fact that the victims were working for him when they were murdered, his money box and gun had been stolen and left at the scene of the crime, and the gun had been used to kill James.

Devon kept interrupting my thought process, though I was hard put to say why. *It was just a kiss*, I told myself.

And several hours of conversation about a wide range of topics. And a comfort level that was unusual for me. We had the immediate bond of service in the Corps, but that quickly grew and I felt like I could talk to her easier than most women I'd met.

And I'd met quite a few. After all, it was the Keys and Key West.

These little islands at the end of the Florida peninsula have drawn wanderers, vagabonds, romantics, and pirates for centuries. Today, there is always an abundant availability of tourist women. Most of the people who come here are looking for a few days of escapism, including women. Vegas has nothing on the Keys. What happens here is quickly left behind and never mentioned again. But mutually using one another, while physically enjoyable, always seemed to leave me feeling empty inside.

It took almost two hours, but the ride was pleasant enough. I slowed to an idle before I entered Rusty's canal. The empty pad at the boat ramp reminded me that I needed to get back to Labelle to get the *Hopper*. As expected, the debris from the storm was completely cleaned up. Except for the stage, which was still sitting on top of Dink's skiff. Something about it was different, though. The stage looked like it had settled; the bottom now rode just above the water all the way around the boat. As I idled past, I could see that it was intentional. The stage was now attached to the boat, and the center console and some of the stage's deck planks had been removed.

Rusty came out of the bar as I shifted the port engine to reverse, putting the *Revenge* into a slow spin in the turning basin. He stepped out onto the barge, kicked three fenders over the side, and headed toward my bow with a boat hook in hand. Seeing that the boat was drifting right to where I wanted it, I put the transmissions in neutral and killed the engines. Climbing quickly down the ladder to the cockpit, I looped the stern line onto one of the barge's deck cleats, just as the *Revenge* bumped the fenders.

"What the heck are you doing to Dink's boat?" I asked, as I stepped up onto the barge.

"It ain't Dink's anymore," Rusty said. "Bought it last night. Like it?"

"What is it?"

"The *Rusty Taxi*," he replied with a broad grin.

I looked at the monstrosity again and it hit me. The stage had been a narrow pentagon about twelve feet wide and twenty feet long. It had been at the corner of the deck, extending along the back to where the deck jogged forty-five degrees. That jog was now the starboard bow. The stage now fit over the entire deck of the low twenty-foot skiff, and it had sort of a boat shape to it.

"I'm gonna sell the outboard and put a little fifty horse on it, build a Tiki bar where the console was, and put the steering wheel at the end of the wraparound bar."

"A water taxi for boat drunks?"

"Pretty much," he replied as we walked toward the bar. Finn took off across the backyard, headed toward his favorite sandbar, stopping only to pee on a tree.

"I leave for one day," I said, "and you're already on to some crazy new scheme. You got enough work right here, without going out and running a water taxi."

"I ain't gonna run it," he replied, opening the door to the bar. "I already have four applications from bartenders with boating experience, or boat people with bartending experience. Hell, it could become a tourist attraction. The Middle Keys' only floating Tiki bar taxi."

I laughed and went through the door, pausing to let my eyes adjust to the dim light inside. Two familiar faces were looking at me from the bar and Andrew Bourke's baritone voice announced, "Good Lord, the man's gone native."

I spent the next half hour catching up with him and Paul Bender, and bringing them up to speed on what we'd learned so far. Both men had been a part of Deuce's team, Andrew from the Coast Guard and Paul from the Secret Service.

Excusing myself half an hour before noon, I went back down to the *Revenge*. Finn was napping in the cockpit—probably sleeping off a meal of clams. Before showering, I looked at myself in the mirror again and decided to shave. It took two disposables and fifteen minutes to get the job done, but after showering and changing into clean boat clothes, I felt better.

My phone vibrated in my pocket and I pulled it out, stepping up into the salon. The number wasn't familiar, but it was local, so I answered it.

"What the hell's this about meeting with the cops?" I heard Vince O'Hare's gruff voice ask.

"You should be here already," I told him. "Where are you?"

"I'm at my house, ya dumb ox. You tryin' to set me up, or something?"

"Look, O'Hare, I know you're not a big fan of authority. But, like it or not, I think this deal you and Lawrence are involved in is what got the Isaksson kid killed."

"What makes you think that?" he asked, suspiciously.

"Oh, I don't know," I said, sarcastically. "Might be that Lawrence's gun was used to kill him, and Lawrence's money box was found on his boat with drugs in it."

"Drugs? Lawrence don't do drugs."

"I know," I said, getting irritated. "Look, the cops are gonna want to talk to you. If you'd prefer, they can come to your house, or maybe hold you for a whole day, like they did him. *Or* you can be at Rusty's in about ten minutes and tell them what you know, like the concerned citizen I know you are."

I ended the call, filled a thermos with coffee and went up to the bridge. O'Hare's a grumpy old guy, but I knew he'd show. If nothing else, he'd want to find out what happened to James.

From the fly bridge, all was quiet but for the soft sound of someone playing a guitar. The sun was high overhead, the sky was blue, and the wind came gently out of the east at about five knots. It'd be a good day to try to catch that big bone.

Instead, I sat in my chair, facing aft, and watched the goings-on in Rusty's little marina community. All the regular live-aboards' boats were back, tied up in their usual spots. Some had chosen to bug out in advance of the storm, taking refuge up along the southwest Florida coast. My own hurricane hole is just a couple of hours away, several miles up Shark River. *Leap of Faith*, the boat that had taken refuge during the storm, was gone, probably moved on out to Boot Key Harbor. Robinson had said they were going to meet up with their friends there, to cross over to the Bahamas together.

Vince had told me that Lawrence received a message, warning him to back off. Back off what? The treasure hunt? Or the other cash treasure that they were both convinced was out there? Or, as I'd wondered earlier, had Lawrence just stepped on the wrong person's toes? He was always trying to help others out of jams. Maybe he'd gotten in over his head trying to help some Key West wharf rat.

A blue sedan pulled into the parking lot and parked next to Devon's brown one. The cars were alike in every detail, except for the color. Devon got out of the passenger side, dressed in jeans and sneakers, with a blue blazer covering a light blue blouse. She didn't look like a cop.

Morgan got out of the driver's side, looking very much like a cop, in his typical suit and tie. As they headed toward the door of the bar, Devon looked all around the parking lot and yard. *Head on a swivel*, Russ used to say. I guess he wasn't the only platoon sergeant who trained his Marines to be always aware of their situation. As the two detectives neared the door, she saw my boat. She said something to Morgan, who glanced my way for a second, and then continued inside.

Devon turned and approached the *Revenge*. I climbed down and met her at the gunwale. "Cup of coffee?" I offered, extending my hand. "We have a few minutes. Everyone's not here yet."

"You shaved," she said, taking my hand and stepping aboard.

"It's more me," I said, leading the way up to the bridge, where I poured a cup for her from my thermos.

She sat down on the port bench, studying my face. "Yeah, I'm inclined to agree. Going back to the high and tight, too?"

"Naw," I said, running my fingers through my hair. "I kinda like it like this now."

"Who are we waiting for?" She took a sip of her coffee. "Mmm, thanks. This is good."

"The owner of the *Anchor* gets it." I nodded over my shoulder toward the bar. "You'll meet him. Rusty and I went through boot camp together. The coffee's from a little farm in Costa Rica."

I placed my mug on the dash. "Lawrence's partner is a local lobsterman, Vince O'Hare. He's a salty old cuss who doesn't much like the government, or cops, or anyone else for that matter."

"Cuss?" she asked. "My grandfather used to say that."

"I was raised by my grandparents. Guess some of my ways are a little old-fashioned on account of that."

"Known this lobsterman a long time?"

"Not really, and not well," I replied. "He's lived here all his life, but pretty much keeps to himself since his wife died several years ago."

"So, what's this earth-shaking news he's going to tell us about?"

I thought about it a moment. "Probably better if you wait and hear what he and Lawrence have to say first. I might be completely wrong, or you might pick up on it yourself and not need my input at all."

I could tell something else was on her mind, so I just looked out over the little marina and waited for her to get the words right in her mind.

She took another sip and set her mug next to mine. "About last night."

"What about it?" I asked, watching a decrepit old Dodge pickup pull into the parking area, followed by Lawrence's cab.

"I may have given you the wrong impression," she said.

Not the first time I'd heard that. *Here comes the attempt at an easy let-down.* "Oh?" I asked, turning and considering her big brown eyes. "I find it's easier to just say what's on my mind rather than try to make an impression and have people take it wrong."

"Okay," she said, and took a deep breath. "I like you and I was very tempted to invite you in last night. And then your poor dog probably wouldn't have gotten his steak until breakfast."

Thankfully, the sound of three car doors got her attention.

Why the hell am I always getting women's signals crossed? "They're here," I stammered. "We'd better get inside."

CHAPTER THIRTY-THREE

After making the deposit at the bank, Harley had dropped Duke off at the home of one of his regular street dealers. Tim had a boat, and owed Harley a favor. Tim took Duke to where he'd stashed the boat and then followed him out to a half mile beyond Pelican Shoal.

Before abandoning the rental boat, Duke had stuck a rag in the gas tank and lit it. The little boat had exploded in a fireball when they were just a hundred yards away. Duke had done this before. The hot fire would consume the fiberglass boat quickly and completely, right down to the waterline. Then the weight of the motor would pull it down to the bottom, more than a hundred and fifty feet below.

As they motored away from the burning wreckage, Duke remembered that he'd left his bag in the fish box. In it was a change of clothes, a little jar with an eight-ball of blow, and some of what he called his muscle drugs. It also held the GPS that had been in the cab driver's money box, when he'd paid a street whore to steal it for him.

Harley's gonna be pissed, Duke thought. He hadn't told Harley about the GPS yet. Maybe it was better if he didn't. He'd learned about the people diving near their place a week ago and had watched them from a distance with binoculars. When the taxi driver came out, Duke had followed him back to Key West, then went back and told Harley. His brother had set things up carefully from the start.

It was nearly sunrise when Tim dropped him off at Sugarloaf Marina. Exhausted, Duke climbed into the little cave-like vee-berth below the foredeck and slept till past noon.

A buzzing noise woke him. The noise stopped, and Duke flopped back on the pillow, closing his eyes. The buzzing started again, and Duke sat up, looking around the little cabin. The noise was coming from the salon. Stumbling through the little doorway, he found the source of the buzzing. He hadn't turned up the ringer on the new phone Harley had given him and it was vibrating on the small table.

When Duke answered it, his brother started chewing him out for being late again. "I did what ya told me, Harley. It was almost sunrise when I got home. I hadda sleep."

"Meanwhile," Harley said, "Waldo's halfway to Georgia. Did you forget about him?"

"Naw, I didn't forget. Tim told me last night that he heard Waldo moved to a trailer park on Ramrod. Shouldn't be hard to find."

"That's your job for today, little brother. Find Waldo. He owes me five grand. If he doesn't have the whole five grand, knock his ass out and take something worth what he owes for collateral. You know what that means?"

"Sure, Harley. Something worth a lot more than he owes, so he's sure to come get it when he has the money."

"Close enough," Harley said. "Bring either the cash or the collateral to the club. And call me at sunset if you haven't found him. I might have something else for you to do."

It didn't take Duke long to find Waldo's car. A blue hearse with pictures of parrots and fish painted on it stuck out anywhere. Waldo's new place was a step up from his old one. In the circle of people Waldo hung with, Duke knew that this meant he'd probably spent Harley's money. A gray Toyota 'Keys car' was parked behind the hearse. Both cars combined didn't look to be worth five thousand.

Duke circled the block. There were two trailers right behind Waldo's with *For Sale* signs taped in their front windows. Duke parked in the common driveway between them and got out. He hadn't seen another car in the trailer park, other than Waldo's and the Toyota. This was a working-class trailer park, so it was doubtful there was anyone in any of them.

Walking between the two trailers, he pretended to be looking at the one with the facing door, just in case there was a neighbor snooping. Not seeing anyone, or any drapes moving, he crossed the small backyard to Waldo's trailer and knelt by one of the tall, skinny windows.

Looking through it, all he could see was a bed on his left, at eye level, and a closet door straight ahead. He moved to the other window and looked in. The bed was to the right of this window and directly ahead was a hallway that led to the front of the trailer. Waldo was turned partly away from him, sitting in one of those swiveling barrel kind of chairs, with his arms draped over the sides.

There didn't appear to be anyone home at the trailer facing the back of Waldo's place, so Duke moved along the side to the back door. It was unlocked. As quietly as he could, Duke mounted the three metal steps and slowly pulled the door open. He stuck his head in just far enough to see Waldo. His head was leaning back now, and his eyes were closed.

This is almost too easy, Duke thought, as he stepped up into the trailer. Moving slowly toward him, Duke could see over Waldo's shoulder. He instantly recognized Waldo's girlfriend, Tammy. All she had on was a bra and panties. Her red, orange, and yellow hair bobbed up and down in Waldo's lap.

When Duke took another step toward the living room, the floor creaked under his weight and Waldo turned, looking right at him. Duke moved quickly, but he didn't need to. As Waldo stood and tried to run for the door, forgetting that his pants were down around his ankles, he tripped and fell forward, knocking Tammy aside. He came down head-first onto the edge of a heavy wooden table, and flopped onto his side like a dead fish.

Tammy screamed, but Duke was on her in a second, smothering her face with his big right hand to muffle her scream. She tried to struggle against him, but he was behind her and in complete control of the much smaller woman.

Looking over at Waldo, he could see the man was still breathing, but he already had a huge bluish knot on his forehead. Looking around the room, he saw Tammy's shirt lying on the floor by the chair. He grabbed it and quickly gagged the woman with it. Reaching over, Duke grabbed the end of Waldo's belt and yanked it free. He used the man's web belt to tightly tie Tammy's arms, crossed elbow to palm. behind her back.

Getting to his feet, Duke looked around the room. Beside the chair was a small table. On it was a mirror, and what looked like a couple grams of coke. He picked it up, along with a short plastic straw that was lying next to it, then turned and looked down at Tammy.

Duke had only seen her a few times, but knew she was Waldo's girl. Whenever he'd seen her, she'd always been wearing baggy jeans and shirts. The weird hair colors and black horn-rimmed glasses she wore were distracting. Her roots were a dark red, changing to a brighter red, then orange, yellow, and almost white at the tips. He'd seen her on the back of Waldo's old Triumph, before he'd wrecked it. Her hair streaming behind her in the wind made it look like her head was on fire.

She had scooted away to the corner and was looking up at Duke, fear in her eyes. She wore only black panties and a blue bra that pushed her tits up, making them look bigger. But it was her tattoos that really caught Duke's attention.

Brightly colored parrots flew around Tammy's shoulders, and multicolored fish swam across her hips in two schools, heading down into her panties. Long, slender octopus tentacles twined up both her legs, beginning at her feet and stretching up to mid-thigh. One reached all the way to her crotch. It wasn't a lot of any one thing, and where her skin wasn't tattooed, she was pale white and flawless.

Duke took a step toward her and she cowered in fear. "Is this my brother's coke?" Duke asked, putting the straw to his nose and sniffing up one of the lines. Thumbing his nose, he answered his own question, as if it was proof positive. "Oh yeah, definitely Harley's."

Tammy tried to say something, but the shirt in her mouth muffled her voice. Her eyes went to Waldo, reminding Duke that he still needed to hogtie the dealer before he woke up. Duke put the mirror down and looked around again. The window behind Waldo's chair had blinds that were pulled down and closed. Taking a switchblade from his pocket, Duke quickly cut the lines from several sets of blinds. They were very thin, but made of braided nylon and plenty strong enough. He bound Waldo's hands first, then went to where Tammy sat with her back against a wall.

When he knelt to tie her feet, she kicked at him. He grabbed her ankle and stood up, lifting her by one leg and banging the side of her head on the floor. He easily hoisted her up until her foot was nearly touching the ceiling, and her groin was at eye level. The proximity excited him.

"We can do this the hard way if you want," Duke snarled at the wriggling woman. "I don't have no problem beating up a girl. Or I can put you down and we can do things the easy way. I might even take that gag off, so you can tell me where my brother's money is."

Tammy stopped struggling and Duke looked down at her face. She nodded her head and he slowly lowered her to the floor. A moment later, he had both her and Waldo's feet tied securely, and knelt beside her.

Her body was like a work of art. The tropical birds and fish only covered a small portion of her skin, but it was like it made her look even better. Duke had thought her to be pudgy under those baggy clothes, but her body was firm and toned.

"I'm going to take that gag out," he said. "I need you to tell me where Waldo keeps his cash. I ain't gonna take it all, just the five gees he owes Harley. Now, if you scream, I'm just gonna have to punch your lights out and find it myself. Okay?"

She nodded and he pulled the gag down over her chin. "He doesn't have much left," she said, breathlessly. "I told him it was a bad idea to cross Harley, but he said he could make it up with the next front. He was gonna call him, I swear."

"Where is it?" Duke asked.

"In the bedroom. There's a nightstand under the window. There's, well, toys and stuff in it. In the back is a big jar. His money's in there."

"Thanks." Duke pulled the gag back up over Tammy's mouth and patted her on the cheek. "That wasn't so hard, was it?"

Duke went to the bedroom and opened the drawer of the nightstand. In it was a collection of multi-colored dildos, some way bigger than anatomically possible, and even a couple that strapped on. He reached into the back and took the jar out. Opening it, he saw that there was indeed a roll of cash inside.

Carrying the jar to the living room, Duke sat down in Waldo's chair. He took the roll of bills out, tossed the jar aside, and started counting. When he finished, he looked at the unconscious Waldo. Then he slowly looked around at the living room's cheap furnishings, until his gaze fell on Tammy. "There's only about a grand here."

Tammy tried to say something, so Duke stepped over and jerked the gag down. "Where's the rest?"

"He spent it," Tammy said. "A deal came up on this trailer and we had to move fast on it. He'll make good on it, though. I promise, Duke. He's coming into a bunch of money on Monday."

Waldo started to stir, and Duke looked over at him. "He's gonna be okay, but that knot on his head's gonna hurt a while." He looked back down at Tammy. "I need something worth more than four grand for collateral. Where's the valuables?"

"Valuables?" Tammy asked. "What do you mean?"

"I'm takin' this thousand dollars," Duke said, waving the bills, then folding them into his pocket. "Waldo owes Harley four thousand more. So, I gotta take Harley something that's worth more than that, to make sure that Waldo brings the money. It's called collateral."

"I know what it means," Tammy snarled. "But Waldo ain't got anything worth that much. Even both our cars combined ain't worth four thousand dollars."

Waldo rolled over on his back and groaned. Duke glanced over at him. "That true, Waldo? You don't have anything worth what you owe my brother?"

The man struggled to turn his body so he could see Duke. "You got it all wrong, Duke," he pleaded. "I got money coming in. Guaranteed, man. I'll pay Harley every penny with interest on Monday."

"Harley told me to get collateral, or kill you," Duke lied. "What you got worth four grand?"

"I don't have anything worth that," Waldo said. "But I will on Monday. I swear, man."

Duke turned his head slowly to Tammy, looking up her octopus-snared legs to the little fish swimming across her flat hips and down into her panties. His eyes lingered on her boobs and the parrots soaring above them, then moved up to her flaming hair. On a chubby chick with glasses, the hair just looked funny. On a tatted-up hard-body, it was arousing.

"Y'all wait here," Duke said, standing up. "I gotta bring my Jeep around. I think I know what you can use for collateral until Monday."

CHAPTER THIRTY-FOUR

Finn followed us across the yard to the door. I held it for him and Devon, and he went straight to his water bowl and rug in the corner. I walked Devon to the bar and introduced her to Rusty, who was talking to Morgan.

"Your friend was just telling me how he was able to figure out where the dive site was," Morgan said.

"He's got salt water in his blood," I said. "With a full moon rising, he leans to the east. If a question involves wind, tides, or currents, Rusty's the guy to talk to."

"Y'all got the tables I pushed together in the corner," Rusty said.

I looked around. Vince sat with his back to the wall in the other corner with Lawrence and Billy. They were huddled close, and it looked like Billy was doing most of the talking.

Bourke and Bender were sitting at a table in the middle, talking with Tony, who must have arrived while I was showering. The door opened and Deuce stepped inside, walking straight toward us.

Deuce shook hands with the two detectives. "Another of my associates is at our communications center," he said, lifting the strap of the laptop bag hanging over his shoulder. "She'll be following along and providing anything technical."

"I usually prefer to conduct interviews like this at the station," Morgan said. "I don't think I've ever had a meeting in a bar."

"The *Anchor* is more than a bar," I said. "It's a gathering spot and a place to conduct business and discuss the news of the day for locals."

We moved to the corner, where Morgan took the chair at one end of the two tables and Deuce set up his laptop at the other end. Rusty went to the front door, turned the open sign around and locked the door.

Once everyone was seated, Deuce said, "Let's get introductions out of the way, first. Detectives Morgan and Evans, these are some of the employees of Livingston and Associates Security."

I glanced up at him. "That was fast."

"Yeah, well, the paperwork got a little push from Uncle Sam." Looking at Ben, he continued. "You know Jesse, Lawrence, and Billy. Billy is representing both Lawrence and his partner, Vince O'Hare. As of yesterday, Billy has accepted a position with our firm, and Mister Lovett put us on retainer. While we're still employed by the federal government, we are acting as a private security firm, hired by Mister Lovett."

"Why?" Ben asked. "Lovett's already been cleared of the murders."

"The murders of two of his employees," Deuce said. "It goes beyond clearing his name. Mister Lovett wants to find those responsible and bring them to justice."

"And just who are you people?" Ben asked. "I've been a cop here for a long time and never heard of Livingston and Associates."

"All of us are, or soon will be, former agents with Homeland Security," Deuce replied, unflustered. And why not? Sitting around the table were some serious snake eaters. Whether they'd been heard of in Key West didn't detract from that in any way. Deuce nodded at the barrel-chested man with the big mustache next to him. "Andrew Bourke, former Master Chief Petty Officer in the Coast Guard's Maritime Enforcement. Next to him is Paul Bender. Paul's a former agent with the Secret Service's Presidential Detail and holds a PhD in forensic psychology."

Nodding at Tony, Deuce continued, "Tony Jacobs, Navy SEAL chief petty officer and explosives expert."

"Impressive," Morgan said. "And you are Commander Russell Livingston, former commanding officer of the Naval Special Warfare Development Group, in Dam Neck, Virginia, and former Associate Secretary of Homeland Security."

"I see you did your homework," I said.

"Yes, I did," Morgan said, then looked back to Deuce. "You left out a couple of backgrounds, Commander. Your attorney was a Marine, as was Mister McDermitt."

"Is," Devon corrected him.

"Yes, well. At any rate, there's an open investigation that was quietly buried in the tombs in Fort Myers some years ago." Morgan looked at me and asked, "Were you and Mister Rainwater in the Everglades together five years ago?"

Billy had been talking quietly with Vince, but looked up suddenly. Billy and I have known each other practically our whole lives and it was the first time I'd ever seen him surprised.

Morgan was waiting for me to react. I looked him straight in the eyes and held his gaze for several seconds. "Yeah," I finally replied. "Billy and I used to hunt and fish the Glades every fall, before school started. We decided to do it again in 2003."

His eyes never left mine. "A successful hunt?"

"Yes," I replied, staring back. "Very successful."

"I don't have a problem with that," Morgan finally said. "I hate cold cases and it's outside Monroe County. Just wanted to see if you'd tell me the truth."

"Is something going on here I should know about?" Deuce asked.

My eyes continued to bore into Morgan's. Finally, he looked up at Deuce. "You neglected to say that you and Captain McDermitt have a shared relationship with the president."

"The fishing trip?" Deuce asked. "Yeah, a couple years ago, President Bush came down here for a little fishing."

Morgan reached into his inside jacket pocket and took out a folded sheet of paper and slid it across to Devon. "That's an official White House email," he said. "Addressed to Mister Bender, and copied to Sheriff Roth and Doctor Fredric. In it, the president wishes Mister Bender great success in his new endeavor with Misters Livingston and McDermitt, who he specifically calls Deuce and Jesse."

Devon looked at the paper. Over her shoulder, I could clearly see the logo of the White House. "Whoa," she said, looking at me. "You've got some friends in high places."

"Yeah," I said. "We're old fishing buddies. Can we get on with this? I'd like to get back to causing some sore lips myself."

Deuce spun his laptop around. "This is our IT expert, Chyrel Koshinski, formerly with DHS and a CIA computer analyst before that."

"Hey, Detectives," Chyrel said from the video link to the island. She was sitting in front of a blank wooden wall, which I recognized, because I'd cut the boards and nailed them in place myself.

"So, where do we start?" Deuce asked.

Morgan looked over at Lawrence and Vince, and then back at Deuce. "It seems that your clients have some information that they've withheld from our investigation. How about I tell you what we have, and let them fill in the blanks. We're all here to catch a serial killer."

"Serial killer?" Deuce asked. "I thought the criteria for that was three murders."

Devon turned toward me. "The body that was recovered yesterday morning was a prostitute. Manually strangled while having sex."

CHAPTER THIRTY-FIVE

D uke still hadn't seen a soul in the trailer park. He backed his Jeep into the neighbor's driveway and turned sharply in the grass behind the hearse, backing as close to Waldo's door as he could get. It was late afternoon, and people would be getting home soon. He got out and went back inside the trailer. Waldo was still laying on the floor where he'd been left, but Tammy had wiggled over closer to him.

"Aw, you're anxious to leave?" Duke asked, as he stepped over Waldo and sat down on the table, facing them both. Tammy's eyes showed equal amounts of fear and hatred. Waldo was just pissed, but both were gagged and couldn't answer.

"Here's the deal," Duke said, looking straight at Waldo. "You owe my brother five large and I got one from the jar. So, you still owe Harley four thousand. Nod if you're with me."

Waldo nodded, his eyebrows furrowed in anger. Duke looked over at Tammy and nodded his head questioningly. She nodded back.

"Okay, since you got no collateral for the four grand," Duke said, "I'm gonna take Tammy with me." Both started shaking their heads vigorously. Duke ignored their silent protests. "You can come and get her back on Monday when you bring the money."

Duke straightened a leg and took his switchblade from his pocket, flicking it open. The gag in Tammy's mouth muffled her scream. Duke flipped the knife end over end, into the kitchen, where the tip stuck deeply into the face of a cabinet, the shaft quivering.

"When you're feeling up to it," Duke said, standing up, "scoot yourself in there and you can cut that cord."

Tammy squirmed and tried to inchworm away from Duke. He took a long step toward her, grabbed a fistful of hair, and brought her around as she struggled to a sitting position. "Remember, I said I don't have a problem with hitting a girl?"

Tears streamed from her eyes, but she nodded.

"Good," Duke said, patting the side of her face again. He bent over and easily scooped her up off the floor. Transferring her to one shoulder, he stepped over Waldo and opened the door.

Turning back, he said, "Bring my knife on Monday, too."

Duke stepped out onto the porch as if carrying a half-naked, flame-headed, tattooed woman was as normal as carrying out the garbage. He quickly descended the steps and carried Tammy to his Jeep. Unsnapping the cover, he flipped it back and laid the woman in the Jeep's small bed.

Snapping the cover back in place he said, "Plenty of air gets in there, you'll be okay." A moment later, he was on Highway One, headed south to the club.

It was just getting dark when Duke pulled into the rear parking lot of *Rafferty's Pub*, parked and got out. He debated leaving Tammy in the bed, but thought she might start kicking if someone pulled in.

Throwing back the cover from the small bed, he lowered the tailgate and pulled Tammy out until her tentacled legs hung over the end. He hoisted her to his shoulder and slammed the tailgate closed.

Duke went in the back door and opened the big walk in cooler just inside. It was cold in there, but Duke figured she'd be okay for the few minutes she'd be in there, while he found Harley.

Tammy was trembling as Duke set her on her bare feet inside the cooler. The cold made her nipples stand out through the thin fabric of her little blue push-up bra. Again, he patted the side of her face, then let his hand fall to her breast, giving it a squeeze.

"I'll be back in just a minute," Duke said. "You be quiet here, and you just might make it out of this alive."

He closed the door to the cooler and went down the hall to Harley's office. He tapped on the door, then opened it, sticking his head in. Harley wasn't there. He went out into the bar, the deep bass nailing him as soon as he opened the door. Brandy was on the stage, and a new girl was giving a guy a lap dance at a table in the corner.

Duke walked over to the bar, where Kenny was polishing a shot glass, and asked him where Harley was.

"Left a coupla hours ago," Kenny leaned over the bar and shouted. "Said he was goin' to Marathon. He should be back any—" Kenny stopped and pointed with his chin toward the front door. "There he is now."

Duke looked toward the door and jerked a thumb to the back when Harley looked at him. His brother nodded, and Duke went back to the office and waited for Harley.

"Did you find him?" Harley asked as he entered the office.

"Yeah," Duke replied, pulling the wad of bills from his pocket and placing them on the desk. "Easy as pie. But all he had was a thousand in cash."

Harley frowned. "You get some collateral?"

"Dude didn't have much," Duke said. "Follow me." He led his brother toward the back door, stopped, and opened the cooler, pointing inside. "Only thing he had worth a crap."

Harley looked inside, then looked back at Duke, confused. "You kidnapped his girl? Are you nuts?"

"Everything the dude owns wouldn't add up to enough to cover his debt, Harley. He said he's coming into some big money on Monday and he'll come and get her."

"On Monday?" Harley said, closing the cooler door. "And what the hell are we supposed to do with her until then? Monday's more'n two days away. We gonna feed her till then?"

Duke looked down at his shoes. "I guess I didn't think of that."

Harley pushed the back door open and stepped outside, leaving the door ajar. Duke could tell his brother was mad, as he watched him pace back and forth, like he did when he was thinking.

Harley stopped pacing and looked at Duke. "She don't have any clothes on, man. Why don't she have— Never mind, I don't wanna know." He paced a moment more and finally said, "It's your thing, man. You take care of it. Take her to the warehouse and keep her there. Feed her, give her water, and let her use the bathroom. And, Duke?" He waited till the man-giant looked up at him. "Don't kill her, okay?"

Duke grinned. "She'll be okay, Harley. I'll take good care of her."

CHAPTER THIRTY-SIX

"All the circumstantial evidence we have," Morgan said, "points directly at you, Mister Lovett. More than enough to get a conviction just twenty years ago."

"It's the forensic evidence that's cleared you," Devon said. "A single strand of the killer's hair rules you out, along with security video cameras all over Key West indicating you were there when the murders occurred."

Morgan leaned forward, his elbows on the table. "Someone's trying to make it look like you did it. I want to know who that someone is."

Lawrence looked across Billy at Vince, who nodded. "If it'll help you catch whoever killed Dwight's boy, we'll tell ya what we know."

"First," Devon said, "let's back up a little. There's a loose end that needs to get nailed down. I can understand you not reporting the theft of the cash box. Things like that rarely get solved and your time would be better spent doing just about anything else. But the gun? Why wouldn't you report it being stolen?"

Lawrence hung his head for a moment. "Dat was a mistake," he said. "I know who stole di box. And di gun? It was in di box when it got stole. Di girl is a homeless one, 'bout twenty-five or so. She was a dancer but got mixed up wit druggies. Di drugs done ruined her, so she begs and steals now. I been trying to help her find her way."

Devon was watching Vince and Lawrence closely as they talked, looking for some sign of a subterfuge. Not that she had to—even I could tell there was more that they weren't saying. And it wasn't because I already knew what it was.

Devon knew it, too. "There's something else you haven't told us, isn't there, Mister Lovett?" she said softly, luring it out with her tone.

Over the next hour, Lawrence and Vince wove in greater detail the story that Vince had already told me. It dated back to 1963, during a short period when there was peace between the Italian and Irish mobs in New York and the surrounding areas. The story ended with the New Year's 1966 heist of the plane, and its cargo of three-and-a-half million in cash.

Lawrence knew one side of what had happened forty-two years ago, mostly to do with the location of the wrecked plane and events that happened afterward. The side of the story that Vince knew included the events that had led up to the theft and subsequent plane crash.

From the look of surprise in both Billy's and Lawrence's faces, I could tell that Vince had never told the old Androsian that it had been Bill Rafferty who had stolen the plane. Morgan and Devon exchanged glances, both seeming to pick up on it.

"How is it that you know so much detail?" Devon asked.

"Bill Rafferty was my brother-in-law," Vince said. "Married to my sister who died giving birth to their second boy."

"And your dive site is close to where the plane went down?" I asked Lawrence.

"I was fishin' di back country at night," Lawrence began. "Up near Snipe Key. It was low tide, early on di first day of di year. I was fishin' near a sandbar dat's usually under di water. A plane try to land on dat sandbar three times. He fly over it slow, like di pilot was measurin' it up. On di third fly over, it look like he was gonna try to put it down on dat sand. He made a mistake or change his mind, I don't know. Di plane almost touch di sand, den take off out over Snipe Key. I hear di engine sputter and quit. Den I hear a big splash."

"Did you go out to the crash site?" Morgan asked.

"No," Lawrence replied, looking at the detective with sad eyes. "Dis was in di sixties, mon. Drug planes everywhere you look. I went out past di island and didn't see di plane. So, I went home. I never told anyone about it, until Vince mention a plane crash on New Years."

"Where's Bill Rafferty now?" Deuce asked.

Vince just shrugged. "Disappeared or died about ten years ago."

"He's still alive," Rusty said. He'd been working behind the bar, polishing glasses that didn't need to be polished.

All eyes turned to Rusty as he came out from behind the bar and walked toward our table. "Bill Rafferty's in a shitty convalescent home up on the mainland. Has been since ninety-nine. Don't even know his own name any-more, is what I hear. But he's still alive."

"So, he survived the crash? There's a *Rafferty's Pub* on Stock Island," Morgan said. "Biker bar and strip club. Key West cops used to be out there at least once a week to break up a fight, a stabbing, or a shooting. Any connection?"

"Wild Bill owned it," Rusty said. "It was just a juke joint back in the day, but with a reputation for a tough crowd."

"Who owns it now?" Devon asked.

Rusty shrugged. "No idea. It was turned into a nudie-bar a good fifteen years back, I think."

"No trouble with the law there in the last year?" I offered.

Morgan and Devon both looked at me. "Now that you mention it, no," Morgan said. "A double shooting about a year ago is the last I've heard of any trouble there."

"Sorta like someone put a heavy lid on things," Chyrel's voice came over the laptop's speakers.

"What'd you find, Chyrel?" Deuce asked, turning the screen so everyone could see.

"Key West is a small town," Chyrel went on. "Only took a second to access the bank that *Rafferty's Pub* uses. Like you always say, Deuce: Follow the money."

"Wait a minute," Devon said. "You can't access bank records without a warrant."

"No," Deuce replied, smiling. "You can't. Nor can you use anything she finds in court, until you get a warrant and find it yourself, based on an anonymous tip."

I realized why Chyrel wasn't actually here for this meeting, and Morgan smiled as the realization hit him, too. "Okay," he said. "We can't use anything you find. But can you find anything worth using?"

Tony grinned, his big white teeth accentuating his ebony complexion. "She already has, Lieutenant. Chyrel never dangles a carrot that she doesn't have tied to a stick."

"Thanks, Tony," Chyrel said. "Nightly deposits into *Rafferty's Pub's* business account, going back four years, had always totaled up to around thirty-thousand per month, rarely more than a couple thousand dollars above or below that. That steady streak ended thirteen months ago. Since September of oh-seven, monthly card receipts have continued to remain about the same, but cash deposits have gone way up."

"Way up?" Morgan asked. "By how much?"

"From an average of thirty a month, a year ago," Chyrel replied, with a grin, "nightly deposits started creeping up. Last month was more than a hundred thousand. This past week, the first week in October, it's gone up even more. Last night's deposit alone was a cool fifteen thousand dollars in cash for just one day."

Morgan whistled softly. "Nobody does that much cash business this time of year. They're laundering money."

"There are legitimate ways a place could grow more business," Devon said.

"Yeah," Rusty chimed in. "I more than doubled last year's receipts already. And all legit. But a fifteen-fold increase? I don't think so."

"Remodeling, rebranding their image, new staff, or manager," I said. "Or like Rusty's doing, a new idea that hasn't been tried before."

Rusty grinned. "Things like that'll get ya small gains, bro. Nothing like what Chyrel just described."

Deuce looked around the table, stopping on me. "I just noticed you shaved. Too bad."

"What?" I asked.

"Chyrel could have wired you up, and we could have put you on a Harley, and sent you in there."

"Again," Devon said, "inadmissible in court without a warrant. Is this how you guys worked with the government?"

"Sometimes," I said. "But the people we usually went after weren't destined for prison anyway, so we did whatever it took to lock their asses up in Gitmo until the sun stops shining."

"All of you look too much like citizens to get in a place like that," Morgan said, taking his phone from his pocket. "Excuse me just a second."

Morgan walked over to the opposite corner, where Finn was lying, as he talked on the phone.

Billy looked at me and started to say something. I raised one finger from where my hands rested on the table and he nodded in return.

Ben came back to the table, putting his phone in his jacket pocket. "That was Jefferson," he said to Devon. "I remembered reading something in the ME's report on the third victim, Janet Sawyer. Jefferson didn't even have to look it up. The friend that first reported the girl missing, and later identified the body, reported that Sawyer had gone to *Rafferty's Pub* to perform a one-night gig. Jefferson and Clark were on their way there to interview anyone who remembered her. I pulled them off. Clark's going to follow up with some more questions with Sawyer's friend, and Jefferson's on his way to see Judge Hargrove for an undercover surveillance warrant."

"Isn't the equipment with—"

"Yeah," Morgan interrupted. "It'll be tied up until Monday."

Chyrel's voice came from the laptop. "What kind of equipment?"

"Micro-cameras and transmitters," Morgan said.

"We might be able to help you out," Deuce said. "But I don't think they'd fall for you as a biker, either."

"I'm not going undercover as a biker," Morgan said. "Evans is going as a stripper."

"Like hell!" Devon said.

"Has to be," Morgan said. "A regular patron wouldn't get past the bar, but a woman going for a job interview as an exotic dancer would probably meet the boss. And we need to know who's pulling the strings."

"Yeah? Well, what happens if the boss wants to see the goods?" Devon asked. "A stripper interviewing for a stripper job would probably have to strip. Wouldn't you think?"

"I have an idea," Chyrel said, grinning from ear to ear.

CHAPTER THIRTY-SEVEN

Harley paced the floor in his office. There wasn't a lot of room for it, but he always paced when he was thinking. Sometimes, he did his thinking in the back room, where there were certainly a lot of paces to be taken.

The VIP room was fifty feet by twenty, with a heavily padded extra-deep bench that ran the length of two walls. In front of the bench were three tables with chairs around them and a small private stage in the opposite corner. This stage had two poles, and guests were often invited to join the dancers onstage.

Admittance to the VIP room was a hundred bucks per person, per hour. The client paid for both himself and the dancer, or dancers, of his choice. But there was absolutely no privacy, unless you just happened to be the only one in the room. The girls were free to take anyone they chose to the VIP room and gave the client's admission to Kenny, stuffing the rest into their G-string. If someone was already in the VIP lounge, others were permitted to join in, but only by bringing in their own personal dancers. On Friday nights, the back room was in near constant use and sometimes held more people than in the bar.

The guy's like a two-year-old, Harley thought of his brother, as he paced the small office. This was one of those times. Instead of taking a bunch of Waldo's stuff, he'd looked for just one thing to use for collateral. And the best idea he'd been able to come up with was to take the guy's girl?

To make it worse, Harley thought, *he brought the bitch here*.

Harley had heard through the grapevine about how the two divers had been killed. Little happened in Key West that didn't become public knowledge, even if the cops didn't want it to. The report of the disappearance of the girl with the French name troubled Harley. He felt certain that his brother had left just before he'd gone to the dressing room to offer her a permanent job.

The only trouble with any scenario involving Duke hooking up with *that* chick was that she was miles out of Duke's league. Harley had done a little research after seeing the thing about her on the news. Jenae Saequa wasn't just a hottie on vacation, nor was she a local dancer moonlighting from one of the bigger clubs. She wasn't even a dancer, though as a dancer she'd been excellent. She was signed with one of the biggest porn movie makers in the world and had made over twenty feature films.

Harley peered through a one-way mirror at eye level in the wall. On the other side, it was at ankle level under his elevated private table. Harley saw the red-headed Anastasia on stage. Looking around, he noticed that it was a bit busier than usual. The door to the VIP room opened, and Brandy came out. She strutted up the steps to join Anastasia onstage, amid a chorus of cheers, whistles, and cat-calls.

Brandy was quickly followed by the new girl, Marsha, who came out of the back room with three smiling shrimpers in tow, all hoisting their drinks and high-fiving one another. Finally, Jasmine came out of the VIP room. Harley opened the door of his office and motioned her inside.

"Busy night," Jasmine said, from the open door. "Wassup?"

"Close the door," Harley said. "We have a problem."

She came into the office and sat on the edge of one of the chairs, slowly crossing one long, red-stockinged leg over the other. "What kinda problem?"

"How's the new girl?" Harley asked, skirting the subject.

"She'll do," Jasmine replied, her hands fidgeting at the edges of her sheer lace camisole. "The guys liked her, she's fresh and energetic. But, you really need half a dozen more, at least."

"Not a chance," Harley said. "You girls are expensive as shit."

"Yeah, but what you're depositing every night is way more than five dancers can bring in, Harley. That shit looks suspicious without a stable of at least a dozen hot girls."

Harley looked at her, surprised. Slowly, she turned in her chair, crossing those long legs over one armrest and letting her hair cascade to the floor over the other.

"And just how do you know what I deposit?" Harley asked, stealing his eyes away from her body. Not an easy task, Jasmine wore only red high-heels, stockings, and a matching black lace garter belt and see-through camisole that tied at the neck.

"I watch things," Jasmine purred, arching her back like a disjointed cat. "I really like to watch things. How 'bout a little toot?"

Harley rose; not taking his eyes off Jasmine, he went to the door and locked it. "You watch things, huh?" he asked as he stepped up behind her and began to massage her shoulders and long, elegant neck. "What sort of things do you like to watch?"

Jasmine giggled. "I'm not just a body, Harley. I have a brain,"

"Oh, I know," he replied, his hands circling around her throat, to the little string holding the sheer black fabric in place.

Half an hour later, Harley left his office. He leaned over the bar and, shouting to be heard over the thumping techno music, told Kenny he'd be back before closing. As he made his way to the back, he passed Brandy and gave her a sharp smack on the ass, marveling at its firmness.

Brandy jumped a little and squealed, then smiled at the boss.

"Keep it up," he told her. "Hell, keep 'em all up! And if you know anyone looking for work, send 'em around.

I need to have more of you hard-bodied beach babes around here."

Brandy gave him an odd smile and said okay, and Harley headed to the back of the building. Outside, he got in his car and started the engine. He gripped the steering wheel tightly as he stared at the back door.

A few problems had come up in the year since he'd taken over running the place, but so far they'd been easily dealt with and things were still going smoothly. He only needed to hold it together for another three weeks, a month at the outside. By then all the blow would be out and the front money would be back. Who knows, maybe they'd find the missing mob cash, too.

Jasmine had been right about one thing. He had to at least make it *look* like the money he was depositing came from the club. He probably should sit on the cash, when it started rolling in heavy. Hire more girls and slowly ramp up the deposits again.

Harley smiled as the back door opened, and put the car in gear. The new girl, who called herself Marsha Brady, came out. Harley was sure that wasn't her real name, but she had the same long, straight blond hair as the teen heartthrob from the seventies. Marsha closed the door and, leaning against the back wall, lit a cigarette.

Jasmine was right, he needed more women. Lots more.

CHAPTER THIRTY-EIGHT

Sunlight was beginning to stream in through the window as the sun neared the top boughs of the tall pine trees that bordered the property to the west.

"We'll need to leave soon," I said. "Low tide and sunset are coming, both of which make it difficult to get to the island."

"You're sure you'll have everything we'll need there?" Morgan asked. We'd been discussing with Deuce how we'd get in and what we might find out.

I looked at Deuce and he nodded. "And then some. Chyrel can wire Detective Evans and Jesse both. He's already got an established alias as a coke importer. Give Chyrel a few hours and Devon will have a solid background as a porn star on vacation, hiring Jesse as a bodyguard, and looking to make a few non-union dollars."

"Non-union?" Morgan asked. "I don't get it."

"It's called deflection," Deuce said. "Move the target's attention to something else. In this case, the urgency that whoever's in charge has to keep her appearance off the books because the actors' union doesn't like their talent taking side jobs for cash."

"A coupla more questions," Morgan said, as he sat down across from Lawrence, Vince, and Billy. "Who all knows about that theft back in sixty-six?"

"Just Rafferty and Russo, far as I know," Vince replied.

"And you," Devon added. "If Rafferty never told anyone, how did you find out? And how do you know he never told anyone else?"

"Well," Vince started, glancing at Billy, who nodded. "My sister told me. She was pregnant with the second kid, and Wild Bill was going to use his share to start over in the islands. She told me he was just waiting for the heat to blow off."

"So Rafferty did tell someone else," I said. "Whatever happened to the two boys? They'd be in their forties now. Maybe he told them, too."

"After my sister died, Rafferty shipped them off to Jersey," Vince said. "To live with his sister."

Just then, the back door opened and my youngest daughter Kim came in, followed by Marty Phillips, still in uniform. I crossed the room to her and gave her a quick hug.

"Why's the front door locked?" she asked, as I shook Marty's hand and led them to the table in the corner. "Marty said there were two unmarked police cars out front. What's going on?"

Hearing Kim's voice, Finn came trotting over; she squatted down to give him a big hug and scratch his ears. He practically melted at her feet, and she rubbed his belly.

I introduced Kim to the two detectives, then gave her the Reader's Digest version of Deuce's new security company.

"Why are you here, Deputy?" Morgan asked.

"He's dating my daughter," I said. "She's in her junior year at UF, studying criminal justice."

"You're working with the sheriff's office now?" Kim asked me.

"I'll give you the details on the way to the island," I said. "We have some equipment to pick up there, and then Detective Evans and I are going to Key West."

Kim looked around at the group, her gaze stopping on Deuce before turning back to me. "Is this another mission?"

"Not exactly," I said. "Lawrence is in trouble. Deuce offered Sheriff Roth the services of his new company, and the sheriff accepted. But we really gotta get going. The tide and sun are both falling fast."

"If there are no more questions," Billy said, rising from his chair, "we'll be heading back to the rock. Lawrence has to start his rounds."

"I think we're done," Morgan said. Then he turned to Devon. "I'll get with Jefferson and Clark when I get down there and let you know what they find out."

"Lieutenant Morgan," Chyrel's voice called from the laptop. "Please give Deuce your phone number. I'll patch you into my system in the morning, when we get started."

Hearing Chyrel's voice, Kim leaned toward the laptop. She must have recognized where Chyrel was, because she said, "Hey, Chyrel. Looks like we're roomies tonight."

"Hey, girl! Look forward to seeing you again."

Kim walked with Marty to his pickup, as Deuce and I went out to his boat, the *James Caird*, to check on Julie. "She's leaving her sweater again," Deuce said.

"Sweater?"

Deuce grinned. "You sit up there on that damned island, out of touch with civilization, and your senses dull. When a woman wants an excuse to see a man again, she leaves something behind. Gives her a reason to come back."

"What the hell are you talking about?" I asked.

Deuce glanced over my shoulder and I followed his gaze. Devon took a large gym bag from Morgan's car, then he backed out of his parking spot and his car disappeared through the overhanging trees.

"Once you two get down to Key West," Deuce said, with that crooked grin, "she's going to have to come back here for her car."

"She's just doing her job," I said, looking on as Devon went to the *Revenge* and put her bag just inside the salon hatch.

"I'll be up there first thing in the morning," Deuce said, as he stepped aboard the center-cockpit ketch. "Rusty said he'd lend me his boat."

As Deuce disappeared down into the aft stateroom of the sailboat, I turned and walked back toward the *Revenge*. Bender was on the fly bridge, and Kim was closing up the engine room hatch. Tony and Andrew were standing by the fore and aft dock lines, and Devon was waiting in the cockpit.

"I thought it'd be easier if I just rode with you," she said, as I approached. "Brought my own Dramamine."

"The more the merrier," I said. "Plenty of room for a few more."

Finn and Rusty joined me on the deck of the old barge. "Good luck, both of you," Rusty said, extending his hand to Devon.

"I'll see ya Sunday," I told my old friend as I stepped up onto the gunwale. He nodded and I jerked a thumb to the cockpit. "You coming, Finn?"

The dog barked and leapt the gunwale. I called up to the bridge, "Start her up, Kim!"

The big engines rumbled to life as Finn made a couple of circles around his spot in the cockpit and lay down. I motioned a hand to the ladder. "After you, Detective."

As Devon climbed up to the fly bridge, I yelled, "Cast off the bow, reverse the port engine."

Like a well-oiled machine, Kim waited until Andrew tossed off the bow line, then engaged the transmission on the port side. The bow slowly pushed away from the barge, as the port engine pulled back against the stern line on the starboard side.

"Cast off the stern," I said to Tony, as I climbed up the ladder. "Take us out, Kim."

Though Kim only visited every other weekend from college, she'd spent nearly a whole year as my first mate, and could handle the *Revenge* as well as anyone. She took the port engine out of gear, waited a moment while Tony let go the line, then shifted both engines to forward and spun the wheel.

Bender was sitting on the forward bench seat, and Devon had taken a seat on the port bench. Kim started to get up from the helm, but I put a hand on her shoulder and sat down next to Devon.

"You know the way as well as I do," I told my daughter. "Just keep an eye out for debris in the water. There's still some junk floating out there that hasn't found our island yet."

Tony and Andrew came up as we idled past the concrete pad by the boat ramp. Andrew squeezed past us and joined Paul. I nodded to Tony to take the second seat. He'd acted as first mate many times, as had just about everyone on Deuce's team, so he was familiar with all the systems on the *Revenge*.

"Hey," Kim said. "Where's the *Hopper*?

"Flew her up to Labelle before the storm," I replied. "If we get time, maybe you'd like to go up with me on Sunday to bring her back."

"You have your own plane, too?" Devon asked. "Who are you? Some kind of Bill Gates?"

"Who's he?" I asked.

Kim laughed as she brought the *Revenge* up on plane and started the wide, sweeping turn toward the Seven Mile Bridge. "You have to excuse my dad," she said to Devon. "He's sort of a caveman when it comes to technology."

"Technology?" I asked. "I thought we were talking about the *Island Hopper*."

"Gates is the founder of Microsoft," Devon said. "And now he's one of the richest men in the world."

"Well, I'm nowhere near that," I said. "But I get it. You see a boat bum with no visible means of support, and he's got a couple of flashy boats and an airplane, and the cop in you is suspicious."

"Who wouldn't be?" Devon said. "But no, I think I've gotten to know enough about you to know that you're not a bad person."

I considered what she'd said. Being a cop, she'd naturally be curious and could probably find out on her own.

"He inherited a bunch," Kim said, as if reading my mind. "And he found some treasure. But dad spends most of it helping others. The boats and the plane are just tools to do the job."

"How do you fish from a plane?" Devon asked, as we went under the high arch of the bridge.

"It's an amphibian," Kim said. "Wait till you see her—a cherry red 1953 deHavilland Beaver."

"You fly, too?" Devon asked.

"Whenever I can," Kim replied. "Which isn't often, with me up in Gainesville and *Island Hopper* down here. You're staying on the island tonight?"

"Yes," I answered for Devon, before anything got awkward. "She can bunk with you and Chyrel, or stay here on the boat."

Kim gave me a look and then glanced at Devon, who was gazing out over the bow. Kim looked back at me with a question in her eyes. I pretended not to notice, and asked her how her studies were going.

Kim rolled her eyes at me. "What?" I asked.

"How are your studies going, young lady?" she said, mimicking me and laughing. She eased the throttles a little. "School's just fine, Dad. Marty asked me to move in with him."

"No!" I said, flatly. "That's just not gonna happen."

"Dad, I'm nineteen. I'll be starting my senior year in January, and I'll have my degree by this time next year. I don't need, nor am I asking for, your permission."

"No daughter of mine—"

"Relax," Kim said, "I told him no."

"You did?"

"Of course," Kim replied. "He's gotta marry me first."

I don't remember much of the ride back to the island after that. The idea that my youngest might soon be married was a little overwhelming. Both she and my other daughter, Eve, had only been back in my life for a couple of years now. Eve was already married and a mom, which made me a grandfather. Deuce's getting out of the spy-versus-spy thing seemed like pretty good timing. I was getting too old to be carting his spooks all over El Caribe.

As we idled up my little channel, Kim pushed the button on the key fob. The door to the dock area under the west side of my house slowly started to swing open. She reversed the starboard engine and used the throttles to turn the big boat around in the relatively small turning basin.

"And now I'm not so sure anymore," Devon said, looking at the dock area under the house. Only the Cigarette was visible, since it and the *Revenge* take up the whole western half of the dock area.

"That one was confiscated," Andrew said, as he and Tony started down the ladder. "We use it for training mostly. Same with the big one on the other side."

Kim stood up at the wheel and faced aft, as the *Revenge* came about. Using just the throttles, she backed the *Revenge* into the tight hole, with very little help from Tony and Andrew.

Devon looked over the top of the Cigarette to the other boats. "And those?"

"The big one's *Cazador*," I said. "Technically, it and the Cigarette are owned by the government. We use *Caza-*

dor for small fishing parties that don't want to pay the big bucks for *Gaspar's Revenge.* Beyond that are my and Kim's skiffs, my caretakers' boat, and my utility boat. The brown one is *Knot-L8.* That's with the letter L and the number eight. Carl and I built that one for fun."

"You do like your toys, don't you?" Devon said as we climbed down, leaving Kim to handle the shutdown.

I stepped over the gunwale and opened the small door to the pier. Finn shot through the door—off to look for the kids, I was sure. "Like I said, you can sleep in the bunkhouse with Chyrel and Kim, there's plenty of room. Tony, Paul, and Andrew will be staying in the other bunkhouse. Or, if you need air conditioning, you're welcome to stay aboard. We'll be hooked up to shore power."

"You have electricity way out here?" she asked, looking all around the dock area.

"Everything's connected to the battery shack on the other side of the island. Those batteries, as well as the ones on all the boats down here, are charged by a generator. The same generator also powers the pumps and other higher voltage needs, on demand."

"Hot water?"

"The *Revenge* has a water heater and there's a rain cistern above my house. The water in it stays pretty warm from the sun."

She seemed to come to a decision and stepped over onto the narrow dock next to me. "I'll stay on the boat, if you don't mind."

"Then you can take the master stateroom," I said, joining Tony and Andrew to help tie up and connect shore power and water lines.

"What can I do to help?" Devon asked.

"I could use some help in the engine room," Kim said, climbing down from the fly bridge.

"Um, sure," Devon replied.

Kim took maintenance seriously. She always checked fluid levels before starting and after shut-down. Not something she'd need help with. I gave my daughter a warning look, before she disappeared through the engine room hatch.

Once everything was secure, I went aboard and carried Devon's gym bag to my stateroom. It was a different color than the one she'd had before, I noticed, and a bit larger. Devon and Kim were talking in the cockpit when I returned.

"I put your bag in the forward stateroom," I said. "Supper will be right after sunset. I'm not sure what Charlie has on the menu, but it will likely be seafood."

"Are we going out on the pier, Dad?" Kim asked.

"Probably oughta hurry," I replied. Then to Devon, I added, "Everyone stops whatever they're doing at sunset out here."

A few minutes later, the three of us walked between the bunkhouses and saw that everyone else was already seated on the pier, ready for the dance Mother Ocean and Sol put on for us every evening. We quietly walked out past the others and sat down on the pier.

"Will there be a green flash?" Devon asked.

"Not this evening," I replied, watching Carl Junior, Patty, and Finn splashing in the shallows. "Humidity's too low."

The kids were tanned, like their parents, their hair colored a light yellow by days in the sun. When I was Carl Junior's age, my tan was so deep I was darker than Billy.

A battery of low clouds obscured the sun, but I knew it would reappear just below them before sinking into the shallows to the west. As Sol emerged, it seemed to ignite the clouds, lighting the undersides. The flames spread out as the sun got lower and touched the far horizon, just off Raccoon Key.

Devon nudged me and pointed toward the foot of the pier. The kids were sitting in the water with Finn between them, all three watching the display in silence.

The air had been scrubbed free of moisture by the passing hurricane, and for the next few days it would be cooler, with low humidity levels. This made for a great view of the setting sun, but without the visual effects.

Slowly, the giant red-orange orb slipped quietly below the horizon and disappeared. At places like Mallory Square, this would have brought on a chorus of cheers and clapping. Here on my island, the event is measured in silence, each observer nestled into their own thoughts on the day.

The kids were the first to recover. They resumed splashing water at Finn, who tried to grab it in his mouth. Chyrel and Kim rose and headed toward shore, saying they had some unpacking to do. A moment later, Charlie and Carl followed them to finish dinner. We were having lobster on the grill.

When the men all rose as one and left for the bunkhouse, that left me and Devon alone on the pier. "I like your daughter," Devon said. "She's straight to the point, like her dad."

"What'd she say?" I asked, suspiciously.

"That you don't have a good track record with women."

I chortled. I couldn't help it. "Sorry about that."

"It's cool. I asked her what she meant by that and she said you have some pretty deep scars is all."

"Ancient history," I replied, looking off toward the darkening sky. "Two divorces and then widowed."

"She told me. She said it was before she found you, three years ago."

"I've dated some since then," I lied. The reality is that my life over the last three years has been a string of one-night stands. A few relationships that showed promise just never developed, one girlfriend I scared off, another one got shot, and the latest didn't think it necessary to end things before sleeping with someone else.

We talked for a while longer, until the sound of Charlie banging on an iron skillet brought us to our feet. A driftwood fire was already going in the pit when Devon and I walked toward the others at the big outdoor tables. "Yep, a regular hippie commune," she said.

"I'm *gonna* whip your ass," I whispered, with a grin.

"Promises, promises."

CHAPTER THIRTY-NINE

After locking up the club, Harley got in his car and drove to the warehouse on the south side of Stock Island. Pulling up to the gate of the decrepit old building, he got out to unlock it. Duke's Jeep was parked by the front door of the mostly featureless building, set back off the road among several others, each surrounded by a high security fence.

Harley pulled his Caddy through the gate, relocked it, and parked beside Duke's Jeep. The warehouse door was locked, so he unlocked it, went inside, and relocked the door behind him.

Only Harley and Duke had a key to the place. It had been paid for a long time ago, and there had just never been any reason to sell it. The warehouse was vacant now, but years ago his and Duke's father had used it to bring in marijuana. The pot would be stored there after coming in on boats, then it would be loaded on trucks and sent to another warehouse in Jersey. Decades before that, according to the stories Harley had heard, the building was used to store illegal rum during Prohibition.

There was a single light coming from the office window that looked down over the rest of the warehouse from the mezzanine. Harley mounted the steps, stomping hard to let his brother know he was coming.

The office door swung open, spilling light down onto the steps. Duke's silhouette filled the door frame, seeming larger than possible. He wore only a pair of shorts and running shoes, and his body glistened with sweat.

"What are you doing here, Harley," Duke asked.

Harley lifted a take-out box of chicken. "Thought you'd be hungry. How's our guest doing?"

Duke stepped back, and Harley entered the office. One side looked like a gym, with barbells, a bench press, and several dumbbells and other workout equipment strewn about. A cable stretched across two pulleys attached to the exposed beams. One end was rigged to the end of a very serious-looking steel bollard resting on the floor. The other end was attached to the middle of a steel pipe, hanging close to the ceiling. The equipment hadn't been there the last time Harley had entered the building. But that was six months earlier.

In one corner was a double bed with a dirty, unmade mattress. Harley recognized Tammy by her hair. She was lying prone on the bed, her face turned toward the wall. She wore next to nothing, just as she had in the cooler. Her arms were tied behind her back, forearms lashed together in a very uncomfortable-looking way with what looked like a belt or strap. At first, Harley didn't think she was alive; she wasn't moving. Then he saw her shoulders quake and could hear her sobbing through a gag.

"What have you two been doing?" Harley asked, as he approached the woman on the bed.

Duke closed the door. "I forgot she was even here. I been working the upper body and got into a zone."

Harley placed the box of chicken on the edge of the bed and took his Buck knife from his pocket, flipping it open in a single movement. He cut through the thin nylon cords that bound Tammy's feet. The woman flinched at his touch and gasped. Putting the knife back in his pocket, Harley quickly unbuckled the belt, releasing her arms. He slowly rolled her onto her side, marveling at the detail in the hundreds of tiny tattoos on her back, shoulders, sides, and belly.

Tiny parrots, each exquisitely detailed and different in shape and color, seemed to fly out of her hair, spreading out across her shoulders and upper back. They parted at the top of her shoulders, some disappearing around and under her arm in front, while others dove down her back, joining and flying down her sides. Just below her ribcage, the parrots turned into fish. Schools of brightly-colored fish, of all shapes and sizes, each as detailed as the birds. The schools circled and launched themselves over the tops of her hips. The little fish got closer together and more densely packed across her flat lower belly, giving the illusion of increased speed before swirling together and diving into her panties.

Studying the intricate design, Harley didn't see Tammy's eyes darting around the room. He wasn't ready when she lunged to get past him, cracking him in the side of the head with her elbow. He saw stars for a second, but instinctively reached out to grab her. He missed.

Tammy dashed to the door, but Duke was there first. He grabbed her around the waist. Moving around behind her and bringing his arms up under hers, he locked his fingers behind her head. His shoulders were easily twice the width of Tammy's, so the full nelson essentially just lifted her arms straight up as he pushed her head down. Though it wasn't immediately painful, Duke was more than capable of applying more pressure and snapping her spine. She struggled for a moment and he pulled up and back, pressing his groin against her and lifting her feet off the ground.

"Let her go, Duke," Harley said, shaking the cobwebs out of his head and rising from the bed.

Duke looked at his older brother, rage building to a boil, deep inside his brain as the heat built in his groin. "She'll try to run again," he said, in a half-snarl.

"I said let her go, Marion!"

"Don't call me that, Harley," Duke warned.

Harley stopped a few feet in front of the now-docile woman. He knew calling his brother by his given name would distract him from anything and everything else. He also knew that only he could defuse it with a simple apology, however insincere.

"I'm sorry, Duke," Harley said, slapping his palm to his forehead. "I keep forgetting. You can let her go, man. Look, she's not trying to run. She's not fighting."

The bulging tricep muscles holding Tammy's head down, relaxed a little and Duke lowered her feet to the floor, her ass and spine rubbing against him. The smoldering rage in his brain slowly subsided, but her position against his body was like a bellows to the fire he felt lower.

Releasing his hold, Duke grabbed Tammy's upper arms, holding her in place in front of him. Harley looked into her pleading eyes, puffy and red from fear and crying. Like a snake, his hand shot out and grabbed her by the hair on the side of her head.

Yanking her forward and off balance, he forced her down on her hands and knees, smacking the side of her face to the rough floorboards so hard the sound rang through the warehouse below with a hollow thud.

"Your old man stole from me, bitch!" Harley yelled, bashing her face against the rough-hewn floor again. "And you wanna try to fix that by hittin' me?" He yanked her up to her knees. "Get on your feet!" he snarled, as he hauled her up by the hair.

Tammy's arms flailed, grabbing at Harley's wrists, scratching long streaks into his forearms as she screamed in pain behind the gag. All the air whooshed from her lungs with a guttural moan as Harley brought his left fist up into the tender spot under her ribs. When she doubled over, he brought his knee up, connecting with the side of her head and sending her sprawling onto the floor.

Harley looked around. Duke's bench was old and well-worn. One corner of the padding had come loose and Duke had used duct tape to mend it. The roll lay beneath the bench.

"Drag her over here," Harley said, picking up the tape and crossing the room to Duke's makeshift lat bar.

Duke picked Tammy up under her arms and dragged her to where Harley stood.

"What's that thing weigh?" Harley asked, pointing at the dock bollard.

"I don't know," Duke replied. "A little less than me, I guess."

"Good. Pull that bar down."

When Duke pulled it down, Harley told him to push it all the way to the floor and hold it. It took nearly all the big man's strength, but he finally held it to the floor.

Harley quickly laid Tammy's arms across the pipe and secured her wrists to the bar with duct tape. "Okay, let it up slow."

Duke eased up on the bar and let the weight drag Tammy's inert body up to a sitting position, then on up until her feet just barely touched the floor, before the bollard settled onto it, too.

Harley stepped back, admiring his handiwork. Tammy hung limp from the bar, her chin on her chest and the heels of her bare feet just off the floor. "Yeah, that'll hold her."

Harley started out the door. "I need you to go up to Marathon tomorrow and find that boat."

"What do ya want me to do with her?" Duke asked.

"That bitch?" Harley shouted, stepping back into the office, pointing at Tammy, hanging helpless by her wrists. He shrugged. "I don't give a shit. Let her starve if ya want; fuck her."

Duke looked at the sheer work of art hanging from his workout equipment as his brother stormed out the door. "Whatever you say, Harley."

CHAPTER FORTY

A sound in the middle of the night woke me. Everyone had retired to their quarters a couple of hours after sunset. We usually rose with the sun, and it looked like it might be a long day. I heard the sound again, a light thud.

I rolled out of bed and opened the drawer to my nightstand. My nine-millimeter Sig Sauer lay right on top of its case in the drawer. There was no need to check if there was a magazine in it, or if there was a round in the chamber. Pap always told me that an unloaded gun was a hammer, and the guy that brought a hammer to a gunfight wasn't going to fare well.

Fully alert, I padded barefoot to the bedroom door, the moonlight through the window guiding my way. When I reached the door, I paused and listened. There was a slight rustling sound and I yanked the door open, my Sig leading the way into the living room.

Nothing. No bogey-man hiding in the shadows, no terrorists bent on mindless jihad, no crazed junkie lying in wait. Just Finn, lying in the corner and looking toward my fly-tying bench. I heard another sound and turned, my Sig leading the way again. The sound had come from the open floor hatch, next to my bench.

Was Devon up and moving around at this hour? I wondered.

Taking no chances, I crouched and moved closer to the hatch, angling to see down to the middle catwalk. A low light illuminated the dock area below, and I knew it was the single bare twelve-volt bulb in the middle of the back wall.

Below, I saw Devon turn at the end of the dock, walking back toward the ladder. She was barefoot, wearing cut-offs and a blue tee-shirt.

"You trying to get yourself killed?"

Startled, Devon looked up, her right hand going instinctively to her hip. Her holster wasn't there. I raised my weapon, and she lifted a hand to her mouth, snickering.

"This isn't funny!" I hissed, not wanting to wake the whole island. "I could have shot you."

"I couldn't sleep," she said, grinning. "I kept wondering if you were a boxers or briefs kinda guy. Guess I don't have to wonder anymore."

Realizing I was wearing only my skivvies, I stepped back out of her sight a little in embarrassment, placing my Sig on the bench. "You sure you're okay?"

"I will be once the next decision is made."

"What decision is that?" I asked.

Devon took a step closer to the ladder, still smiling. I had to step closer to the hatch to look down and see her. She craned her neck upward, and the sparkle of mischief was unmistakable in those brown eyes. "Whether I'm coming up there, or you're coming down here."

I grinned back at her and extended a hand. "You still haven't seen the *rest* of my house."

"No," she said, and started slowly up the ladder. "I haven't."

She stepped off the ladder and into my arms.

When my eyes opened, I thought I'd dreamed the whole thing. The sun wasn't up yet, but it was starting to get light outside and it spilled in through the open window, along with a cool breeze. The bed was disheveled and empty. Sitting up, I looked around.

No, I don't think you were dreaming, McDermitt, I thought, picking up a pale blue tee-shirt from the floor, where it had been pushed nearly under the bed with my skivvies. The shirt had a picture of a bottle on the front and next to it were four lines: *One Tequila, Two Tequila, Three Tequila, Floor.* I put it to my face. No perfume, just a good, clean scent, with a touch of lavender, maybe. I'm not big on identifying smells, but I know what smells good to me.

Putting on my skivvies, I went to the open bedroom doorway. Finn hadn't moved from his spot in the corner, but his head was up, ears alert. Devon had her back to me, looking at the books in my bookcase. Her dark blond hair cascaded over tan shoulders. She was wearing only the cutoffs.

"Looking for something?" I asked, walking toward her.

She spun quickly, her breasts partly hidden by the wild blond tresses, hanging over her shoulders. "This is you," she said, pointing to a framed picture on the top shelf. "With the president?"

"Yeah," I replied, stopping in front of her. My eyes roved all over her body and she didn't shy away in the least.

"Who's the redhead?"

I glanced at the picture. "Doctor Jackie Burdick," I replied, stepping just a little closer, well within her personal space. "A Navy doc who stitched me up a few years ago."

"Your body language in the photo tells me there was more intimacy between you than that," Devon whispered as I drew her into my arms.

"Ancient history," I whispered, as my lips found her neck.

"Do we have time?" she asked, moaning softly into my shoulder and pressing her body hard against mine.

"No, not really," I whispered, taking her shoulders and moving her out to arm's length. I let my eyes take in all of her again.

"Maybe later?" she asked, with a seductive pout and sparkling eyes.

"Oh, definitely later," I replied. "I woke up and thought I'd dreamed last night. That was you, wasn't it? With the trapeze, black angel's wings, and Mardi Gras mask?"

Devon slugged my shoulder, causing me to wince slightly.

"Beware what you ask for, Jesse," she said, snatching her tee-shirt from my hand. "When this is over, I'm going to turn you inside out and leave you begging for mercy."

My eyes followed her as she walked across the deck toward the floor hatch, hips swaying seductively. "Promises, promises."

"I'm going down there to get dressed," she said, pulling the shirt over her head and flipping her hair out of it. "Do you have food in this house? I'm starved."

"Breakfast is outside, just after sunrise," I said, heading toward my bedroom as she climbed down. I was suddenly quite happy with Carl's idea for the trap-door.

I dressed quickly in jeans and a long-sleeved button-down work shirt. Since we'd showered together just a couple of hours before, I was out the door and ready for the day in minutes.

We had a hearty breakfast of omelets with cheese, green peppers from the garden, and bite-sized chunks of lobster tail left over from last night. Talk around the tables was mostly subdued.

The sound of an approaching outboard got my attention. "You expecting someone else?" Charlie asked.

"Deuce said he'd be out this morning, before we leave," I replied, rising from the table. "Sounds like Rusty's old outboard coming through the cuts to the south."

Kim and Devon followed me to the south pier, where Rusty's old skiff was turning into my channel. Deuce stood in the bow, with Julie at the helm—which explained why they were coming up from the south. Julie knows the back country better than anyone, even me.

Another man was sitting next to her. He sat rigidly straight, head up, steely eyes missing nothing. His crew-cut was sprinkled with gray and his square jaw unshaven, but only for a day or two.

"Who's that with Deuce and Julie?" Kim asked.

"That'd be Colonel Travis Stockwell," Tony answered, as he came down the steps with Andrew and Paul. "Wonder what he's doing here?"

Catching the line that Deuce tossed from the bow, I tied it off to a cleat, while Tony did the same with the stern line.

"How've you been, Jesse?" Stockwell asked, as Julie shut off the engine.

"As well as can be expected, Colonel. What are you doing here?"

Travis stood and looked down at the dock, before looking up with a question in his eyes. I nodded and he stepped up onto the pier in front of me, our eyes locked on one another's.

"My time is short, too," he said. "I'm here to beg for my old job."

"Position's been filled," I said. "I do have an opening for a sea-faring galley wench, if you know anyone looking for a job."

Stockwell grinned. "I just might have someone in mind. She even has her own boat. Last I heard, she was on her way here. In the meantime, Deuce tells me he needs some specialized equipment."

Everyone on the pier, except Kim and Devon, knew we were talking about Charity Styles. Charity had been selected to do wet work for the CIA, and had been out sailing the Caribbean for over a year now. Stockwell was her handler, and I didn't like the idea much. The woman had psychological issues and was going to wind up getting killed. Hearing that she was on her way here meant only one thing: the plug had been pulled on any further missions for her.

I nodded my understanding. "What kind of equipment?"

"Just about anything you want," Travis replied. "Bargain basement prices, too. Except weapons. We both know you have more than enough of those to go around."

"You mean like the electronics we were already planning to use?" I asked, suspiciously.

"We'll just call this a trial. Play with the stuff and see if it's something you'll be interested in."

I grinned at my former first mate. "We can talk price once Devon and I get back."

"Devon?" he asked and turned to look at her. "Detective Evans, I presume."

She must have picked up on my less-than-warm attitude. "And you are?" she asked in an even tone, shaking his hand.

"Travis," he replied. "Formerly Associate Director Stockwell with Homeland Security, and Colonel Stockwell, US Army before that."

"We're just about to get underway, Colonel," I said. "You planning to stay a while?"

"Actually, I thought I might go with you. Deuce explained what's going on when he picked me up early this morning. Don't you think a star of Detective Evans' caliber would have two bodyguards?"

"This is her sting," I said. "If it's okay with her, it's fine by me."

"Can I speak to you privately?" Devon asked me.

I followed her up the steps and opened the door. Inside, she turned to me and asked, "Who is this guy? I get the impression you're not exactly friends?"

"Long story," I replied. "But he's more than capable."

"I could tell that, just looking in his eyes. Even smiling, he looks terribly dangerous, which fits the part."

"He was an Army Ranger, tough as they come," I said. "Few men I'd trust more, if things got difficult."

"If you're not against the idea and I can get the okay from the sheriff, I'd say bring him."

"You won't need to contact Sheriff Roth," I said. "Unless you want to confirm it. Stockwell's the ultimate planner. He wouldn't even be here offering to help, if he hadn't already talked to the sheriff. Probably with either the president or Secretary Chertoff on the line, as well."

"He's got that kind of clout?"

"That picture you were looking at?" I said, nodding toward my bookshelf. "Stockwell arranged the charter and took the picture."

"Unless you're opposed, let's take him."

"Our personal differences aside, I think it makes good sense."

We went out to the deck and descended the steps to the pier. "Put your bag in the Cigarette," I told Stockwell.

"We're not taking the big boat?" Devon asked.

"Not flashy enough," I replied, as Travis lifted a go-bag out of Rusty's skiff. "A Hollywood star wouldn't be riding around in a fishing boat."

"Speaking of which," Chyrel said, as she joined us on the pier. She handed a file folder to Devon. "Your alias.

You can study it on the way down. Instead of building a fake one, you're just going to impersonate someone."

"Who?" I asked, as Devon opened the folder. She took a picture and handed it to me.

"I'm Dona Vegas."

I looked at the picture. The woman in it bore a striking similarity to Devon. Same hair color and style, same height, and close to the same build. Her facial features were close enough that it would work, but the woman's eyes in the picture were slightly darker brown.

"Who is she?" I asked Chyrel, handing the photo back to Devon.

"She's a Brazilian national," Chyrel replied. "German father and Brazilian mother, born in seventy-five. She's split her time living in California and Germany for most of the last decade, though. She speaks fluent Portuguese and German, and her English has very little accent. But she can turn that up a notch on film. Some people like that."

"I don't even want to know how you know this, Chyrel," I said. "So she's a real-life porn-star?"

"Yeah, pretty big name in the late nineties, with over a dozen films to her credit."

"What if these guys know she's Brazilian?" Devon asked.

"Leave that to us," Travis said, coming out of the dock area. "We'll come up with a diversion or change the subject. Jesse's good at improvising. All you have to do is look beautiful and be aloof."

"Yikes!" Devon said. "I didn't even think about clothes. What's a stripper wear when they actually wear stuff?"

"Got you covered," Julie said, lifting a small overnight bag from the boat. "Try some of these out while you're on the way down there. Everything should fit, just whatever you're comfortable with."

"You guys think of everything," Devon said, taking the case.

"I spoke with Lieutenant Morgan half an hour ago, when we were headed up here," Deuce said. "He'll have two other undercover detectives inside the bar and said you'd know who they were. He also said he tried to call you, but it went straight to voicemail. Oh, and Tony and Andrew will go with you and stay in the boat, as backup."

"How far away will they be?" Devon asked.

"Less than a hundred feet," I replied. "The rear parking lot of *Rafferty's Pub* is on a canal, and we'll be docking there."

"You'd better get a move on," Chyrel said. "I called the club last night to arrange an interview, pretending to be your personal assistant. The owner wasn't there but the bartender, a guy named Kenny Whitt, said he's almost always there by noon. He went ahead and made the appointment and promised to call the boss and make sure he's there. Apparently, he's at least heard the name Dona Vegas."

Just then, Devon's phone rang. She fished it out of her purse, looked at the caller ID, which I could see only showed a local phone number. She pushed the accept button and put the phone to her ear. "Detective Evans."

She listened for a moment, then said, "Mister Montrose, slow down. Who are you again?" She paused, listening. "Oh, yeah. What's this about?" She listened for a few seconds, thanked whoever it was, and ended the call.

"Surprised you got a signal down here," I said. "Usually the only place we can get one is up there on the deck."

"That was Kevin Montrose," Devon said. "The gentleman who found the third body. He says he knows who the killer is and just saw him in Marathon."

"How's he know that?"

"Dunno," she replied. "Seemed like a harmless old fisherman, when I met him. I'll call the sub-station in Marathon and have them send someone to take his statement."

"He is harmless," Julie said. "I've known him all my life. He used to carry the mail, but he retired a long time ago. Now he just fishes and gossips."

"We'd better get this show on the water," I said, leading the way to the docks under the house.

Finn started to follow us, but I stopped him. "You can't go on this fishing trip," I told him. "Stay here and watch the kids."

Finn took off up the steps like a jet fighter.

CHAPTER FORTY-ONE

Duke was up early, way earlier than was customary for a bar bouncer. Harley had called him before sunrise and told him where to go. Slowing as he came off the Seven Mile Bridge, Duke started looking for the Walmart. A mile into Marathon, he found it and turned onto Sombrero Beach Road. A couple blocks later, he almost missed the turn onto Sombrero Boulevard.

"This ain't gonna be easy," Duke mumbled, steering the Jeep around the bend in the road next to Sombrero Resort. Ahead, he could see a lot of boats docked along the waterfront and more anchored in the little harbor.

He parked in a small crushed-shell parking area on the left and climbed out, squinting in the late morning sun. Across the road was a place called *Dockside*. It sat on stilts, mostly out over the water. Duke walked across the road toward it.

The place was really small on the inside—mostly just the bar in the middle—and open to a large deck out back.

Duke looked around, seeing only one old guy sitting at the bar drinking coffee. Out on the deck, there were four people, a tourist couple sitting together and two obvious boat bums, sitting at separate tables.

"Get you something?" the dark-haired bartender asked. Her nametag said *Robin*.

"I'm looking for a boat," Duke replied.

"We sell food, booze, and coffee," Robin said. "Not boats."

Duke looked at her, confused. "I don't want to buy one. I'm looking for a boat called *Gaspar's Revenge*. Supposed to be a charter boat here."

The bartender eyed him cautiously. "You don't look much like a fisherman."

"I'm not," Duke said, thinking as fast as he could. "The guy owes my brother some money and I just want to find him."

"What guy?"

"The guy who owns the boat," Duke said, getting flustered.

Robin just stared at him for a moment. "The guy owes your brother money, but you don't know his name?"

This wasn't going the way Duke had thought it would. A big flashy boat like that should be easy to find, but looking at the hundreds of boats in the harbor, some flashier than others, he realized he had a serious problem, especially not even knowing the guy's name.

"Well, ya see, this guy—"

"I can't really help you mister," Robin said. "There's lots of boats around here, but I've never heard of a charter boat with that name. You want a coffee, or a beer, or something?"

Duke looked at her a moment. "Naw," he replied. "Is it okay to walk down the pier?"

"Dock," Robin corrected him. "Piers stick out into the water. Knock yourself out."

Duke walked around the bar and out onto the deck beyond it. He turned left and went through a side exit next to a small stage. The dock stretched out a long way. He started walking, reading the names of the boats he passed.

Duke paused next to a houseboat, where a long-haired guy sat on the roof smoking a joint.

"*Que pasa, hermano*," the man called down.

Duke didn't speak Spanish. "You know English?" he asked the man.

"Sure do, Gigantor," the man said, in a decidedly California surfer accent, exhaling a huge cloud of blue-gray smoke.

"I'm looking for a guy who owns a charter boat called *Gaspar's Revenge*. You know it?"

The man leaned forward in his rooftop chair, lifted his sunglasses slightly, and peered down at Duke. "Nah, man," he finally said, leaning back in his chair and puffing on the joint. "Never heard of it. There's a *Kate's Revenge* about six slips down, man. That it?"

"Thanks," Duke said and continued along the dock, reading the boat names. When he glanced back a moment later, the long-haired guy was gone. *Kate's Revenge* was a sailboat like Duke's, only a lot bigger. He ran into a few other people, some walking the docks, others working on or relaxing in the many boats he passed.

None were named *Gaspar's Revenge*, and nobody he spoke to had ever heard of it. It was already close to noon and Duke was getting hungry. He took his phone out and called Harley, who didn't answer.

Duke walked the length of the dock again. Seeing that there was another long line of boat slips on the other side of *Dockside*, he quickened his pace. If Harley called back, he wanted to be able to tell him that he'd looked at all of them.

Another forty or fifty boats later, having spoken to a lot more people on and around the docks, Duke had struck out. None of the people he talked to knew about the boat, and none he saw looked like it or had the name. A few people had even offered their boat for a charter.

Duke's phone rang; recognizing his brother's number, he answered it.

"Find the boat?" Harley asked.

"There's an awful lot of boats here, Harley."

"I take that as a no."

"Nobody here has even heard of it," Duke said. "You sure you got the name right?"

"You gave me the name," Harley said, and Duke could picture him rolling his eyes.

"Oh yeah," Duke said. "Maybe the taxi guy gave you the wrong place, then. Cause there ain't no boat anywhere around here called *Gaspar's Revenge*, and nobody here has ever heard of it."

"All right," Harley said. "Get on back down here. Kenny set up an interview for some new talent and I'm meeting her at noon."

Duke looked at his watch. It was almost eleven-thirty. "I'm leaving now. But I won't get there by then."

"Just come straight to the club," Harley said. "I got something for you to do."

"Not the warehouse?" Duke asked.

"She's not going anywhere."

CHAPTER FORTY-TWO

The powerful racing engines rumbled at an idle as I steered the sleek racing boat into Harbor Channel and turned northeast. Travis was in the port seat of the dual console boat, looking over the second set of gauges displayed on the dash in front of him. I had the same gauges at the helm, but in a go-fast boat, traveling at nearly half a football field every second, the helmsman's eyes were better off being on the water ahead.

Devon stood between us, looking over the windshield at the long, narrow foredeck. "How fast will this thing go?"

"Faster than you can drive a car across the Seven Mile Bridge," Tony replied, standing behind me.

"Y'all might want to strap in," I said. "Devon, one of the middle seats back there will be the most comfortable."

Once they were seated and had their restraints buckled, I slowly brought the boat up on plane and increased speed to forty knots. Exiting Harbor Channel into the wide-open Gulf, I bumped the speed up to fifty and swung the bow toward the west.

"Both engines operating normally," Travis called out. "Water temp is still a little lower than what you said was normal."

"These engines are a little cold-natured," I said. "They never reach normal operating temperature without a lot of speed."

Turning my head, I looked back at Devon. She'd pulled her hair back and put a couple of bands in it to keep it from tangling. "You okay back there," I asked.

"Yeah," she shouted back. "Took a pill half an hour ago and feel fine. I thought you said this boat was fast."

"Hang on!" I shouted, advancing the throttles slowly. Most boats, you could just jam the throttles to the stops, but the engines in this Cigarette were so powerful, doing that would cause the props to cavitate and the engines would overrev.

At seventy-five, I looked back again. Devon at least looked more relaxed than that first time out in the *Revenge*. She was even smiling. Tony and Andrew had their arms resting on the gunwales. Andrew was just looking out over the water and Tony was listening to an iPod with his earbuds, his head nodding up and down.

I pushed the throttles further forward until we were traveling at ninety knots, close to the boat's top speed. The seas were finally almost flat again. Hurricane Ike was now nearly a thousand miles across the Gulf and nearing the coast of Texas. The go-fast boat was barely in the water, just skimming the surface with the aft fifteen feet or so in contact with it.

"Everything's normal," Travis shouted over the engines, then glanced back at Devon. "She seems pretty content."

I chanced a quick glance over my shoulder. Devon had her head back against the seat rest, eyes closed and legs outstretched. She seemed to be enjoying the ride.

Less than half an hour later, we were idling toward a long canal, dredged nearly a century ago into the ancient coral rock of Stock Island. Devon had gone down into the bare cabin to change as soon as I'd slowed and turned south. The cabin had been quite luxurious when we'd gotten the boat, but I'd gutted it anyway, leaving only the bare bulkheads and the two bare benches that had once been the settee. The head was still there, but no longer enclosed. Entertaining guests wasn't what we used this boat for.

I switched on the earwig in my right ear, hidden under my hair, and said, "Comm check."

Though they're hardly noticeable, Travis went the opposite route because his crew cut didn't afford any coverage. He wore what looked like a regular Bluetooth device, like people use when they don't want to hold a phone to their ear. Goofy-looking on some people, but on Travis it merely looked more professional.

"Crystal clear," Travis said, his voice coming over the tiny speaker in my ear. Tony and Andrew both confirmed, also.

"Got all of you loud and clear," Chyrel said, from her little office on my island. "Detectives Morgan and Evans, are y'all on?"

"Roger," I heard Morgan say. "I'm parked across US-1 and another unit is parked in a driveway north of the club."

Devon didn't respond, so I tapped on the cabin's hatch. "Turn on the earwig I gave you."

A moment later, Devon's voice came over the comm. "Okay, got it. I'm on now."

When she came out of the cabin, Devon looked completely different. She'd somehow managed to put makeup and lip gloss on while the boat moved through the light chop. For someone prone to seasickness, just being inside the enclosed cabin should have made her a little green around the gills, even after taking a Dramamine.

Her feet and legs were bare, all the way up to a very brief pair of high-waisted dark blue shorts. Above that, she wore a long-sleeved blue flannel shirt, with the sleeves rolled up and the bottom tied in a knot above her waist. It showed off plenty of tanned, flat belly below it, and ample cleavage above. The middle of her black bra could be seen just above the knot, a row of round black buttons accentuating the lower part of the bra. The button at the center was the camera.

She'd used makeup to make her eyelids look smoky and sultry, drawing the corners further to the sides of her face, and teased her hair slightly, to make it bigger and bouncier.

"Whoa," I said, leaning against the gunwale for a better look.

"The real Dona Vegas has darker eyes," Devon said.

"I don't think anyone's going to be looking at your eyes," I quipped, looking her up and down.

"We'd better get outta sight," Andrew said, moving past Devon toward the cabin hatch. Tony followed him and closed the hatch once they were inside. They'd remain there unless we needed them.

"Somebody's standing on the dock ahead," Travis said. "Showtime, Detective."

Devon sat down on one of the middle seats, tossing her hair back over the engine cover and stretching those long, tan legs out before her.

A man was waiting on the only dock on the port side of the canal. Chyrel had told me just before we left the island that she'd let the guy at the bar know that we'd be arriving by boat.

"Miss Vegas?" the man asked, as I eased the boat up to the dock. His eyes were locked on Devon, oblivious to me and Travis.

"Please step back," Travis said, standing in the cockpit behind his seat, dock lines in hand.

"I'm the guy your assistant spoke—" the man started to say.

"I don't care who you are," Travis hissed, reaching a hand under the back of his shirt. "Step back away from Miss Vegas's boat, now!"

The man looked at Travis and must have seen something in his eyes, because he immediately backed up as far from the edge of the dock as he could. "Sorry, sir. Can I help you tie off?"

Travis could be very intimidating, but he was the consummate professional. He handed the man one of the dock lines. "Tie off the bow, please."

Once the boat was secured, I shut down the burbling engines. Stepping back into the cockpit, I lowered a small step mounted to the inside of the gunwale and held a hand out for Devon. She took it and lightly stepped up onto the dock. She quickly slipped a pair of high heeled sandals on her feet and turned to the man waiting there.

"It's an honor to have you here, Miss Vegas," he said. "I'm sort of a fan, I guess."

"Yeah," I said, stepping over onto the dock. "That's great. Are you the manager?"

"Um, no," he replied. "*Rafferty's* doesn't have a manager anymore, just the owner. The bar's open and there are a couple of customers inside, but the entertainment hasn't started. So, if you want, you can wait in the VIP lounge. My name's Kenny. I tend the bar. The owner will be here in a few minutes."

The owner? I thought. Rusty said he was an old man in a retirement home in Homestead. One of the sons? Or maybe the old man sold it?

"Yeah," Travis grunted. "The VIP lounge will be fine, but don't keep Miss Vegas waiting."

"Right this way," Kenny said, walking toward the gate and the nearly empty parking lot beyond it.

We went in the back door and Kenny showed us down a hallway. There was music coming from ahead. My senses were on full alert, cognitive skills working overtime. The hall had two restrooms and a walk-in cooler on the left and two doors on the right, probably an office and dressing room for the dancers.

Coming out of the hall into the main part of the club, Kenny turned left, toward a long L-shaped bar. The main floor area took up the whole front of the building, with a ceiling around twelve feet. A few down-and-out looking characters sat at the bar to my left, nursing beers. I couldn't tell which of the three were the two cops.

An elevated area in the corner to my right held a single table, with a small couch and two chairs. Next to it and slightly lower was an array of electronic equipment, the DJ's booth. Next to the booth was a half-circle stage, twenty feet across, with a floor-to-ceiling pole in the middle. Around the stage were a dozen or so chairs pushed up under a narrow drink bar attached to the stage.

Twenty or thirty tables were scattered around the open room. None of the tables had a chair on the side facing the stage. The back wall had two doors, one of them in the corner behind the bar. A liquor stockroom, no doubt.

Kenny opened the door next to the bar, which took up the whole back and side wall. It was easy to see that this had been quite a place at one time. The bars, both for drinking and ogling the dancers, looked like solid mahogany. But the place was suffering from decades of wear and neglect.

A sweep of the room, and I took it all in. Possible choke points, areas of egress, possible hidden dangers, and places that would provide cover. I could see Travis making mental judgments and observations, probably right along the same lines.

"Mister Rafferty will be here in just a couple minutes," Kenny said, holding the door open. "Sorry for the wait. Can I get you anything?"

Mister Rafferty? I thought. *Must be one of the sons.*

"Thanks," I said. "We're good."

Kenny closed the door, but not all the way, and went back to his bar. Island music wafted through the door opening, a guy singing about *Gary's Island*. I wondered if his was anything like mine.

Travis led the way to the center of the room, held a chair out for Devon and we all sat down at a table.

"Rafferty must be one of the sons," Travis said in a low voice, just loud enough to be heard over the music.

"The sons are Harlan and Marion Rafferty," Devon said. "All that came up on them were a few minor disturbances up in Jersey and a couple of arrests for possession."

"When he said VIP lounge," I whispered, looking around, "I thought he meant like a star's dressing room or something. What the hell is this place?"

"You've never been in a VIP room?" Devon asked with a grin.

Before I could answer, the door opened and another man stepped into the room. "Company," Travis whispered.

The guy had curly, dark hair. My eyes focused like lasers on his every movement, and the little hairs on the back of my neck stood up. About my age, wearing jeans, a black tee-shirt, and leather jacket, he came into the room with the air about him of a man used to getting his own way. He was slightly shorter than my six-three, and maybe the same weight, I guessed. If he'd ever been in shape it had turned to flab, now. Still, a big guy. With dark, curly hair.

"Miss Vegas," he said, walking toward us, motorcycle boots clopping on the hardwood floor. "Sorry to keep you waiting."

Travis and I both stood up, chairs scraping on the floor, and walked toward the approaching man. He stopped in his tracks and took a half-step back, right hand hovering above his pocket. "What the hell?"

"Miss Vegas has had trouble recently with overzealous fans," Travis said.

"You're the owner?" I asked.

"Yeah, Harley Rafferty."

"I'm sorry, Mister Rafferty," Devon said, stepping between us. She spoke with just a trace of a German accent, extending her hand. "I am Dona Vegas."

Rafferty smiled, looking Devon over from head to foot. "We don't get many stars of your notoriety," he said. "Please, have a seat."

As Devon and Rafferty passed between us, Travis and I stepped around behind her and to the sides. Rafferty noticed our movements.

"Before we discuss anything," Devon said, sitting down and addressing Rafferty seriously, "I must insist this be a cash deal. My agent, publicist, and above all the IAEU, can never know."

"The IAEU?" Rafferty asked.

"I'm a member of the "International Adult Entertainment Union," Devon said. "Normally, all money I earn would go through the union's paymaster, but..."

"Oh, I understand completely," Rafferty said, holding up both hands. "Not a big fan of unions, anyway. Would you mind stepping up onto the stage, so I can see how you look under stage lights?"

"Certainly," Devon said, standing and walking slowly toward the stage. Her heels were at least four inches tall, perching her at nearly my own height as she strutted past me. Her walk in those heels and shorts would have put many a runway model to shame.

Either someone was watching, or the lights were motion activated, because they came on when Devon stepped up onto the stage. There were two shiny, floor-to-ceiling poles on the stage. She grabbed the pole on the left and twirled around the left side of the stage, stopping at center stage, by grabbing the other pole. She planted her left foot at the other pole's base in a spread eagle, slinging her head forward, hair falling over her face and shadowing her body from the bright spotlights. How she didn't break an ankle in those heels, I'll never know.

Devon stood there a moment with her head down, long blond hair spilling over her shoulders and chest, then she flung her head and hair back, looking up at the bright lights. The effect was like a car salesman yanking the cover off a shiny new sports car. If anything, the lights made her look even more beautiful.

Rafferty stood and clapped his hands. "I'm sold!" he shouted. "Now it's just a matter of how much and what you're offering."

Chyrel had been explaining in our ears what a VIP room was and what went on in one, though I think Devon already knew. It wasn't at all what I'd thought. Chyrel also dropped a few keywords in our ears.

"No advertising, other than a single sign, inside the club," I said. "She'll dance tomorrow night and maybe take one or two clients for a PSE. No more than two at a time. And we'll be in the room. Anyone gets too physical, they're gone."

"My brother handles security," Rafferty said as the door opened. "Here he is now. We never have any trouble when Duke's around."

Another man came into the room. Rafferty didn't catch it, since his back was to her, but Devon started for just a second when she saw the guy. She slowly twirled around the pole again, turning away from us. I heard her whisper over the comm. "That's the guy on the boat with the shotgun."

To say the guy walking toward us was big would have been an understatement. He was freakishly large across the shoulders, chest, and arms, with powerful-looking legs. If I'd had to guess, I'd have said he tipped the livestock scales at somewhere close to three hundred pounds—and not an ounce of it was fat. This guy was miles past dangerous size.

"Duke, this is Dona Vegas," Rafferty said. "Miss Vegas, my brother, Duke Rafferty."

Devon had no choice but to let him see her face. No telling how the guy would react if he recognized her. I sensed Travis tensing, ready to draw the handgun from the holster tucked into the back of his jeans. I was also armed and ready. Devon's weapon was in her purse, slung on the back of her chair.

She quickly stepped down off the stage and the bright lights went off. I hadn't been looking toward them, as the Rafferty brothers had been, but my vision was still diminished in the sudden darkness.

Devon walked toward the muscle-bound man, extending her hand. The giant didn't seem to recognize her and reached for her hand. She suddenly stumbled in the heels and fell into him. Travis and I moved quickly toward them, but he caught her easily, her right arm snaking around his waist, trying to hold herself up by his belt.

He stood her back on her heels and held her at arm's length until she steadied. His eyes never even came close to looking at her face, as they were fixed on her body. The expression on his face was quite obvious. It was a look of animal lust.

Both brothers had dark, curly hair. This one could crush a beer keg.

Paul Bender's voice came over the comm. "You need to get out of there now. That man's a bomb about ready to blow."

"It's stuffy in here," Devon said. "Will the air conditioner be on tomorrow night?"

"Yeah," Harley said. "We can make it cold enough in here, your nipples will poke right out of your shirt. We can go in my office to talk money, if you like."

"Yes, I would," Devon said, already headed to the door.

Travis and I waited outside the door to Rafferty's office, listening to everything going on inside through our comms. The other Rafferty, Duke or Marion, came down the hall and stopped in front of us.

"I have to talk to my brother," the big man said.

"After they negotiate a price," I said sternly. The guy seemed a little slow-witted. "You're a competitive body-builder, I bet."

"Not anymore," he replied, his chest muscles flexing a little. "I got into power-lifting a couple years ago."

"Power-lifting?" Travis asked, also seeing the need to keep the guy talking about himself. In the open, this guy wouldn't have had much chance against the two of us, probably not even one of us. But, in close quarters, like this hallway, if he could get a hand on either of us, I had no doubt he could break our spines and tie us up like pretzels.

"Yeah," Duke said. "Building muscle for mass and strength, instead of form. It's the big thing in gyms these days."

In my ear, I heard Devon wrapping up a deal with Harley. She'd agreed to work one night for five hundred dollars and fifty percent of any tricks in the VIP room. She even demanded a minimum of four hundred bucks a trick. The bone mic on our earwigs could only pick up other sounds if they were very close. So, it had been a one-sided conversation. But, as they ended their discussion, I clearly heard Rafferty ask to be first. I was learning way more than I wanted to.

As Duke went on about bench pressing over three-hundred pounds, the office door opened and Devon stepped out. "I think we're done here," she said to me and Travis, then turned to shake hands with Rafferty. "I will see you tomorrow night at seven, Mister Rafferty. Get some rest."

We left the way we came in, the steel door clanging behind us. "Did you get the bugs planted?" Deuce asked.

"One in the office," Devon said, when we were halfway across the parking lot. "I put one under his desk and I also got one on the muscle head's belt, and another on Rafferty's leather jacket. Something tells me he only takes it off for one thing."

"One on the wall by the back door," Travis said.

"That stumble was intentional?" I asked, opening the gate to the dock.

"Of course," Devon said. "I was walking in heels when I was six."

"Chyrel, are you getting anything on those bugs?" I asked.

"Sure am," Chyrel replied as I stepped aboard and fired up the twin Mercury Racing eleven-hundreds. "Recording for playback, when you want it. But make it quick. Something's going down."

"I feel like I need a shower," Devon said, pulling off the ridiculous heels and stepping into the boat.

Travis let loose the bow line and tossed it in the cockpit, as he stepped aboard. "Let's go."

"McDermitt," Morgan said. "Do you know Garrison Bight?"

"Yeah. Want to meet us there?"

"Evans knows the place," he said.

The bight was just a few minutes away, but the canal was so narrow I had to back up to clear the dock before turning around. In minutes, we were out of the canal and I tapped on the hatch. "You guys can come out now. I think Miss Vegas wants to get out of her stripper clothes."

Tony and Andrew came out of the cabin and sat down in back while Devon went below to change. I slowly brought the boat up to planing speed, then left the channel and headed across the five-foot-deep flats. I kept it up on the step as we passed Sigsbee Park and only slowed just before we got to the sharp turns in the narrow channel into the bight.

Devon came out of the cabin, still wearing the flannel shirt, but with jeans and sneakers now. I found it a lot more appealing.

"There," she said, pointing toward Houseboat Row, as we entered the small cove. "The little blue houseboat with the covered porch."

As I came alongside the porch, Morgan opened a glass sliding door and stepped out. We quickly tied off and followed him inside. He had his laptop open on a table in the little kitchen and I could see Chyrel's face on the screen.

"Start playback from the slamming of the door," I heard Deuce's voice say over both the laptop and my earwig at the same time.

A window opened on the screen, resembling the controls on a tape player. We heard a door slam, and Morgan reached over and turned the volume all the way up on the computer. We heard another door opening and closing, and then Rafferty said, "What'd ya think?"

"She's smokin'," Duke Rafferty replied. "She only gonna work one night?"

Rafferty replied, but it wasn't audible, due to a loud whooshing sound, probably one of them sitting down in a chair next to the bug. "For five hundred?" Duke asked.

"Yeah, little brother," Harley said. "Having a real live porn star in the VIP will bring in thousands. That is, if she has the same endurance in real life that she shows on film."

"You're real smart, Harley."

"You hear anything from Waldo?" Harley asked.

Morgan took a pad and pen out of his pocket and wrote on it.

"No," Duke said. "But he'll bring the money on Monday. She's important to him."

"How you figure?" Harley asked. "Just another split-tail."

"Know that hearse he drives? It has the same fish and birds on it that she does."

"Waldo did those tats?" Harley asked.

"Pause it," Morgan said. The playback stopped and Morgan took his phone out. He scrolled through his contact list and tapped one, putting the phone to his ear. "Morgan here. I want you to research a local by the name Waldo. Don't know if it's his first name or last. Drives a hearse with fish and birds painted on it."

Morgan ended the call and told Chyrel to continue the playback. Duke's voice came over the speakers. "I think so, Harley. He's gonna want her back, so he'll bring the money on Monday to get her. Just like he said."

"A kidnapping?" Andrew asked.

A chair squeaked and the whooshing sound came over the speakers again. Either Duke or Harley said something, but it was drowned out by the background noise.

"No," Harley said. "I'll go to the warehouse. I gotta meet Delgado. But I got a tip on the guy that found that French chick."

Devon and Morgan exchanged glances, and Morgan scribbled on his pad again.

"What French chick?" Duke asked.

"The tiny little girl who danced here the other night and left about the same time you did." Harley said. "My source tells me she turned up stuffed into some mangrove roots not far from where you keep your boat."

There was a moment of silence, then the sound of paper tearing.

"Here," Harley said. "This is the old guy's name. You can find him fishing the old bridge on Bahia Honda. I know you did it, Duke. So go take care of this. I'll go to the warehouse and take her some food. Delgado's meeting me there in an hour. One of his guys is bringing in another load, and he needs a place to store it."

"You're taking her food?" Duke asked. "But I thought you said fuck her and let her starve."

"Waldo's not very likely to bring the money if she's dead," Harley said. "Wait. When I said fuck her, did you think I meant…" There was silence for a second, then Harley erupted. "Dammit, Duke! You gotta stop taking shit so literally!"

More silence, then the sound of a door opening. Harley asked, "Is she alive?"

The closing door covered up any answer. "Did you get his answer on the bug by the back door?" Travis asked.

"No," Chyrel replied. "It's too far from the office door. It only recorded footsteps approaching, and a steel door opening and then slamming shut. This was recorded ten minutes ago. Both devices are now moving, turning north on US-1."

"Jesse," Deuce said, his face appearing on the screen. "I just got a call from Rusty on the sat-phone. He said he got a call from Robin over at Dockside about an hour ago."

Two images of Duke Rafferty appeared on the screen, on either side of Deuce. One was taken from the video, just after Devon stumbled. In the freeze-frame, Duke was staring right at the camera on Devon's bra. Or more precisely, he was staring at her breasts, practically salivating. The other was taken of Duke, again looking toward the camera, but he seemed to be looking at something slightly above it. I instantly recognized the boat on the right side of the picture. It was in the slip right next to Angie and Jimmy's houseboat.

"Jimmy called Rusty about the same time, Jesse. Emailed him this picture of Duke Rafferty on the docks at Boot Key Harbor this morning. Half a dozen other people from Boot Key Harbor called him this morning, too. They all describe a guy who looks just like this asking about *Gaspar's Revenge*. Robin said he's driving one of those jacked-up Jeep Wranglers, red, with big off-road tires. He knew your boat's name, but not yours."

"I got the warehouse location," Chyrel said. "Owned by Bill Rafferty since nineteen-sixty-four. It's on the south side of Stock Island, on Front Street."

"How'd you come up with that so fast?" Morgan asked. "Never mind. Evans, you're with me."

"Wait a minute," I said, putting a hand on Morgan's shoulder. "Who's the old guy Harley sent Duke after?"

"Oh God," Devon mumbled. "Kevin Montrose. Remember he called and said he knew who the killer is and had seen him?"

"Call him back," I said. "Find out where he is and let Travis know. We're headed for the old railroad bridge." I turned to Devon. "Be careful and good luck."

She gave me a quick peck on the cheek and whispered, "Get some!"

"Oorah!" I shouted, halfway to the back porch and the Cigarette.

CHAPTER FORTY-THREE

Morgan got in his sedan and started the engine. Evans got in the passenger side. "Get Jefferson on the radio, and tell him to meet us at the curve on Front Street. Then call Judge Hargrave and tell him what we heard. Ask for the warrant to be extended to cover Delgado and searching any other properties owned by the Rafferty clan."

Evans relayed the message through dispatch as Morgan hit the gas and turned onto Palm Avenue Causeway. He turned on the lights and siren as they approached North Roosevelt and slowed for the left turn.

Evans was on her phone, pleading her case to the judge, as Morgan turned off the siren and accelerated. He left the blue light on the dash turned on, for all the good it did.

Evans ended the call and scrolled through her recent calls to find Kevin. "Judge said okay on the warrant," she

said, putting the phone to her ear. "We'll have it in ten minutes."

Morgan turned left again and crossed the short bridge from Key West to Stock Island.

When Kevin answered, Evans asked him where he was precisely.

"Fishin' Bahia Honda Channel," he replied. "I gave the other detective the guy's description and where the boat is that he lives on. Did ya catch him?"

"Not yet, Mister Montrose," Evans replied. "We think he might be looking for you and he knows you're fishing there."

"Yeah, well, out here on the water, his muscles ain't much good. I carry a pistol in my boat, all legal and registered. That freak comes out here, I'll shoot his ass before he gets on *my* boat."

A click told Evans he'd hung up, and a look at her screen confirmed it. "Stubborn ass, old fool," she grumbled, as Morgan turned onto Front Street.

"He hang up?"

"Yeah," Evans replied, as Morgan pulled up behind Jefferson's car.

Evans's phone rang as she started to get out of the car. She answered it without looking, hoping it was Montrose. She listened for a minute, then got back in the car, before ending the call.

Seconds seemed like hours as she waited for the mobile fax to print out the new warrant. It finally started whirring and then spit out a sheet of paper. Evans grabbed it and got out of the car.

"We have the warrant," she shouted to Ben.

"Try to get Montrose again," Morgan said, looking around the area. The warehouse was around the curve and another fifty or sixty yards down Front Street. "Pull the cars in there," he said, pointing to a boat repair yard. "Maybe we can get two birds."

Evans looked at him. "Ben, that girl could be dying."

"Chance we gotta take," Morgan replied. "They seemed bent on keeping her alive and if Delgado's gonna be here and we can catch him delivering drugs, we can put him away forever."

They got back into the cars and pulled them into the boatyard to wait. The wait wasn't long. Five minutes after they parked, Jefferson's voice came over the radio. "That's Delgado's car approaching. There's a panel van following it."

"How far out is uniformed backup?" Morgan asked Evans.

"Five minutes," she replied.

Morgan picked up the mic and spoke into it. "Jefferson, give them a minute to turn off the road, then you and Clark go park at Fishbusterz Seafood and make your way in on foot to the back of the property. Backup will be here in five minutes. Evans and I will go in with the squad cars and I'll send a uniform around both sides."

"Roger that," Jefferson said, then backed out and turned down the road toward the warehouse.

"They know to come in silent?" Morgan asked.

"Yeah," Evans replied. "I had dispatch repeat it back."

Two minutes later, three squad cars rolled to a stop in front of the boatyard, and five deputies got out of them. Morgan went to the deputies and explained a quick plan, where the two solo deputies would lead and go straight to the front corners of the building. The other squad car, with the other two deputies, would follow him to the front door.

"If there's a gate," Morgan said to the deputy driving the lead car, "crash through it."

"Oh yeah," replied the young deputy, a man by the name of Howell. "Just call me Rubber Duck."

They got back into their cars and Evans said, "Jefferson and Clark are in position and under cover at the back of the property."

Morgan started the Crown Vic and pulled out of the boatyard, following behind the two solo deputies. The third patrol car fell in behind him. There was a gate, and Howell crashed through it with wild abandon.

The two lead squad cars split, moving across the littered yard of the warehouse toward the two corners. Morgan hit the gas, driving over the crumpled gate, and accelerated toward the door at the front.

The two detectives jumped out of Morgan's sedan and took cover behind their doors, guns drawn. The third squad car slid to a stop beside them, kicking up more dust. Morgan reached in and flipped on the PA, grabbing the mic off the dash.

"This is the Monroe County Sheriff's Department," Morgan announced, his amplified voice reverberating off the old wooden structure. "We have the building surrounded. Come out with your hands on your head."

Two more patrol cars came charging through the demolished gate. Morgan turned at the sound and motioned them toward either side of the building.

Hearing a noise inside, Morgan got down behind his door again. He keyed the mic and said, "This is Detective Morgan, with the Monroe County Sheriff's office. We have a warrant, and if you don't come out peacefully, we're coming in."

There was the sound of breaking glass and Jefferson called out on the radio, "They're coming out the back window! Four men, heading toward the dock."

From behind the building, Morgan could hear shouting, as the detectives gave the subjects orders. Then a shot rang out. That one shot was followed by nearly a dozen in rapid succession, as the four police officers at the back of the building opened fire.

"Breach the door!" Morgan shouted at the two deputies with them at the front. One of the deputies picked up a heavy steel battering ram and ran quickly to the door. His partner and the two detectives were right behind him.

The deputy didn't hesitate. He was a big guy and the ram weighed fifty pounds. The door failed with the first blow, the frame splintering and the door falling off its upper hinge to hang crooked inside the building. The four cops stormed quickly through the opening, spreading out with shotguns and handguns up and ready. No more shooting was heard from the back of the building.

The van and Delgado's car were in the warehouse, along with a black Cadillac CTS. Behind the van was a small stack of bundles wrapped in black plastic. There were even more in the van. The uniforms quickly cleared the warehouse area and Morgan went over to the plastic-wrapped packages. If Delgado was involved, he knew what would be wrapped inside them.

As the two deputies swarmed up the stairs to a mezzanine office, Morgan picked up one of the bricks. It weighed about ten pounds and was tightly wrapped. Taking a pocket knife from his pants pocket, he slit the covering and stuck a finger inside.

He touched the tip of his finger, covered in white powder, to his tongue and turned to Evans. "Coke. Gotta be five hundred pounds."

"Up here, Detectives!" one of the deputies shouted from above.

Morgan and Evans raced up the steps and into the office. The two deputies were trying to cut through duct tape securing a young woman's wrists to a metal bar hanging from the ceiling. The woman wore only a bra; a pair of panties lay discarded at her feet. She had hair dyed several bright colors, and splotches all over her body.

Evans raced over to the girl, Morgan following her. He quickly shrugged out of his jacket and, as the deputies cut the girl free, wrapped the jacket around her shoulders. As he did so, he realized that the splotches were actually hundreds of brightly colored tattoos.

Evans helped support the girl and walked her to the only piece of furniture in the room, a bare mattress on a worn-out bed.

Morgan took his handheld radio off his belt and called Jefferson.

"We got 'em, Lieutenant," Jefferson said. "All of them were armed and one fired on us. Delgado's hit, but he'll live. His driver and the van driver are both dead. The fourth man is alive, but probably not gonna make it."

"Come with me," Morgan said to the two deputies. They went quickly down the steps to the warehouse, leaving Evans to take care of the girl.

"Secure those packages," Morgan said, pointing to the coke. "Both of you count them separately. If your numbers don't match both of you do it again."

Seeing no back door except a big rollup door, and figuring Rafferty would have used that if it opened, Morgan went out the front and around the left side of the building. Delgado was sitting up, a red stain on the front of his right shoulder. Morgan went over to where Harley Rafferty lay in the dust, two large blood stains on his midsection and pink foam at his mouth.

Morgan knelt beside the man. "You're not gonna make it, Rafferty. One bullet went through your lung and the other one's in your belly. Why don't you tell me about the French girl? Did your brother kill her?"

Harley's eyes squeezed shut, "Fuck you, asshole!" he snarled, spitting frothy foam on Morgan's pants leg."

The older detective only knelt there, watching the man die. There wasn't anything he could do to help him, anyway. Rafferty's breathing became more shallow.

"James Isaksson and Jennifer Marshall?" Morgan asked. The two divers? Did you kill them, or your brother?"

Rafferty opened his eyes and looked up at Morgan. He seemed to come to a decision and moaned, "Duke killed 'em, man. A few others, too." He gulped three quick breaths and added, "My brother's a sick fuck. I shoulda put him down myself."

Rafferty's head rolled to the side and his chest quit heaving. His lifeless eyes stared up at the azure sky, no longer seeing it.

CHAPTER FORTY-FOUR

Making no pretense at observing normal safe boating practices, I brought the go-fast up on plane as soon as we left the bight, pointing the bow toward Fleming Key Cut. By the time we went under the bridge, we were going over sixty knots and accelerating through the turn into the main shipping channel.

Roaring past Mallory Square and a docked cruise ship at nearly ninety knots just an hour before sunset on a Saturday, I knew that there would be hundreds of pictures of us going by. Tourists would be turning to one another wondering if we were part of the show, or a scene from *Cops*. Welcome to Key West, Bob and Martha from Waukegan. The next strange scene will be starting shortly.

The throttles were against the stops as I turned east around the tip of Key West and into the Atlantic Ocean. Bahia Honda was thirty miles dead ahead. I kept the boat in the deep sandy trough just inside the barrier reef.

Wave action was minimal, but I still had to throttle back to ninety-five.

"How did this old fisherman figure out who the killer is?" I asked nobody in particular.

"Y'all's coconut telegraph," Chyrel said over my earwig. "A few locals hanging out at a bar, each with different sides of the same story. Folks down here can put things together, and they're tight with each other. I doubt anyone that guy talked to in Boot Key Harbor told him anything."

"Be interesting to find out," Travis said. "You learn anything on Montrose, Chyrel?"

"A little," she answered. "He's never been arrested, which is saying a lot for an eighty-three-year-old Conch. He served with the Army in Germany and Italy during World War Two, retired from the postal service in seventy-eight, and worked as an outboard mechanic until he fully retired at sixty-five, back in nineteen-ninety. Wife, June Montrose, never worked outside the home, died six years ago. Two sons, both killed in action in Vietnam. The oldest son was married and they had a daughter. His wife committed suicide right after he was killed, and the daughter went to live with Kevin and June."

"Sounds like a lot of those guys," I said. "Living through the Depression built resilience in people. Something comes up in their life, they just dealt with it and continued the march forward."

"Sounds a lot like your grandfather, Jesse," Andrew said.

Yeah, I thought, *a lot like Pap.*

Though Duke Rafferty had a ten-minute head start and we had considerably farther to go, having to loop all the way around Key West, I felt sure we'd get there at about the same time. One of the great things about living in the Keys is the lack of traffic on the water, compared to snaking your way up or down that two lane ribbon of asphalt, the Overseas Highway.

In the corner of my eye, I saw Travis lean forward and tap on one of the gauges. "What is it?" I asked, keeping my eyes on the water ahead.

"Port engine is running a little hotter than the starboard."

"Shit," I muttered, my subconscious already moving my hand to the throttles. "How hot? And what's the oil pressure?"

"Port engine's at two-thirty. Oil pressure on both engines are at sixty-five pounds."

I took my hand off the throttle and put it back on the wheel. "Just keep an eye on it. Thirty pounds is safe."

We soon approached the marker at Big Pine Shoal, and I turned northeast toward the old bridge with the sun at our backs. Still a mile away, I could see a small boat, just beyond the removed section of the ancient bridge on the left side of the channel. It was white and had a high bow, like old boats I'd seen as a kid on Chesapeake Bay when Dad was stationed at Quantico. I'd seen it around a few times, usually fishing the back country.

"A red Jeep in the parking lot," I heard Tony say.

"Port engine temperature is redlining," Travis said, coolly. "Pressure's down to forty pounds."

"Screw it," I said, keeping both throttles wide-open. We shot through the gap in the bridge at seventy knots. I was going for a distraction, if the old man was still alive.

Pulling back hard on the throttles, I waited a second before cutting the wheel hard to port, bringing the sleek racing boat roaring into a tight turn, kicking up spray in a huge arcing circle, before coming to a stop.

The unmistakable sound of a shot rang out, but the old man was more concerned with our sudden appearance, standing and waving both arms while he shouted at us.

Scanning the fishing pier, which was once the foot of the bridge, I spotted Duke Rafferty easily. Not just because of his size, but also because he was the only one on the pier not running away. Instead, he was resting his huge forearms on the pier railing and pointing a gun. The distance wasn't great, maybe eighty feet. A difficult shot for a handgun, with the target bobbing on a boat.

Another shot rang out and I saw the old man go down in his boat.

The port engine suddenly froze up, and I shut off the fuel and ignition to it. "Tony, take the wheel!" I shouted, stripping off my harness and kicking my shoes off under the dash. "Crash it on the beach if you have to, but get there before that asshole gets away."

I didn't wait for a response, but dove headlong into the gin-clear water. My shirt and jeans slowed me a little, but swimming is as natural as walking for me. I struck out toward the old man's boat, swimming as hard as I could.

When I reached it, I grabbed the gunwale near the stern and started to hoist myself in. Another shot rang out, much closer, and wood splinters cut into my left hand and wrist. I dropped back into the water.

"Mister Montrose!" I shouted. "I'm not the guy trying to kill you. He's on the pier and my friends are after him. My name's Jesse McDermitt. May I come aboard?"

"I know who you are," the old man croaked. "Recognition didn't get from my eyes to my brain quick enough, is all. Come aboard."

Levering myself up cautiously, I saw Montrose lying on the deck in a puddle of blood, a revolver laying at his side. I rolled into the boat and scrambled to get to him. Just as I reached his side, I heard a terrible crunching sound, one of the worst sounds a waterman can hear: fiberglass breaking.

When I looked over the gunnel, I saw the Cigarette on the rocky beach, a huge hole in the starboard side. Travis, Andrew, and Tony were scrambling up the embankment to get to the pier.

"You have a first-aid kit on board?" I asked the old Conch. His face was etched deep with lines, his skin dark brown from the sun with a coarse, leathery look. His eyes were bright blue and clear. For just one instant, I thought I was looking into Pap's face. He'd have been about the same age, if he were still alive.

"Starboard side," Montrose grunted. "In the console."

Leaning back, I opened the compartment and pulled the white case out. I tore his shirt open. There was a hole in his chest, just above and to the left of the sternum. Blood pulsed out of it at regular intervals. I gently rolled him onto his side. No exit wound.

"I ain't gonna make it, son," the old man croaked.

"Sure ya will," I said, opening the first-aid kit. "You Conchs are too ornery to die."

The kit was supplied with the items a fisherman might need to remove a fish hook from his finger. I pulled out a roll of gauze and tape, and stripped off some of each. Wadding the gauze, I pressed it over the bullet wound. It was saturated and leaking before I could put the tape in place.

"No, son," Montrose said softly. "I ain't. And that's okay. You know who I am?"

I pressed my hand to the wound, trying to stop the blood flow by will alone. I looked around quickly. Another boat was coming to help. I waved my free arm at them in a distress sign, then looked back down at the old man.

"You're a Soldier," I replied, my hand pressed firmly to his chest to keep the life-blood in his body.

Montrose looked at my forearm, staring at my Force Recon tattoo.

"Where'd ya serve?" he asked.

"Lebanon, Panama, Kuwait, and Somalia," I replied, "You?"

Looking at the amount of blood sloshing around on the deck, I realized that he was right. He was losing blood too fast. The bullet must have nicked one of the main arteries to the heart. He was dying, and I was helpless to stop it. All I could do was try to make him comfortable. I'd noticed a half-full bottle in the console with the first-aid kit, and now I reached back to grab it.

"I jumped into Sicily," he replied, wheezing. "Under General Ridgeway. Then we went on to Anzio."

As happens so often when old warriors meet, we formed an instant bond, a tether that bound us through blood and sweat. Though separated not just by decades, but by generations, we were brothers.

Holding the bottle up in front of him, I saw his eyes light up. He cackled a little, then coughed up some blood. His eyes sparkled as though he were in on his own joke. "Have a drink with an old soldier, there, Gyrene?"

I pulled the cork from the bottle with my teeth, spat it on the deck and held the bottle to his lips. He drank slowly, enjoying the burn of the rum. We both knew it would be his last taste.

As I tilted the bottle to my own lips, he said in a quiet, halting voice, as if already recounting his life to Saint Peter, "I survived the Great Depression, son. Lived through the Labor Day Hurricane of thirty-five, the war, and some dumbass punk sticking a knife in me, thinking letter carriers had cash on 'em. Only to get killed in my own damned boat."

"Anything I can do for you?" I asked.

"Tell my granddaughter, Denny, that everything's hers. She don't have to come back down here to look after me when I get old, and she don't have to keep the house. Tell her she can sell it and spend it, whatever she wants. She's my only kin. Will you tell her that?"

"Yeah," I said, fighting back tears. "I'll tell her."

This old man had fought and worked all his life, only to die alone with a stranger, and only one person in the world that he could call family.

He coughed blood again, foamy and pink around his mouth, as he looked up at a battery of clouds, burnished by the sun now setting beyond the gap in the old bridge. Staring the angel of death in the face one more time, he began to quietly sing the refrain of *Blood on The Risers* in a cracked and wheezing voice.

Gory, gory, what a helluva way to die.
Gory, gory, what a helluva way to die.
Gory, gory, what a helluva way to die.
I ain't gonna jump no more.

The old man coughed once more, and as I held my hand firmly against his chest I felt the pulsing pressure slow and then stop, as his last breath rattled from his lungs. Those clear blue eyes turned dull and lifeless, as the other boat bumped us. I heard voices shouting.

"Semper Fi, Mac," I whispered softly, gently closing the fallen hero's eyes.

EPILOGUE

Kevin Montrose's funeral was held three days later, on a Tuesday. His wish was to be cremated and his ashes released in his beloved back country.

Devon went with me. There were few in attendance, mostly very old and seeming to count the days until it was their turn. The funeral was held outside, in Kevin's own backyard. I'd learned that sixty years ago he'd cleared the land and built the house himself. His old boat had been pulled up onto a trailer, and at the helm was the urn with his ashes and a folded American flag. Devon and I sat in the back, both of us wearing ball caps to shade our faces from the bright sunlight.

"That must be the granddaughter," Devon whispered, nodding toward the back door of the house. A priest in a robe with a sash across his shoulders led a young woman to the front of the small gathering, where she sat down.

Even from twenty feet behind her, I could see that she was crying, her shoulders quaking. The preacher walked over to Kevin's boat and cleared his throat. He looked to be nearly as old as Kevin, probably in his late seventies. He had a full head of thick white hair and walked with a cane, favoring his right leg. When everyone quieted, he began the eulogy.

"I've known Kevin Montrose probably longer than anyone here," he said. "Knew him before he got married, knew both his sons, and even married the one. I was there when his granddaughter Denise was born. She's here with us today.

"Kevin and I jumped into Sicily together in forty-three. I didn't know him then; we met for the first time when we landed on the beaches of Anzio, almost nine months later. It was in Anzio that I got this." He rapped the side of his leg with the cane, creating a hollow metallic ring.

"First time I met Kevin was when he picked most of me up and carried me to the rear on his shoulder. I saw him again an hour later and was able to thank him, when he carried another man back to the rear. We shared a smoke and learned that we were both from the Keys, so we exchanged information to stay in touch once we got back home.

"Kevin was an honest, hard-working man, who never asked for anything nor took a handout. He'd give you the shirt right off his back, if he knew you needed it. I've seen him do it. The world's gotten a lot poorer in the last few days, with one less man of Kevin's caliber in it. I'm gonna turn things over to the Army now. These soldiers flew all the way down here from Fort Bragg to bid farewell to our brother."

The preacher turned and placed one hand on the urn, then whispered softly, "Airborne leads the way."

From the long driveway, beside the house, I heard the familiar sound of marching feet. A detail of seven riflemen appeared, all of them NCOs. They were led by a crusty-looking sergeant major, with a chest full of decorations and too many service stripes on his sleeves to count. All of them wore the maroon beret and shoulder patch of the 82nd Airborne Division.

Marching alongside the detail was a bugler, who wore sergeant's stripes, and a full-bird colonel. This got my attention. Just who the hell was Kevin Montrose?

The Colonel stepped up to the front of the group assembled in the yard and cleared his throat to speak. From a pocket inside his uniform blouse, he removed a folded sheet of paper.

"I will now read the Silver Star citation awarded to Staff Sergeant Kevin Montrose.

"The President of the United States takes pleasure in presenting the Silver Star Medal to Kevin Lewis Montrose, Staff Sergeant, United States Army, for gallantry in action against the enemy while serving with Company H, Third Battalion, Five-Hundred-Fourth Parachute Regiment, Eighty-Second Airborne Division, in Anzio, Italy on four March nineteen-forty-four. Throughout the entire battle, Staff Sergeant Montrose's outstanding leadership and heroic devotion to duty was an inspiration to all who witnessed it. When several infantrymen were injured by artillery explosions, he went in search of aid. He provided the medical personnel covering fire. He personally aided in the evacuation of the wounded. He charged the enemy, attacking relentlessly. He moved his men strategically to counter every push by the enemy.

His actions are in keeping with the highest traditions of the Armed Forces of the United States."

Refolding the paper, the colonel put it back into his uniform pocket. Reaching into the boat, he reverently picked up the folded flag and, clutching it to his chest, strode toward Kevin's granddaughter, where he knelt and presented it to her. He spoke quietly to her for more than a minute, much longer than the standard "On behalf of the president and a grateful nation" speech, which I had given way too many times.

The colonel straightened, turned, and marched off to the side, away from the rifle squad. On the first command from the sergeant major, Devon and I both stood and rendered a salute, as the riflemen snapped off three quick volleys, the noise sounding as if it were one rifle instead of seven. The bugler blew that forlorn melody that always causes a lump in my throat.

When it was over, Devon and I walked up to the front to pay our respects. I introduced Devon and myself to Kevin's granddaughter. She was about Kim's age, maybe a year or two older.

"You're the one that was with Gramps when he passed?" Denise Montrose asked. Her eyes were red and puffy.

"Yeah, I was there with him," I replied. "He told me it was okay; he was ready to go be with your grandmother. He also gave me a message to give to you."

"Did he suffer?"

"Not for long," I replied honestly. "But he met what was coming like a true warrior. Never complained once. He told me to tell you that everything was yours and you don't have to come back here if you don't want to."

She sniffed, and a tear streaked down her face. "I always hated these islands. I couldn't wait until I was old enough to leave."

"He said for you to sell everything and spend it how you want, if that's what you wanted to do," I hesitated a moment.

She must have sensed there was more, and asked me to continue.

"I didn't know your grandfather. I'd seen his boat around a few times and we probably bumped elbows in a bar a time or two. But in his last minutes, I could tell that he felt a great deal of love for you. It wasn't so much what he said, but the glint in his eyes when he said it. He was very proud of you."

"Thanks," she said, sniffing. "I never really realized how much I owed him. He was always a strict man, always pushing me to try harder. When I went off to college up in Gainesville, I was told to expect it to be very difficult, but it wasn't. Thanks to his pushing me."

"My daughter goes to UF," I said.

"Is her name Kim? I recognized your last name."

"You know her?"

"We had some classes together," she said. "If you'll excuse me, I have to locate a boat to take Gramps's ashes out to the back country."

"Why not use his?"

"I don't know if I could find my way back," she replied.

"I've got a boat," I offered without thinking. "And I live in the back country."

"You'd do that?"

"It'd be an honor," I replied. "Tomorrow?"

"I have to get back to school. But I'll be back the weekend after next. Can you do it then? I'll be happy to pay."

"Kim will be back home that weekend, too," I said. "We'll do it on Saturday."

◆ ◆ ◆ ◆

Getting the *Hopper* back to the *Anchor*, and Billy back home, was delayed a few days. Billy expedited the release of Lawrence's cash savings from police evidence and I convinced him to keep it in a bank. "If for no other reason," I told him, "than the next time you're wrongly accused, it won't end up in police evidence."

Billy didn't have any problem staying over a few more days. It made me wonder if there was trouble at home with his wife. I decided that he'd tell me if he wanted me to know, and if he didn't then it was none of my business. Billy's now on retainer to Deuce's new company for legal advice and other things that might suit his talents. He left me his old Noserider, which I've decided to name *Fidelis Bellator*, or Faithful Warrior. Maybe I'll take the *Revenge* up the coast in search of the perfect wave. Or use the Noserider for a coffee table.

Over the following week, I learned that Delgado, the cocaine kingpin of Monroe County, had been charged with trafficking and being complicit to kidnap, rape, and assault, among a bunch of lesser charges. The DA was confident that he'd win, and the minimum mandatory sentence for trafficking cocaine was life in prison. At Delgado's age, that wouldn't be very long.

The shootout that took place at the pier, while Kevin lay dying beside me on the deck of his boat, left Duke Rafferty injured. He survived, but he'd been hit twice in the melee and one of the bullets nicked his spinal cord, leaving him paralyzed from the chest down. Even though he was unable to move his legs, it still took all three men to take him into custody. He'd ranted and screamed, wanting to know why he was being arrested. He said he was only doing what his brother told him to do. By the time they loaded him into the ambulance, he was blubbering like a baby.

I'd asked Travis why he hadn't put a bullet in his head, and he'd told me there were just too many people watching, but he had a better plan anyway. It was uncovered that Duke was abusing steroids, which was pretty obvious based on his size and insane activities.

Duke was later convicted of the three murders; though permanently paralyzed, he was put in with the general population up in Raiford. A rumor quickly spread among the inmates that he'd sexually abused children. Travis said he had nothing to do with either event.

The Cigarette was demolished. The one engine had thrown a rod and was of little more use than a mooring anchor. I'd had the boat removed from the rocks and taken to a boatyard on Stock Island, where it was stripped of the one good engine, the transmissions, and anything useful. I told the yard owner to sell the engine and anything else to cover the recovery. If there was anything left over, I told him to donate it to Kevin's granddaughter. He said he would, that another marina owner had already started a GoFundMe to help her. I had Chyrel explain to me what that was, and then anonymously donated enough to get her through at least a year.

The Friday after Kevin's funeral, I met with Deuce and the other members of his new security company. I'd already spoken to my son-in-law, and he and his father readily agreed to help. I told Deuce straight up what I wanted to do. If I was going to foot the bill, it would be with the stipulation that we take occasional pro bono cases for folks who couldn't otherwise afford security or a private investigator, people like Kevin and Denise. We'd also help people who were swindled, to get back what was rightfully theirs.

Andrew grinned, if you could call it that. His mouth is usually hidden behind his bushy mustache. "You mean like Travis McGee?"

"Except we don't keep half," I replied, grinning also.

Everyone agreed.

Lawrence told me that he was desperate to tell the detectives something useful, but he'd made so many mistakes he didn't know where to start. Leaving his cash box in the car was bad enough, but leaving the gun and his handheld GPS in the box was worse. All the locations he'd searched were on the GPS, along with the spot where James and Jennifer had been killed. So he couldn't even tell them where to look for the evidence that might have convicted him.

Over the next week, we brought our resources to bear on finding Vince and Lawrence's missing plane. It didn't take long. We put things together, comparing the stories from the two old guys, Rusty's knowledge of the water, and researching the type of plane and how far it might have glided. We soon came up with a pretty good idea of where to search. Lawrence had been close; James and Jenny hadn't been far from it. The twin-engine Cessna was in sixty feet of water, about a thousand feet north and slightly east of where they'd been looking. It was heavily encrusted with coral, and sand covered most of both wings. It was also completely empty. So, the mystery of the casino heist is still a mystery.

For now.

Devon and I met for dinner in Key West the Friday before Kevin's daughter and Kim came back down. This time, she did invite me in. And she lived up to her promise of turning me inside out—but I never begged for mercy. The following day, she came back to the island and stayed with Carl and Charlie while Kim and I took Denise out on Raccoon Flats to spread her grandfather's ashes.

I wish I'd taken the time to get to know that old man. He lived a simple life and worked hard. His sons learned by his example that serving others was an honor, whether it was on the beach at Anzio, the jungles of Vietnam, or delivering the mail in a tropical storm.

There had been more than a few whispers at the funeral from people who'd never known about his Army service. I found this typical of most men who fought in that war.

For that one day, on the beaches of Anzio, Kevin Montrose rose above his humble beginnings. And because of his actions that day, many men lived who might have perished. Many of those men went on to have children, grandchildren, and great-grandchildren, some of whom might never have been born were it not for that one man on that one day. One man, who was a hero when a hero was needed, who then returned home to a humble life, never to speak to anyone of the horrors he'd seen.

Yeah, a lot like Pap.

A lot like many of the men of The Greatest Generation.

THE END

If you'd like to receive my twice a month newsletter for specials, book recommendations, and updates on coming books, please sign up on my website:

WWW.WAYNESTINNETT.COM

THE CHARITY STYLES CARIBBEAN THRILLER SERIES
Merciless Charity
Ruthless Charity
Heartless Charity (Spring, 2017)

THE JESSE MCDERMITT
CARIBBEAN ADVENTURE SERIES

Fallen Out
Fallen Palm
Fallen Hunter
Fallen Pride
Fallen Mangrove
Fallen King
Fallen Honor
Fallen Tide
Fallen Angel
Fallen Hero
Rising Storm (Late 2017)

The *Gaspar's Revenge* Ship's Store is now open. There you can purchase all kinds of swag related to my books.
WWW.GASPARS-REVENGE.COM

BB

Carteret County
Public Library

43786935R00215

7/22

Made in the USA
Middletown, DE
18 May 2017